Cry Havoc

Cry Havoc

Justice Keepers Saga Book X

R.S. Penney

Prologue

Dying felt very much like going to sleep.

Waking up, however, was much less pleasant.

The first moment of awareness, the first thing that might be considered a genuine thought, was the realization that he was floating. Floating someplace warm. It was almost relaxing until he realized that every last inch of him was submerged. Was that a problem? Something told him that it was a problem.

He suddenly remembered that he had to breathe. The liquid. It would get into his lungs, choke him. Frantically, he struggled for the surface only to discover that he felt no burning in his chest.

His head broke through, trails of slime dripping from his chin. Some of it got into his eyes, but thankfully, it didn't hurt. His face. He pawed at his face. He could not say why, but he knew with absolute certainty that this was not his face.

Coughing and sputtering, he flailed until he reached the edge of this strange pool. His hands grabbed the rock, and then he immediately retracted them. It wasn't rock at all. It was warm and soft…like flesh.

With a gaping mouth, he looked up to blink at his surroundings. "Where?" A voice spoke. Not his. "Where am I?"

He crawled onto the shore at the edge of the lake of slime, his head hanging. Long, dark hair, thick with sludge, dangled and trailed along the floor. "Where am I?" he asked. "Who has done this?"

It all came back to him.

Gao.

That was his name. One of many. He had been born Liu Bang, the son of a peasant from Pei County. He had been a soldier, a husband and an Emperor. His people needed him. "Why have you done this to me?"

"Calm yourself, my son."

An Old Woman stood at the edge of the pool, a crone with a face like leather and thinning gray hair. She wore simple country clothes and sandals on her feet. "Be at ease. All will be well."

He looked up at her, narrowing his eyes, and felt a flush of anger burning his face. "You!" Struggling to his feet, he tried to seize the woman. She was gone before he got within two feet of her.

"We mean you no harm, my son."

When he turned, she was there again, at the very edge of the pool, close enough to dip a toe in the slime. "You are to be our emissary," she said. "One who will guide your people to greatness."

Baring his teeth, Gao hissed at her. "You were there!" he growled, striding toward her. "On the roadside! You set all of this in motion!"

The Old Woman looked up at him, and her mouth cracked into an almost-toothless grin. "We recognized your potential even then," she said. "You were meant for glory, my son. You have not yet achieved a tenth of your true purpose."

"I have to return to my people."

"They will not know you. Not as you are." She poked a finger into his chest, and he stumbled backward at her touch. "That life is over. It is time for you to embrace your next challenge."

Gao ran hands over his body. Hard, sculpted muscle greeted his fingertips, smooth without a single strand of hair. He felt his face and found it nothing like the one that he remembered. His cheeks were gaunt, almost hollow; his chin was pointed. He had no beard, but long, black hair fell to the small of his back. He was a young man again, filled with a vigour he had all but forgotten. "Who are you?"

The Old Woman closed her eyes, breathing deeply. "Your people have no name for us," she said. "And you must tell no one of our existence until we deem them ready to possess such knowledge."

"Return me to my people."

"As you wish."

She gestured to a tunnel in the cavern wall. With faltering steps, he followed it, soft flesh squishing beneath his bare feet. The walls seemed to glow with a reddish light. Just enough for him to see clearly.

The tunnel curved slightly to the left, and when he went around the bend, the Old Woman was standing before him again. She kept her eyes fixed on the floor, on a pile of clothes that she had gathered there. "You will not get far as a naked man."

Once he dressed, she guided him through a smaller tunnel that branched off from the main one. At the end of it, he found an empty chamber with nothing on the walls or floor or ceiling.

He forced his eyes shut, stiffening, and then took a hesitant step forward. "What is this place?" He turned, but the doorway in the wall sealed itself up, flesh knitting together so perfectly you would have never known there was a gap.

So, they planned to trap him?

He would have protested, but the floor writhed, and when he spun around, a lump was rising with a slimy sound. It split to form both arms of an upward-pointed triangle. He approached with caution.

A bubble formed around his body, distorting the light. He cried out in shock, but his momentary outburst was nothing compared to the scream that ripped its way out of his mouth when he began to fly through an endless tunnel of blackness.

Moments later, he arrived at what appeared to be a grassy field under a blue sky with just a few clouds. It was hard to tell. Peering through the bubble's surface was like trying to see through a curtain of falling water.

"What sort of devilry…"

The bubble popped.

He *was* in a field, a field of tall grass that reached almost to his knees, the stalks around him flattened by his arrival. Quickly, he turned around and found another triangle like the one in the other place.

He reached out with a tentative hand, but brown flesh became gray, and the triangle collapsed into a pile of ash. What sort of creatures were these? Not spirits, he thought. But what? Beings able to bend flesh to their will. They had given him a new body, but he was still himself, so far as he could tell. His mind remained intact.

Sinking to his knees in the grass, he shuddered as he drew in a breath. "They have restored me to life for a reason." He looked up and felt his eyes widen. "Ying is not yet ready. That is why."

Mountains rose up before him. He knew this place; the Old Woman had brought him to a spot not far from Chang'an. He could be home within a few hours if he ran. Perhaps it was time to put these young legs to work.

The walls of the city stood tall and proud under the harsh light of the noonday sun. The moat sparkled as if someone had strewn a thousand diamonds across the dark water. With summer nearing its peak, it was warm.

People flowed across the bridge toward the gate, some on foot, one or two leading horses. Soldiers in iron lamellar stood on either side of the opening, casting glances at everyone who passed.

Gao walked with his head down.

He kept his posture demure, eyes fixed on the stones under his feet, and hoped it would avoid attention. The wind made strands of his long hair flutter. Fortunately, most of the slime had dried and flaked away.

One of the guards, a hard man with a scar on his chin, looked up to sneer as Gao passed. "Strange clothing, countryman," he growled. "Who are you? And where do you come from?"

Gao froze.

The Old Woman had given him garments that were little better than rags. Not even the simple *yi* and *shan* that you might see on a peasant. His clothes were not cotton or silk but rather some scratchy material that made his skin itch. And there were no rich colours. He was clad in gray from head to toe. To these men, he must have looked like a beggar or a vagabond. Perhaps that was the point.

"Who are you?" the soldier said again.

Lifting his chin to meet the other man's gaze, Gao narrowed his eyes. "I am your emperor," he said. "And you will not speak to me in such-"

He was down on all fours, head ringing like a struck gong, before he even realized that he had been slapped. Blood dripped from his mouth to land upon the stones. Slowly, he looked up. "How dare you-"

"Be silent, countryman."

Closing his eyes, Gao hissed when he felt the point of a sword at his throat. "You must believe me," he panted. "I am Gaozu of Han, the Unifier. Bring my wife, and I will prove my claim-"

He cut off when the blade pressed a little deeper into his skin. Hard enough to draw blood. The soldier stood over him with a snarl fit for an angry dog, teeth clenched, face flushed to a deep red. "The city is in mourning after the death of the Emperor!" he spat. "You will not disgrace his memory with these lies. Speak but one more falsehood, and I will kill you, stranger."

"I am Liu Bang of Fenyu-"

The soldier drew back his sword.

"Have the mighty warriors of Han fallen so far?" Gao paused when he realized that a small crowd had formed, surrounding him. It was the timbre of the speaker's voice that got his attention. A woman?

He looked up to find her standing just a few paces away, a tall and slender woman in a *chang* of bold, blazing red and a *ru* of white with red along the collar and the cuffs of each sleeve. Her black hair was left loose, falling almost to her waist.

Her face was lovely with a thin, delicate nose and dark eyes that seemed to burn with some hidden, inner fire. "Killing beggars and madmen," she said coldly. "Is there no better use for your sword?"

"Quiet, woman," the soldier barked. "This is no concern of yours."

She did not obey.

Instead, she placed herself between Gao and the soldier, standing tall and proud as if she could stop a flood with nothing but the fury of her stare. Gao could only see the back of her head, but he realized that he would rather not be the target of that stare. "Can you not see that this man is ill? He should be cared for, not slaughtered."

"Who are you to-"

"I am your emperor!" Gao shouted.

That was the last thing he remembered before something thumped him across the back of his head. Everything went dark then. Perhaps he had died again.

No. No, he hadn't died. He realized as much when the pain became unbearable. He felt as though the world were spinning,

6

as if he might fall at any moment. And he might have if not for the fact that there was something soft beneath him.

His vision came into focus, and he saw the woman who had come to his aid staring down at him. "He's awake," she said.

"Who are you?"

"Who are *you*, stranger?"

Gao sat up, touching his face, noting again the hollow cheeks and hairless chin that were not his. The lump on the back of his head gave him pause. "You won't believe me even if I tell you the truth."

The woman sat at his bedside with arms crossed, frowning as she considered that. "You expect me to believe that you are the dead emperor?" she asked. "Even when you look nothing like him? Even though you are decades younger than him?"

A flash of pain made him wince, and he let himself fall back on the bed. "I do not expect you to believe anything," he said. "They did this to me."

"Who did?"

"The spirits, the... I don't know. I awoke in a place of darkness, trapped in this body. And they sent me here. To suffer. To see all that I have lost."

He became aware of an old man standing behind the young woman, a distinguished fellow with creases in his face and thinning gray hair. Her father? Yes, that would have to be it. "It would be unwise to continue telling your story," he said. "They might have done far worse to you if my daughter had not intervened."

"They might have done far worse to *her*."

In response to that, the young woman sniffed and turned her head to stare at the wall. He suspected she wanted to look at anything but him. "I'm not afraid of a few surly guards," she insisted. "What they did to him was wrong."

Gao expected some kind of rebuke from the old man, but none came. Instead, the fellow just put a hand on his daughter's shoulder and smiled lovingly. Old fool. No good would come from nurturing the girl's eccentricities.

"I am Feng Ju," the old man said. "My daughter, Lihua."

"A pretty name for a pretty face."

"Tell me, stranger," the girl replied, "are men capable of admiring a woman for her intelligence or her bravery? I intervened on your behalf; I tended to your wounds, but you say nothing of that. Your appraisal of my name means little to me, and your appraisal of my face means even less."

"Discipline your daughter," Gao hissed.

The old man only laughed and bent forward to kiss the girl's forehead. "As well try to discipline the wind, stranger," he said. "We are returning to the country in a few days. Come with us. It would not be wise for you to stay in the capital."

The journey to Feng's country home took several days. The man had a small farm near the banks of the Wei, and he had offered room and board if Gao was willing to work the fields. It was almost enough to make him laugh — or weep. The emperor had returned from death to be reduced to a mere farmhand.

He would have spat in the old man's face if not for the fact that he knew he needed food, and he would find no help in the city. Lihua was right. He was no longer Gaozu of Han, no longer Liu Bang from Pei County. He still felt like himself, still grew angry at the things that had made him angry before, still desired the same things he had wanted when he was emperor. But that life was over. Lihua pestered him to choose a name every time they spoke. Last night, he had tossed his bowl aside and growled, "Sui Bian."

That only produced laughter from the young woman. "You wish to be called 'whatever?'" she scoffed. "Surely you can do better."

He could, but he refused to. He might have been forced into this life, but he would not accept it. On the second night, while

Feng and his daughter slept, he sat alone in the tall grass by the river's edge.

"Did you think we brought you back to resume your old life?"

He froze.

It was an effort to make himself stand up and turn around, but the Old Woman was there when he did, watching him. "You have done a marvelous thing, my son," she said. "You do not know it yet, but the Empire you created will propel your civilization to new heights."

"Then let me return to lead it."

With a sigh, she came toward him and shook her head. "All things pass, my son," she said. "It is time to begin the next great work."

Stomping through the grass, he put himself right in front of the old crone. He had to resist the urge to seize her by the shoulders. She just stared at him, unflinching. "Time to begin my next great work?" he yelled. "What work is that?"

"Building new empires, of course."

He turned away from her and went to the riverbank, smiling and shaking his head. "New empires," he whispered. "How am I supposed to forge a new empire when you curse me with this body! When you take away all that I was!"

He turned around, but the Old Woman was gone.

Sobbing, Sui Bian fell to his knees and covered his face with both hands. His body trembled with every breath. "Why couldn't they just let me die?" he whispered. "Just let me DIE!"

"Who are you talking to?"

The sound of Lihua's voice made him jump. He found the young woman standing just a few feet away, wrapped in the blanket that she had used to keep herself warm. Her hair was loose, her face serene and pale in the moonlight. "I fear for you, stranger," she said. "Does the madness have you so firmly in its grip?"

He said nothing.

It surprised him when Lihua approached and knelt beside him, reaching out to lay a hand on his cheek. "Let us help you," she pleaded. "My father can give you a good home. You will be safe with us."

What else could he do but accept?

(194 BCE)

Sui Bian used a hoe to violently remove some weeds, churning up a spray of dirt with them. He didn't much care about that. The work was hard and tiring, but it kept his mind off other things. News came from Chang'an now and then, but he tried not to listen. What he heard disturbed him greatly.

His widow – the Empress Lu – now dictated much of what went on in the capital, and his weakling son could do little to restrain her. Liu Ying was a timid emperor. It left Sui with a bitter taste in his mouth. Had the boy learned nothing of what he had tried to teach? Any thought of returning had long since fled from his mind. If he tried, Lu would have him killed.

Hearing what she had done to Qi – ripping the woman's eyes out, cutting her arms and legs off and leaving her to die in pig shit – had been enough to make him empty his stomach in the fields behind Feng's house. After years of battle, Sui Bian had thought that no amount of human brutality could unnerve him, but that… That was something else entirely. And his third son, poor little Ruyi, now dead at Lu's command.

Sui Bian had wept for him. He had prayed to the Old Woman several times, begged her to intercede on his behalf – if the spirits could raise him from the dead, surely they could do the same for Ruyi – but she would not come. The Old Woman ignored him now. He had not seen her since that night by the river. He was beginning to think that perhaps he had imagined all of it. Perhaps he was mad, just as Lihua suspected.

The sun was sinking toward the distant mountains, but its glare was still bright and strong. High summer had come. Over a year since his death and rebirth, and here he was, hoeing weeds on a little farm that he would never have noticed in his former life.

Sui Bian was facing west, shading his eyes with one hand. "Why?" he whispered to himself. "Why don't you just let me die?"

"You needn't push yourself so hard."

He turned around to find Old Feng watching him with a frown. Had the man heard his muttering? "Have some water, my friend," Feng said. "Do not break yourself under the sun's cruel gaze."

"I do not need your pity, old man."

Anyone else might have punished Sui for his disrespect, but Feng only sighed and turned away, making his way back to the house. Eventually, Sui decided to follow. He did need to quench his thirst.

Halfway to the house, he found Lihua in the fields, inspecting the barley. The girl was always doing things like that, taking on a man's work as if her father would not be scandalized by it. Strangely, Old Feng didn't seem to mind. In fact, he encouraged it. To some extent, Sui understood.

Old Feng shared his home with the children of his dead neighbour, Zhao Si, a man who had died at Gaixia. A man who had died under Sui's command when he was still Liu Bang. Zhao Fuling and Zhao Tian were both good boys, but their father was gone and his wife as well. Lihua's mother had perished shortly after her birth, and Feng's only son had lost his life in the very campaign that won Sui his empire. The two families relied on each other, and Lihua being Lihua, she insisted on helping.

The young woman looked up to favour him with a smile. "That fury I see in your eyes, Stranger." She refused to call him

Sui Bian, and he refused to choose another name, which left them at a standoff. "Tell me, is your existence so miserable that you can find no joy in anything?"

The stalks rustled as Guo Dong stepped into the open.

The boy came from a neighbouring farm, but in recent months, he had offered his services to Old Feng. Sui suspected that he intended to ask for Lihua's hand, but that was none of his concern.

Guo Dong was a slim youth, just shy of average height, with short, black hair and a pitiful excuse for a beard. There was something in the way he looked at you, almost as if he were planning some trick. "In Sui's defense," he said, "Hoeing weeds on a hot day like this would dampen my spirits as well."

"I'm not so sure about that," Lihua countered. "The task falls to you more often than it does to him, but you're always smiling when I talk to you."

"Perhaps your company raises my spirits."

Lihua blushed, turning her face away as if that could hide feelings that were now painfully obvious. It should not have annoyed Sui – if Guo Dong wanted her, he could have her; a woman like that would be a fitting wife for this useless fool of a man – but it did. He chose to leave without comment.

Guo Dong, however, was determined to provoke a reaction.

The boy stepped in front of Sui with an impish grin and a glint of mischief in his eyes. "There must be *some* way to make the job easier," he said. "Perhaps you should do away with the hoe and simply scowl the weeds to death."

Lihua giggled.

Clenching his teeth, Sui pushed past the young man. He shook his head as he made his way toward the house. "Idiots, the both of them!" he spat. "To think that this is what my life has come to!"

Feng's home was a modest building but well made. Walls of wood supported tiled roofs that rose to a peak on each of the three wings that surrounded a small courtyard. The fourth wall was an iron gate that stood open despite the onset of evening. Sui had left it so. Seething with frustration, he had taken a walk by the river to relieve himself. He was just returning when the sound of hushed voices made the hair stand on the back of his neck.

Old instincts took over, and he reached for the bronze knife on his belt only to find it missing. Well, of course it was. He was a farmhand now, not a soldier. His former life was over, but he still retained much of what he knew. And he felt invigorated in this new body. He crept around the back of the house and froze.

In the golden rays of the setting sun, Guo Dong and Lihua stood side by side, both gazing out on a field of barley that swayed in the wind. Neither one saw him watching. He was about to leave, but something made him pause.

"Why, of all the women in this world," Lihua began, "would you want me?"

A good question.

Guo Dong turned to face her with the kind of smile you could only find on a love-sick boy. "Because you make me laugh," he answered. "And you fill my mind with ideas that keep me awake long into the night. Because you are kind."

Lihua's shoulders slumped. Her back was turned, but Sui could imagine the pain in her eyes. "I would not be a good wife to you," she said. "Or to any man."

"You think I fear the fire within you," Guo Dong protested. "But it is that fire that draws me to you."

Lihua turned to him.

It shocked Sui to see tears on the girl's cheeks. He didn't think anything could make her cry. "Promise me..." she rasped. "Promise me that if we have a daughter, you will not break her. Promise me you won't force her to marry a man she hates or quash her every inclination to question the world around her."

Tenderly, Guo Dong laid a hand on her cheek, and Lihua leaned into his touch. "If we have a daughter," he said, "I want her to be just like you."

Sickening.

Lihua set a hand on his shoulder and left it there for a moment before she backed away from him. "You had better go now," she said. "My father has grown accustomed to my stubbornness, but even he has his limits. If we are to be together, then…Well, he will want to do things properly."

Guo Dong nodded.

Sui decided that he had better depart as well. He could not say why, but he did not want Lihua to know that he had witnessed her conversation with the young man. Why she vexed him so was a mystery he could not unravel. As well try to discover why the old hag had raised him from the dead and cursed him with this body.

Try as he might to forget her, Lihua remained in his thoughts that night. She kept sleep at bay and forced him to endlessly ponder his fascination with her. Why did she vex him so? It wasn't love. Sui Bian knew that emotion well, and he felt not a spec of it for this vixen. No, what he felt in Lihua's presence was akin to what he might experience when contemplating the battlefield tactics of his enemies.

It was as if their every interaction had become a contest. Her stubborn defiance was a challenge, and Sui would have answered that challenge decisively if not for the fact that he would incur Feng's displeasure upon doing so. The old fool was determined to coddle his daughter, and Sui had nowhere else to go.

Lihua did more than just annoy him.

She filled his thoughts often now, more often than he would have liked. Too often! His patience was waning. Sooner or later, she would exhaust the last of it.

Two days later, he found Guo Dong in the fields, tending a pair of oxen that were hitched to a plow. The young man was gently stroking the nose of one beast, murmuring something to it.

Sui Bian approached the boy with his head down, forcing the snarl from his face. "Put them back to work," he snapped. "We have very little daylight left. You should not waste it."

Guo Dong turned around to face him with a jovial smile. "Hello, Sui," he said. "I am sorry that I teased you the other day. You just seemed so very unhappy. I thought that I could change that."

"My happiness is no concern of yours," Sui muttered. "Now, put them to work."

A frown compressed the boy's mouth, and he scanned the tall grass as if searching for something. "A pair of wild dogs ran past a short while ago," he said. "They frightened the oxen. I thought it best to let them calm down."

Crossing his arms, Sui answered the young man's stupidity with a stony expression. "If the oxen are too frightened to work," he began, "then whip them and have done with it. They will put up no resistance if they fear you more than some mongrel hound."

He turned to leave, stomping through the grass, but he had barely gone ten steps when Guo Dong blocked his path. The boy's face was red, his eyes hot with anger. "Why are you so angry?" he demanded. "You insult Lihua; you sneer at me. Feng has given you a home and food and kindness, but you show him nothing but disrespect."

Sui pushed the boy out of his way.

He was trembling, sweat beading on his forehead, as he made his way to the other side of the farmyard. There were weeds that needed hoeing, and he preferred that task to the displeasure of Guo Dong's company.

The sound of footsteps behind him put him on edge. He turned to find Guo Dong running to catch up with him and skidding to a stop perhaps five paces away. "Enough," the boy growled. "Feng may tolerate your disrespect, but I will not. It stops now."

For the first time in a very long while, Sui Bian grinned. "Ah," he said. "Come to teach me a lesson, have you?"

Guo Dong retreated a step.

"Where's your bravado now, boy?" Sui demanded. "How old are you? Seven years and ten? *Eight* years and ten? Do you know anything about combat? Have you seen the fear in a man's eyes as he dies on your sword? No. I thought not."

The young man was backing away, his face now pale, his eyes wide with fright. More fool him. He had honestly believed that Sui Bian was not dangerous. It was time to disabuse him of that falsehood.

"I don't want to fight you," Guo Dong whispered.

"Then you should have kept your mouth shut."

With two quick strides, Sui closed the distance and slammed a hand into the young fool's chest. Guo Dong was shoved backward. He tripped over his own feet and fell on his backside.

"Get up," Sui hissed.

"Leave him be."

To hear a woman commanding him so was enough to set his blood on fire. He spun around to find Lihua watching him. Her face was stern, her posture stiff, and the wind teasing her loose, flowing hair made her look almost like a vengeful goddess. "I pity you, Stranger," she said. "I sometimes wonder what tragedy broke your mind. But pity has its limits. If you wish to remain in this house, you will not threaten those whom I love."

Striding toward her with teeth bared, Sui felt intense heat in his face. "And you will not presume to command me!" he spat. "Learn your place, woman!"

Lihua hesitated.

Something changed in the way she looked at him. At first, he thought it was fear – and that pleased him – but he quickly realized that she was not cowed. No…Not cowed in the slightest. Lihua understood what it was she faced. She recognized, somehow, that she was standing before a man who knew how to kill. But she would not yield to him. "You will gather your things tonight," she said. "We will provide you with enough food to last three days, but you will leave this farm tomorrow at sunrise."

"How *dare* you?"

"Do not push me further, Stranger."

His hand moved like a striking snake, fingers closing around her throat before he even realized what he was doing. Feng's anger be damned. It was time to teach this girl a lesson that he would not-

Clamping one hand onto his wrist and the other onto his elbow, Lihua twisted his arm and pushed down on it. Pain lanced through him from fingertips to shoulder. This should not have been possible. How could a woman-

Her foot landed in his stomach, driving the wind from Sui's lungs. The next thing he knew, he was bent double and stumbling away, trying to catch his breath. Lihua was saying something, but her words did not register until he pushed his way through the pain. "…will never touch me again," she concluded.

Rage boiled within him.

Sui drew a bronze knife from a sheath upon his belt. The weapon had belonged to Feng during his time in the army, but Sui had taken it after finding himself empty-handed the other night. He felt more at peace with a blade at his side.

Lihua was focused on Guo Dong, her eyes full of pity and sadness. He was tempted to leave the pair of them to their fate. No woman could respect a man after seeing him so thoroughly defeated. But the rage could not be denied.

He charged Lihua.

The girl rounded on him just in time for him to grab a fistful of her clothing and drive the knife through her flesh, up underneath her sternum to pierce her heart. Her eyes widened, and her mouth hung open. A soft whimper escaped her as her body went limp.

He had to kill Guo Dong too, and then there was nothing to do but run. Run and pray that he was nowhere near the farm when Feng found his daughter's corpse. He went east, seeking a place to hide, and from that day onward, he was no longer Sui Bian.

Part 1

Chapter 1

The July sun beat down on them from a cloudless sky, its golden rays falling on a windmill with blades that turned slowly. Jack almost snorted as he watched it go. Ah, the classic torture of miniature golf. It was an Earth ritual that he was more than happy to introduce to his Leyrian friends.

Rajel was bent over in the shade from the windmill, gripping his putter tightly in both hands and frowning at the neon-green ball just a few inches in front of his shoes. He gave it a gentle tap.

The ball rolled up the ramp...and hit a blade.

"This is fun to you?" Rajel snapped.

Standing a short ways back with one hand on the end of his own putter, Jack smiled and shook his head. "It's tradition," he said. "You haven't really had the Earth experience until you've played mini-golf."

Cassi was sitting on a nearby bench in a blue sundress with white flowers on it, her putter laid across her lap. "No wonder your people are crazy," she said. "Games like this would drive anyone up the wall."

Rajel tapped the ball again.

This time it went gracefully up the ramp and through a tunnel at the base of the windmill just before a blade blocked its path. It came out on the other side, stopping right next to Jack's orange ball, just a few paces from the hole.

"See?" Jack said. "It's fun."

"I'll take your word for it."

With a heavy sigh, Jack followed a cobblestone path to the green. "Just be glad we got a few days off," he muttered. "Every bloody Friendship Day. 'You're the first Keeper from Earth, Jack! The children look up to you.' I thought it was over when I moved to Leyria."

But it wasn't. Why would it be? Just last week, Larani had informed him that he would be expected to appear at the Global Friendship Day ceremony – in India, this year – and that he had better have a speech prepared. And perhaps it could be a tad less inflammatory than last year's.

Oh, and Anna would be coming too! She was the woman who discovered Earth, after all. And why not bring Cassi along for good measure? They could do one last review of the Earth-based Keepers just to make absolutely sure that all of Slade's cronies were finally gone. And then Melissa had insisted on visiting her family. So, why not just bring the whole team?

He took his place next to his ball, putter in hand, and gave it a tap with just enough force to make it roll right into the hole with a nice *plunk*. Two strokes. Not bad for a guy who was out of practice.

Rajel took position next to his ball and tapped it gently. Of course, it made a beeline for the hole and dropped in to land on top of Jack's ball and the one that Cassi had put in with just one stroke.

The other man paced over and sank to one knee, retrieving all three of them. Bright sunlight glinted off the purple lenses of Rajel's sunglasses, but though he used them to cover eyes that did not see, you would never know it from the way he golfed… or fought. Or just about anything. "This game irritates me."

"Oh?"

"Once we have a direct path to the hole," Rajel began, "each of us can sink the ball in only one swing. Because how could we do otherwise? Spatial awareness makes it all but second nature to us. But these traps…"

Jack shrugged.

A moment later, Cassi joined them, taking her hot-pink ball from Rajel. She tossed it up and caught it in one deft hand. "I believe the traps are the point."

Jack led them to their next challenge – a straight line of AstroTurf where the only thing that stood between you and the hole was a mechanical crocodile that opened and closed its mouth every few seconds. Seeing it almost made him laugh.

Rajel came stomping over with a petulant sigh, grimacing as he shouldered Jack out of the way. "Let me try first," he said. "I want my turn over with."

He dropped his ball and hit it too hard.

The damn thing rolled so fast you almost expected to see a trail of burnt turf in its wake, but even with all that speed, Rajel's timing was off. The crocodile snapped his jaw shut, the ball bounced off his snout.

"Gods forsake me!" Rajel growled. "I hate this game!"

"Excellent!" Jack said. "*Now*, you've had the complete Earth experience."

Cassi put herself right in front of Rajel and looked up to glare death into his eyes. "The problem is not the game," she said. "The problem is that your mind is clouded with frustration and pent up anger."

Rajel went red and turned his face away from her. A shiver went through him as he let out a breath. "Yes," he said. "You're right."

"You wanna talk about it, bro?" Jack offered.

"Not really."

Pressing his lips together, Jack looked up toward the sky and blinked. "He doesn't want to talk about it," he muttered under his breath. "Well, here's the thing, dude. You've been extra grumpy since we got back from Antaur; so, I'm thinking it's share time."

Rajel shuffled over to the weeds and crouched down with his back turned. "It's not the sort of thing a grown man should fret about." He retrieved the ball with a grunt and then stood up straight. "Bruised feelings."

"Adults can't have bruised feelings?"

"They can," Rajel said with some reluctance. "But in general, they deal with those feelings better than I have."

"You'll get no argument from me," Cassi grumbled.

Jack shot a glance in her direction, narrowed his eyes and then shook his head. "It's been my experience," he began, "that even the most calm and collected person sometimes loses his cool. So, what's up?"

With extreme reluctance, Rajel turned around and shambled back toward them with his head down. "Keli," he said. "I... seem to have developed feelings for her. Feelings that she can't return."

"Well..." Jack replied. "I gotta say I'm impressed."

"You're impressed?"

"Yeah, it takes a special brand of courage to go barking up that tree." Jack blushed as soon as the words were out of his mouth – not the most sensitive response he could have offered; Summer was quite annoyed – but he put his chagrin aside to focus on the issue. "She's asexual, isn't she?"

"You could tell?"

"I had a suspicion."

A grunt from Rajel confirmed those suspicions.

Jack reached out to lay a hand on the other man's shoulder, and that seemed to ease some of Rajel's tension. "It's okay, dude," he said. "I won't give you the 'plenty of fish in the sea' speech – 'cause no one actually likes hearing that when they're hurting – but until you *do* find that special someone, you can always count on us. We got your back."

"You have my back?" Rajel asked. "What exactly do you intend to do with it?"

"It's an Earth expression," he said. "The point is you can count on me. And on Cass. And on Anna…"

"Where *is* Anna today?" Cassi inquired.

"You wouldn't believe me if I told you."

Blinds on Crystal Hunter's kitchen window segmented the sunlight into thin bands, but despite that, the place was still bright and cheerful. It was a simple room with wooden cupboards and an old fridge decorated with dozens of colourful magnets, all shaped like Earth letters.

Anna was on her knees in front of the pantry, loading up its lower shelves with cans that Crystal had purchased at the supermarket. Paying for food. She had spent the better part of a year on this planet, and that was *still* a foreign concept to her.

Anna wore jean shorts and a thin, white tank-top, her strawberry-blonde hair done up in a nubby little ponytail. "There," she said, setting the last can in place. "That should be all of it."

Jack's mother was only a silhouette in her mind – an image painted by the spatial awareness that every Keeper gained after Bonding a Nassai – but the other woman was close enough for Anna to make out the smile on her face. "You know, you didn't have to do this," Crystal said. "You *could* have spent the afternoon with your friends."

"Nonsense," Anna replied. "I wanted to spend some time with you."

She stood up and turned around, wiping her damp bangs off her forehead. It was warm in Crystal's little apartment, and she had worked up quite a sweat carrying those groceries up from the car. "I thought, maybe we should get to know each other."

"Well, it's appreciated."

Crystal sat in a wooden chair with one leg crossed over the other, drumming her fingers on the kitchen table. Her soft laughter was almost musical. A short woman with golden hair that fell in waves to her shoulders, she looked nothing like her son. Well, at least, not in terms of colouring. Jack had his mother's cheekbones. "But sweetheart," Crystal went on. "You don't have to impress me."

"Was I that obvious?"

Crystal stood up in one graceful motion and flowed across the tiles on bare feet. "A little." Gently, she took Anna by the shoulders. "But it's appreciated nonetheless. I'm glad you and Jack got together. I've been wishing you would for, like, *years* now."

Closing her eyes, Anna felt a blush singeing her cheeks. She took a deep breath. "I guess we're both a little dense," she mumbled. "But it means a lot to me to hear you say that."

"Love's hard sometimes."

"Yeah."

It felt so nice when Crystal pulled her into a tender hug. Anna found herself leaning her cheek on the other woman's shoulder. She could not remember the last time she had been this close with her own mother. "As far as I'm concerned," Crystal whispered. "You are part of the family."

"Thank you."

Sometimes family sucked.

Claire sat at a picnic table in her uncle's backyard, holding a piece of corn on the cob in both hands. Her mouth was open, but she paused halfway through the act of taking a bite. Her eyes flicked to each of her cousins. "What?"

There were three of them on the opposite bench – all pale; these were kids from her mother's side of the family – and they all stared at her as if she had grown horns on the top of her head. Logan was the oldest, a young man of fourteen with a mop of blonde hair and a nose too big for his face. "Is it true?"

"Is what true?"

His younger sister, Lisa, was closer to Claire's age. A pretty girl with long, golden hair and freckles on her pale cheeks, she leaned in close over the table. "What they said about Melissa," she whispered. "Does she really have an alien living in her body?"

"Yeah," Claire snapped. "It's called being a Justice Keeper."

"That's so messed up," Logan muttered.

"I don't think I could do it." That last response came from Brendan, a tall boy with a cleft chin and clear blue eyes. He shuddered as he completed his thought. "Let an alien live in my body? What if it takes over, or something."

"It doesn't work that way," Claire said.

"Yeah, but, like, it's still weird."

Instead of arguing with him, Claire went back to her dinner. The corn crunched as she bit into it. So good! When was the last time she had had corn on the cob? It had to be a year ago. She couldn't recall ever having it on Leyria.

"At least *you're* still normal," Logan said.

Claire scanned the backyard for her elder sister and found Melissa standing by the wooden fence with a glass of fruit punch in her hand. She had spent most of the afternoon doing that, hanging back, keeping her distance, talking to aunts and uncles who came up to exchange pleasantries but not really seeking them out. Melissa had always been soft-spoken, but never this reserved. But then, when your cousins were all whispering about you behind your back, what else could you do?

Normal.

At least Claire was still "normal." If they only knew...Tentatively, Claire reached out with her senses. Fear seemed to radiate from the three kids on the other side of the table. Or...Well, not *fear* exactly. Keli had been teaching her to sift and sort through the different emotions she picked up from other people. Precision was important. There were flavours of anger, flavours of joy and flavours of fear. This was more like mistrust mingled with a strong desire to keep their distance.

A thought leaked through from Logan. Claire had a vivid image of Melissa trying to give him a hug and Logan backing away with his hands raised defensively as if he thought she might infect him with something.

Slamming her hand down on the table, Claire looked up to glare fire at the idiot boy. "What the hell is wrong with you?"

"What?"

Claire stood up, and her lip twitched as she tried to stuff the anger back down into her belly. "She's my sister!" Her words were harsh, but she didn't care. "Not some victim of the plague. If Melissa tries to give you a hug, shut up and take it!"

Logan was staring at her with an open mouth, and his face had gone deathly pale. "How did you..." He shook his head so fast it must have made him dizzy. "I guess *you're* turning into a freak too."

"And proud of it."

"That's what you get when you live among these aliens," Lisa said. She was looking at her hamburger as if it might bite her. "Mom always said so. They'll fill your head with their messed up ideas."

"Your mom's an idiot!" Claire growled.

Her mind was still open to the impressions of everything around her, and she felt a distinct change in the mood. The easy-going atmosphere that had permeated the backyard was suddenly dark and hostile. Or...well, that wasn't it either. Not hostile, exactly. There was nothing to indicate that they meant her any harm, but there *was* anger simmering just beneath the surface.

"Claire Carlson!" Aunt Sasha wailed. "What has gotten into you?" The woman was not exactly tall and not exactly short, not exactly skinny and not exactly plump, but her round face and blonde curls were unmistakable.

"Your kids are rude," Claire began. "They keep telling me that my sister's a freak, and they don't seem to care that literally *hundreds* of people owe her their lives. But why should any of this surprise me? Your kids pick up all your racist bullshit." At least half a dozen people gasped, but Claire kept going. "So, of course, they're gonna have problems with aliens too."

Sasha exchanged glances with her husband Bill, and when she turned her attention back to Claire, her face was red. "Della," she said in a stiff voice. "What do you have to say for your daughter?"

Claire's mother was sitting in a lawn chair with a beer in her hand, sunlight glinting off the dark lenses of her glasses. She stood up slowly. For half a second, Claire thought she was in trouble, but telepathy had its benefits.

"Well," Della replied, "I'd say I'm glad my kid has learned to stand up for herself. Don't blame Claire for seeing what's right in front of her nose, Sasha. You *are* an idiot!"

Della strode across the grass at a leisurely pace and offered Claire her hand. Claire took it, and then they were walking to the gate. Melissa joined them half a moment later, and the smile on her face was priceless.

Claire had a permanent bedroom in her mother's house, and even though she hadn't seen it in over a year, nothing had changed. The walls were still a soft pink with adorable cartoon elephants painted on them. She was a bit old for that sort of thing now, but the consistency was comforting. The window still looked out on a large backyard dotted with apple trees.

In PJ bottoms and a blue tank top, Claire sat on the bed with her legs curled up, hugging her knees as she gazed out the window. A knock at the door got her attention, and she didn't need her talent to know who was waiting in the hallway outside. "Come in, Mom."

The door opened, and she found Della standing there in green track pants and an old t-shirt. Her mother was frowning, and there were loose strands of blonde hair falling over her face. "So," she said, "I'm guessing this has discouraged you from coming back to live with me?"

Claire squeezed her eyes shut, stiffening as she wrestled with the guilt of having to tell her mother something she really didn't want to hear. "Part of me wants to," she began. "And part of me is happy on Leyria...But, Mom, they're never gonna accept me here."

Things just weren't the same since her father made that deal with the Overseers. Oh, he was the same Harry that she remembered – kind but stern, overprotective to a fault – but Claire had no idea what the cost of her new powers was. What did her father have to give up to save her life? What would the Overseers make him do?

When they arrived on Earth a few days ago, Claire had asked to stay with her mother instead of going with her father and sister to Uncle Mark's house. She wanted to see her cousin's on Harry's side of the family – they always treated her better than Logan and Lisa and the others – but she needed a break from Harry.

Maybe a long break.

Two nights ago, while she was eating a quiet dinner with her mother, everything had come spilling out of her. She had cried for the better part of an hour. And that was when Della had offered to let her move back home.

"At least there are other telepaths on Leyria," Claire said. "Not many, but some. Here, I'm just a freak."

"You're not a freak."

"Yes, I am."

Della paced across the room in a fury, shaking her head in disgust. "No, you're not, Claire!" she spat. "Don't let your idiot cousins get inside your head. There are millions of people out there who wish they could do what you do."

Sniffling, Claire tried to ignore the fat tear that slid down her cheek. "You didn't see what Logan was thinking," she croaked. "You didn't feel the fear and disgust coming off him when he looked at Melissa."

Della sat on the edge of the bed, her blonde hair dangling in waves as she glowered into her lap. "I wish that I had never let you go to Leyria," she said. "No, not because I hate Leyrians, but I should have never trusted your father to take care of you girls."

"It wasn't his fault."

"Claire, he brought you to a place where men with guns tried to kill you. And when you miraculously survived, he used that alien *thing* to change you."

"He was trying to protect me."

Della was on her feet again in an instant, throwing up her hands as she paced to the opposite wall. "Well, isn't that always his excuse?" She spun around to face Claire with her arms folded. "Your father is a control freak, Claire."

Hearing that left Claire feeling numb inside. It was a strange sensation. With her new powers, she was always picking up stray emotions from other people. Add that to the typical drama of being a preteen girl, and it was safe to say that she was always feeling *something*. But that last one just flattened her.

Was her father really a control freak? She might have said that in moments when he was trying to enforce one of his unreasonable rules, but Claire was old enough to know that kids were always saying stuff like that. Hearing it from a grownup, though… "What do you mean?"

"I shouldn't have said anything."

A frown tugged at the corners of Claire's mouth, but she forced herself to look up at her mother. "I'm not a little kid anymore," she muttered. "I deserve to know what's going on with my parents."

With a heavy sigh, Della shuffled back to the bed and knelt on the carpet. She took Claire's hands in hers. "All right," she said. "But if you repeat this to your father or your sister, I'm gonna be mad."

"I promise."

"Your father is a control freak." Claire saw terrible sadness in her mother's eyes as she said that. "Look, I know I wasn't always the best mom. I used to drink too much. And your dad was always taking care of you when I couldn't. I'm sorry for that, baby, I really am. Your dad had to pick up the slack when I screwed up, and maybe that turned him into the man he is today."

"I don't understand."

"Look at how he is with Melissa," Della said. "Your sister chose one of the most dangerous careers in the world, and from everything I've heard she's *very* good at it. I couldn't be prouder, but I'd be lying if I said I didn't lie awake every night, worrying."

There were tears on Della's cheek, but she sniffed and wiped them away with the back of one hand. "The difference is that *I* accept it," she went on. "I know I can't protect my little girl; so, I trust her to protect herself. Your father doesn't. He goes with her on dangerous missions. Because he can't accept that she might get hurt, and there's nothing he can do about it."

Claire hugged herself, rubbing her arms for warmth. She turned her face away from her mother. "Okay, I get it," she whispered. "But what can we do to help him?"

"We can't do anything, honey," Della replied. "Your father thinks the world should be a certain way, and sometimes it doesn't even occur to him that anyone might disagree. Once upon a time, the worst thing you could say about him was that he was hard to live with. But now…Now, he has the power to make the world the way he wants it to be. Or he thinks he does."

Chapter 2

The little blue Honda Fit settled into a parking spot that was much too big for it. The engine went quiet, and the driver's-side door popped open.

Jack emerged from the car into a muggy evening where the sun beat down and left orange sparkles on the black lenses of his glasses. A hot wind hit him and ruffled his hair. It was going to be a warm night, he could tell.

His mother's apartment complex was a simple tower of white bricks in the middle of downtown Winnipeg, a twelve-story building that reached for red-rimmed clouds that stretched across the blue sky. There were other skyscrapers all around him and noisy cars zipping past on the road. He had almost forgotten what that was like. Leyrian streets were deathly silent by comparison.

Giving his old car a pat on its roof – it was his mother's now; Jack had given it to her when he moved to Leyria – he shut the door and the left parking lot. The Honda beeped as he activated the alarm.

When he went around the corner, he found Anna waiting for him on the building's front step, and she was so damn cute in a pair of jean shorts and a blue flannel sweater. Her strawberry-blonde hair was left loose for once, and it fell just past the nape of her neck.

Jack reached up with one hand and pulled down his sunglasses so that he could peek over the rims. "Whatcha doin' out here?" he asked. "I thought we were gonna have leftover spaghetti with Mom."

Anna stood by the door with her arms crossed, smiling sheepishly at the pavement under her shoes. "That was the plan," she agreed. "But I wanted to surprise you; so, I did a little research..."

She looked up at him with those lovely blue eyes, and any thought of asking what she meant by research went flying out of his head. "I thought maybe we could have a date night?"

"What did you have in mind?"

Anna stood on her toes, brushing his lips with hers, and then, before he could ask for more details, her arms encircled his neck. "You'll see," she whispered. "Plus I think your mom might appreciate a little privacy after a week of hosting us."

"Probably," Jack agreed. "So..."

"Don't worry; I know the way."

"You're not gonna tell me, are you?"

"Nope."

Five minutes later, they were on the road and headed toward the outskirts of the city. Anna gave directions, but Jack had to get behind the wheel. His girlfriend had never learned to drive. Leyrians rarely used cars. Most of their cities had efficient public-transit systems that could get you anywhere you wanted to go in about fifteen minutes.

Still, he was impressed by how well Anna knew her way around his hometown. She had a great sense of direction – Jack was still amazed at how quickly she had learned the layout of Ottawa on her first visit to Earth – but even though they were staying with his mother, they had spent very little time here in Winnipeg. She must have looked up their destination on a map, which meant a fair amount of planning had gone into this date.

It wasn't long before they were driving through a neighbourhood near the one that he had grown up in. The pieces all snapped together in Jack's head. Suddenly, he knew exactly where they were going. "No..." he said.

"Yup."

After parking the car, they followed a crowd of people under a massive sign that read, "Welcome to the Apple Blossom Festival!" The carnival was located in an open field near the eastern bank of the Red River.

It was basically a tiny city of colourful tents laid out in neat, square patterns to form a grid of makeshift streets in the grass. You could find pretty much anything you wanted here: apple pies, homemade jewellery, teddy bears sewn by hand by an old woman who had been bringing her stuffed critters to the festival for almost twenty years. The sounds of the midway drowned out almost everything else. In the distance, a Ferris wheel turned lazily with glowing lights on every spoke.

Grinning so hard his jaw hurt, Jack tilted his head back and took in the sight. "It's just like I remember it," he mumbled. "I gotta give you props for this one, An. You came up with the perfect date night."

Anna was holding his hand as they made their way through the crowd. She glanced over her shoulder with a sly little smile of her own. "Well, I can't take *all* the credit."

"What do you mean?"

"Your mom told me that when you were young, you always wanted to take a girl to the fair, but you never had anyone to go with."

Closing his eyes, Jack nodded. "That's true," he said. "But I'm surprised Mom knew that. I don't recall telling her."

Anna spun around to stand in front of him, and then, before he could utter one word of protest, she was tickling him. He flinched and giggled, trying to get away, but his girlfriend was relentless. "It's hard to keep secrets from the people who love you," she said.

Jack was laughing so hard he had tears on his cheeks. "Okay! Okay!" He retreated, scrubbing at his eyes with the back of one hand. "Your point is taken. Henceforth, I will submit to your Orwellian invasion of privacy."

"So…"

"So?"

Standing on her toes, Anna kissed his cheek. "Would you like to be my date to the fair?" she whispered. "We could have some apple pie, listen to the live music, maybe ride the Ferris wheel."

"I would love to."

Their journey took them down a wide lane between two rows of colourful tents. A blue one on his left was occupied by a woman in her fifties who still wore sunglasses even though the last traces of twilight were fading from the sky. One glance and Jack understood why. She was selling designer sunglasses.

On his right, several kids from the local high school sold corn on the cob from a bright yellow tent. Maybe half a dozen people were clustered around a table that was loaded up with t-shirts.

Anna slipped her arm around his waist and snuggled up with her head on his chest. "This place…" she murmured. "I can totally see teenage you daydreaming about bringing a girl here."

Eventually, they found themselves in the midway, surrounded by all sorts of crazy rides. There were the giant strawberries that went round and round in a circle. There was the Scrambler; Jack thought that one was aptly named because it looked and moved like the spinning head of a blender. One was shaped like a huge octopus with cars at the end of every tentacle. Kids screamed, and the scent of popcorn filled the air.

They were fenced in on all sides by carnival games, each one sheltered from the elements under a metal roof that was decked out in blinking lights. The men and women who operated those games all cried out, beckoning people to try their luck.

A young woman with dark skin and long hair that she wore in corn-rows was running a game of Skee Ball. She caught Jack's eye and favoured him with a salesman's smile. "Win it for your girlfriend?" she said, pointing to the big stuffed panda that hung over her head.

Jack stepped up to her with his hands clasped behind his back, craning his neck to examine the prizes. "Tempting," he said, eyebrows rising. "What do you say, Anna? Want me to win you a teddy bear?"

In the blink of an eye, Anna placed herself in front of him. That impish grin of hers told him that he had just made this a contest. "I don't know," she replied. "Do you want me to win *you* a teddy bear?"

"Sure."

The young woman looked at him with a quizzical expression.

He shrugged and lowered his eyes, a mild flush warming his cheeks. "I like teddy bears," he explained. "So, how 'bout I try to win you one, and you try to win me one?"

"Deal," Anna agreed.

The rules were pretty simple. To win a teddy bear, you had to earn at least twelve hundred points in three throws. Which meant that you had to get the ball in one of the two rings in the upper corners – both worth five hundred points – at least twice.

Jack pressed his lips together as he studied the lane, sizing it all up with spatial awareness. He felt an eagerness from Summer. The math played out instinctively in his mind. Well…It wasn't really math; there were no symbols or numbers. It was what math would be if it could be expressed with emotion. A certainty that he had to throw the ball exactly *this* hard. He had done this many times before, but usually, it involved shooting a gun with precision.

Lifting the ball in his hand, Jack examined it. Not just with his eyes or his fingers but with his mind. There were tiny nicks along its surface. It would roll unevenly. He had to account for that.

He tossed the ball.

It landed squarely in the lane, rolled along at dizzying speed and hopped from the end of the ramp…right into the ring in the upper-left corner. The young woman turned her head, her eyes widening in surprise.

"Beginner's luck," Jack assured her.

Of course, that explanation was far less convincing when he performed the exact same feat a second time. For his final throw, he chose the ring in the upper-right corner. The ball went in with a satisfying *thunk*.

Next to him, Anna completed her final throw and stood up straight with a grin on her face. "Well," she said. "I guess you can choose any prize you want."

"You both can," the young woman muttered. She reached for the huge panda – the most expensive prize she had to offer – but Anna forestalled. "No, he's cute, but I want something a little smaller. That one."

She pointed to a modestly-sized, brown teddy bear with a blue bow-tie. A cutie to be sure. The instant Anna got her hands on him, she squeezed him tight as if he were a treasured childhood toy. "I love him!" she exclaimed.

Jack's bear was black with a brown snout and a cream-coloured bow-tie. He knew right away that he would keep the little guy forever as a reminder of this night. "Come on," Anna said, leading toward the rides.

Fifteen minutes later, they were climbing into the car of a Ferris wheel and waiting patiently as the attendant fastened the safety bar. They began to rise, the city lights coming into view bit by bit.

Anna was next to him with hands folded in her lap, smiling lovingly at him. "I'm really glad we came here tonight," she murmured. "You're such a romantic."

Jack slipped his arm around her shoulders, and she cuddled up with her head on his chest. "What do you mean?" he asked. "Because I had a silly fantasy about taking a girl to the fair when I was in high school?"

"It's adorable."

They were partway up when the wheel stopped to load people into the next car. Not high enough to get a good view, but he did see lights reflected over the dark waters of the Red River. It was a beautiful night. Warm but not painfully so. For a moment, he almost thought that Anna would fall asleep in his arms. And he was okay with that.

At the apex of their climb, he had a lovely view of the city under a starry sky with only a few clouds drifting across the heavens. He never really thought that he would miss this place – when he was a kid, he had wanted to see the world – but having been all over the galaxy, he had to admit that there were days when he longed for the familiar. Only a few, but it did happen.

Anna sat up, and the wind teased her hair. Her impish smile returned. "You know, I have seen a *lot* of Earth media," she began. "And I have it on good authority that there's another carnival tradition we're forgetting."

"What's that?"

Gently, she laid a hand on his cheek and turned his face toward her. Then she was kissing him. It was a chaste kiss, tender and sweet, one that soothed away his worries and left him with a warm glow.

It was almost midnight when they left the fair. Jack found himself driving down a narrow street that ran parallel to the river, a street lined with tall maple trees that stood like shadows, their dark branches reaching over the road. He was about to turn onto the Provencher Bridge when Anna put a hand on his thigh. "No, stay on Tache," she said.

Gripping the steering wheel hard, Jack squinted through the windshield. He shook his head slowly. "Stay on Tache?" he muttered. "Why? There's nothing on Tache."

Anna was reclining in the front seat with her hands folded behind her head, and her soft laughter made him wonder exactly what she had in store for him. She could be quite devious when she wanted to be. "Just trust me."

They continued on, passing a library, a park and several small apartment buildings. When they passed under a set of train tracks, Jack became even more confused. What on Earth were they doing all the way out here? He saw nothing but tiny houses.

"Just past the pumping station," Anna said. "Now, left."

Her directions led them to a short dirt road surrounded by trees, a secluded little hidey-hole on the bank of the river. He looked around, trying to figure out why Anna had chosen this place, and then it hit him. "This is a make-out spot! You want to go to a make-out spot?"

Anna sat with her arms crossed, her lips pursed as she stared indignantly through the window. "I don't know *what* you're talking about!" she insisted. "That you could even *think* such a thing about a woman of my breeding!"

"Um..."

Leaning over the gearshift, Anna seized a fistful of his shirt and pulled him close. Every last trace of reluctance fled from Jack's mind when her soft lips found the side of his neck.

Anna practically climbed on top of him, holding him pinned with her hands on his shoulders. Her hot breath on his ear made him shudder. "The theme of this evening," she whispered, "is doing all the things you didn't get to do when you were younger."

"Mm-hmm…"

She sat up, and even though she was just a shadow in the darkness, Jack could feel the intensity of her gaze. "So," she cooed. "Do you wanna make out with a hottie?"

Jack tossed her down into the front seat, and then he was on top of her, nipping at her neck, her collarbone, the soft skin of her shoulder. The scent of her was intoxicating. Like strawberries.

Her mouth found his, and this kiss was anything but chaste. No, not chaste at all. It was ragged desperation. For a very long while – like an hour, at least – it really was just making out, but then Anna peeled his t-shirt off and flung it into the backseat. Her flannel sweater went next, and then one thing led to another…

Some men described sex as a haze in which their conscious minds retreated and they acted on instinct, but Jack was intimately aware of everything. He felt it every time Anna's fingernails left scratches in his back. He heard every sigh, reveled in the softness of her skin. He was aware of *everything*.

Well…Everything that mattered.

And the only thing that mattered was the goddess in his arms. Everything else was just a distraction. Anna was the only thing in his universe. He listened for the pace of her breathing. He focused on the slight sting of her nails digging into his shoulder. He mixed it all together into a sparkling cocktail of information with only one purpose. Not just to give her pleasure; that was easy. Jack had discovered what she liked on their first night together. No, the *real* challenge was to leave her teetering on the brink for a little while, to tease her to the point of desperation. That way, it would be so much sweeter when he finally did take her over the edge.

At one point, he paused just to admire her face. There was no light, but Jack didn't need it; he could sense every inch of her, every perfect inch. Anna was smiling up at him. "I love you," she whispered.

He smoothed a lock of damp hair off her forehead, kissed her softly on the nose and whispered. "I love you too..."

"Really?"

"More than anything in this universe."

Once wasn't enough for either of them, but when they were finally satisfied, when they were catching their breath and basking in the afterglow, Jack found the presence of mind to check the clock on his multi-tool. He blinked at what he saw. It was almost three a.m.! "Wow..."

He was lying in the front seat, staring lazily at the interior of the car's roof. Anna was curled up on top of him with her head on his chest. "The blanket..." she mumbled. "In the back..."

He reached behind the driver's seat and found a thin blanket there. Odd. He hadn't put it there, and he had been out all day with Rajel and Cassi. Which meant that Anna must have hidden it in the backseat last night at the very latest. Which meant that she had been planning this date for a while.

Jack took the blanket and settled it over her. It was big enough to cover her from feet to shoulders but thin enough to be cool on this hot summer night. Anna sighed as she nuzzled his chest. "I know we have to go back soon," she murmured. "But can we just stay here for a while? Can you just hold me?"

Jack closed his eyes and let his head fall back against the seat cushion. He breathed deeply through his nose. "Sure," he whispered. "For as long as you like."

He found himself trailing his fingertips up and down her back, gently caressing her. Thoughts drifted through his mind. Things that had occurred to him earlier that afternoon, things he wanted to tell Anna. He half thought about mentioning them, but he was just so mellow. He didn't want to move...or talk...

He just wanted to enjoy the feeling of his girlfriend's warm body, listen to the soothing sound of her breathing as she fell asleep...

Knock, knock, knock.

Jack woke up to realize that it was morning. The sun was shining bright over the Red River; the trees were standing tall with green leaves fluttering in the wind. And there was a cop outside his car.

A tall and broad-shouldered man with fair skin and gray stubble along his jawline, he leaned forward to peer through the window. It was open just a crack; so Jack could hear the man just fine when he said, "Okay, lovebirds, time to go home."

Rolling onto her back, Anna stretched languidly and sighed with contentment. Her eyes popped open. She was covered to her shoulders, but for half a second, Jack thought she would be mortified and clutch the blankets to her chest. That was what happened in the movies. Instead, she just smiled and said, "Good morning, Officer. Is there something we can do for you?"

"You can get dressed and go home."

Stifling a yawn with her fist, Anna nodded. "Sure," she said in a sleepy voice. "If you'll just give us a moment, we'll be on our way."

The man backed away from the car with his hands on his hips, but his gaze never wavered. Not for an instant. Jack wasn't quite sure what to do. He couldn't start putting on his own clothes until Anna climbed off of him, and he was pretty sure she wouldn't do that with the cop outside. *Oh, this should be fun. I can't wait to explain to Mom why we have to pay a fine.*

Anna sat up, holding the blankets in place to keep herself covered. Glancing out the window, she raised a thin eyebrow. "Were you planning to watch?" she asked. "Because, honestly, that might get me a little excited. And then Jack and I would *have* to have sex again; it's not smart to drive when you're distracted by lustful thoughts. So, if you plan on watching, I'm going to have to insist that you stay for the entire show."

The cop was blushing so hard you might have thought that he was some sheltered, home-schooled kid. He averted his eyes for a brief moment and then regained some of his backbone. "Who the hell are you, lady?"

"The woman who saved your planet…what? Three times now?"

"Yeah," the cop snarled. "And I'm Anna Lenai."

"Well, actually…"

Crossing his arms, the cop tossed his head back and stared up at the sky with his mouth hanging open. "Look, I don't have time for stupid college kids," he growled. "Get dressed, go home and don't let me ever catch you out here again."

He stalked off toward his cruiser, which was parked a little ways up the road.

Anna flung the blanket aside without a care in the world and began retrieving her clothes from under the seat. "You heard him, sweetie," she said, patting Jack's thigh. "Oh, and can we stop at that Canadian coffee place you like so much? I think your mom would appreciate it, and I want to get one of those maple donuts before we get back to Leyria."

Chapter 3

Silver rays of morning sunlight streamed over a wooden fence, scorching the dew from a lush, green lawn. A flowerbed just beneath that fence was populated with roses and lilies and tulips in beautiful shades of red and pink and yellow. The sun hadn't found them yet, but it would soon enough.

Harry was down on one knee in the grass, his head bowed almost as if in prayer. The symbolism wasn't lost on him now that religion was becoming a major theme in his life. "You really outdid yourself, Mark."

His mouth tightened, and then he shook his head in frustration. "No matter how hard I try, I just can't make them grow like that," he muttered. "But then I never had the time for gardening."

Well, that wasn't exactly true.

It *used* to be true. Two years ago, when he was still juggling the responsibilities of a cop and a single father, it would have been fair to say that he didn't have enough time for gardening. But this last year on Leyria had been almost leisurely compared to the life he had known. His routine was pretty simple. He saw Claire off to school each morning, did a little light housework, cooked dinner in the afternoon – even though that blasted robot insisted on taking the job from him – and spent his nights with the girls.

True, there were several months in which he had been bedridden, and despite his resolution to stay out of it, he usually found a way to help with whatever Melissa was doing. But otherwise…He could have been a gardener if he wanted to.

"Maybe you should take it up," a voice said behind him.

Harry stiffened.

His words had been private, meant for his ears only, but Mark must have overheard part of his lamentations. His brother's footsteps in the grass were soft. Only a trained ear would pick them up.

Harry got up and turned around.

A tall man in blue jeans and a polo shirt, Mark stood with his arms crossed. He had a bit of a belly now that he was well into his forties – and the beard that stretched from ear to ear showed more than a few flecks of gray – but the muscles on his arms were as big as they had ever been. "Gardening might be safer."

"It's not really an option now, is it?"

"Isn't it?"

With a tight frown, Harry turned his face up to the clear blue sky and blinked. "The aliens are gonna hold me to that deal, Mark," he said. "I won't put Claire's life at risk. Not ever again!"

Mark began pacing a circle around Harry, pausing near the back fence. "Maybe you never should have made it," he grumbled. "Deals with the devil usually end up costing a lot more than your soul."

"So, I should have let her die?"

"I didn't say that."

"Well, then…"

Harry turned to face his brother and found the other man shaking his head with teeth bared. "You never should have taken her there in the first place!" Mark insisted. "Let's review the sequence of events."

"Okay…"

"A year ago, Melissa was accepted into the Justice Keepers' training program. You went to Leyria with her, and you took Claire. You told us all that they would be safer on Leyria, but while you were there, you involved yourself in the Justice Keepers' business, got yourself shot, used yourself as bait to trap the psychopath who nearly killed you in your own kitchen, brought Claire with you to a hostile planet and screwed around with her brain."

Harry felt warmth in his face, and the single tear that rolled down his cheek only added to his shame. "Yeah, that's accurate," he admitted. "If you remove all the context and the reasoning behind those decisions."

Mark strode forward until they were toe-to-toe. The intensity in his elder brother's eyes made Harry brace himself for some harsh words. He had seen that exact same look every time he screwed up as a kid. "I believed you when you said that Leyria was a place where the girls could be safe," Mark began. "I *still* believe that. But why do you have to keep chasing danger, Harry? Why can't you just be a retired cop?"

"Hello?" Melissa called out.

She emerged from the patio door in white shorts and a red tank-top, her black hair cut short in a bob. "I just got in five minutes ago," she said, striding across the lawn. "Mom says hi."

"And Claire?"

"Still with Mom."

Harry shut his eyes, a heavy sigh exploding from his lungs. "Well, I guess it was too much to hope that she would come home," he muttered. "How was Sasha's barbecue?"

A tiny smirk was Melissa's first response to that. "Eventful," was all she said. "But I should probably tell you that Mom thinks Claire should stay here with her, and I think Claire is seriously considering it."

"Over my dead-"

"Harry…" Mark cut in.

Turning away from both of them, Harry paced across the yard with his arms folded. "If Claire is really happier here," he began reluctantly, "then I'd be willing to give Della full custody."

When he finally worked up the courage to look, they were both staring at him bug-eyed, as if they had never seen him before. "That's…very mature of you," Melissa said. "I think Mom would be glad to hear it."

Mark was smiling and nodding slowly as if he had always known that Harry would make the right decision. "It might be for the best," he said. "I guess I should let the two of you chat. Harry. Agent Carlson."

Melissa blushed every time someone used her new title, and this was no exception. She hugged her uncle, and then Mark was stomping back to the house, the patio door grinding as he ducked inside.

Standing awkwardly with her hands in her pockets, Melissa kept her gaze fixed on the grass. "I am never going to get used to that," she muttered. "One day, I'm going to be interrogating somebody. They'll call me Agent Carlson, and I'll go beet-red." She snapped her fingers. "Just like that, all the credibility is gone."

"You'll be all right."

"I hope so."

It took even more courage to dig deep within himself and find the words he really didn't want to say. "We never really talked about what happened on Antaur," Harry said. "You must hate me."

"I don't," Melissa assured him.

"Why don't I believe that?"

His daughter gave him a hard-eyed stare that he knew would serve her well when she eventually *did* find herself in an interrogation room. "Because you're a good person," she replied.

"Because *you* feel so guilty about it that you can't forgive yourself. Because I now have irrefutable proof that you're the kind of man who would sell his soul to protect his daughters, and since I happen to *be* one of those daughters, it's hard not to love you."

"You may not love me after I fulfill my end of the bargain."

Gritting her teeth with a hiss, Melissa shook her head. "I wish you would just tell me what that is!" she pleaded. "You said it doesn't involve killing anybody or betraying your friends or anything like that. So, what could possibly be so bad?"

"No," Harry said. "I don't want you anywhere near this."

"But I could help."

"No!" It came out as a growl, one so fierce Melissa actually took a step backward. Moderating his tone with some effort, Harry began again. "I am going to attract a *lot* of negative attention in the next few months. You have a promising career ahead of you, and I will not let you ruin it by attaching yourself to me."

Melissa studied him with wide eyes. "Is that why you're letting Mom take Claire?" she whispered. "So that she won't suffer any of the blowback?"

"Being a good father is no longer a luxury I can afford."

"What does that mean?"

Harry didn't answer; he just went back into the house and left her to think.

Rajel stood with fists on his hips, listening to an ocean that lapped at the shore mere inches away from his bare toes. It was a hot afternoon, the sun beating down relentlessly from a cloudless sky. Gulls dove over the water, looking for food. And he could hear the sound of children playing in the distance.

Tilting his head back, Rajel closed his eyes and felt the sun on his face. "Beautiful," he said. "A definite improvement over the endless drizzle of Denabrian winter."

With spatial awareness, he sensed the approach of a small young woman with short hair. She came up behind him and stopped about three feet away. "You know, Leyria *is* a big planet," Cassi began. "It's always warm somewhere. You didn't have to spend three days on a starship if all you wanted was sandy beaches."

He turned to her.

Cocking her head to one side, Cassi studied him with her lips pressed together. "I *had* to come," she went on. "Larani wanted me here just in case Jack needed some help wrapping up the investigation."

Rajel crossed his arms, nodding to her. "How is that going?" he asked. "I admit that I haven't been keeping track, but I'm fairly certain it's been months since you and Hunter made an arrest."

"You'd be right," she replied. "The last was on Velezia."

"I always knew Roderick was crooked," he muttered under his breath. "So, do you think you've weeded out the last of Slade's agents?"

Unwrapping her sarong, Cassi handed it to him and then strode out into the water until she was submerged to her ankles. She seemed to be transfixed by something on the horizon. Rajel couldn't say what. There were no horizons in his world. Only a fog that started about a hundred metres away from his body and got exponentially thicker the further you went. "It's hard to say," Cassi said at last.

"Let me guess," Rajel said. "You've got no more leads, and there's been no strange activity for a while now. The optimist in you wants to conclude that your work is done, but deep down inside you just *know* that you missed at least one of

Slade's people, and that person will reveal themself at the worst possible time."

He heard the distinct sound of splashing, and when he turned around, Cassi was right in front of him. "Yeah," she said. "That's pretty much it."

"Pretty much."

"Anything I can do to help?"

Cassi smiled, bowing her head and playfully brushing a lock of hair aside. "That's funny," she said. "I was about to ask you the same thing."

He stiffened, retreating a step, and tried to ignore the flush that singed his cheeks. "You mean after my outburst yesterday?" he muttered. "I'm fine. I just... Getting to know Keli has been a very confusing journey."

"I don't doubt it."

"I shouldn't have lost my temper."

Cassi had one hand on her hip as she studied him. "Wasn't it just a few months ago that you were saying that you despised telepaths?" she inquired. "What happened to change your mind."

"I had a chat with my Nassai."

"Ah. Yes, that'll do it."

He was trying to get a read on this woman. Cassiara was naturally flirtatious. So, was her attempt at assessing his feelings just friendly concern... or was there something *else* going on? He would have to probe with judicious care. "I sense that you don't have a high opinion of Keli."

"I don't have any opinion of her one way or the other," Cassi replied. "I've worked with her a few times, and I will admit that she's good in a crisi, if a bit unpredictable. But other than that, I don't know her."

"So, why do you ask?"

"I can't get to know one of my colleagues?" Cassi protested. "You might not have noticed, but I'm something of an expert when it comes to getting over a broken heart."

Rajel answered that with a wolfish grin. "I see," he said. "So, are you offering your services in that regard?"

"Oh no!" Cassi said, shaking her head. "I've already been one man's rebound girl this year. I'd rather not repeat that experience. But maybe…When you're a little more settled, we can revisit the issue?"

"I'd like that."

To his surprise, she started tapping her lips with one finger and watching him as if she wasn't quite sure what to make of him. "Interesting," she murmured. "I half expected you to insist that you'd be mooning over Ms. Armana for the better part of the next year."

"Why would I waste energy on someone who doesn't want me when I can explore opportunities with someone who does?"

Cassi strode forward, laying a hand on his forearm. "Ah! It seems we have a lot in common." She took back her sarong, then stood on her toes and clicked her teeth together an inch away from his ear. "Perhaps we won't have to wait as long as I thought."

She was gone a moment later, leaving Rajel to stand there with a big, dopey grin on his face.

Hunched over the desk in the small office they gave her aboard Station One, Larani typed a report on a small metal keyboard. The inclined plane of SmartGlass – a segment of her desk that was tilted to form a screen – displayed several paragraphs of text. Larani checked them several times. She had always been a fastidious woman, but with Dusep's popularity surging, it was important to make sure that everything was done by the book.

She glanced over her shoulder to find stars in the window behind her desk. That irked her. She was used to seeing the blue sky or other buildings or *nature* of some kind, not the empty vacuum of space. But her people had built stations in orbit of Earth rather than setting up bases on the planet's surface. A part of that was to assure the Earthers that their Leyrian cousins were friends and not invaders, but the Earthers also seemed to want to maintain a sense of separateness, an independence of culture. Which was ludicrous in her opinion, but there it was.

A hologram appeared in front of her desk, a ghostly figure comprised of swirling blue letters and numbers in Leyrian script. It almost made Larani jump out of her chair. Almost, but not quite.

She looked up to blink at the apparition. "Ven," she said. "This is a surprise. I didn't think we'd be seeing you again for a while."

"Assemble your people, Director," the hologram said. "We have work to do."

Yawning so hard it hurt, Anna slapped a hand over her mouth. "Goodness," she mumbled, stepping into Larani's office. "My apologies, everyone. I didn't get very much sleep last night."

Jack followed her in with his head down, and of course, his cheeks were pink. Earthers could be so modest sometimes. But then, her boyfriend seemed to be very impressed by how she handled that random cop this morning.

Cassi was leaning against the wall with her arms folded, and she glanced in Anna's direction with a knowing smile. "Just glad you could make it," she teased. "I do hope we didn't interrupt something important."

"Oh, nothing of consequence."

Rajel stood behind the desk with one hand pressed against the slanted window pane that looked out into space. "Well, now that we're all here," he said. "Maybe Larani could tell us what this is all about."

"Not yet. There's still one more-"

Melissa came stomping into the office and stopped abruptly two paces away from the desk. She looked up at Larani with hard eyes. "Ma'am, with respect, I would like to know why my father wasn't invited to this meeting."

Reclining in her chair, Larani studied the young woman for a brief moment before nodding. "Agent Carlson," she began. "The reason that *you* were invited to this meeting is your wise decision to report your father's dealings with the Overseers as soon as you learned of them."

Everyone exchanged glances.

"I had already heard as much from Hunter and Lenai," Larani went on. "But now, I know I can trust you. In light of your father's recent decisions, I'm sure you can see why his presence would not be advisable."

"Yes, ma'am…"

Larani was on her feet an instant later, pacing around the desk as she spoke. "Now that we're all assembled," she said. "I'll turn the floor over to our guest."

A hologram appeared in the middle of the room, and Anna felt a sudden rush of joy! She hadn't seen Ven in almost a year! She had hoped for a chance to get to know the AI, and maybe now she would get it.

"Ven!" Jack exclaimed.

"Jack," the hologram replied. It turned slowly on the spot, as if taking in the sight of each of them, and then something almost like a sigh came through the speakers. Ven was becoming increasingly adept with human mannerisms. "I wish that I could be here under better circumstances," Ven said. "But I have some terrible news."

Anna felt cold inside. Ven's last visit had resulted in Jack being captured by the Ragnosians. And the time before that, they ended up fighting a guerrilla war in the streets of Queens. "What is it?" she mumbled.

"Five months ago," Ven began, "you raided a castle in the Lyrian highlands that Slade was using as a base of operations."

"Yes."

"While you were there, you retrieved encrypted data from one of their servers. The algorithms used to protect that data were very complex. Larani granted me access on my last visit, and I've only just finished decoding it."

Jack was at her side with one hand in his pocket, his eyes fixed on the floor. "We should have known that would eventually come back to haunt us," he mumbled. "What does it say?"

"You probably expected Slade to meddle in the upcoming election," Ven said. "But I'm afraid it's worse than anyone could have anticipated. Slade is planning to assassinate Sarona Vason."

Chapter 4

Gaping at the hologram, Jack blinked a few times. He gave his head a shake as if trying to dispel an image that had formed in his mind. "Slade is planning to assassinate the Leyrian Prime Council?" he exclaimed. "I knew the guy was evil, but even for him, that's ambitious."

Anna had to admit that she was dubious as well. Not that Slade would do it – there was no low that man wouldn't stoop to – but that he would actually be able to accomplish such a lofty goal. The Prime Council was one of the most well-protected people in the galaxy. Even Slade would have a hard time getting through those defenses.

Anna stepped forward to face the hologram with her lips pursed. "You're sure?" she asked, raising an eyebrow. "It would be extremely difficult, if not impossible, for Slade to pull that off."

"Difficult," Ven agreed, "but not impossible." The hologram waved a spectral hand, and a globe appeared, a world of blue oceans and green landmasses. Similar to Leyria but not the same. Anna recognized it on sight. That was Alios. Slade's original plan was to kill your Prime Council during the final debate, three nights before the election. But your recent treaty with Antaur has changed the situation.

"Yesterday morning, Sarona Vason and Jeral Dusep announced plans to visit the Fringe Worlds in the hopes of smoothing over tensions after your world agreed to cede Belos to the Antaurans. The final debate will be held on Alios, not Leyria."

Cassi marched through the globe with her teeth bared, shaking her head. "That was a crap decision," she growled. "Fifty million people living on Belos. Now, every last one of them has to move or petition the Antauran government to let them become citizens."

"The point," Larani cut in, "is that the Prime Council's security team will have to adapt to these new circumstances. They've been holding these debates at Dantharus Hall, in Denabria, for over two centuries; the security team had detailed plans for how to cover every single entrance and exit. Now, they will have to make up plans on the fly for whichever venue the candidates choose."

"And there are bound to be gaps," Jack lamented.

"Exactly."

Rajel turned away from the window, pacing across the room. "All right," he said. "So, why don't we place a long-range call through the SlipGate network and warn the Prime Council of the danger?"

Sitting primly on the edge of her desk, Larani sighed. "I did precisely that half an hour ago," she explained. "The Prime Council remains adamant that if she doesn't visit the outer colonies, her chances for reelection are gone. She's going. And we're going to make sure that she has adequate security for every step of that journey."

"No offense, Larani," Jack said. "But it's an eight-day flight from Earth to Alios. We're a bit far off, don't you think?"

"I've convinced the Prime Council to delay her departure by three days. That will give us enough time to rendezvous with her on Leyria. As I said, we're going to be with her every step of the way. I have also contacted our best people on Alios and reassigned them to the security detail. I want you five there because, out of all my agents, you have the most experience with Grecken Slade and his lieutenants. You'll know what to watch for. I will be assuming command of all Justice Keepers assigned to this mission. As of right now, this is our number one priority."

They all nodded.

Larani stood up with her back straight and her shoulders square. Her face was stern, but she nodded once to each of them. "Special Agents Hunter and Seyrus," she barked. "For the duration of this assignment, you will be reporting directly to Operative Lenai as members of her team."

Anna had a serious case of the warm fuzzies when she saw the tiny smile on her boyfriend's face. "Works for me," Jack said. "Hell, maybe we can make that a permanent arrangement."

"We'll discuss that later."

Anna gently laid a hand on Jack's back. She would be more than happy to have him as a permanent member of her team. They had always worked well together. A part of her wanted to name Jack as her second in command, but Rajel had seniority. The role should go to him.

"Would one of you please contact Ms. Armana?" Larani asked. "It wouldn't hurt to have a telepath along for this mission."

"I'm sure I can persuade her," Anna said.

"Excellent," Larani said. "Then gather your belongings. We leave for Leyria in six hours."

Della's kitchen was well lit by multiple windows that looked out on her yard. It was the sort of place that you might expect from a woman who had grown up accustomed to a certain amount of affluence: white tiles, granite countertops, an island in the middle of the room with a sink built into it.

Harry stood by one of those windows, frowning as he watched squirrels scurrying up a tree outside. "So, you're sure this is what you want?" he asked. "You've made a lot of friends on Leyria, honey."

He turned.

Claire sat at the table with her hands folded on a place-mat. One look at her, and you knew without a doubt that she was expecting the worst. Maybe she thought he would make this difficult, put up a fight. It broke his heart to see such distrust in his daughter's eyes. When had that started? Was it after he had made her a telepath or before? He had a bad feeling that it had been growing for some time now. "I think..." Claire began. "I think I need a break from everything."

Della was sitting at the island with her elbows on its surface, her chin resting on laced fingers. Her eyebrows shot up. "Please tell me that you're not going to make a fuss about this, Harry."

He closed his eyes, fighting back tears, and shook his head slowly. "No, I won't." It took a great deal of effort to keep his voice steady, but he did it. Claire had been through enough in the last few months. Seeing him cry would only make this harder for her. "If this is what Claire wants, then I support it."

"Thanks, Dad."

"We'll keep in touch," Harry promised. "I'll call you once a week."

It surprised him when Claire hopped out of her chair and bounded across the room in three quick strides. She slammed into Harry, throwing her arms around him in a fierce hug. "I'm gonna miss you, Dad."

Now, the tears were flowing freely, and Harry made no effort to stop them. "I'm going to miss you too." He returned the hug with just as much gusto. "Promise me you'll stay safe. And listen to your mother!"

"I promise."

Harry dropped to one knee, resting his hands on Claire's shoulders. As hard as it was, he forced himself to look her in the eye. "And I promise to visit," he said. "At least once every few months."

Claire smiled as tears streamed over her cheeks. "I would like that," she whispered. "And maybe, in a little while, I could visit you."

"You're always welcome."

She hugged him again, throwing her arms around his neck, and she didn't let go for a very long while.

Jack peered through the small window in his mother's kitchen, taking in the sight of his hometown. It would be the last time he would see it for a long while – somehow, he knew that – and that left him with a lump of sadness in his belly. Sunlight glinted off the windows of skyscrapers. If he strained, he could just make out the Red River in the gaps between buildings. Winnipeg was a beautiful city. It dawned on him that he hadn't appreciated it enough when he was living here... And somber thoughts kept his mind off the conversation his mother and girlfriend were having not ten feet away.

Crystal threw her head back, roaring with laughter and trembling so hard that some of the contents of her glass spilled onto her hand. It was only water, but it still made quite a mess. Hell, she practically fell out of her chair. "So... You just *dared* him to watch the two of you having sex?"

Anna sat across from her with one leg crossed over the other, grinning as she shook her head. "Well, you know me," she said. "The sluttiest slut who ever did slut."

Slouching in her chair with a hand over her mouth, Crystal... tittered. "Oh, I like this girl, Jack!" she exclaimed. "When are you getting married?"

Jack buried his face in the palm of his hand, groaning under his breath. "Great job, Mom," he said. "Nothing convinces a woman to stick around quite like pressure from the in-laws."

Anna stood up and paced over to him, wrapping her arms around his waist. She nuzzled his chest. "I don't know if you've noticed, sweetie," she murmured. "But I'm not exactly trying to get away."

He licked his lips, then shut his eyes and offered a curt nod of approval. "Well, that is good to know." Damn it! He was so embarrassed he could barely find the willpower to speak. Why couldn't he have one of those classic sitcom moms who was scandalized by the thought of her baby boy having sex? Summer thought the whole thing was hilarious. "But uh, you know, it would probably be good to *not* share details of our sex-life with my mother."

"Oh, grow up!" Anna teased.

"Men," Crystal muttered over her glass of water. "Always so modest."

She rose from her chair with a sigh, then came over to join them in a group hug. "And now you're going away again," Crystal murmured. "And I won't see you again for another six months."

"I'll try to come sooner," Jack whispered.

His mother pulled away, brushing a tear off her cheek with the back of one hand. "No," she said. "You have a life to live and a promising career. I get the sense that the galaxy needs you. Both of you."

"We *will* visit," Anna promised.

"I know," Crystal said softly. "I just…" Her eyes lit up with that spark she got when she had a sudden flash of brilliance. Jack had seen that look on his mother's face many times. Mostly when she was helping him with really difficult math homework. "What if I went with you?"

"To Alios?"

"The hospital owes me several weeks of vacation," Crystal explained. "Oh, I kept meaning to take them, but we always got swamped. You know how it is. I could request a short leave of absence."

Squeezing his eyes shut, Jack shook his head. "I don't think it's a good idea, Mom," he said. "We're going to protect the Prime Council from a potential assassination attempt. If Slade finds out you're there, he won't hesitate to go after you."

Anna was next to him with her hands in the pockets of her shorts, nodding slowly in agreement. "Crystal, we would love to have you along," she said. "But Jack's right. It's too dangerous."

Jack felt a sudden pang of guilt.

His mother looked crestfallen, but she accepted the news with a stiff upper lip. "I suppose you're right," she whispered. "A shame...I want to see what life is like beyond the confines of this little world."

"Maybe you could visit us on Leyria," Anna suggested.

"I'd like that."

With a deep breath, Crystal stood up straight, squared her shoulders and put on a brave face. "Well," she said. "I guess there's nothing left to do but to see you off. Come on. I'll drive you to the SlipGate terminal."

Melissa sat alone at a round table in the little cafe that overlooked the concourse on Station Twelve, watching the people scurrying past below. Traffic was light at this hour; she saw a Justice Keeper reading something on a tablet as he walked by and a man in a gray suit on his way to the tram station.

Hunched over with her elbow on the table, her chin resting in the palm of her hand, Melissa sighed. "Yeah," she whispered to Ilia. "It makes me sad too."

Everything about Station Twelve reminded her of Jena. She remembered the many, many sparring sessions in which she had struggled to pick up the basics of martial arts. Jena had always been patient and kind, encouraging her to keep trying. She remembered meeting Raynar for the first time. She remembered running frantically through corridors that seemed to go on for miles, bursting into Jena's office and proclaiming that she knew what Grecken Slade really wanted. Melissa would never have imagined that she would look back on those days and long for the simplicity of easier times.

Claire was staying behind and moving in with their mother. That bothered her, she realized. She would have never thought that being separated from her sister would leave her with a dull ache in her chest, but there it was. Claire would be safer here on Earth – she knew that – but a part of her wanted to protest and insist that her little sister belonged with her on Leyria.

Letting her mind drift, Melissa slipped away from the physical world to commune with her Nassai. The setting that Ilia chose was a replica of the little cafe. But now Ilia was sitting across from her. Or maybe it was more accurate that Jena was sitting across from her. Nassai experienced every thought that passed through a host's mind. It was fair to say that they knew a person better than that person knew themself, and Ilia had used that knowledge to recreate Jena in every detail.

She was right there, just as Melissa remembered her: tall with boyishly-short hair, sharp eyes and a dimple in her chin. "Don't be so somber, kid," she said. "We had a lot of good memories in this place too."

"We did."

"So, why so sad?"

Pressing her lips together, Melissa looked up at the ceiling and blinked. "You ever get the feeling that the world is changing?" she whispered. "And you really, really want it to stay the same?"

Jena grimaced as if she had a bad taste in her mouth, then shook her head quickly. "Change never really bothered me," she replied. "It's just a part of life. You kind of have to accept it."

"I guess."

"You don't sound convinced."

Melissa's chair scraped across the floor tiles as she stood up. When she looked over the railing, she saw no one else down there. But then, why would there be? This facsimile of the station was probably empty except for her and Jena and any other avatar that her symbiont chose to adopt. "It just seems like fortune cookie wisdom."

"Doesn't make it any less true."

"Can't we just…invent some kind of time-stopping device?" Melissa protested. "I'm gonna miss my sister."

Jena stretched out in the chair and smiled that special smile of hers. The one that called you an idiot and said that she loved you at the same time. "I'm pretty sure they've still got my stuff in storage," she said. "Go access it. Should be in locker Unit Twenty-Three. The password should be Tomas14."

"Why? What's there?"

"Something that might make you feel a little better."

Ten minutes later, after a ride on the monorail that had taken to the other side of the station, Melissa found herself in the hallway outside Jena's old office. That brought all of her memories flooding back to the surface, and she had to push through the pain again. She wasn't sure why she had come here. It was on the way to the storage unit, but there was nothing here she needed. Maybe she just wanted to look at the place one last time.

When she poked her head through the door, she saw Larani Tal standing by the window behind Jena's old desk, peering out into space. Melissa was quiet, but spatial awareness alerted the other woman to her presence. "Agent Carlson," Larani said without looking. "Is there something I can do for you?"

Melissa stepped into the office with her hands clasped behind herself, frowning as she took in the sight of it. "I guess you had the same idea I did," she mumbled. "You miss her too, huh?"

"I do."

"I never realized that you and Jena were close."

Larani turned abruptly, her sharp eyes accusing Melissa of implying too much with that statement. Her face softened a moment later. "We weren't," she said. "Not, I suspect, as you mean it, anyway. Jena and I knew each other as cadets."

"She never mentioned that."

"I'm not surprised," Larani grumbled. "Jena was something of a sensation among the other cadets. She flew through the program with ease. Six months after she arrived on Leyria, she was already going on dangerous missions with senior Keepers. They thought she was a rising star in the organization."

"What changed?"

"Jena made an enemy of Grecken Slade."

With a heavy sigh, Melissa strode across the room and stopped in front of the desk. She studied her reflection in the SmartGlass. The face that stared back at her seemed unfamiliar somehow. Older. More worn down. It wasn't anything obvious – there were no wrinkles or blemishes – but Melissa could see the fatigue behind her own eyes. "I guess I should have expected as much."

Larani sat down in Jena's old chair, crossing one leg over the other and folding her hands in her lap. "She thought very highly of you, Melissa," she said. "She told me more than once that she expected you to become an excellent Justice Keeper."

Closing her eyes, Melissa felt a tear sliding down her cheek. "I didn't think I would take her symbiont," she whispered. "Sometimes I feel like…like I have to live up to her legacy. And I'm not doing a very good job of it."

"On the contrary," Larani replied. "I can't think of a more worthy successor. Jena would be proud of everything that you've accomplished."

"That's what Ilia tells me."

Reclining as far as she could, Larani smiled ruefully at the ceiling. "You Earthers," she said, shaking her head. "For over seven hundred years, the Justice Keepers protected Leyria from threats both foreign and domestic, and no one thought to name their Nassai until Jack Hunter came along."

"I'm glad to know we shook up the system."

"Are you, now?"

Melissa looked around the room. There was nothing to see – the walls were bare, the furniture untouched – but that didn't mean anything. Even though she had occupied this office for the better part of a year, Jena had never bothered to decorate. Almost as if she were trying to avoid settling in. As if she thought her life circumstances might change on a moment's notice, and then she would be flying off to some other part of the galaxy. Maybe the facsimile that Ilia had created was right. Jena really was the kind of woman who just rolled with the changes.

Melissa had only been a civilian in those days, but she had always felt as though she were a part of the team. Now…Now, the team was different. Jena was gone and Ben too. Thinking of Raynar might make her start crying again. She had liked the young man even if he was a bit of a doofus. And Melissa got choked up whenever she remembered what her father had told her. That Raynar said kissing her was the happiest moment of his life. She was flattered, but what did that say about the poor guy's life?

The team *was* different.

They had Rajel now and Novol. Melissa tried not to think about the butterflies in her stomach that showed up whenever someone mentioned him. And Keli had become their resident telepath; there was no denying it. Melissa just wished it didn't make her feel so sad.

"Are you all right, Agent Carlson?" Larani asked.

Melissa cleared her throat and then stepped back, bowing her head to the other woman. "Quite all right, ma'am," she answered. "I just…Being back here brings up a lot of memories I haven't thought about in a long time."

"For both of us," Larani assured her.

She left the other woman to her memories of Jena and made her way to the storage units. They weren't far from the living quarters. Once inside, she found a series of metal doors in the wall, all sealed shut.

She entered the password into Unit 23, and the door swung open with a hiss. At first, she wasn't quite sure what to look for. Some of Jena's clothes were sealed up inside plastic bags. There were some books, a picture of Jena's parents in an ornate frame. But nothing stood out to her.

Leyrians weren't big on personal property. They didn't really *own* very much. When they moved out of a house, they left the furniture behind so that the next occupants could use it. Their multi-tools were fairly modular with circuitry that was upgraded regularly. Every house and apartment had several workstations with computer interfaces. No one had to buy their own laptops or tablets. Sometimes, Leyrians hung on to things with a lot of sentimental value. Melissa imagined that if she and her father were to move out of their house on Leyria, Michael the robot would go with them. But there just wasn't much here. She was about to give up when she noticed something.

A big, fuzzy teddy bear with soft brown fur was sitting on a shelf at the back of the storage unit. His eyes opened when Melissa stepped inside, and his limbs began to move with a soft, mechanical whir. "Hello," he said. "Where's Jena?"

"Fuzz Bear," Melissa whispered.

"It's nice to meet you," he said. "Are you a friend of Jena's?"

She sniffled, making no effort to stop the tears that streamed over her face. "Yes," she whispered, nodding. "I'm a very good friend of Jena's."

Fuzz Bear looked up at her with his big black eyes, and he blinked once in an almost human gesture. "Is Jena all right?" he asked. "I haven't seen her in a while."

How did she answer that?

Over the last year, Ilia had shared some of Jena's memories with her. This robotic teddy was one of Jena's most prized possessions. He had been with Jena ever since she was a little girl. Melissa didn't have the heart to tell him that his human companion was dead. He wasn't really sentient. Melissa knew that, but she still couldn't bring herself to say it. "Jena's just fine," she murmured.

Crossing the length of the storage unit in three quick steps, Melissa picked up the bear, and he wrapped his arms around her. He nuzzled her cheek with his fuzzy nose. "My name is Melissa," she said. "Jena asked me to come and get you so that we could be friends."

"I would like to be your friend, Melissa."

"I'd like that too," she whispered. "Jena had to go away for a while…To help some people. But she said that you and I could take care of each other."

"Any friend of Jena's is a friend of mine."

"I'm glad to hear it," Melissa said. "Now, let's pack up some of this stuff. We've got a long flight back to Leyria."

Chapter 5

Isara moved like a wraith in a red dress, her cloak flapping in the breeze. Her face was hidden under a scarlet hood, and she kept her eyes downcast. Overhead, the Antauran stars twinkled as the last traces of sunlight vanished from the eastern sky.

This small country road was lit only by the odd streetlight that provided just enough illumination to show a fence to her right and trees on her left, all with leaves fluttering in the wind. It was warm now that spring was in full bloom.

She smiled.

Eventually, she reached a gate where two men in blue uniforms immediately came to attention. One glowered at her as he stepped forward. "Gods forsake us, woman. What are you doing out here in a get-up like that?"

Isara looked up so that the light would penetrate her hood, and she felt her lips curl into a sinister smile. "Thrax Shegan is here, is he not?" she whispered. "Perhaps you could get him for me."

The soldier bared his teeth in a snarl. "Oh, I see. You're a telepath." He fingered the pistol holstered on his belt. "Just when I thought you couldn't get any more flamboyant with your fashions, you try this."

"Please ask Thrax to come out here."

"Doesn't work like that, ma'am," the soldier replied. "Even telepaths can't just walk onto military installations without proper authorizations. Now, you show me some orders, and I'll get you in to see Mr. Shegan."

Isara's hand lashed out.

Her fingers closed around the man's throat, and then she lifted him off the ground. His eyes bulged. "Kill her!" he squeaked. "Kill her!"

The other soldier reached for his gun.

Isara studied her captive for a moment, her eyebrows slowly climbing. "I am not a telepath," she whispered. "I am something far, far worse. Bring me to Thrax Shegan, or I will make you regret-"

"Isara!"

She turned her head and found a man on the other side of the fence, a tall man in ostentatious green robes with golden trim. He was just shy of middle age with a receding hairline and wrinkles in his brow. "I felt you coming before you got within a mile of this place," he said. "Let them go."

She did as she was bidden.

The soldier she released landed on his feet and stumbled, stretching out a hand to keep his balance. He looked up at her with murderous intent. "By the Gods above! Who let this woman-"

"Be silent," Thrax said.

With a quick gesture of his hand, he brought both guards to their knees. They were on the ground, clutching the sides of their heads and wheezing in pain. A moment later, they passed out, one by one.

"Impressive," Isara said.

"Slade told me that you would be coming," Thrax growled. "He knows I'm loyal to the Inzari. What do you need from me?"

"Take me to the prisoner."

There was no need to specify which prisoner she meant. Thrax used a control panel in the guardhouse to open the gate, and then she was walking through it, following a narrow road that slithered through the grass to a gray building in the distance.

Other guards moved to block her path when she approached the front door, but Thrax cowed them with a look. No one wanted to anger a telepath. Not when that telepath had official authority over this facility.

Inside, she found white-walled hallways populated by men and women in pristine lab coats. Most of them walked past with their heads down, focused on something they were reading on a tablet or simply avoiding eye-contact. They knew Thrax. Even without his rank and position, telepaths were viewed as being akin to godliness here on Antaur. So, if the chief interrogator chose to bring in another flamboyantly-dressed companion, well...Who were they to question it?

A left turn brought them to another hallway that ended in a stairwell. Down they went, to the deepest sub-basement, where Thrax had to use his security ID to enter the cell-block.

Another guard rose from his station as they entered, frowning at the pair of them. "Sir," he said. "I must insist that you log your guest in and receive an official visitor ID."

Thrax replied to that with an easy smile and a friendly chuckle. "I trust her, Bil," he said. "She's here to help me interrogate the prisoner. The one we found last month in the Diplomatic Complex. We need extra telepaths to break the protections offered by that creature he carries."

"Be that as it may, sir-"

"Relax, Bil."

The soldier stiffened, and his face became an expressionless mask. He stared unblinking at the pair of them. "You've seen her ID," Thrax said. "I logged her in, and you presented her with official credentials."

"Yes, sir," Bil replied.

"Protocol was followed to the letter."

"Yes, sir. Yes, it was."

Clapping the other man on the shoulder, Thrax smiled and again and offered a nod of respect. "Good," he said softly. "Now, why don't you take a moment and get a coffee. I would imagine you could use a break."

"Yes, sir."

They proceeded through the cell-block without further incident, all the way to a door at the very end. When it opened, Isara found Flynn sitting on a bench with his head down. The fool was still in his Earth fashions.

The instant he looked up at her, his face was split in two by a triumphant grin. "Oh, I knew you would come!" he exclaimed. "They kept trying to tell me that no one would rescue me. But I knew! The Inzari protect their own."

With two hands, Isara reached to pull back her hood. Her hair was longer now and braided, falling almost to her shoulder-blades. "Indeed," she said. "Thrax, if you would give me a moment alone with the prisoner."

"I don't think that would be wise," the telepath protested.

Glancing over her shoulder, Isara showed him a death glare that should have frozen his blood cold. It did nothing of the sort. The man just leaned against the door-frame with an impish smirk. "This is my facility, Isara," he insisted. "I don't care how much authority Slade gave you. I'm not leaving you unsupervised."

"As you wish."

She stepped into the cell, placing her hands on her hips as she stood over her errant servant. "Now," Isara said. "Tell me what happened."

"I stabbed Lenai!" Flynn proclaimed. "I did it! They told me she was the best of our enemies, and I beat her on my first try. I think maybe you've overestimated these Justice Keepers."

He was genuinely pleased with himself. Curious. Self-awareness was often lacking among men and even more so among Earthers, but this…this was beyond the pale. Did he truly have no understanding of the depth of his failure?

"I beat her," Flynn whispered. "Now, let's go! Before more guards come."

"Your symbiont and I will be leaving momentarily."

Flynn sat there with his mouth agape, shaking his head. "My symbiont…" he said. "What are you talking about?"

Lighting quick, Isara drew a small knife from her belt, and she stepped forward to slash his throat. Flynn was faster than she had anticipated. His hand seized her wrist before the blade made contact with his flesh.

He stood up, dark eyes blazing with fury, and his lips peeled back into a hateful snarl. "So, this is my reward for service?" he spat. "You came here to kill me?"

"Failure is not rewarded."

He slammed a hand into Isara's chest, forcing her to step backward, but his attempt to Bend Gravity failed when the slaver's collar around his neck kicked in and sent a jolt of pain through his body. Flynn fell to his knees, spasming.

Seizing a fistful of his hair, Isara tilted his head back to expose his throat. Vacant eyes stared up at her. Flynn was too incapacitated by pain to be truly aware of what was happening. Her knife found its mark in one quick slash, and then blood spilled onto Flynn's shirt.

He bent over, clutching the wound with both hands as more blood stained the cell's floor. His croaks and gurgles were sweet music to Isara's ears. Seconds later, he collapsed to the floor, lying flat on his face.

Thrax was quivering with rage, his forehead glistening with sweat. "How am I supposed to explain this to my superiors?" he screeched. "Forsake me for a fool! What am I supposed to say about the blood all over the damn floor!"

His eyes focused on Isara, and she felt pressure on her mind. He was trying to push through the protections offered by her symbiont. Without hesitation, she rounded on him and slit his throat as well.

Thrax dropped to the floor, one leg thrashing as he died.

Carefully, Isara knelt over Flynn's corpse. It was important not to touch it with her bare skin. The symbiont he carried was feral. It would try to Bond with any suitable host, even one that already carried another symbiont.

Drawing aside her cloak, Isara unclipped a disk-shaped containment unit from her belt. It was only slightly larger than a dinner plate, small enough to be concealed with ease. She pushed a few buttons, entering the pass-code, and two clear tubes extended from the unit, attaching themselves to the back of Flynn's neck.

His body began to glow.

The light collected, pooled together and then flowed through the tubes, into the containment unit. When it was over, the LED changed from red to green to indicate an airtight seal.

"Now," Isara said. "I suppose I can have some fun on the way out."

Tossing the yellow ball up, Slade caught it in one hand and then took a moment to examine the thin grooves in the rubber. He lowered his hand to look out the tiny window in this old cargo hauler. There was nothing out there but blackness. An endless, eternal night which the stars tried desperately to hold back. They would inevitably fail, going out one by one. A fitting end to this miserable universe.

He heard the hiss of a door opening behind him, and he didn't have to look to sense the silhouette of Isara coming in with her hood pulled up. She said nothing; she merely waited for him to address her. In someone else, that might have been a sign of deference. Not so with Isara.

"Did you get it?" he asked.

"I did."

On his left, two small, clear tanks stood side by side. One was empty, but the other contained a swirling, purple gas that flickered like storm clouds crackling with lightning. Leo's symbiont. Recovered by Isara after Jack Hunter brought a regrettable end to that young man.

Stalking across the room like a predator on the hunt, Isara went to the empty tank and connected the portable containment unit she had used to recover Flynn's symbiont. In moments, both tanks were full, both flickering like caged thunderstorms.

Reclining with his elbows on the arms of his chair, his fingers steepled neatly in a thoughtful gesture, Slade observed the woman. "Did you even consider rescuing him?" he asked. "Useful agents are not a resource that we should waste."

Isara glanced over her shoulder, her face barely visible in that hood. Her lips were pressed together in a frown. "The key word being 'useful,'" she said. "That one was too much like Leo. Bloodlust without thought."

"You yourself have done as much."

He felt a warping sensation as Isara blurred into a smear of red. When she snapped back into his time-frame, her arm was extended toward him, a throwing knife flying from her fingertips. Glittering steel caught the overhead lights.

Effortlessly, Slade reached up and caught the hilt, holding the tip of the blade mere inches away from his eye. He said nothing, made no indication of anger. He just raised an eyebrow and waited for a response.

"I would not begrudge anyone a little violence," she said. "But not at the expense of our larger plans."

"I see."

Crossing her arms, Isara shook her head. "You now have two symbionts," she said. "Whom will you give them to?"

"I have some plans," Slade replied. "Set a course for Leyria."

The blinking multi-tool on the counter pestered Aiden with its constant nattering. He hadn't bothered to put on the gauntlet this morning, and the screen kept flashing the same thing over and over. "Video message waiting. Video message waiting."

In an old pair of shorts and a t-shirt that he had worn to bed, Aiden sat at his kitchen table with a mug in hand. He glowered at the counter, trying to decide what to do. Finally, he shook his head and said, "Multi-tool active. Play message. Holographic display."

An image of his mother coalesced, floating just a few inches above the floor. Liah Shandi was a tall woman with copper skin, long, dark hair that she wore in a braid and glasses that made her look far too serious. "Aiden," she said. "Please call me back. I'm worried about you."

Lifting the mug to his lips, Aiden slurped as he sipped his coffee. "I bet you are," he muttered under his breath. "Let up, Mom."

"Sweetie," Liah went on. "You don't have to be a Justice Keeper to make us happy. There are many career paths for you. You always had an aptitude for science. I spoke to Jan Tressio the other day, and she said Balthane has an opening in its physics program."

"Physics..." Aiden muttered.

His mother let her head drop, sighing softly. "It's been three months, Aiden," she lamented. "You've cut yourself off from everyone. I don't know what you're feeling, but I do know that you can't live your entire life in that apartment."

His grip tightened on the mug.

When his mother looked up to fix her gaze on him, Aiden felt like he was five years old again. "Your father and I are coming to see you," she said. "I think it's time you spoke with a councilor."

Aiden threw the mug.

It shattered against the wall above the kitchen sink, thin shards flying off in every direction. Some of them passed through the hologram, causing it to ripple, but the audio played without interruption. "Aiden, please talk to us-"

"End message and delete!"

The hologram vanished.

Aiden was bent over with his elbows on the table, fingers laced over the top of his head. A shuddering breath ripped its way out of him. "Bleakness take me, Mom," he said. "When are you gonna figure it out?"

Couldn't they understand? Justice Keepers were the most respected people in society. Honoured above all others. All his life, he had expected to join their ranks. He *deserved* that respect as much as anyone else, but now...Now, a Nassai had declared that he was unworthy. Unworthy of that respect. Unworthy of the power. A bloody Nassai had taken away his future.

No. Not just his future. The damn thing had taken Melissa from him as well. She was of a higher class now, and Aiden would not accept being the lesser in any pair. An equal, yes. But lesser? The thought of it was intolerable.

A knock at the door drew him out of his reverie.

Red-faced and gasping, Aiden looked up and blinked. "What is it now?" he hissed, rising from his chair. "Who else wants to come by and pity me?"

He pulled the door open and found a mail-delivery bot in the hallway outside. A waist-high cylinder of white plastic, it fixed a camera lens on him and then beeped when it confirmed his identity.

A slot in the robot's body popped open, revealing a square-shaped device inside. He took it without hesitation, holding the thing up to the light to examine it. Aiden had never seen anything like it before. "Who sent-"

The robot was already rolling down the hallway toward the service elevator. Well, he supposed he would just have to figure it out on his own.

Slamming the door, he set the square down on his kitchen table and noticed a red button on one side. Well, the next step was obvious, but with the way his luck had been going lately, it was probably a bomb.

He pushed the button.

A hologram appeared, resolving into the image of a tall man in a well-tailored blue coat with gold trim. A man with a stern face, hollow cheeks and long, black hair that fell past his shoulder blades. Aiden recognized him instantly. You didn't spend years learning the history of the Justice Keepers without memorizing the face of their most infamous leader.

"You!" he snarled, recoiling from the image.

"Yes, me," Slade replied.

"What do you want?"

The other man spread his hands and bowed his head in a mockery of respect. "To correct a grave injustice," he said. "I've had my eye on you for some time, Aiden. Do you recall the application you sent to the training program two years ago?"

"I do."

Slade showed him a toothy grin, chuckling softly. Aiden saw nothing humorous in any of this. "I reviewed that application, Aiden," he said. "You showed great promise. It pained me to hear about what happened to you."

Leaning forward with his hands braced on the table's surface, Aiden looked up at the hologram. He trembled with rage. "Great promise, is it? Well, it's funny. The Nassai don't seem to agree with your assessment."

"The Nassai," Slade scoffed. "Please. I think we both know what their opinion is worth. They're aliens, Aiden! They don't have a true understanding of human morality. The greatest mistake we ever made was binding ourselves to their rigid definition of right and wrong. A Nassai chose Jack Hunter as a host. It remained with him even after he tried to use his power to torture another man. Tell me, Aiden, have you ever made such a grievous mistake?"

"No."

"And yet," Slade went on, "Hunter is allowed to retain his honour, his authority, and the power that he misused...while you are left here to languish."

Aiden felt his body growing tense.

Turning on his heel, Slade paced a line with a grin that seemed to ooze smug self-confidence. The hologram remained fixed in place, but it was clear that he was walking. "They told you that you were unworthy, Aiden. They presume to sit in judgment over you while turning a blind eye to their own sins."

"What sins?"

"Where do I even begin?" Slade exclaimed. "Last year, after she took my position, Larani Tal allied herself with a man who had been convicted of smuggling weapons to the Fringe Worlds in direct defiance of the embargo. She used her considerable influence to lighten that man's sentence and then she set him loose to do her dirty work."

Was that even possible?

Weren't Keepers supposed to be the best? The brightest lights in the darkness? How could one stray so far from their ideals? And not just any Keeper! The Chief Director of the entire organization!

"And speaking of Larani's crimes," Slade went on. "Your girlfriend's father actually tortured a prisoner under Larani's watch. And she did nothing. She didn't prosecute him. She didn't report the crime. She let him go free."

Mr. Carlson? Torturing prisoners.

"It's not possible..."

Slade was laughing outright now, shaking his head as he continued to pace. "And Melissa?" he said. "She was hospitalized for taking illegal drugs. I was there. And still, a Nassai accepted her. Have you ever experimented with drugs, Aiden?"

"No," he whispered.

Slade faced him with a stony expression. Every last trace of amusement was gone. You would never have known that he was laughing only moments ago. "They lied to you, Aiden," he said. "They're not the noble people you thought they were. But you are. That's why they can't allow you the power of a symbiont Bond. Because they know that you will expose them."

Aiden narrowed his eyes as he studied the other man. "Even if I believe it's true," he began. "Why would I ever agree to work with you? All the death you've caused. The lives you've ruined."

"In the service of a greater good."

Now, it was Aiden's turn to laugh. Even he was amazed by the disdain in his own voice. "What possible greater good would require the slaughter of innocents?" he spat. "Go away! I want nothing from you!"

"The Inzari are powerful, Aiden," Slade answered. "Their wrath is a terrible thing to behold, but they are capable of mercy as well. Some must die for the rest to live. It is regrettable, but it is the nature of the universe. You know this to be true. It is a reality that few are willing to acknowledge."

"Why?" Aiden breathed. "Why should we serve these Inzari?"

"Join me, Aiden," Slade beckoned. "You will have your answers and the power that you have been unjustly denied."

The door slid open, and Telixa strode into her quarters, unzipping her jacket and removing it. She tossed it down on the couch and paced across the room. Another series of blood tests failed to find anything out of the ordinary. There were no nanobots in her system, or so Dr. Maderon kept insisting.

Of course, it might help if she told him that he wasn't supposed to be looking for nanobots. She kept hoping that some anomaly would make him dig deeper, that he would discover the virus that Slade had injected and then maybe cure it. Or contain it. She could just tell him what to look for, but doing so might cost her her command.

That wouldn't bother her if not for the fact that Slade would surely punish her when he learned of her disobedience. And he could leave her in agony for hours or even days at a time. Or so he claimed. Thus far, she had only been forced to endure a few minutes of torment at a stretch, but Telixa had no doubt that he could do it. Until she got the virus out of her system, she was essentially his slave. And sooner or later, Dr. Maderon would begin to suspect that there was more than simple paranoia behind her repeated requests to be tested.

Standing by the wall in pants and a tank-top, Telixa planted her fists on her hips. "Keep working, Doctor," she whispered. "Please."

"It's time."

A month ago, the sound of a disembodied voice in her empty quarters might have made her jump, but she was growing used to Slade's unexpected visits. She turned around to find him sitting on the couch and smiling that oily smile of his. "Proceed with the next phase of the plan."

"You must be joking," Telixa spat.

Slade rose from his seat, adjusting his pompous red coat. At first, she was tempted to press her point, but he silenced her with nothing but a glance. "I thought we had been over this," he said. "You will do as you're told."

Telixa strode across the room, shaking her head and growling like a caged tiger. "The plan is no longer viable!" she insisted. "The alliance between the Leyrians and the Antaurans shifts the balance of power. We would be fools to provoke them."

"I am uninterested in your excuses. Proceed with the next phase."

She tossed her head back, staring at the ceiling with a gaping mouth. Deep creases formed in her brow. "I forget how stupid you can be sometimes." Antagonizing him was not a good idea, but whatever her circumstances, she refused to be this man's lapdog. "I cannot just order a military strike that will almost certainly drag my people into a war we can't win."

Suddenly, Slade was right behind her, wrapping his arms around her stomach and pulling her close like an affectionate lover. She could feel his hot breath on her neck. "Telixa," he whispered in her ear. "The arrangement is simple. My job is to create the plan. Your job is to sell it."

"Let me go!"

"Do as you're told."

She tried to elbow him, but there was nothing to elbow. This was all just an elaborate hallucination. Neurons firing in her brain, tricking her into seeing and feeling and smelling things that weren't there.

Slade reappeared right in front of her, and before she could even blink, he snapped his fingers. Pain drowned out her awareness of everything else. She was barely cognizant of falling to the floor. "Do as you're told."

Sobbing, Telixa made no effort to stop the tears streaming over her face. "We have to...move carefully!" she squealed. "If...we p-push too hard, the crew will start to suspect that-" She cut off in a scream.

"Do as you're told," Slade insisted.

"Fine! Fine! I'll do it!"

The pain was gone.

Telixa got up on her knees, covering her face with both hands and wiping away the moisture. "I will do it," she croaked.

"But I promise you, Slade. One day, I'm going to make you suffer for this."

His only response to that was soft laughter. The image of him faded away, leaving only a voice that echoed in her mind. "I look forward to it, my dear...I look forward to it."

Interlude 1

(1069, CE)

He was William now. The name had been his for almost twenty years, ever since the Old Woman had given him the face of the man to whom it had originally belonged. That man was now dead, buried in an unmarked grave near the beaches of Normandy.

Tall and proud in a ringmail shirt, he stood upon a hilltop with his head uncovered. His face was pale now – too pale to be handsome, in his estimation – and marked by a thick, graying beard. "Watch them run."

The hill sloped gently downward to a flat plain of brown grass covered in the white flecks of a light snowfall. On that plain, several men in tunics of green and brown ran for the distant treeline. Those trees were bare now. Not a leaf to be seen on any branch. That would make for easier hunting if he were so inclined. Fortunately, he was not.

The thunder of horses' hooves got his attention.

He turned around to find one of his knights approaching on a massive black destrier. The man drew rein and then removed his helm, offering a curt nod of respect. "Sire," he began. "The Northerners are in retreat."

"So I see."

"Shall we pursue?"

A frown tightened William's mouth as he studied the other man. He shook his head slowly. "Never let your enemy choose the terrain," he answered. "Our horses would be of little use in there. Our enemies are counting on that."

"How shall we proceed then, Sire?"

Drawing his sword with a metallic rasp, he pointed the weapon toward the field where his men were arrayed on horseback. Nearly three dozen of them, awaiting his next command. There were farms in the distance: small houses of wood with thatched roofs. That would be a good place to begin. "The fields," William said. "Burn them."

"Sire?"

"Were my instructions unclear?"

The man swallowed visibly, then shut his eyes and tried to work up his courage. "No, Sire," he replied at last. "But...This is good farmland. If we burn it, the region will be unfit for habitation for several years at least."

"What's your name, son?"

"Quentin, Your Highness."

Despite himself, William felt a peal of laughter bubbling up. "Rebellion is a most grievous crime, Quentin," he said. "Our response must be swift and decisive. Burn the fields and burn the villages. Take what you need from the larders and burn the rest. And put anyone who resists to the sword. Do you understand?"

"Yes," Quentin mumbled. "Yes, I do."

Sitting on a wooden stool in his tent, William scraped a sharpening stone along the edge of his sword. His helm was off, and what meagre protection the tent provided did little to keep the chill from nipping at his ears.

"Well done, my son."

He looked up, blinking. "I was wondering when I would see you again." His next stroke of the sharpening stone produced a loud, angry rasp. "How long has it been? Three years, at least."

The Old Woman stood before him with a motherly smile, looking very much as she had the last time William saw her. Her appearance had not changed at all in over a thousand years. She would still blend in perfectly on the streets of Chang'An. "We must let the tether go slack if we wish you to grow."

"What does that mean?"

She didn't answer, which should not have surprised him. Instead, she just paced a line across the width of his tent, inspecting his lodgings. She stretched a hand out toward the wall but did not quite touch it. "We have asked much of you."

William stood up, tossing his sword aside, and offered a deep bow. Upon rising, he greeted her with a smile of his own. "And you have given much," he replied. "Eternal life is no small reward."

"Nothing is eternal," the Old Woman murmured.

That chilled him.

After a moment of silence, he looked down at the ground under his feet. Working up the courage to speak was not easy. That irked him. Whether as William or Saul or Liu Bang, he had never been afraid to speak his mind. But this creature – he had long since given up any notion that she might be human – made him hesitate. The spirits gave him life; they could take it back just as easily. "May I ask a question?"

She just looked at him, dark eyes never wavering.

Was that permission? Or should he hold his fool tongue? Eventually, he decided that he had never been one to keep silent when he had something to say, and now was not the time to start. "You send me out to conquer... Why?"

"Your kind must go to the stars."

"To the stars?"

"Yes."

"Why?"

The Old Woman laid a hand on his cheek, and he was startled by the warmth in her touch. Her mouth cracked in a toothless grin. "All will be revealed to you in due time, my son," she said. "In due time."

Snow fell upon an open field where northerners fled like the cowards they were. Most did anyway. A few of them chose to stand and fight, not that it did them any good. Poor farmers in roughspun tunics and cloaks, carrying pitchforks or hatchets, they made a stand against his knights.

And they fell.

One young man with flecks of snow in his dark hair came charging toward William. The boy showed his teeth and drew back the pitiful knife he carried.

Spinning to face him with the elegance of a trained soldier, William thrust his blade forward. Right through the lad's chest. He savoured the *crunch* of breaking bones and the look of horror in the boy's dark eyes. There was nothing sweeter than breaking an enemy. Any enemy.

With a growl, William pulled his sword free, and the boy's corpse dropped to the ground. He stepped over it without a second thought.

Men in ring-mail shirts hacked down anything that got in their way. The air was thick with the stench of death. William glided across the battlefield as if in a trance. After a thousand years, it was all second-nature to him.

A man with an axe came racing toward him.

Cocking his head, William raised an eyebrow at the fool. "Do you welcome death so eagerly?" he muttered. "Well, if you were stupid enough to begin this rebellion…"

The man raised his axe above his head.

William's sword struck first, slicing cleanly through his wrist on the down-stroke. With a quick pivot, he severed the man's leg at the knee, laughing as his opponent fell to land face-up in the grass.

Twirling his sword with a flourish, William pointed the blade downward and drove it home through the other man's chest. Another rebel dead at his hands. This was almost too easy.

"No!"

William spun to find one of his own knights striding toward him, stepping over the bodies of fallen northerners. The man's face was red, his eyes wild with hate and fury. A tall fellow with golden hair and a neat goatee, he looked like a demon loosed from Hell. It took a moment for William to put a name to the face.

Raymond.

Lifting his weapon in a defensive posture and smiling behind the bloodstained blade, William chuckled. "You would turn upon your own king, sir?" he called out. "To protect these treasonous dogs?"

Raymond held his sword in both hands, neither advancing nor retreating. His gaze did not waver. "These are good men," he said. "No different than you or me."

"These are dead men," William countered. More laughter bubbled up, and he made no effort to stifle it. "They just don't know it yet. And so are you!"

Raymond attacked.

Steel rang against steel, and William drove the traitor backward across the field. He slashed at Raymond's legs, but the other man was nimble even in his armour, jumping back just in time.

Hammering him with blow after blow, William kept his adversary on the defensive. He offered a fierce, horizontal slash that would take the other man's head off.

Raymond brought his sword up just in time to intercept the cut. He delivered a kick to the gut that made William want to empty his stomach. Dazed by the hit, William danced backward to get some distance.

He looked up to see a blade coming down to split his skull open. It took everything he had to get his own weapon up in time. A challenge! It had been too long since anyone had made him work for victory.

Stepping aside, he let Raymond's blade fall like a headsman's axe, its tip landing in the grass. He lashed out with a back-hand strike that clipped the side of Raymond's open-faced helm. It was still enough to stun the traitor.

Rounding on the other man, William slashed at his neck. Raymond parried that with some difficulty. The man was retreating now, moving backward through the grass like a hunted animal.

Desperate, frantic, Raymond swung at William's left shoulder.

William batted the sword aside, tearing it out of the other man's hand. He could end this here and now, but his blood was hot. No one defied him. No one. He would see to it that the northerners learned the depth of their mistake.

Snarling, he grabbed Raymond's throat with a gloved hand and pulled the other man close. He looked into the traitor's blue eyes...and something happened. Suddenly, it was not Raymond but Lihua who squirmed in his grip.

She stared at him defiantly, legs kicking, teeth bared.

"You!" William shrieked.

He threw Lihua to the ground, but when she landed, she was Raymond once again. The traitor knew that his death was imminent. His face was pale, his eyes haunted. And this time, there would be no coming back.

Planting a foot on the other man's chest, William pinned him to the ground. "I confess," William purred. "I will enjoy killing you a second time."

"Raymond!"

A glance to his right made him aware of a northern boy rushing toward him with nothing but a poorly-made spear. A skinny lad with curly, dark hair, he looked as though he were ready to wrestle a bear.

"Edwin, no!" Raymond bellowed.

William silenced him with one quick, clean thrust, laughing as blood frothed from Raymond's mouth. Pulling his blade free of the other man's flesh, he turned around. "Think clearly about this, boy. Is this how you want to die?"

Edwin just kept coming. When he got within striking distance, he tried to ram his spear through William's belly.

William swatted it aside with little effort and then reversed his swing to slice open the boy's guts. Edwin fell to his knees, clutching his belly.

And then it was Guo Dong who stared up at William with hatred in his eyes. Guo Dong who, even as his blood spilled onto the ground, greeted William with that mocking smile. "You know the worst part, Liu," he croaked. "You will never be happy. You could live another thousand years. Ten Thousand! But you will always be...alone."

William ended it before the wretch could say another word.

Chapter 6

The flight back to Leyria had been a solitary affair for Harry. Three days on a starship, with no one to talk to but Melissa, and she was tight-lipped about the assignment she had been given. There was a part of him that wanted to go with her, but Harry didn't even suggest it. Melissa could take care of herself; she was a fully-trained Justice Keeper now. And he wasn't a hero anymore. If he had ever been.

He had taken an hour to settle in, unpack his things, set the damn robot to cleaning his house and relax. Then he had put out a message on the Interlink. Leyrian social media wasn't so different from its Earth counterparts. It turned out that since Harry had never bothered to make accounts of his own, other people had done it for him after they saw his fight with Isara. That was all over the Link now. It wasn't hard to get some of those accounts to tweet or share or whatever – to put the word out that he would be giving a talk in downtown Denabria this afternoon.

Sunlight came through the glass ceiling of the civic centre, glinting off the metal frame that supported it. Below that slanted roof, at least two dozen people filled almost every one of the chairs that faced a lectern. They were young and old, men and women, some formally dressed, others in casual clothes. But they all had one thing in common: they had all come here to see Harry Carlson.

Which made them idiots, but then, he had agreed to this. It was time to fulfill his end of the bargain.

Harry stood at the back of the room in a gray suit with a purple shirt and matching tie. Earth fashions, but if he had to go on stage, he wanted attire that brought out his self-confidence. This would do.

Closing his eyes, Harry took a moment to collect himself. "You can do this," he whispered. "It's just like all those times you had to address a room full of surly beat cops. Only easier."

He started down the aisle between the chairs.

People twisted around in their seats to watch him as he passed. You could tell that they were expecting something grand. The worst part was that Harry would probably have to rise to those expectations. It was part of the job now.

Harry stepped up behind the lectern, thrust his chin out and studied them all for a very long moment. "What you have heard is true," he said at last. "I wield the power of the Overseers."

He raised his left hand, summoning a crackling force-field with the N'Jal. People gasped at the sight. Some of them exchanged glances. Well, there was nothing quite like a competent showman for keeping a crowd engaged.

Harry let his arm drop and gripped the lectern with both hands, leaning forward to stare intently at his audience. "It's time to expose the false gods for what they really are," he said. "Liars! Deceivers!"

There were murmurs of approval from the crowd.

"The Overseers," Harry went on, "were never gods! They were demons who toyed with us for their own ends. We are all part of some grand experiment they're conducting, and I say it's time for these lab rats to fight back!"

One young man jumped up and shouted, "No more lies!" Several others echoed him. Harry's words seemed to resonate with the young people – impassioned speeches usually did – but he could tell that some of the older members of his audience were more skeptical. And good for them! It pleased him to know that some people weren't taken in by the first loudmouth who crossed their path.

An older man – a handsome fellow with tanned skin, gray hair and thick glasses – sat in the front row with hands folded over his round belly. When the noise died down, he spoke up. "You say the Overseers are false gods," he said. "But you use their technology. Do you not see a contradiction there?"

Harry hated himself for what he was about to do.

With a great deal of care, he rolled up his sleeves to make it clear that he was not carrying a multi-tool on his person. Then, extending his left hand toward the audience, he used the N'Jal to project a hologram over his upturned palm. A simple image of Leyria orbiting its parent star.

"I am the Deliverer," Harry said. "You have seen with your own eyes. You know. Hundreds of people across dozens of worlds have tried to use Overseer technology, and every single one of them was unable to control it. But their technology serves me."

He closed his hand and the hologram vanished.

The old man who had challenged him now sat back in his chair with arms crossed. "So, you can control their technology," he said. "Well, forgive me, Mr. Deliverer, but that hardly proves you're some kind of messiah."

An older woman with curly hair stood up and frowned at Harry. "You're too late anyway," she added. "It's been centuries since anyone on this planet has worshipped the Overseers as gods. The Covenant of Layat put an end to that."

Harry waggled a finger at her like a professor giving a lecture. "Ah," he countered. "But you're forgetting the Antaurans.

They very much *do* worship the Overseers, and they are your allies now."

Murmurs of discontent told him that not everyone in this room was happy with that situation. Well, he wasn't going to try to change their minds. Leyria and Antaur would not be going to war any time soon. People could grumble all they wanted as long as they didn't start killing each other.

"Who cares what the Antaurans believe?" someone shouted.

Setting his jaw with determination – fighting his way past his reservations – Harry nodded slowly. "I'll tell you why you should care," he began. "The Overseers want us to fight each other. I don't know why. It's part of their experiment."

That got people talking.

"It doesn't matter what you believe," Harry pressed on. "If the Overseers command the Antaurans to fight, they'll do it. You don't have to be religious to find yourself in the middle of a religious war. And as for the treaty…Well, what are words on paper compared to the will of the gods?"

"I can't tell you what the Ragnosians will do now that they have access to our side of the galaxy, but I have no doubt that the Overseers will find a way to manipulate them. They've been doing it for centuries. Grecken Slade is one of their agents. He spent years corrupting the Justice Keepers, putting his people in key positions."

They were frightened now. Harry could tell.

Once again, Harry lifted his hand, and this time, sparks crackled in the air. "The Covenant of Layat promised you that someone would come to cast down the false gods and expose their lies," he said. "*I* am that person! And the time for change is now!"

"He did what?" Larani spluttered.

A hologram of Gabi Valtez stood before her in white pants and a red blouse. Today, the other woman had her hair up in a long ponytail, and there was an intensity in her dark eyes. "He called himself the Deliverer and tried to turn his…congregation…" The disdain she invested into that word would chill any woman's blood. "Against the Overseers."

Even in the privacy of her quarters aboard the Night Flyer – a small room with two green couches and a screen of Smart-Glass on the wall – Larani cringed at the thought that someone might overhear this conversation. Particularly Melissa. The girl would not take it well if she found out that Larani was keeping tabs on her father. "It's Claire," she said. "Somehow, this is related to the deal he made to save her life."

Gabi's hologram took a step back and looked down at the floor under its feet. "I don't see how it could be," she replied. "Even if our suspicions about this pact between Harry and the Overseers prove accurate, why would he turn people against them?"

"That I can't say."

"Perhaps we should turn this over to LIS."

Tapping her lips with one finger, Larani shut her eyes as she considered that. "No," she said after a moment. "I don't know very many people in the Intelligence Service. I'd rather keep this between us."

"You may not have a choice in the matter."

"Oh?"

With a sigh, Gabi turned around. The hologram flickered, and when it reappeared, she was facing Larani again. "Your people aren't subtle enough to keep an eye on Harry without alerting him to their presence," she said. "And as a civilian, I no longer have the resources of LIS at my disposal."

Larani sat down on the arm of one sofa. Her body seemed to deflate as if someone had sucked the energy right out of her. Truth be told, she felt that way sometimes: wrung out and exhausted. "You may be right," she admitted. "But I would rather have someone I trust monitoring the situation."

"*Should* we be monitoring this situation?"

That gave her pause.

Larani trusted the other woman…to a point. She and Gabrina may have found comfort in each other's arms, but that didn't make them close. Companion have mercy on her, when had trust become so difficult? There was a time, not so long ago, when she would have never questioned the loyalty of *anyone* in the LIS. So, what had changed? Was it Slade? Was it discovering just how many moles he had planted in her organization? She and Gabi were usually on the same page, but the other woman's question was not sitting well. "Whatever do you mean?"

Gabi answered her with a shrug. "I don't agree with what Harry's doing," she said. "But religious freedom is a basic human right. If he fancies himself the next Layat, do we have any authority to stop him?"

Crossing her arms in a huff, Larani stood up and paced a tight circle around the hologram. "I don't want to stop him," she said. "I just want plenty of warning when this scheme of his blows up in all of our faces."

The other woman wrinkled her nose in distaste. "Fair enough," Gabi said. "I'll keep my eyes peeled."

The SlipGate chamber in the lower decks of the Night Flyer was pretty much the same as every other one of its kind that Jack had seen: gray walls with no fixtures of any kind except a single console and the Gate itself. That console was operated by a man in a blue uniform who watched the Gate as if he thought venomous snakes might come through at any moment.

Jack didn't blame him. The metal triangle was silent, but something about the way light reflected off its shimmering surface drew the eye. The damn thing was just plain unnerving.

But maybe that was his growing fear of the Overseers and their vague plans for humanity. "Think she'll be here soon?"

No sooner did he finish saying that than a voice came through the speaker. "Night Flyer, this is Denabrian Gate terminal," a woman said. "We have a passenger waiting to come aboard. Forwarding the authorization code now."

"Confirmed, Denabria," the Gate technician replied. "Authorization code accepted. Our Gate is open. You can send her through."

Thin grooves along the triangle's surface lit up, growing brighter and brighter until they seemed to blaze. A moment later, a bubble seemed to expand from a point until it was large enough to hold several people, but there was only one person inside.

When it popped, Keli stood in front of the Gate with the strap of a gym bag over one shoulder and a suitcase in the opposite hand. As usual, she was dressed elegantly in a sleeveless blue dress.

"That wretched feline of yours," she said, striding forward, "has been delivered to Harry Carlson's residence."

A burst of laughter escaped Jack, and he shook his head slowly. "Wonderful," he said. "Maybe Harry can turn *him* into a telepath. *That'll* make him easier to deal with."

"It would serve you right."

Outside the SlipGate chamber, they found a wide hallway with white bulkheads. There were very few people on the lower decks – every now and then, they passed one of the ship's crew – but they never crossed paths with any other passengers.

Being a gentleman, Jack took Keli's suitcase, which earned him a small smile of thanks. Well, at least that was an improvement. A year ago, he would have gotten a glare for his trouble.

When they were alone, Keli paused and set a hand on his shoulder. That brought him to a halt. "Do you think Slade will make good on this plan?"

Wincing at the thought of someone assassinating the Prime Council, Jack drew in a breath. "Why not?" he replied. "It's not the craziest thing he's done. A year ago, he turned an entire city into a war zone."

"Can we stop him?"

"What kind of question is that?"

"The kind that deserves an answer."

Biting his lower lip, Jack felt his eyebrows rising. "Can we stop him?" He started forward again without waiting for Keli, forcing her to catch up. "I don't think it matters if we can, 'cause we're gonna put our asses on the line for it anyway."

For some reason, that brought a grin to Keli's face. She really was becoming a more cheerful person. "That's what I like about you, Hunter," she teased. "You can face grim death with a song in your heart."

"Well, *that's* not the least bit ominous."

"It's not my fault that it happens to be true."

Clack, clack!

Wooden swords struck each other with a sound that echoed through the ship's gymnasium as Anna and Rajel sparred. She watched the man standing before her with his eyes closed, watched as droplets of sweat rolled down his face.

In gray shorts and a purple tank-top, she faced him with her blade up in a guarded stance. Hot and sticky, just like he was. She had never sparred with Rajel before. Oh, she had seen his prowess on the battlefield – there was no doubt in her mind that Rajel could hold his own – but seeing it was not the same as experiencing it. Not by a long shot.

Rajel swung at her legs.

Anna jumped, back-flipping through the air. With a grunt, she landed and lifted her sword again. Heartbeats only, but Rajel was already coming at her, swinging his sword in a vicious, downward arc.

Sidestepping, Anna turned her blade over her right shoulder and caught his on the downstroke. Once again, they met with something like a clap of thunder, but this time, Anna pushed forward. Her opponent retreated.

Rajel slid out of her field of view, swinging at the back of her neck.

Anna threw herself forward, somersaulting over the gym mats and coming up on one knee. In the blink of an eye, she was already back on her feet and sprinting across the length of the room.

Rajel was right behind her.

His silhouette was there in her mind's eye, a misty figure always just beyond arm's reach, struggling to keep up and never quite making it. Anna kept it that way, letting him think he might just close the distance and then adding an extra burst of speed at the very last second. Get his blood good and hot. The wall was coming up fast. In less than five seconds, she would be cornered. Good.

Anna ran up the wall on nimble feet, then pushed off and back-flipped over Rajel's head. She landed just behind him. He was already spinning around to face her, swinging that sword in a smooth, horizontal arc that would take her head off.

Anna bent over backward and felt a soft caress of air as the wooden blade passed over her nose. She popped up and thumped him on the noggin with her weapon. "Ow!" Rajel growled, falling back against the wall.

Standing before him with the tip of her blade pressed into the gym mats, one hand closed around the hilt, Anna smiled and shook her head. "Not bad," she said. "You really had me going for a moment there."

"For all the good it did. You still got me."

"That's because you're too predictable."

He arched one dark eyebrow, waiting for her to explain that. It was all she could do not to sigh. Once again, her big mouth had gotten her into trouble. Now…How to put this diplomatically…

Grinning sheepishly, Anna bowed her head to him. She felt a warmth in her cheeks that had nothing to do with the sweat she had just worked up. "You fight as if you've got something to prove," she said. "You get a little bit obsessed with winning. That can cloud your judgment if you let it."

"Point taken," he grumbled. "Any advice?"

Anna turned around, marching back to their starting point with her sword in hand. Her answer to that was a shrug of her shoulders. "Never mind what your opponent thinks of you," she said. "In fact, *let* them underestimate you. It will only give you an edge."

Rajel was coming up behind her with teeth bared, hissing with obvious frustration. "I suppose you're right," he muttered. "Though I don't have to like it."

"Well…If you want an assessment of your abilities."

"Yes?"

"I need a second in command," Anna said. "Want the job?"

Before he could answer, the gymnasium doors swung open, allowing Jack to enter. Melissa was right behind him, and then Keli and Cassi. Good! They were all here. It was time for her to be all leadery.

Tossing her sword aside, Anna stepped forward and faced them with a smile. "Glad you made it," she said, nodding. "We will be arriving at Alios in four days, and we're going to make the most of that time."

"What did you have in mind?" Cassi asked.

"I want you all to train for at least two hours a day. Rotate partners so that you get used to multiple fighting styles. This isn't about perfecting your technique. You're all very good at what you do. No, this is about expanding your mind. Slade is constantly hitting us with surprises. I want you to learn to expect the unexpected."

"Even me?" Keli asked.

Cocking her head to one side, Anna raised a thin, red eyebrow. "There some reason why you shouldn't take part, Kel?" she asked. "In fact, you most of all. It'll do you good to learn combat skills outside of your mental abilities. And I want the others to practice against a telepath."

"Welp," Jack said. "You heard the lady."

Sword fighting.

It was ridiculous.

Panting, struggling to fill her lungs, Keli stood on the mat with her sword gripped in both hands. She watched her opponent with some trepidation. Melissa had not hit her even once with a practice sword, but she had won every engagement thus far. The child would stop when her blade was only half an inch away from Keli's skin. It was not fear of pain that made Keli apprehensive. It was the fear of losing. What could she do? The girl was faster and stronger, and that damn alien she carried within her body blocked the only thing that might give Keli an advantage.

Melissa came forward, swinging.

Keli barely got her weapon up in time, and the jolt nearly knocked the sword out of her hand. She backed away as the girl pressed her attack. Melissa leaped, twirling in the air like a figure skater, her sword coming around like a propeller blade.

Keli backed away, but a feather-light cut on her thigh told her that the child had scored a hit. Melissa kept coming.

"Stop!" Anna yelled.

Face drenched in sweat, Keli shut her eyes tight. "This is pointless," she hissed. "I will never be able to keep up with any one of you."

"So, don't," Anna advised. "Use your own advantages."

Keli let the tip of her sword drop until it touched the floor. A growl rumbled in her throat. "If I do that," she snapped, "I will inflict harm on the girl! I could push through her mental defenses, but not without harming her."

At the edge of the mat, Anna stood with her arms folded, watching them spar. "You can push a little, Keli," she said. "They've got to learn how to defend against a telepathic attack."

So, Keli listened. She really listened. There wasn't much coming from Melissa. Not with the fog of the alien's mind shrouding her thoughts, but if Keli strained, she could pick up a whiff of... something. Intent. Focus. The girl was about to attack.

Keli moved first, charging forward before Melissa could put her on the defensive. She could feel the girl's surprise even with the Nassai's obstruction. Keli slashed at her.

With a quick twist of her body, Melissa brought up her own weapon to deflect the cut and nearly tore the sword out of Keli's hand in the process. That produced fear; so, Keli used that fear. She hurled it all at the girl. Penetrating the fog was nearly impossible, but the sudden jolt of emotion was enough to make Melissa hesitate for half a second.

Half a second was all Keli needed.

She poked the girl's belly with the tip of her blade. Melissa stepped back, blinking in surprise. "Nice," she said. "Do that again. I want to practice."

"If you insist," Keli replied, backing away from the girl with a smile on her face. This was going to be fun.

The instant he walked through his front door, Harry let out a deep sigh of relief. He collapsed against the door. "I need a shower," he whispered to himself. Jack's dumb, orange cat came over to sit his big rump on the floor and stare up at Harry with his huge green eyes.

"What do you want?" Harry grumbled.

Spock just blinked at him.

Ignoring the cat, Harry lifted his left hand and ordered the N'Jal to project a signal into SlipSpace. The Leyrian Radio Authority might pick up a blip, but it would sound like noise to them. The Overseers had gotten good at hiding their transmissions.

A second later, his ex-wife was standing at the foot of the stairs with her head bowed. It wasn't really Della. This was just the form the Overseers took when they chose to communicate with him. Until today, Harry would have said that it was just a telepathic projection, but that theory went to shit when Spock arched his back, poofed out his tail and hissed. The big tabby scrambled backward, but he never took his eyes off the spot where Della stood. Could he actually see her? The Overseers seemed not to notice his reaction. Or they just didn't care. Harry couldn't tell which.

Della looked up at him, and her mouth quirked into a chilling smile. "Nicely done, Mr. Carlson," she said. "As always, we are impressed by your ingenuity."

"So, you're pleased?"

"Yes," she replied. "Very pleased. Continue your good work."

Chapter 7

The weather on Alios was almost always beautiful; that was one thing that Anna missed about her time on that world. The sky above Caleem Park was a perfect sapphire-blue with fluffy clouds drifting over the tops of buildings that surrounded her on all sides. Many of those buildings had unique architecture. One was shaped almost like an hourglass; another looked more like a pyramid.

Seven rows of folding chairs were spread throughout the grass in the middle of the park, all facing a stage where the Prime Council and her opponent would give an opening address to their audience. Every one of those chairs was filled. Anna saw people from all walks of life, men and women both young and old.

There were cameras as well: small, disk-shaped devices with lenses that floated above the crowd. She saw a line of reporters conversing quietly with one another behind the furthest row of chairs.

In white pants, a black t-shirt and sunglasses, Anna stood by the stage, waiting for the show to begin. She tapped her earpiece to activate the comms. "We're a go in five minutes, boys and girls," she said. "Give me a status update."

"Nothing on this end," Jack said.

Anna caught a brief glimpse of him near the edge of the park. He was keeping an eye on the perimeter with a pair of uniformed cops. Tickets to attend this event in person had been distributed through a lottery. In theory, no one would be able to get in without proper identification, but Slade and his goons had a talent for slipping past even the best security measures.

"Nothing on the northwest corner," Rajel said in her ear.

"Northeast is clear as well," Cassi added.

Pressing her lips together, Anna looked up to the rooftops of the nearby buildings. The warm sun on her face did nothing to ease the chills that ran down her spine. To say that she was nervous was a massive understatement. "Keli," she said. "You got anything to report?"

"The crowd is relatively calm," Keli replied. "I'm sensing anger from some people. Some of them do not care for Sarona Vason, and others are even less sympathetic to Dusep. But none of them intend violence so far as I can tell. I would have to probe deeper to be absolutely sure."

"No," Anna said. "That's good enough."

She spotted Melissa coming her way, pacing a line right in front of the stage. The young woman kept scanning the audience as if she expected someone to jump up and start shooting at any moment.

Anna spun to face the girl with a soft sigh, forcing a smile that anyone with half a brain would see through. "How are you holding up?" she asked. "Feeling nervous?"

Casting a glance over her shoulder, Melissa narrowed her eyes as she studied the audience. A sudden shiver went through her, and she gave her head a shake. "Right now, I'm thinking 'paranoid' might be a better adjective."

"I bet I know what you're thinking."

"What's that."

This time, when Anna smiled, it was genuine. "Right now, you're asking yourself, 'Why couldn't my first assignment as a real, true Justice Keeper be something simple like an arm's deal or a terrorist cell?"

Melissa chuckled, shaking her head. "I've already had my share of terrorist cells," she replied. "Remember the Sons of Savard?"

"Don't remind me."

A flicker of static in her ear made Anna jump, but then Keli's voice came over the comm system. "Get ready," she said. "They're starting."

The massive speakers on either side of the stage crackled momentarily before a deep voice said, "Assembled guests, I present to you Sarona Vason, the Prime Council of the Leyrian Systems Accord."

Thunderous applause serenaded Sarona Vason as she walked on stage in a green jacket and a white, high-collared shirt. A reminder, however subtle, that she had come from the Green Party. The Prime Council was supposed to put aside such allegiances when she assumed office. In theory, her role was that of a mediator. However, Dusep had rallied the Blues with his anti-immigrant rhetoric. And the Greens had been their fiercest opponents.

The wrinkles on Sarona's dark face only served to make her look that much more distinguished. Her white hair was up in a bun. "Good afternoon," she said. "I'm glad to see so many of you here on this fine day. And I am pleased to address the millions of you who are watching at home."

"We've walked a long and difficult road these last five years. When I took office, we had just made contact with Earth. We had learned that the legends of our lost homeworld were true. We stood at a crossroads then, and now we stand at another. The galaxy has changed. We are vulnerable to threats that, just a few years ago, would have been unimaginable."

Anna found herself watching the crowd, trying to gauge their mood. It was hard to pin down anything solid. The most she could say was that many of them were fascinated by the Prime Council's words. Or at least…focused. She couldn't shake a sense of unease that kept gnawing at her, and Seth echoing her feelings certainly didn't help matters.

Humanity had to unite against the Overseers – that much was obvious – but given half a chance, Dusep would push them in the opposite direction. As Prime Council, Sarona Vason could not decree policy, but she could force a vote on any issue. Anna had no strong feelings about the woman one way or the other, but she knew that Sarona had used her position to maintain a balance of perspectives. Dusep would do no such thing. He would force votes when he was sure that he would like the outcome and censure councilors who opposed his rhetoric.

"In the face of this growing uncertainty," Sarona went on, "many of you feel the urge to look inward. To cut off contact with our neighbours and to seal ourselves off. The thought of doing so makes you feel safer."

Her face was stern, her eyes sharp as she studied the crowd. "But feelings are not always an accurate description of reality," she said. "In reality, isolationism would put us all at great risk. Hating Earthers. Hating Antaurans or Ragnosians. Hating that which is different: these are the very prejudices that we worked long and hard to overcome. Will we turn our backs on all that progress so easily?"

Shutting her eyes tight, Anna stiffened at the thought. She tapped her earpiece to activate the microphone. "Perimeter team," she murmured. "Give me an update."

"All clear out here," Jack replied.

"Same," Cassi added.

Anna took a deep breath to calm herself. So far, so good. This event would be over in ninety minutes. A *long* ninety minutes for Anna and her team, but she took comfort in the knowledge that two hours from now, she would be sitting down to a quiet dinner.

Operative Telien's team would be covering the first debate tonight. Which meant that Anna's people would get some much-needed rest. They just had to hold out a little longer.

Pressing his hand against a keypad next to a door at the top of the stairwell, Aiden reached out to the symbiont he now carried and applied a Bending. The power to warp space-time. It was incredible. Energy surged through every cell in his body. He felt the twisting sensation as circuitry within the panel was ripped apart at the molecular level.

That done, he unclipped a small metal disk from his belt. "Multi-tool active," he said, touching it to the door. "Program One."

Nanobots emerged from the disk and scuttled over the door's surface, crawling into the lock. Normally, buildings had security systems to prevent this sort of thing, low-level EMP fields to disable invasive nanobots. But Aiden had just destroyed those systems with a Bending.

There was a soft *click* as the lock turned, and then he opened the door just a crack. Blazing sunlight assaulted his eyes.

Shielding himself with one hand, Aiden retreated deeper into the shadows. He let his arm drop and blinked. "Those who walk the path of Justice," he whispered, quoting the Covenant of Layat, "need not fear the light of day."

He stood on the landing in an almost skin-tight bodysuit with his face covered and his eyes hidden behind a pair of goggles. With his teeth, he pulled a black glove over the one hand that he had left bare. He couldn't Bend space-time with his hand covered. Well...he *could,* but it would damage the circuitry in his glove as easily as it had damaged the circuitry in the keypad. "The Leyrian tech has done its job," he whispered. "Let's see if the Ragnosians are equally competent."

One tap at a button on his belt, and he began to ripple and fade away, growing more and more transparent until he was invisible. He watched his arms and legs vanish, which was disconcerting, to say the least. Even the plastic case that he carried in his right hand was gone. He still felt the handle in his grip, but he couldn't see it.

Gently, he pushed the door all the way open, stepped out onto a flat roof under a clear, blue sky and then pushed it closed again. In the distance, he heard Sarona Vason's booming voice coming through the speakers in Caleem Park. That sound was quickly overshadowed by the soft hum of a security drone. Aiden wanted to jump, but he forced himself to remain still.

The drone flew past without incident.

His suit could conceal him in more ways than one. It could render him invisible to the naked eye, yes, but it could also drastically lower his heat emissions so that infrared scanners would not pick up any trace of him.

He crept across duroplastic coated in photo-voltaic paint and knelt at the north-east corner of the rooftop. The building was on the west side of a street that ran all the way to the border of Caleem park, about a kilometre away.

He opened the invisible case, and his goggles painted a blue, wire-frame outline of a sniper rifle that no one else could see. He clipped the stock into place and attached the scope. Then he used it to select a target.

The scope's magnification factor gave him a very good view of the guests seated in several rows of chairs spread across the grass. On the stage, Sarona Vason was standing tall behind the lectern and speaking emphatically. Aiden ignored her. The Prime Council was not his target. Slade would deal with her when the time was right. Aiden's task was to kill a Justice Keeper. It didn't matter which one. Slade just wanted a death to inflame the city's fears.

He slid his rifle to the left and found Lenai standing at the base of the stage on the west side. Settling the cross-hairs onto her head gave him no satisfaction, he realized. She had done nothing to him personally, and from what he could tell, Lenai was a competent officer, if misguided.

Another pivot brought his scope in line with Melissa. She was positioned on the east side of the stage, watching the audience with obvious trepidation. Killing her would prove his loyalty to Slade's cause but…No. He couldn't. Not like this. If he was going to kill Melissa, he would do it face to face.

Adjusting his aim, he noticed Jack Hunter at the southern border of the park. The man was watching the street, focused on potential threats at the ground level. Aiden felt hot hatred in his chest. Hunter had tried to rip a man apart with a Bending, but he got to keep his symbiont and his position? And they said Aiden was unworthy? Yes, killing Jack Hunter would make Slade very happy.

His finger curled around the trigger.

Standing at the edge of the park with one hand on the grip of his holstered pistol, Jack frowned into the distance. "Everything's still quiet," he said. "I'm thinking we're in the clear."

"Just the same," Anna said in his ear. "Stay sharp."

He felt his lips curl into a smile and nodded slowly. "Always," he promised. "You just make sure you do the same." It was the closest that he could get to saying 'I love you' over an open channel. Not that he minded the rest of the team knowing how he felt, but they might think he was being unprofessional if he got all sappy.

Resuming his task, he took another visual survey of the area. Drialo Avenue was a wide street between two lines of skyscrapers. Ordinarily, that street would be filled with a hundred pedestrians going about their business, but now it was quiet. Everyone had been cleared out for-

Summer was terrified!

Without a second's hesitation, Jack put up a Time Bubble. That sudden spike of alarm was something he had never felt before from Summer, and strangely, the instant he was safe within the confines of the bubble, her fear vanished to be replaced with a sense of relief so powerful it made him want to sigh. Instead, he looked around.

Beyond the bubble's shimmering surface, the world was a blurry mess of wobbly buildings and distorted trees. Everything seemed normal. But Summer would not react like that without cause.

Jack took two steps to his left.

When he let the Time Bubble collapse, something whistled past his ear and struck the ground behind him, burying itself in the grass.

"Sniper!" Jack bellowed.

Voices cried out in shock.

Dropping to one knee, Jack drew his pistol and used spatial awareness to calculate the bullet's trajectory. Four buildings down on the west side of the street. He fired several times without hesitation.

Aiden gasped when Jack Hunter blurred out of the line of fire in the very instant that he pulled the trigger. Instead of killing the other man, Aiden's bullet hit the ground and sent clumps of dirt flying. People were already screaming; he could hear them even at this distance.

Desperate, frantic, Aiden tried to adjust his aim. Maybe he could get off a second shot before he had to retreat. When he centred the cross-hairs on Hunter once again, the other man was down on one knee in the grass…and pointing his pistol directly at Aiden.

Aiden threw himself sideways just before something smashed through the scope of his gun. Another bullet grazed his right shoulder, ripping a gash in his suit and exposing a thin strip of his flesh.

The cloak failed in that area, and part of Aiden's upper arm was now visible. Oh, Bleakness take him! This should have been easy. He was well beyond the range of Jack's spatial awareness. There was no way the other man could have sensed him. And with the cloak providing invisibility, there was no chance that Jack might have caught a glimpse of him. So, how could the man have known? Aiden couldn't believe that Hunter would just happen to erect a Time Bubble mere seconds before a bullet went through his head.

Ignoring those questions, he scurried away from the ledge so that his enemies could not get a clear shot at him. Then he disassembled the rifle, returned it to its case and fled into the stairwell.

Halfway down the first flight, he disabled the cloak and let himself become visible again. There was no point in maintaining it now. Not with the suit damaged. Aiden had failed in his task, and Slade would not be pleased.

People were out of their seats and running in all directions, trying to get out of the park before the sniper took another shot. Over the cacophony of voices, Melissa heard Anna talking.

The other woman was crouching near the corner of the stage with her pistol in one hand, scanning the distant buildings for some sign of the shooter. "Rooftop Team," she snapped. "What have you got?"

A brief moment of silence was followed by Anna sighing. "What do you mean you can't see him?" she snarled. "The door opened and closed on its own...Well, that's just bloody brilliant."

Ignoring her, Melissa climbed up on stage to join the patrol of uniformed guards who had clustered around the Prime

Council. Sarona Vason was spooked. You could see it in her eyes.

Backing up with her pistol drawn, its muzzle pointed toward the shooter's rooftop, Melissa took a deep breath. "Madame Prime Council," she said. "I will be escorting you and your team through the evacuation route."

"Thank you, Agent Carlson," Sarona murmured.

Melissa almost dropped her gun when the shock hit her. The Prime Council knew who she was? Recovering her wits in a heartbeat, she put that out of her mind and went with the guards through the backstage exit.

That took them down a small set of stairs to the field on the north side of the park. Men and women in heavy armour formed two lines around their group, each one carrying a portable force-field generator.

Melissa scanned the nearby buildings for any sign of trouble, but there was nothing she could spot with the naked eye. She was pretty damn sure that Sarona Vason was not the sniper's target anyway. If he was aiming for the stage, then his shot was off by at least three hundred feet. So, either he was the worst sniper in the world…or he had been trying to kill Jack.

"Ma'am," one of the Prime Council's aides said, "We're going to have to cancel the debate tonight."

Sarona Vason continued onward with her eyes fixed dead ahead, not even bothering to acknowledge the young man with a glance. "Absolutely not," she insisted. "I will not be bullied by a terrorist. If we show weakness, Dusep will use it against us."

Melissa was right behind them with her gun pointed down at the ground, frowning as she glanced left and right. "I don't think you were the target anyway," she muttered to herself.

"Very astute, Agent Carlson," the Prime Council replied. "Perhaps you would like to share your observations with the group?"

A blush put some colour in Melissa's cheeks. She had not intended for the other woman to hear that, but she was in it now. "A trained sniper might miss by a few inches," she said, "but that shot was off by a hundred metres. There's no way they were trying to hit you."

She could only see the back of Sarona Vason's head, but she still felt an incredible surge of relief when the other woman nodded. "I reached the same conclusion," the Prime Council said. "This attack was not about me."

On the north side of the park, they found the Prime Council's limo – a long, black car decked out in force-field generators and ballistic glass – waiting by the curb. With a great deal of urgency, Sarona Vason was ushered into the back of the vehicle. Her aides went in next, and then some of the armoured guards.

Melissa turned to go.

"Agent Carlson," the Prime Council called out.

Pausing in mid-step, Melissa turned back to the other woman. Her brow furrowed in confusion. "Ma'am?" Anxiety tied her stomach in knots. If her performance had been lacking in some way...

She could see Sarona leaning forward to peer out the open door. "Join us, please," the Prime Council said. "I would appreciate your insight."

"Um...Yes, ma'am."

An hour later, when the commotion had died down, Jack was sitting in the back of an automated car with Anna. His girlfriend kept glancing in his direction and frowning; he could tell that she was worried.

Closing his eyes, Jack let his head hang. He touched two fingers to his forehead. "I'm all right," he assured her. "The bullet didn't even touch me."

Anna sat with her shoulders hunched up, staring mournfully into her lap. "Yes, but it got pretty close," she muttered. "I don't know, I just...I can't bear the thought of losing you, you know?"

"You're not gonna lose me."

A moment later, she was looking at him, those icy blue eyes of hers trying to bore a hole in his skull. "How *did* you do it?" she asked. "How did you know that someone was going to take a shot at you?"

Tilting his head back, Jack blinked a few times as he considered it. "It wasn't me," he answered. "It was Summer. Right before it happened, she had this moment of...panic, and I just trusted her."

Anna gave him a smooch on the cheek. "Well, I'm glad you did," she whispered. "But maybe you should ask her about it."

That was a wonderful idea. Jack let his mind drift, willing himself into a relaxed state that would allow him to commune with his Nassai. With Anna holding his hand, it was easy.

The world began to fade, growing darker and darker until he was floating inside an endless void. Sheer nothingness in all directions. For a very brief moment, *he* was nothing, but then sensation began to return.

Sound came first, then touch. He heard the chirping of birds and felt stone beneath his feet. The darkness receded, and he saw that he was standing in the middle of a garden, surrounded by rose bushes and flower beds full of yellow tulips and purple lilies. He could smell the flowers.

His actual body was still in the car with Anna, but this virtual world was as real to him as his waking life. He came here often to speak with Summer.

On cue, she stepped out from behind one of the bushes and stood before him in a strapless white dress, blonde hair cascading over her shoulders. Her smile was warm and inviting. "It's good to see you again, my host."

"How did you know?"

Turning gracefully on her heel, Summer clipped a rose with a pair of scissors that appeared in her hand the moment she needed them. "Straight to business then?" she said. "No time for pleasantries."

Jack stood on the narrow path with his arms folded, glaring at her. At first, he tried to convey irritation, but then he realized that he didn't have to convey anything. Summer knew his every thought. "Hey, you saved my life today," he countered. "I don't think it's *totally* unreasonable that I might like to understand *how* you did it."

"You call it spatial awareness."

Jack blinked as if somebody had just thrown a glass of water in his face. "Spatial awareness," he said. "I couldn't sense him with spatial awareness."

It startled him when Summer answered that with soft, delicate laughter. She offered him the flower that she had cut, and Jack took a moment to enjoy its scent. After all, she had gone out of her way to fill this mental construct with sights and sounds and smells that he would find soothing. The least he could do was enjoy it.

"You are correct," Summer agreed. "The shooter was too far away for either of us to detect his presence. I did not sense him at all. I sensed the bullet."

"The bullet."

"Yes."

"But the bullet hadn't arrived yet."

She was smiling at him the way Lauren did whenever he asked a stupid question, which made it that much more irritating when she reached up to pat his cheek. "You call it spatial awareness," Summer explained. "But a more accurate name for the phenomenon would be spatial-temporal awareness."

"Because space and time are one."

"Humans," Summer went on, "can only perceive three dimensions. You experience time as a linear flow from one moment to the next. But this is not an accurate depiction of reality. It is a limitation of human perception. You cannot imagine a four-dimensional object; so, you cannot use spatial awareness to its full potential. Nassai, however, perceive all four dimensions simultaneously."

Jack stood there, slack-jawed, trying to work it all out in his head. Was she really saying what he thought she was saying? "Summer," he stammered. "Are you trying to tell me that you can see the future?"

"With varying degrees of clarity."

"So, you saw..."

"I saw your death," she said in a tone that was far too matter-of-fact for the subject matter. "At a moment when the probability was solid enough to be near certainty."

Drawing in a shuddering breath, Jack walked to a bench near the path and sat there. He set his elbows on his thighs, resting his chin on laced fingers. "If... you can do this," he whispered. "Why don't you do it more often?"

Summer laughed again.

"What's so funny?"

"Your linear perception of time strikes again."

Summer extended her hand over the concrete path, and an image of Leo appeared. Jack felt an instant flash of rage, but the other man was just standing there, ready for a brawl but not moving.

Another version of Jack appeared, a simulation who stood with his fists up, ready to respond to whatever Leo threw at him. Both men were frozen, locked in place as Summer inspected them. "The future is not a single, linear path," Summer began. "It is a multitude of timelines existing concurrently."

Suddenly, there were three Leos, all moving in slow motion. One drew back his arm for a punch. Another shifted his balance to begin a kick. The third was backing away, trying to gain a moment to catch his breath.

And then there were nine Jack's, three in front of each Leo, each one offering a different response to what his enemy did. One Jack, in front of the punching Leo, leaned back and raised a hand to deflect the blow. Another ducked to evade it outright, The third Jack prepared himself for an arm hold.

One of the Jacks in front of the kicking Leo was jumping to begin a kick of his own. Another was backing away. It was...a confusing mess. And just when he thought it couldn't get any worse, twenty-seven new Leos appeared.

"Okay! Okay!" Jack said. "Stop!"

But Summer ignored him. With another wave of her hand, she changed the image slightly so that some of the Jacks and some of the Leos became transparent. On second look, he realized that they were all transparent, but some were more solid than others. "The more probable an event is," Summer went on. "The more clearly I can perceive it."

She spun to face him with fists on her hips, wearing a stern expression that would make his mother proud. "Given your accelerated reflexes and those of your opponents, sometimes, I only become certain that you're about to be punched in the face after it's already too late to prevent it. Ironically, the fact that you were *not* aware of the sniper made your death more probable and allowed me to perceive it with greater clarity."

"Whoa..." Jack whispered.

"And we are limited by what I can share in the heat of the moment." She walked over and stood right in front of him. "I cannot put specific thoughts in your head. I can only choose how strongly I wish you to experience my emotions. I can warn you *that* something is wrong, but I cannot give you specifics as to the nature of the problem."

"Right."

With a sigh, Summer turned around and sat down beside him. She put a hand on his shoulder. "Now, ask yourself this," she said. "In the moment just before the sniper fired, I allowed you to experience an overwhelming sense of panic and dread. If I did that all the time – if I tried to warn you like that when the threat was minimal, a certainty that one of your enemy's kicks would land true – would you have reacted as quickly as you did when I warned you about the sniper?"

"No," Jack admitted.

"So, now you understand my dilemma," Summer concluded. "I must reserve such warnings for moments when the danger is extreme and when I am certain of the outcome of not warning you."

Rising in one fluid motion, she glided across the width of the path to the bushes on the other side. She remained there for a little while with her back turned. "You humans," she murmured. "The truth is, Jack, that I am *very* impressed. Even with my warning, the probability of your death was incredibly high."

She turned partway around and looked over her shoulder, a lock of her golden hair falling over one eye. "But you trusted me," she whispered. "You always have. You treat me like an equal partner. You dignify me with a name. You listen to me. My emotions are not just background noise to you."

She plucked a rose, studied it for a moment, and then, with a frown, she let it fall from her hand. "So many of you do the exact opposite," she lamented. "It wasn't always that way… But now, too many Justice Keepers ignore their Nassai."

Jack stood up slowly, his face tight with sadness. "You're right," he said, nodding. "They do… And maybe it's time we changed that."

When Jack came out of the trance, he found Anna watching him intently, and he could tell that she was nervous. He put his arm around her, and she snuggled up with her head on his chest. "Everything's going to be all right," he assured her. "It's going to be better than all right."

"How so?"

"Because," Jack whispered. "We have an advantage we didn't even know about, and I'm going to teach you how to use it."

Chapter 8

They gave her a plate of leafy greens, chopped carrots, tomatoes and cucumbers in a vinaigrette dressing. Melissa took it and ate with silent enthusiasm. The salad was quite delicious, but every time she started to relax, something reminded her that she was sitting across from the Prime Council. Her general policy of "if you don't know what to say, say nothing at all," seemed prudent.

This dining room on the upper floors of a hotel in downtown Arinas was decorated with round, stained-glass windows in shades of pink. A simple, white table – just a long rectangle with ten chairs – was cluttered with the empty plates left behind by the Prime Council's aides. Humanoid serving bods moved throughout the room, retrieving dishes and flatware.

Sarona Vason sat at the head of that table, picking at the last bits of her meal. The woman looked up just long enough to hit Melissa with a cautious stare before she went back to her plate.

One of her aides, a man of average height with copper skin and thick eyebrows, stood at her side. "Ma'am," he said. "I really think-"

"Absolutely not."

"But surely after this afternoon's debacle."

Leaning back with her arms folded, the Prime Council sniffed disdainfully. "The debate will go on as planned," she insisted. "I've already explained to you that I am not willing to show fear in the face of violence."

The young man accepted that with some resignation, nodding as if he knew that his attempts to advise caution would prove fruitless. "Very well," he said. "I will confer with councilor Dusep's people, and we will see if we can-"

He was cut off by the sound of muffled voices beyond the door. Somebody was yelling, which put Melissa on edge. Oh, how she wished they had let her keep her pistol. It seemed only natural that any guest of the Prime Council would have to be unarmed, but if this was an attack...

"You can let him in," Sarona Vason said.

"Ma'am?"

"Trust me."

No sooner did she finish saying that than Jeral Dusep burst through the door and came striding across the room. A short, compact man in a blue coat, he seemed to sneer at everything he saw. "It's funny," he said. "You manage to give at least half of your speech before a sniper takes a shot that misses you by almost half a kilometre, and then the event is canceled before I can present a rebuttal. A suspicious mind might wonder if the timing was deliberate."

"You can't be serious," Sarona barked.

Dusep came to an abrupt halt about five feet away from her chair, standing tall with his shoulders square. His face might have been carved from stone. "I am deadly serious," he replied. "We agreed on equal time."

Dabbing her mouth with a napkin, Sarona rose from her seat. She turned to him and scoffed. "Well, you'll forgive me, Jeral," she said. "I'm afraid I didn't brief the assassins on our agreement."

That put some colour in Dusep's face, and he stiffened as if holding back his anger. "My supporters won't stand for this," he said. "I will be conducting a rally tonight at Draynoth Stadium."

"Be my guest."

"Ah," Dusep countered. "So, now you try to appear unfazed."

With a sigh, the Prime Council picked up her glass of wine and lifted it almost as if she were toasting the man. "Jeral, you've been skirting the line of hate speech for over a year now." She took a sip. "I look forward to the day when you cross it because, on that day, your career is over."

"In a few weeks, I will be in office. There will be-"

"You think the Prime Council is not bound by our laws?" Sarona raised an eyebrow to indicate what she thought of that. "It doesn't matter if you win this election. You'll slip eventually. It's who you are."

Turning on his heel, Dusep strode to the door and paused there. For a moment, it looked as though he planned to make one last biting comment, but he thought better of it and left without another word.

Melissa felt the knot of tension in her chest unravelling. Ilia's disgust with that man was so strong it was almost hard to think when Dusep was in the room. She knew that if Dusep had his way, Earthers who had come to Leyria for protection would suddenly find themselves alone and friendless.

"Now," Sarona murmured, taking her seat once again. "Perhaps you could give me some time with Agent Carlson?"

Her young aide nodded and then followed Dusep out the door. If Melissa had been nervous before, she was downright petrified now. Facing death was one thing. Trying to impress the leader of the Leyrian Systems Alliance was quite another. What could Sarona Vason want with a new Justice Keeper fresh out of training?

Melissa had an answer before she could even voice the question.

The Prime Council sat with her elbows on the arms of her chair, fingers steepled in front of her mouth. "You're a shy one, aren't you?" she muttered. "I don't believe you said one word throughout the entire meal."

Licking her lips, Melissa glanced down into her lap for a moment. Only a moment. It took some doing, but she forced herself to make eye-contact. "I am not experienced in the ways of politics."

"That will soon change."

"Regardless," Melissa went on. "I didn't want to offer opinions on subjects that I'm not qualified to speak on."

That put a smile on the other woman's face. "May the Companion have mercy!" Sarona exclaimed. "Until I met you, I didn't believe that Justice Keepers were capable of such humility."

Clearing her throat, Melissa picked up her glass of water and took a sip. "Is there something that I can help you with, ma'am?"

"Tell me about Earth."

"About Earth?"

"The relationship between our two worlds is even more important in light of the threat from Ragnos. The truth is that I had hoped – perhaps foolishly – to one day make your world an official signatory of the Leyrian Accords."

Melissa gasped.

Doing that would make all Earth-born humans into Leyrian citizens, granting them the right to vote in Leyrian elections and access to the basic rights and freedoms outlined in the Accords. And since there were almost as many Earthers as there were Leyrians, it might not go over well. Melissa could see why the Prime Council had kept such plans to herself. Dusep would have a field day with that information. "That…might not work out," she said. "I can see a bunch of objections from both your people and mine."

The right to medical care was guaranteed in the Leyrian Charter, and the right to basic living essentials as well. Rights that were not embraced by many of Earth's nations. Such a union would be difficult, to say the least.

"It would take time to bring your people into the Accords," Sarona said. "But I *do* believe that it's worth doing."

"And you think I can help you?"

"You can give me some perspective," Sarona explained. "I don't believe I've ever had an in-depth conversation with someone from your world. And you strike me as an astute young woman."

"Well…" Melissa said, "then I'd be happy to help."

The local Keepers had given Larani an office on the fifth floor of their headquarters in Arinas. Anna strode through the door to find the chief director standing by the window and looking down upon the street below. She could already tell that Larani was feeling dismayed. She didn't know the other woman all that well – they had never been close – but she had worked with Larani enough that she would blame herself for the fact that a potential assassin got close enough to actually take a shot. Well, she would have to share that blame because Anna was intent on helping herself to a sizable chunk of it.

"Report," Larani barked.

Anna marched across the room with her head down, stopping right in front of the desk. She forced herself to look up and blinked. "I've had forensics going over every inch of the rooftop the shooter used."

"What did they find?"

"The building is used by a team of researchers working on new pharmaceuticals," Anna replied. "Rooftop access is restricted to those with a passcode. Our team analyzed the keypad and found micro-abrasions in the circuit pathways. Just enough damage to prevent the automated systems from disabling nanobots that tried to tamper with the lock."

Slowly, Larani turned around, and the golden sunlight behind her almost made her into a silhouette, a shadow that glared disapproval at the woman who brought her bad news. "What could do such damage?"

"The circuitry was ripped apart on a molecular level," Anna said. "And the only thing I know that can do that and leave no visible marks is a Bending. Which can only mean one thing..."

"Slade."

Anna dropped into the chair in front of Larani's desk, folding her hands in her lap as she let out a sigh. "We knew he was coming," she said. "This shouldn't surprise us."

"We had drones scanning those rooftops," Larani countered. "Why didn't they pick up movement or a thermal signature?"

"The forensics team found a piece of fabric on the rooftop," Anna explained. "It's the same material that we confiscated from the two men who attacked Director Andalon in his apartment. Cloaking technology."

It shocked Anna when Larani yanked her own chair out from underneath the desk and shoved it across the room with enough force to send it crashing into the wall. The other woman was snarling. "Brilliant!" she growled. "So, Slade has access to Ragnosian weaponry. Which means he must be working with them."

Anna paused for a second before answering. She had never seen Larani this angry before. The woman was an exemplar of professionalism: calm, cool and collected at all times. Formal to a fault.

"We shouldn't assume anything," Anna said. Bleakness take her, she wasn't used to being the calm, level-headed one. "Slade might have stolen the technology."

Larani turned her back on Anna, standing before the window with her arms crossed. "Perhaps you're right," she rasped. "But I still don't like it."

"Permission to speak freely, ma'am."

That made Larani tense up. The woman looked over her shoulder with suspicion in her eyes. "You've never asked me for such permission before." A moment of tense silence passed before Larani finally said, "Permission granted."

Craning her neck to meet the other woman's gaze, Anna narrowed her eyes. "This isn't your fault," she said, shaking her head. "You followed security protocols to the letter. You assigned your best people to protect the Prime Council."

"I knew the danger was real!" Larani snapped. "That data that we decoded made it pretty clear that Slade would make a move against the Prime Council, and I let her go out there anyway!"

"With all due respect, ma'am," Anna cut in. "That wasn't your choice to make. You did everything you could."

Larani slumped against the window, head hanging. "I know," she whispered. "But I should have...I should have brought Slade in two years ago. I should have listened when Jack tried to tell me that he was dirty."

Anna wasn't sure what made her do it. Before she even realized it, she was out of her chair and moving around the desk. She threw her arms around Larani, and the other woman sobbed in her embrace.

Larani pulled away, sniffling as she wiped tears from her cheeks. "I'm sorry," she muttered. "I shouldn't indulge in such displays of emotion."

Grinning, Anna felt a sudden warmth in her face. She lowered her eyes and did her best not to chuckle. "This is me you're talking to, remember? After all the times I've lost my temper, the least I can do is let you vent."

"I appreciate that, Operative Lenai."

"Just call me Anna."

When she looked up, Larani was smiling. "Very well, Anna," she said. "Now...As pleased as I am to see that Agent Hunter survived the attempt on his life, how exactly did he avoid sniper fire?"

"Well," Anna said. "That's an interesting story."

Draynoth Stadium wasn't exactly packed, but it wasn't exactly empty either. The place could seat about a hundred thousand people, give or take, and at least ten thousand of those seats were filled, most down in the lower levels.

Dusep was on stage, behind the lectern and gesticulating wildly. "How many of you feel left behind?" he shouted with his hands in the air. "Left behind by policies that are more concerned with appeasing strangers than serving our own people?"

It was a speech that Jack must have heard at least fifty times since he had started working with Larani. Oh, the words changed, but the sentiments remained the same. It would take maybe ten minutes to find similar rhetoric in any of Earth's history books. Natives, good! Foreigners, bad! Fear that which is different! Grr! Jack had hoped that Leyria was past this sort of thing.

"So, she warned you with fear?" Rajel asked.

Jack stood with hands gripping a metal railing, leaning forward to watch the crowd below. "That's the gist of it," he muttered. "If we listen to our Nassai more, it'll go a long way toward keeping us alive."

Rajel was next to him with his back against the railing, scoffing as if Jack had just said the most obvious thing in the world. "Sighted people…" he lamented. "It's like you tune out awareness of everything else."

"We should probably focus on the rally."

"Why's that?" Rajel countered. "You really think he's going to say something that we haven't heard a million times before?"

The man had a point. But Larani had sent them to keep tabs on Councilor Dusep, and even if he didn't trust her instincts on this one, Jack would want to monitor the situation. Speeches like this got people fired up. It was only a matter of time before violence erupted. Maybe one of these people would bump into an Antauran immigrant on the way home. Maybe all that bubbling anger would rise to the surface.

"We have a lot to be proud of!" Dusep exclaimed. "The first human civilization to achieve interstellar flight! Ours is a legacy worth defending!"

Biting his lower lip, Jack listened to the councilor's rhetoric. He shook his head slowly. "It's not Dusep we have to worry about," he murmured to Rajel. "It's the people hanging on his every word."

Slamming a closed fist down on the lectern, Dusep growled like a caged animal. "I never thought we would be having this conversation, folks!" he said. "But I have to stand here in front of you and explain why the Systems Council gave away one of the colony worlds! I have to tell you why your friends and your families have been displaced!"

The crowd started jeering and hissing.

Dusep, now as calm as a frozen lake, only shrugged and answered them with a sheepish grin. "There's no excuse, folks," he went on. "No excuse. You're going to have to accept an uncomfortable truth. Your government cares about appeasing the Antaurans! They care about appeasing the Ragnosians! They *do not* care about you!"

That stoked more than a few tempers. Jack saw at least two hundred people rising from their seats and clapping. Some whistled, others shook their fists. It wasn't very long before everyone else was on their feet.

"They don't!" Dusep said over the noise. "They don't!"

Jack couldn't help himself; without even intending it, he started tuning the man out. There was only so much of that you could listen to without succumbing to the urge to stick an ice-pick in your brain.

He found himself watching Dusep's aides. There was a small pack of them near the stairs that led up to the stage: three men and two women, all dressed in blue. One, a tall fellow with neatly-trimmed brown hair, couldn't take his eyes off the councilor.

"See someone you know?" Rajel asked.

Jack stood up straight, blowing air through puckered lips. "Just Dusep's people," he answered. "Larani told me about some of them. The man doesn't attract as much support as Sarona Vason, but he does have his share of true believers."

"Anyone in particular?"

"Matao Zaranthel," Jack said softly. "The guy practically worships Dusep." It was very likely that if the councilor somehow won the election, Zaranthel would become his chief of staff.

Tossing his head back, Rajel frowned as he mulled that over. "Never heard of him," he said. "There some reason you're focused on him instead of the vaguely-human-shaped vitriol dispenser?"

"He just rubs me the wrong way," Jack muttered. "It's not really something I can put my finger on."

"Right," Rajel muttered. "Well, I think we've heard everything we need to hear. So, why don't we grab a drink and then file a report-"

He cut off when his multi-tool started buzzing and squawking in his pocket. Jack's was going bonkers too, and one quick look around the stadium made it clear that they weren't the only ones. Even Dusep had stopped his speech to check the status updates. Which could only mean that this was a general alert.

Rajel had the metal disk of his multi-tool clutched tightly in his hand, and he raised it to his ear to hear the update. Jack checked his as well, and he nearly gasped when he read the message. *Proceed to shelter areas. Multiple incoming warp signatures detected.*

The colony was under attack.

Chapter 9

When Anna passed through the door to the Prep Room, she found herself in a short but dark tunnel, a tunnel that ended in a large, open area. A circular table dominated the windowless room, and Justice Keepers stood around it in small clusters. There must have been at least sixty of them, all team leaders. Some she knew; others she didn't.

Larani was on the far side of the table with her hands clasped behind herself, gazing up at the hologram of a woman in a military uniform. There were four versions of that hologram, one pointed in each of the four cardinal directions so that people on all sides of the room could see her.

Captain Zai-Ella Taborn, a woman of average height who wore her black hair up in a clip, faced the assembled Keepers with a blank expression. Anna remembered her from their brief interactions on Earth. The other woman had led that expedition that was sent to find Anna after her shuttle went missing. It was hard to get a read on her. Taborn could be abrupt sometimes, but she wasn't exactly cold. Other military officers might have given up on Anna after several weeks of searching, but Taborn pressed on at Jena's insistence. Had she not done so, Anna's life would have been very different.

"It's confirmed," the captain said. "Our long-range sensors detected twenty-three distinct warp signatures, all headed this way."

Anna strode forward until she was directly in front of one of those holograms. Her mouth tightened. "Can you determine their point of origin?" It occurred to her that she wasn't in charge of this meeting, and butting in like that might rub some people the wrong way, but she didn't care. She needed answers.

Captain Taborn glanced to her right for half a second, no doubt checking something on a monitor. "Based on their trajectory," she said. "We believe that their point of origin was the SuperGate in the Savron System."

"Ragnosians," someone said.

Pursing her lips, Anna blinked as she considered that. "It doesn't make sense," she said, shaking her head. "They know this kind of aggressive action will incite retaliation. Why would they start a war they know they can't win?"

A man she didn't know – a tall fellow with tanned skin and short black hair – stood a quarter of the way around the table with his arms folded. "Well, maybe they think they *can* win."

"Against us *and* the Antaurans?" Anna shot back. "Not likely."

Larani gave her a look that suggested she be quiet. More than suggested, actually. It was only two hairs short of a withering glare. "This is academic," the chief director said. "We can sort out their motivations later. The relevant question is how we respond to this threat. How many ships do we have in the system?"

"Fifteen," Captain Taborn answered.

"So, we're out-gunned."

The captain shut her eyes, nodding slowly in resigned acceptance of that fact "Yes, we are," she said. "The closest major outpost is Palissa. We've sent a distress call, but at maximum speed, it will take their ships nearly six hours to get here. The Ragnosians will be here in seventy-three minutes."

A female Keeper leaned forward with her hands braced on the table, staring up at the hologram. "So, we have to hold out until then," she said. "Does Fleet Command have a strategy?"

"We do," Captain Taborn answered. "Seven Phoenix-Class cruisers will fly out to engage the Ragnosians near the edge of the solar system. Their goal will be to disable weapons' systems and warp engines. Leave them stranded where they can't do any harm. We get in, we do as much damage as we can and then we haul ass back here to rejoin the rest of the fleet."

"If we can disable even five or six of those ships, we may have a fighting chance. Between the remaining cruisers, the orbital defense platforms and at least two hundred assault shuttles, we might just be able to scrounge up enough firepower to win this fight. But we're going to need every bird in the air. Director Tal, under the authority of Fleet Command, I am ordering all of your pilots to join us in defending this planet."

Anna felt sick to her stomach. Not at the thought that she might die; she had faced that reality over and over again. Not even at the thought that Jack might die. As much as she wanted to protect him, she trusted him to take care of himself.

No, it was the possibility that she might have to kill, that she might have to take another human life, that set her teeth on edge. Maybe she was naive, but she had honestly hoped she would never have to do that again. But here she was, about to go into a war-zone. There had been no official declaration, but that didn't matter. When the shooting started, people died.

The four holograms flickered and then reappeared, each one of them frowning at the people who gathered around the table. "Those of you without a pilot's license," the captain went on, "will be assigned to ground units as support. We will do everything in our power to prevent troops from landing on this planet, but some will get through our net. It's inevitable."

"Captain," Anna said.

"Agent Lenai?"

Anna replied to that with a small smile and a nod of respect. "It's Operative Lenai now," she said. "But it's nice to know you remember me."

"Well, you're hard to forget."

"Captain, I can't help but wonder if we can stop this *before* it gets out of hand. We act as if a confrontation is a foregone conclusion. What if it isn't? We don't even know for certain if these *are* Ragnosian ships. Shouldn't we at least *try* to find out their intentions before we start shooting?"

The captain let out a sigh and briefly lowered her eyes to the floor. When she looked up again, her face was hard. "Believe me, Anna, I would like to avoid a battle as much as you would." She paused for a moment to let that sink in. "But a fleet of twenty-three ships that advances on a planet without sending a signal to identify themselves has made its intentions clear. And with the Prime Council here, we would be foolish not to assume the worst."

Anna didn't like it – not one bit – but she couldn't argue with the other woman's logic. Bleakness take her! She had hoped that the alliance with the Antaurans would have created stability in this part of the galaxy. Surely, Ragnos wouldn't risk a war with *two* major powers. How wrong she was.

"Get your people ready," Captain Taborn said. "I want twelve shuttle squadrons in orbit within half an hour."

The holograms faded, leaving them with a stern Larani who stood on the other side of the table with her lips pressed together in a frown. "You heard the woman," the chief director said. "Get moving."

Ten minutes later, they were all standing in a circle under a catwalk in the shuttle bay. Despite her attempts to focus on the briefing that she didn't want to give, Anna was distracted by the sounds all around her: the shouts of engineers backing orders at each other, the hum of engines powering up, the hiss of the roof hatch opening so that another batch of shuttles could depart.

The whole team was here: Jack with his fists clenched, Rajel with his head cocked as if he were listening to something that no one else could hear, Melissa doing her best to look stoic and Keli making no such effort. Cassi just shifted her weight from one foot to the other. She looked as though she might jump at a sudden noise.

Drawing in a shuddering breath, Anna closed her eyes. "Okay," she said, nodding. "We all know what we have to do. Jack and I are both pilots; so, we'll be taking shuttles up to join the defense force."

Glancing in her direction, Jack narrowed his eyes. "I suppose this is a bad time to tell you that I don't like this," he muttered. "We're Keepers, not soldiers."

Cassi leaned one shoulder against a metal pole that supported the catwalk. The look she gave him would make any man flinch. "So, what do you propose? Should we politely ask the Ragnosians to leave us alone?"

"No," Jack said. "But we could play to our strengths. Our job is to defuse a volatile situation with minimal loss of life. Get us aboard those ships, and we can disable critical systems."

Anna raised both hands defensively and backed away from the group. She shook her head in dismay. "I don't like it either," she said. "But we have a colony of over two billion people counting on us."

"Fair point."

"Rajel," Anna went on.

The man stiffened at the sound of his own name and then let out the breath he had been holding. Perhaps he really was listening to something. "Apologies," he mumbled. "My mind was elsewhere."

"Anything you need to share?"

"I just wish I could go with you."

With two steps forward, Anna put herself in front of him and gently laid a hand on his shoulder. That seemed to get his attention. "Your job is just as important," she assured him. "You've been assigned to the Three Hundred and Twenty-Fifth infantry division. If the Ragnosians land troops on this planet, you'll help them to contain the threat."

Rajel straightened with pride and then, to her surprise, the tiniest smile crept onto his face. "I'll do what I can," he promised. "Just take care of yourselves."

"Keli."

The telepath was leaning against the wall with a hand on her stomach. Almost as if this conversation were making her sick. She looked up when Anna called her name. "You wish me to participate in the battle."

"I can't order you to do it," Anna said. "But-"

"I am happy to help."

Anna blinked, then composed herself as quickly as she could. "Well, good," she said. "Can you do anything about the people on those ships?"

"Probably not," Keli replied. "A battle like this...Too many minds. Imagine being in a room where thousands of people are all shouting over one another. Trying to get a sense of who is saying what will be quite difficult. The problem is further compounded by ships moving away and coming closer at incredible speeds. Individual minds becoming louder and then quieter."

"I get it," Anna said. "What if we put you with Rajel?"

"That could work."

Anna spun to face the others, standing as tall as she could, lifting her chin to project confidence she didn't feel. "Melissa, Cassi," she said, striding forward. "You both have enough shuttle training to serve as copilots. You'll be coming with us. Any questions."

No one said a word.

"All right, let's go."

The cabin of a class-2 assault shuttle was nothing special; if you had seen one of them, you had seen them all. There wasn't all that much to see except for a square table with a bench on each side, a cot along one wall and a set of stairs that led to the cockpit.

Melissa sat at that table with her elbow on its surface, her forehead pressed into the knuckles of her fist. *You chose this,* she scolded herself. *You chose it when you decided to become a Justice Keeper. This is part of the job.*

The cockpit doors slid apart.

Jack descended the steps at a trot, heaving out a deep breath. "We're in position," he said. "When the Ragnosians arrive, we'll intercept them and...Kid, what's wrong?"

Melissa looked up, blinking at him. "It's nothing," she whispered hoarsely. "I'm just a little nervous. That's all."

Leaning against the wall next to the stairs, Jack turned his face up to the ceiling. "It doesn't look like nothing," he said as if talking to himself. "Melissa...We're about to go into a life-or-death situation. If you're afraid, now's a good time."

"No, no. It's not that."

"Then what?"

Melissa shut her eyes, and despite her best efforts, tears slid down her cheeks. She sniffled. "I don't want to kill people." It came out as a squeak. "I'm sorry, Jack. I know this is my duty, but-"

Her words cut off when Jack came forward and threw his arms around her. "I know you don't," he whispered. "Believe me, I know."

Pulling away from him, Melissa brushed a tear off her cheek with the back of one hand. "But this is what I signed up for, right? This is part of what it means to be a Justice Keeper."

"Not to me, it isn't."

Jack sat next to her with a hand on the table. The sympathy in his eyes made her want to start sobbing again. "Go," he urged. "There's no reason why you have to be here, Melissa."

"But don't you need a copilot?"

"A copilot helps," Jack explained. "But I can fly the shuttle on my own if I have to. Open the SlipGate and go back down to the planet's surface. You shouldn't have to be a part of this."

"I'm a Justice Keeper," she protested.

"You're eighteen."

Melissa gave him a level look and then, when that didn't phase him, she arched an eyebrow. "How many eighteen-year-olds did we send to fight the Nazis back home?" she asked. "Why should I get a pass?"

"Because progress?"

"I don't think it works like that," Melissa muttered. "I'll do my duty."

The comm-unit beeped, prompting Jack to access the shuttle's systems through his multi-tool. A moment later, Anna's voice was coming through the speakers. "Guys," she said. "The advanced fleet has engaged the Ragnosians. They're sending us telemetry."

"Computer," Jack barked. "Access data from the advanced fleet."

A hologram coalesced above the table.

Twenty-three Ragnosian battlecruisers, each one the size of Melissa's little finger, flew in tight formation. They were all vaguely rectangular in shape with a rounded edge in front. Seven more ships appeared. Miniature versions of Phoenix-Class cruisers, all shaped like birds with their wings spread in flight. The Leyrian vessels were all labeled but not the Ragnosians. Most likely because the computer didn't know their names.

The Tyree flew over a ship on the edge of the Ragnosian armada, spitting orange flickers of light. The Ragnosians replied with green energy bolts that pounded the Tyree's belly. "Damage assessment," Jack said.

"No significant damage," the computer replied.

The Stellar Flame rushed straight toward a Ragnosian cruiser until it looked like they were headed for a head-on collision. But then the Flame pitched its nose upward and dipped underneath the other ship, firing a steady orange beam that drew a line across the enemy's hull.

In seconds, it was pure chaos. The neat, orderly ranks of the Ragnosian fleet broke apart as they all went off in different directions. Leyrian ships were zigzagging up and down, left and right in a flurry. One came straight at Melissa before it fizzled away. The flash of weapons' fire made it hard to keep track of anything else.

Two Ragnosian ships cornered the Adella, each one emitting a pair of green particle beams from cannons on its upper hull. The small Leyrian cruiser was crushed under the weight of all that firepower, torn to shreds.

Melissa flinched, turning her face away. Duty or no duty, there was no reason why she had to watch that.

The Ragnosians were powerful; there was no denying that. But they were slow and less maneuverable. The Leyrians were flying circles around them. If they could just make those shots count…

The Striath, Captain Taborn's new ship, flew right over one of the battlecruisers and then yawed around to point its nose at the Ragnosians' backside. It fired a volley of plasma bolts at places where the shields had been weakened.

"Warp engines disabled," the computer announced.

"Yes!" Melissa shouted.

Other Leyrian ships were doing the same, disabling their enemies and moving on to the next target. They managed to immobilize four battlecruisers, but the other Ragnosian captains must have figured out the plan. Those who weren't engaged with the advanced fleet jumped to warp.

"They're headed our way," Anna said over the speaker.

"You sure you can do this?" Jack asked.

"I can do it," Melissa hissed. "Let's just get it over with."

Chapter 10

Swivelling her chair around, Anna looked out the cockpit window to find nothing but stars against the blackness. Her shuttle was part of a swarm that had taken up position around one of the space stations orbiting the planet. A station with the specific purpose of defending Alios from a hostile fleet. Anna's job was simple: prevent Ragnosian fighters from disabling the space station's weapons.

Squinting through the window, Anna shook her head. "Where did it all go wrong?" All their efforts to build a lasting peace had come to this. They should have stopped this nonsense before it devolved into a shooting war. "You nervous, Cas?"

"Of course."

Anna was about to say that Cassi's apprehension was natural – only an idiot would be completely untroubled by the prospect of going into battle – but her console started squawking before she could get a word out. Her instruments displayed multiple ripples in SlipSpace, indicating the approach of the Ragnosian fleet.

"They're dropping out of warp," Cassi announced. "Ten thousand kilometres away and closing."

A red rectangle appeared on the canopy window, and the SmartGlass zoomed in to give her a good look at the enemy ships. They appeared one by one from out of nowhere: three battlecruisers, all shaped like blades with rounded tips.

Anna spread her hands across the console and summoned a hologram, a 3D-map of the area. The space-station was shaped like a ring with gun ports on its outer edge. Fifty shuttles had clustered around it to form a defensive perimeter.

"Enemy ships releasing fighters," Cassi said. "Here they come."

Anna shut her eyes, exhaling, and then nodded slowly. "I guess there's no avoiding it now," she muttered. "Well, who wants to live forever anyway?"

"I do, actually."

"So noted."

In her window, the enemy ships were still too far off to see, but red dots appeared on the glass. Ten…Twenty…Fifty? In seconds, there were too many for her to count, each one representing a Ragnosian fighter.

The SmartGlass drew a wire-frame outline of the craft. It was a tiny thing, round with two sharp prongs in front that almost touched. As she studied its dimensions, she almost gasped. The damn thing was only about ten metres long and eight wide. Given that much of that space had to be taken up by the engine and the weapons' systems, there was no room for a pilot, which meant-

"Those things are drones!" Cassi explained.

"Analyze their flight patterns," Anna barked. "Look for commonalities."

"Why?"

"Because I need to know if those things are being piloted remotely or if they're fully automated."

Her window zoomed in on the three battlecruisers flying side by side, each one firing bright green particle beams from cannons on its dorsal hull. Those beams pounded the space station, which responded in kind.

The small fighters were closing in to attack from all sides. Anna chose one and set a course right for it. It was time to see exactly what these things could do. And hopefully take out a few of them.

The fighter reoriented itself with shocking speed, pointing the two curved prongs at her and spitting a glob of green plasma.

Anna thumbed the hat-switch.

Her shuttle slid upward so that the plasma sped past beneath her. She retaliated with particle weapons of her own, bright orange flares that converged upon the enemy fighter. The drone casually side-stepped them and attacked again.

Anna winced from the glare of white light when her shields absorbed the impact. The drone was gone. Her instruments said that it had flown right past her, making a beeline for the station. Clearly, the shuttles were a secondary target.

Stepping on the pedal, she turned one hundred and eighty degrees. Stars wheeled past in her window, and then Alios swung into view. They were six hundred kilometres above the planet's night side. It was too dark to make out oceans or land masses, but she could see splotches of light from the cities below.

And the space-station.

Even without the SmartGlass painting a wire-frame over it, the blazing beams streaking from its outer edge would make it hard to miss. While it pummelled the capital ships, the station pelted the drones with missiles. Anna saw distant flashes as each one exploded. "Analysis complete," Cassi shouted. "The drones are executing what appear to be pre-programmed maneuvers. I'm not detecting any signals that would allow for remote piloting. Those things are automated."

Automated weapons.

Such devices were illegal on Leyria and all of its colonies. Creating them was one of the few things that could earn you a life sentence in a very nasty prison. There was no such thing as perfect AI. Give a machine the option to kill without human supervision, and it would inevitably kill the wrong people. Anna felt cold in-

The shriek of alarms drew her out of her reverie.

Checking her instruments, she discovered that one of the Ragnosian battlecruisers was coming up behind her. And then it was scrolling past overhead, on a direct course for the space station. Anna pitched the shuttle's nose upward, releasing a stream of plasma bolts from the wing-mounted cannons. They sped forward in pairs, each set colliding with a screen of flickering static that appeared just in the nick of time.

"No damage," Cassi said. "Enemy fighters closing on us from behind."

"Switch to EMP rounds."

"Aye."

Anna gunned engines in some sad attempt to stay out of weapons' range, but it did little good. The shuttle trembled from the impact of multiple shots. The lights flickered, and her console went dark for half a second. However, the extra speed *did* let her keep pace with the battlecruiser. In fact, within seconds, she was overtaking the other ship. Any minute now, she would be flying out in front of it.

She saw a pair of particle beams erupting from the cruiser's nose, pounding the ring-shaped station. Shields didn't gradually lose power as they did in the movies Jack liked. That was a misconception in Earth's culture. Shield generators produced force-fields that were capable of withstanding a certain amount of damage. Those force-fields would remain at full strength so long as the generators had power. There were only two ways to defeat them: overwhelm the shields with more energy than they could handle or use charged bullets to phase through them. The Ragnosians seemed to be trying the former.

Perhaps she could try the latter.

Gritting her teeth, Anna felt sweat on her brow. It took a moment for her to realize that the rumbling sound she heard was her own throaty growl. "Hold on tight," she said. "This is gonna be scary."

"What are you-"

They flew out in front of the battlecruiser.

With a quick tug on the flight-yoke, Anna pulled up so that they passed through the space between the two particle beams. She flipped the shuttle upside down; the cruiser's top-side came into view. "Target the cannons."

"Confirmed."

Anna squeezed the trigger, unleashing several volleys of glowing bullets from the launchers on her wings. They passed right through the Ragnosian's shields, and then there was a flash of something that looked like emerald fire as one of those particle cannons exploded.

"I'm reading fluctuations in their power grid," Cassi said. "And their forward shield generators are down. They're vulnerable."

The crew aboard the space station must have come to the same conclusion because they lashed out with a particle beam that drilled right through the battlecruiser's nose and kept drilling until it came out the other side. It was a horrible thing to witness. A steady stream of high-energy plasma sawing the ship in half.

"Drones coming our way!" Cassi said.

Anna checked her screens and found a swarm of them coming up from underneath the battlecruiser, all rushing toward her like angry hornets. "A good guest knows when to make an exit," she said. "Let's go."

In the cockpit window, Jack saw a black sky full of stars above him and the tops of clouds swirling over a blue ocean below. On his right, a Phoenix-Class cruiser kept pace with his shuttle. His instruments identified it as the Delfane, named after some Leyrian goddess. He could only see the forward-most section of the larger ship. It was huge, as long as a city block, and shaped like a falcon with its wings spread in flight.

Bogeys were coming at him.

Squeezing his eyes shut, Jack drew in a breath. "Hang on!" he shouted. "They're coming in hot!"

Two small fighters came flying head-first toward him, each one spitting a stream of green plasma from between the prongs on its front side. Jack adjusted course. His shuttle slid upward and plasma flew past beneath him. As did both fighters.

They were approaching a battlecruiser similar to the one that had taken him captive a few months ago. Missiles erupted from the ship's belly, streaking down to bombard the planet below.

Jack gasped when the Delfane angled its nose upward but continued on the same trajectory. Its pointed beak emitted a thick, orange particle beam that drew a line across the battle's cruiser's underside. Force-fields appeared to protect the Ragnosian ship.

"It's no good," Captain Taborn's voice came through the comm. "Those shields are too strong. We can't punch through."

Stiffening as he recalled his time aboard one of those battle-cruisers, Jack drew in a hissing breath. "Leave it to us, Captain." He swivelled his chair around to face Melissa. "You ready?"

The girl was behind the port-side console, looking stoic. Well…as stoic as anyone could in this situation. "Shield emitters fully charged," she said. "Just tell me what you need, and I'll be ready."

Jack nodded.

Taking the controls again, he looked out the window. The Delfane had reoriented itself to fly with its nose pointed forward. Weapons' fire from the small fighters pounded the larger ship.

Slamming his foot down on the pedal, Jack had the shuttle make a yaw turn of one hundred eighty degrees so that he was now pointed in the direction he had come from. The Delfane continued on its previous course, its enormous wing passing beneath him.

In less than a minute, they were coming up on the battle-cruiser's backside. Guns on the dorsal and ventral hull spat particle beams at him, but Jack managed to avoid them all with a little bobbing and weaving.

He flew over the Ragnosian ship's topside, watching as its massive hull scrolled past under him. Cannons along its surface rotated and began firing plasma at him. Some of those shots landed true, but force-fields snapped into place to protect him.

So, he did the only thing he could.

He brought the shuttle as close to the battlecruiser as possible, so close the tips of his wings almost scraped some paint off the other ship's hull. At this angle, it would be harder for the enemy guns to target him.

"EMP rounds," Jack ordered.

"Confirmed," Melissa answered.

His shuttle flew in a tight circle around one of the cannons with its nose constantly pointed inward, toward the centre of that circle. Jack pulled the trigger on the flight-yoke.

Two lines of glowing bullets sped from his wings and destroyed the battle-cruiser's heavy artillery in a shower of sparks and scorched metal. Jack broke off that circle, flying backwards, away from the explosion.

Alarms blared.

His instruments were warning him that there were more guns behind him, and they were taking aim. Another five seconds, and he would be a pile of ash. And Melissa too.

With a quick tug of the flight-stick, Jack flipped the shuttle upside-down. Now, the enemy ship was above him, and he was flying straight toward another one of its dorsal cannons. The damn thing reoriented itself, trying to line up a good shot.

Jack fired first.

A second volley of bullets produced yet another explosion. Jack had to resist an urge to duck. Chunks of shrapnel bounced off of his shields. And then he was skimming the battlecruiser's surface, so close he could almost reach up and touch it.

He spotted a cylinder protruding from the Ragnosian ship's hull.

A shield generator.

With a cheeky grin, Jack shook his head. "All right, Melissa," he said. "How would you feel about a little wanton disregard for property rights?"

"Just fine."

He fired on the shield generator, watching as several hundred white tracers pelted it and destroyed its circuitry with a spray of blue sparks. Then he pitched the shuttle's nose downward, away from the other ship.

A flash of green sped from left to right in front of him. One of the other cannons was targeting him. The next shot struck the shuttle's port side and jostled him in his seat. On his screen, Jack saw that the shields had not been strong enough to absorb all of the blast. He had taken some damage.

Another shot pounded him.

The alarms started screeching.

Jack pitched the shuttle's nose downward, away from the other ship. Stars wheeled by in his window, and then all he could see was black. Jack gave it a quick count of five, and then he flipped the shuttle around.

The Ragnosian ship slid into view in front of him, framed against the backdrop of the planet below. Those bloody guns were still firing. He saw several streaks of green coming toward him.

Jack used the hat-switch to perform a lateral slide, pushing his shuttle to the right while its nose remained pointed forward. The incoming fire rushed past on his left. "What is the status of their shield net?" he barked.

"Weakened but not disabled," Melissa shouted. "Multiple generators protect the same area."

"Damn... All right, switch to particle weapons. Full power. And give me a targeting solution on their weapons systems."

Jack squeezed the trigger.

Two bolts of plasma erupted from his wings and converged upon the battlecruiser. There was a flicker of white as force-fields appeared to protect the enemy ship. He fired again and again. "Did we do any damage?"

He looked over his shoulder to find Melissa frantically scanning the readouts on her console. The girl was flushed, and her forehead glistened. "Only minimal damage," she said. "And we wouldn't have even done that much if we hadn't taken out that first shield generator."

He nearly jumped out of his seat when the Delfane flew between him and the battlecruiser, following a course parallel to that of the Ragnosian ship. "Nice work, Hunter," Captain Taborn's voice came over the comm. "But I think we've got it."

Delfane reoriented itself so that Jack could only see its back end. It was a little like looking at the ass of a giant metal bird. But he was pretty damn sure that he knew what would happen next.

Gunning the shuttle's engines, he accelerated, passing under the Delfane's belly. When he got close enough, he saw that his allies were emitting a particle beam. A beam that punched a hole in the Ragnosian ship's armour.

"Reading power fluctuations in the enemy ship," Melissa said. "They're breaking-"

She didn't have to finish that sentence. On the window's magnified display, Jack watched the enemy ship crack apart like an egg. At first, he cheered, thrusting his fist into the air, but then he remembered what it was he was cheering. A crew of two thousand people. Dead and dying.

Jack forced his eyes shut, tears trickling over his cheek. He sniffed. "Sorry, kid…I didn't mean to be so-"

He swivelled around to find Melissa slumped over the port-side console. The girl refused to look up. "It's all right," she whispered. "They did come here to kill us."

"You gonna be all right?"

"Yeah."

"Good…Because we still have work to do."

Larani watched the battle play out on a holographic display that hovered over the table in the Prep Room. It was zoomed out to the point where she couldn't identify individual ships. Just dots that flitted back and forth around a rotating globe. Orange dots for Leyrian ships, Green for Ragnosian.

She stood before the hologram with fists on her hips, shaking her head. "Give me an update!" she barked. "Quickly! How many of our pilots are still up there?"

"We launched a total of 68 shuttles," Agent Talmean reported. That made sense. There were only two hundred and twenty-seven Keepers on this planet. Not all of them could fly, and of those who could, most had taken a copilot. "We can confirm that forty-seven shuttles are still intact."

"Forty-seven…"

Something caught her eye.

Two green dots streaked around the globe and converged on an orange one. There was a moment of stillness, a moment where they just seemed to float there, and then the orange dot winked out. Another cruiser lost. They had started with fifteen, and now they were down to eight. Ten if you counted the two ships that had been disabled at the edge of the solar system.

Closing her eyes, Larani shuddered. "All right," she said after a moment. "Let's see if we can offer our pilots some support. Is there any way to-"

She cut off at the hissing sound of automatic doors opening, and when she turned around, she had to stifle the urge to gasp. Jeral Dusep was striding into the Prep Room, flanked by two of his aides, and the man looked like he was ready to chew through steel.

"What are you doing here?" Larani demanded.

Dusep approached the table, leaning forward to get a good look at the display. He seemed to be transfixed by it. "I wanted an update on the battle," he said, "and Sarona's people are less than forthcoming."

Facing the man with the sternest expression she could summon, Larani cocked her head. "I can't say that I blame them," she fired back. "The last thing we need right now is reactionary bullshit."

A few people exchanged glances.

Larani rarely swore.

Standing up straight, Dusep looked over his shoulder. His dark eyes smoldered. "I should think you would be hesitant to stoke petty rivalries at a time like this," he replied in a soft, dangerous voice. "After all, you're as much to blame for this as Sarona."

Larani wanted to slap him. She restrained that urge – it would be conduct unbecoming at the very least – and chose to collect her thoughts. She would *not* fall into one of his traps. Not at a time like this. However... The smart thing to do would be to let that comment pass, but she just had to know. "How is it my fault, councilor?"

He chuckled as he began a slow circuit around the table. "You Justice Keepers," he murmured. "So many people look to you as exemplars of the best among us. But people are easily fooled."

Dusep spun to face her, his face an emotionless mask. "You embrace the politics of naivete," he went on. "You refuse to acknowledge that there are *real* threats in this galaxy."

Larani opened her mouth to protest but clamped it shut again a second later. She would not be baited. No good would come from letting herself be drawn into a pointless argument. She had a job.

Leaning over the table with her hands braced on its surface, Larani ran her gaze over the assembled Justice Keepers. "Can we get a breaching pod up there?" she asked. "Send in a small team to disable one or two of those ships."

Agent Sokai, a tall woman with golden hair, turned away from her station and then shook her head. "It might be possible," she admitted. "But all of our pilots are otherwise engaged. We have no one to escort the pod."

"Furthermore," Agent Moran added. "We know next to nothing about the layout of those ships. There's a very good chance that our people would be overwhelmed before they damaged any critical systems."

"Then what use are you?" Dusep muttered.

Larani shot him a glare.

He answered that with a cheeky grin.

Scrubbing both hands over her face, Larani brushed damp hair off her forehead. "All right," she hissed. "Give me an update on the ground teams. Do we have all of our people in position."

A dark-skinned man who stood next to a screen that displayed troop deployments turned to face her. "We've stationed Keepers with the military units that will be defending key infrastructure and heavily populated areas," he said. "We don't have enough people to defend every city on this planet."

"And why is that the case?" Dusep chimed in without invitation. "I'll tell you why. It's because you failed to prioritize the safety of the colony world."

"There are less than three thousand Keepers in existence," Larani snapped. "Having almost ten percent of them here hardly qualifies as negligence."

"If we had developed automated defense systems that would actually kill an enemy, we would not be at a disadvantage when-"

Slamming her fist down on the table, Larani growled. Almost everyone jumped at her sudden outburst, but it earned her a few seconds of blessed silence, and that alone was enough to soothe any guilt she might have felt at such a flagrant breach of decorum. "Escort the councilor from the room."

Before she even finished speaking, two of her people were gently but firmly taking Dusep to the door. Good riddance. She had no time for his nonsense. Now, to-

"Ma'am!"

Larani looked up to see a flurry of activity on the holographic display. Three green dots were surrounding one of the white lights that represented an orbital defense station. The ring turned red, indicating that it had been rendered inoperable.

"That's the fourth station we've lost," Agent Sokai reported. "There are gaps in the net. The Ragnosians are sending down troop carriers."

Larani sighed.

Things were about to get so much worse.

Jack saw nothing but blackness ahead of him, blackness speckled with thousands of distant stars. It was serene and still and perfect, but then a streak of green rushed past him and sped off into the distance. He was dodging fire from fighter drones that were closing in on him.

On his console screen, the feed from the rear-view camera showed him three of those round robots in hot pursuit, each

one releasing hot plasma from the prongs on its front side. And then he was evading another volley of incoming fire.

"They're like bloodhounds, these things," Melissa growled.

Jack narrowed his eyes, shaking his head in dismay. "Worse than bloodhounds," he said. "Even the most vicious dog will eventually get tired."

He made a sharp turn to the left, and suddenly Alios dominated the view through his window. Blue oceans obscured behind swirling clouds. The robots managed to score a hit on his port-side, and he would have been thrown out of his chair if not for the seat-belt that held him in place. It sounded like thunder crackling overhead.

Not far ahead, the LMS Serenity was taking fire from one of those massive battlecruisers. He would have tried to help, but he and Melissa had problems of their own at the moment. Instead, he flew right past, plummeting nose-first toward the planet.

"What are you planning?" Melissa called out.

"Something brilliant."

He pulled up when he felt the first trace of resistance from the atmosphere, and then the red halo of super-heated air surrounded his shuttle. He used the gravitational drive to slow his descent considerably.

Particle weapons splashed him from above, bouncing off the shields, and then the swirling mists of the upper mesosphere gave way to an endless expanse of blue sky. He saw sunlight reflected on the tops of clouds.

"They're still coming!" Melissa wailed.

Pulling back on the flight-stick, Jack pitched the shuttle's nose upward and fired his own stream of plasma flares up toward the heavens. There was a distant explosion as one of the robots failed to get out of the way.

But now he was falling ass-first toward the ground.

"Jack?"

"Those things aren't designed for atmospheric flight," he explained. "We are. They won't be able to maneuver as well."

A quick flick of the flight-stick flipped the shuttle upside-down, and then he was in a straight nose dive for the ground. Or, well...the surface of the ocean. Sunlight sparkled on the blue waters.

Jack levelled off and flew straight toward a cluster of fluffy clouds. He passed right through them, and for a few moments, there was nothing but gray in his window. The lack of visibility did nothing to deter his pursuers. Another volley of incoming fire pounded his shields like blows from a giant's hammer. "Ready missiles," he ordered. "Target the remaining two drones."

"Won't they just evade?"

Jack answered that with a cheeky grin. "I'm counting on it," he said, tapping a few commands into his control console. "Set for a low yield. We don't need to put a crater on the planet's surface."

"Done," she said. "Missiles armed-"

Her words were cut off by the thunder of more particle weapons hitting the shuttle. Jack didn't need his instruments to tell him that last volley had penetrated the shields and done some damage to the dorsal hull.

He performed a one-hundred-eighty-degree yaw so that he was flying backwards. Not the smartest move in an atmosphere; the shuttle's gravitational drives could execute any type of turn, but its body was designed to minimize wind resistance when pointed in the direction of flight. Both robots emerged from the cloud he had just passed through, each one charging up a blast in between its two prongs.

Jack fired the missiles.

One veered to the left and the other to the right, bearing down on their targets. Both drones broke off to evade, but the missiles were as relentless as the robots had been just a few moments earlier.

Jack capitalized on the distraction.

He yawed to the left, pitching slightly upward, and fired a stream of plasma bolts into the path of the first robot. The damn thing was so busy trying to outmaneuver the missile that it flew right into the storm, exploding in a fireball. The missile detonated a second later.

Swinging the shuttle's nose around, he tried to settle his targeting reticle onto the other bot. But the drone executed a sharp turn and pointed its prongs at him, releasing a stream of plasma. His eyes smarted when the shields popped up to protect him, and he felt the mild shock-wave of a low-yield explosion.

When the flickering force-field vanished, the third drone was coming right at him. On a collision course.

Without thinking, he performed a downward slide – allowing the shuttle to lose a hundred feet of altitude – and pitched its nose up ninety degrees. He fired just as the Ragnosian fighter sped past, punching holes in its belly and destroying the thing once and for all. "How are we doing, Melissa?"

"Dorsal shield generators are damaged just behind the starboard wing," she said. "Nanobots are working to repair them, but they'll be inoperable for at least half an hour."

The comm system beeped, and when he answered the call, Captain Taborn's voice came through the speaker. "Agent Hunter?"

Chuckling softly, Jack wiped the sweat from his brow. "Captain!" he exclaimed. "So nice of you to call. I was just thinking that we really don't talk anymore, and that's a shame."

"Well, complete this next mission, and I'll have you over for tea," she replied. "We have Ragnosian drop-ships about two hundred clicks from your position. They're sending down troops, Jack."

"Disable the drop-ships," he said. "Got it."

"*Destroy* them, Agent Hunter," she ordered. "These are enemy combatants, not suspects you plan to arrest. The fewer boots they put on the ground, the less our people will have to deal with."

Shutting his eyes tight, Jack trembled as he drew in a breath. "All right," he said hoarsely. "I'll do what I have to do."

He set a course for the coordinates she sent him. At this low altitude, it would take a little longer – you could only fly so fast in an atmosphere – but going back up would draw the attention of more drones. Besides, this would give him time to check in.

Jack turned around and faced Melissa with his hands gripping the arms of his chair. "You okay, kid?" he asked. "I know those are some crap orders."

Melissa was reclining in her seat with her eyes closed, catching her breath. "I can deal," she murmured. "It's just... Couldn't we find another way?"

"Well, I guess we'll assess that when we get there?"

The girl's eyes snapped open, and she regarded him for a very long moment before speaking. "You're going to disobey Captain Taborn?" she asked. "That might get you in a lot of trouble."

"We're Keepers, not soldiers," Jack countered.

"I know," she muttered. "And I agree that we should look for alternatives before we resort to lethal force. We take matters into our own hands. It's kind of our thing. But most of the time, the worst that might happen is a slap on the wrist. This... Depending on how it goes, this could be treason."

Chewing his lip, Jack bobbed his head from side to side. "Fair point," he said. "But that's part of the job too. You don't get to stop following your moral compass when life gets complicated."

"Yeah, I guess not."

Resting his head on the seat cushion, Jack felt a lazy smile coming on. "Hey," he said. "I told you that we would assess the situation when we got there. Not that we would disobey orders on principle. We'll figure it out."

Five minutes later, he was checking his instruments when he noticed that they were approaching a shoreline. A narrow strip of sandy beach bordered a rainforest that seemed to go on forever. In seconds, they were flying over lush, green trees that clung to rolling hills.

His sensors picked up two troop carriers descending from high orbit about thirty kilometres ahead. With a few quick taps at the console, he increased speed. They had to intercept those ships before they got near a human settlement. "How far to the nearest city?" he asked.

"Ta'leean is one hundred twenty-five kilometres north-east."

"That's where they'll be heading," Jack muttered. "Bust out the Kenney Loggins, kid. We're going back into the fray."

"Kenney who?"

He turned around just enough to look over his shoulder with narrowed eyes. "Oh, come on!" he said. "Seriously? You've never seen Top Gun?"

Melissa shrugged and answered him with an impish smile. "I don't watch old man movies," she said. "Pick something a little more current."

"More current," he grumbled.

Linking the shuttle's systems to his multi-tool, he accessed his music library. It was time to school this whippersnapper on the awesomeness that happened when you mixed power rock with high-flying action. A little "Danger Zone" would get the blood pumping.

Checking the screens showed him a computer rendering of the enemy ships. Both were plump air-craft with stubby wings. Not very maneuverable, but perfectly-suited to carrying about a few dozen soldiers. No fighter escort. Odd.

Jack looked up through the window, then shook his head. "Something about this isn't right." His hands danced over the controls, putting them on an intercept course. "If these ships are delivering ground troops, why send them down without protection?"

Melissa didn't have an answer.

In seconds, it didn't matter anyway. They were swooping low over the treetops, coming in hot. The two troop carriers were dead ahead, flying on a vector that would bring them to Ta'leean within ten minutes.

"EMP rounds."

"Aye."

Jack lined up his shot and fired a volley of glowing bullets at the ship on his right. They went right through the shields, disrupting vital systems. The ship on his left opened a hatch in its backside, and two fighter drones came out.

"Damn it!"

He executed a banking turn over the forest, exposing the shuttle's belly to the two drones. They took advantage, and Jack was nearly thrown out of his seat by the impact of particle weapons. Then he was racing away from the two fighters.

"They're gaining on us," Melissa announced.

Reversing the gravitational drives, Jack slowed his shuttle and growled when more incoming fire pounded its exposed backside. The two fighters zipped past above him. He could see them in his window.

Without thinking, he pitched the shuttle's nose up and released a stream of bullets that pelted one of the drones. Sparks flickered over the robot's body, and then it dropped out of sight, concealed by the trees.

The other one kept going, making no attempt to turn and fight.

"These things are a distraction," Jack said. "They're trying to lead us away from the other drop-ship."

With another quick turn, he put himself back on course and pushed the shuttle for as much speed as he could get at this low altitude. His scanners told him that the second drone was in pursuit of him again.

"Not this time."

The rainforest was rushing past beneath him. The sky ahead was clear and blue with the morning sun shining bright. A section of the window zoomed in to show the second troop carrier still on course for its target.

"Ten seconds to weapon's range," Melissa shouted. "Now!"

He unleashed another storm of bullets that phased through the shields with little difficulty. There was a brief flash as one of the drop-ship's anti-grav stabilizers exploded. "Their force-field emitters are damaged," Melissa said. "Engines too. One clean shot, and they're dead."

"Particle weapons," Jack ordered.

There was only half a second of hesitation before Melissa replied with, "Particle weapons, aye."

Jack closed his hand around the flight-yoke.

The Ragnosian troop carrier was right there in his cross-hairs, exposed, vulnerable. All he had to do was squeeze the trigger. From a tactical perspective, that was what he should do. Disabling the drop-ship would prevent those troops from reaching their target, but that didn't eliminate the threat. A couple dozen hostiles roaming around the Haltorean Rainforest was a mess that *someone* would have to clean up eventually. The smart thing to do would be to end the threat now.

But he couldn't.

He would not fire on helpless people.

Two seconds later, fate decided for him as the drop-ship crashed into the trees and flattened several beneath its girth. Jack let them go. If they won this fight, they could come back with greater numbers and capture those soldiers as prisoners of war. It may not be the smart thing to do, but-

Something very much like thunder filled his ears, but he barely even noticed it when the shuttle trembled under the fury of weapons' fire. The second drone had caught up to them.

Jack reduced his speed once again, but this time, when the drone passed over him, it spun around to point those prongs right at him. Screens of buzzing white static popped up to shield him from multiple plasma bolts.

"Secondary weapons!" Jack bellowed.

"Confirmed!"

He fired without even checking to see if he had a targeting solution, and only the searing blaze of an explosion told him that his aim had been good. He had destroyed the robot but not before the damn thing got off two more shots.

The lights went off in the cockpit.

"Main power is out," Melissa screamed. "Dorsal shield emitters non-functional. And we've lost artificial gravity."

Jack didn't need her to tell him that. He tuned her out and focused on the task of keeping them alive. The shuttle's nose dipped. Without the gravitational drives, they would have to glide until they could find a safe place to land. But they were already too low and too slow.

First, they brushed the treetops, and then they crashed right through. The next thing Jack knew, his shuttle was skidding along the ground and bulldozing anything that got in its way. Trees snapped, vines fell and chunks of mud went flying.

It ended when the shuttle's nose slammed into a massive lupuna with enough momentum to knock the thing over. Only the safety restraints prevented Jack from going face-first into the window. Thankfully, that window held. He couldn't find a single scratch on it. The reinforced SmartGlass was designed to endure pressure a hundred times that of Earth's atmosphere. It could endure a few bumps and bangs.

"Well..." Jack panted. "That happened."

Interlude 2

So much had changed.

It had been over a hundred years since William had died, but he had lived on, discarding the man he had once been and adopting a new identity. He had seen every last corner of the world, from the outermost reaches of what had once been his homeland to the shores of the Iberian Peninsula. He had traversed the jungles of Africa, watched the Romans rise and fall. He had been a king, a beggar, a thief and a nobleman. He had died more times than he could count.

There were no surprises left, or so he believed. He had seen more than any man had a right to. He had been all but certain that he knew the limits of human existence... until the spirits took him beyond the stars.

It shook him to the core when he learned that there were other worlds to explore, some with wonders beyond anything he could have imagined. Ten years after William had passed, he had been a simple fisherman who died of a sickness that filled his lungs with mucus.

When the spirits restored him to life again, he found himself in lands that he did not recognize, lands where the people used weapons that could hurl a small pellet many times further than even the best archer could shoot, lands where ships of iron sailed the oceans, lands where they spoke a language he had never heard in all his travels. He could still remember the horror of that first night when he had looked up to see a purple moon.

The Old Woman told him that he must expand his understanding of the universe. He had tried. Oh, how he had tried. The locals thought him a madman, and when his attempts to communicate failed, they had thrown him into a cell and bound his hands so that he could not even feed himself. That life did not last long. He had died within a year of entering that cell, and when he rose again, he was still in the strange, new world. The Old Woman told him that his was only one of many globes in the heavens, and he would need to see them all before his work was through.

Now, he was Dravis Trovan: a tall and slender man with a dark complexion of sun-kissed skin and a thin mustache. His black hair was cut short and combed back neatly. His knee-length, red coat was marked by gold embroidery at the hem and the collar, and lace protruded from the cuffs of each sleeve.

He walked along the docks with a purpose, pausing just long enough to admire the metal ship birthed in the marina. The captain was barking orders at her crew. A woman captain. He had never seen the like.

"Milord…"

Turning sharply, Dravis cocked his head and raised a dark eyebrow. "Arel," he said. "I take it you have news."

The young man who stood before him in soot-stained breeches and a shirt with the sleeves rolled up to the elbows refused to look up and meet his eyes. Arel was a good lad. With a little help, he might find himself a good wife. Dravis was half inclined to give that help. "They're gathering, milord," he said. "They've shut down the factory."

"As expected."

"They say they won't return to work unless their demands are met."

Gazing up at the heavens with lips pursed, Dravis felt his eyebrows rising. "How audacious of them," he murmured. "Well, there's no sense in prolonging this idiocy. Did you speak to the local constabulary?"

"Yes, milord. They say they will move in on your command. Shall I give the word, milord?"

Clapping the boy on his shoulder, Dravis spoke in a reassuring voice. "Not yet," he said. "Tell them to gather outside the building but wait for my order. We will at least try to settle this in a civilized way."

"Yes, milord."

He was curious to see what Mari would do. The woman had been rallying her fellow workers for months now, pushing them to strike. It seemed that she had finally convinced them to take that final step, which would make matters difficult.

He rode in one of the new automobiles. Fascinating machines. He had walked the earth for over a thousand years, and yet he could never have imagined such a thing. He was beginning to understand the Old Woman's designs. A sliver of them, anyway. If men could invent machines such as these, then perhaps the stars were not beyond their reach.

The streets of Elohan were crowded, forcing his driver to travel slowly. Too slowly, in Dravis's estimation. The rabble that blocked his way should learn to fear their betters. Most were foreigners, not Tareli citizens. Barbaric scum who clung to the coattails of civilization in the hopes of seizing a few scraps but who offered little of value in return. They did make good workers — when properly managed.

Small houses cramped together with barely an inch of space between them lined both sides of the muddy street. Boys in dirty trousers and coats offered their services loading freight onto ships. Dravis ignored them even when one threw a piece of fruit that splattered on his window.

The factory was a large, gray building with smoke rising from its chimneys. A big crowd had formed outside: workers thrusting their fists into the air, shouting "People, not tools!" over and over.

When the automobile stopped, Dravis opened the door and got out. He stood before them with a frown that should have sent any man who knew his place hopping. "It seems this will be more difficult than I had imagined."

He approached the crowd.

They were a motley group of men and women who ranged in age from just shy of adolescence to old and gray. Most had the copper complexion of native citizens, a mark of a strong Tareli heritage. Though it certainly wasn't definitive. And it was clear that some of these workers were not citizens at all.

"What is the meaning of this disturbance?"

His voice carried with enough volume to make a few of the people in front stop chanting, and when those few quieted down, the rest fell in line. Soon, he was face to face with a crowd of almost three hundred people, all of them gawking at him.

The crowd parted to allow somebody to come through. A short woman with dark, bronze skin who wore her black hair up in a bun. "Lord Trovan," she said with disdain in her voice. "We were wondering when you would grace us with your presence."

"Is this your doing, Mari?"

It enraged him when she answered that with a mocking grin. "You will forgive us for interrupting your day," she said.

A dark woman with her hair in a multitude of braids stepped up beside Mari, and her smile was just as insolent. "Yes, it must be difficult for you," she added. "Who would have thought that owning a munitions factory would require actual work?"

Several people sniggered.

He crossed his arms and stepped forward, meeting her smile with an angry scowl. "Those munitions are the only thing keeping our soldiers safe when they explore hostile lands," he shouted. "This strike puts them all in danger."

"The Companion forbid that anything should come between the Empire and its love for endless war."

"That war keeps you safe," Dravis protested.

Planting fists on her hips, Mari smiled and shook her head. "You really expect us to believe that?" she asked. "Invading foreign lands, stripping away their resources? *This* is what keeps us safe?"

Frowning as he considered his next move, Dravis nodded slowly. "We have here an opportunity to end this peacefully," he said. "Return to work now, make no more trouble, and I will forget this indiscretion."

"No one's going back to work," Mari said. "Not unless things change around here."

"I warn you, Miss Delfiana, my patience is not without limits."

"You work us to death!" Mari spat. "Twelve-hour shifts with only one day off in ten. The 'pay' you offer is barely enough to let us feed our families, and the rent that you charge on these dismal houses keeps increasing."

"Such is the nature of the world."

"Not my world."

"Nor mine." That had come from the dark woman. Dravis had almost forgotten her, but the look in her eyes made it clear that she loathed him. Who was she? A foreigner, by her colouring – that much was clear – but one who had never learned proper respect.

"Very well," Dravis said. "You're all fired."

Mari threw her head back and laughed. "Is that supposed to frighten us, Dravis?" she exclaimed. "Sack us if you want. Every last one. But it won't matter. This factory is ours now."

"Can you produce even one arbiter who would agree with that assessment?"

"It doesn't matter," the dark woman cut in. "Words on paper are meaningless. Look around you, *my lord.* Every one of these people is willing to lay down their life to protect what is theirs."

"Who... Who are you?" Dravis stammered.

The woman stepped forward and thrust out her chin. "Nakia ka Thradari," she said. "A pleasure to make your acquaintance."

He stood there slack-jawed, blinking as he tried to work through his disbelief. "You have been given an opportunity that few of your people will share," he said. "The chance to taste the bounty of civilization. You would squander it so easily?"

"'Bounty?'" Nakia mocked. "I think you mean 'the exploitation of civilization.'"

He ground his teeth until his jaw hurt, then stepped forward with a glare that made several people jump out of his way. "This discussion is moot," he said. "The constabulary is here. If you won't end this strike peaceably, they will end it for you."

Many of the workers quieted down, their bravado squelched as they remembered the men and women in gray uniforms who waited on the other side of the street. Mari and her foreign bitch had emboldened them, but such passions tended to burn out in the face of cold, hard reality. It was easy to talk about giving your life for a cause, but few people had the will to actually do it.

"Don't let him rattle you!" Mari shouted. "Hold firm, my friends! Without us, this factory would be bankrupt in a matter of days!"

"He'll use you up and spit you out!" Nakia added. "Go back to work now, and the oppression will never end! We're people, not tools!"

"People, not tools!" someone echoed. And then they all took up the chant. "People, not tools! People, not tools!"

With a wave of his hand, Dravis signaled the constables, and they marched across the street with truncheons in hand. The situation descended into chaos within seconds: constables whacking workers over the head, workers throwing punches or landing a good kick, people crying out in pain on the ground.

In the midst of the confusion, Dravis saw Mari shouting, "Do not back down!" That damnable woman! She was the source of all this trouble. Before he even knew it, Dravis was striding toward her.

Mari spun to face him, her eyes widening when she deduced his intentions. His hand lashed out, seizing her throat, and she squealed as he lifted her right off the ground. "You!" Dravis snarled. "You did this."

She was gurgling in his grip, feet kicking as her face turned purple. Dravis couldn't help but laugh. "Foolish woman!" he sneered. "Who's going to save you now?"

Something struck the back of his knee and he stumbled, Mari falling to the ground when he released her. The woman pushed herself up on extended arms, tears streaming over her face as she hissed at him.

Dravis turned around and gasped.

Nakia stood before him with her fists up in a fighting stance, her teeth bared as if she meant to rip open his throat. "That would be me," she growled. "Let's end this."

She kicked high, striking his chin with enough power to send a tooth flying from his mouth in a spray of blood. He was barely cognizant of the woman spinning to deliver a back-kick that struck his chest and drove the wind from his lungs.

Dravis stumbled.

The woman was on him like a tigress defending her young, charging in to punch his chest with one fist and then the other. She followed that with a jab that should have broken his nose.

Leaning back, Dravis caught her wrist with one hand. He slammed a fist into her belly, and she wheezed. Ignorant foreign scum, He would teach her some respect!

Dravis pulled her close to look into her dark eyes, and suddenly it was Guo Dong who stared back at him with that mocking grin. "No..." he whispered, shoving the other man to the ground.

Edwin landed at his feet, moaning.

Kicking him several times, Dravis savoured the sweet snap of broken ribs. With a gasp, Edwin flopped onto his back. Hot rage drowned out awareness of everything else. Edwin was coughing, blood spilling from his mouth.

"Leave her alone!"

Dravis looked up to find Raymond coming at him with teeth bared, blood staining his neat, golden goatee. The other man leaped, tackling him to the ground.

Dravis landed on his back with a frantic Lihua on top of him. It took every ounce of strength he had to restrain her. The bitch screeched as she tried to claw his eyes out. She would kill him right there if he gave her the tiniest opening.

"Get off me!" Dravis panted. "Get off!"

A gray-clad constable came up behind her and smashed the back of her head with a cudgel. Lihua collapsed on top of him with a whimper. Dravis tossed her body aside and found a bleary-eyed Mari staring vacantly at nothing at all.

"Mari!"

Clutching her chest as if trying to hold her ribs in place, Nakia crawled over to her dying lover. Yes, those two were lovers. How could he have failed to notice before? The woman snarled at him with murder in her eyes. "This isn't over. I swear... One day, in this life or the next, I'll make you pay. I'll-"

Her words cut off when one of the officers shot her in the back.

Chapter 11

The planet's night side was mostly just a big black patch that blotted out the stars behind it, but Anna saw a thin crescent of blue as they approached the terminator. There were tiny pulses of light in the distance. Explosions or weapons' fire? She could not say which.

She angled the shuttle upward, away from the planet, and saw a momentary flicker of green. When the window zoomed in, she realized that it was more than just a flicker. It was a bloody storm.

A cluster of automated fighters had surrounded the LMS Destiny, and they were pummeling it on all sides with particle weapons. Her instruments said that the Destiny's shields were holding, but all it would take was for one shot to break through.

Pressing her lips together, Anna felt her eyebrows rising. "Work is never done," she whispered. "Cas, you ready for more action?"

"Do I get a choice?"

"Not so much."

She put them on a direct course for the maelstrom of weapons fire. The closer they got, the more Anna realized that those drones were devious little shits. If they maintained a constant rate of fire, the Destiny couldn't lower its shields. And with the shields up, it couldn't counter-attack. Not even with

EMP rounds. Those would disrupt a force-field as they passed through it, and even a momentary disruption could be fatal when you were being hit on all sides with enough firepower to blow a hole in your hull.

The besieged ship grew larger and larger in her window until she could make out each individual drone. One spun around to point its prongs at her.

Anna fired first.

Plasma bolts tore the little robot to shreds before it could get a shot off, and this prompted three others to break off from the Destiny and turn their attention toward her. If she didn't know better, she would have said they were angry.

Anna grinned.

Pulling back on the flight-stick, she angled the shuttle's nose upward and flew off into deep space. She cranked the gravitational drive up to full power, and it wasn't very long before she was fleeing the scene at a rate of two hundred kilometres per second. The drones managed to keep pace with her.

She was jostled about as incoming fire rebounded off the shields. Each volley sounded almost like waves crashing on a beach, but despite the noise, she still caught the occasional grumble from Cassi.

"Shields are holding, but they're smart little bastards! They-"

A violent tremor threw Anna forward so hard she almost banged her head on the console. The cockpit went dark for a second before the emergency lights kicked in, and then she became aware of the frantic screeching of alarms. "Bleakness take me!" Cassi shrieked. "They're timing their shots so that they all hit the same spot at the same time. That last one broke through the shields."

"Rear-view camera?"

"Disabled!" Cassi shouted.

Anna flipped the shuttle upside-down so that she was now flying backwards. Three small robots came into view, and each one spat a glob of green plasma. Three shots that would all hit her in the same spot.

A flick of the hat-switch slid the shuttle downward – from her perspective – so that the three projectiles sailed harmlessly over its top-side. "Arm a high-yield missile," Anna barked. "Hurry."

"Target?"

"No target. I just want it to fly in a straight line." The AI that governed the shuttle's shields and auto-pilot was programmed to ignore any object that was not coming directly at it. She was hoping these three bots worked the same way. "Set for remote detonation."

More incoming fire.

Snarling like a beast, sweat drenching her face and hair, Anna threw herself into the task of evading it. It wasn't easy. The bots saw what she had done last time, and they used that to anticipate her next move. She had to bob and weave and roll out of harm's way, all while flying backwards.

Fortunately, the drones were starting to fall behind. They were trying their best to keep up, but they were smaller than her shuttle; their engines weren't as powerful. Just a little more distance, and her plan could work.

"Good to go!" Cassi said.

Using the targeting reticle that appeared in her window, Anna launched the missile on a path that would take it through the empty space between the three drones. Hopefully, they would ignore it.

Her hopes were dashed when all three fighters broke for-mations and flew off in different directions. Perhaps their AI realized that a missile didn't have to hit you to do damage. Well, the plan had been a good one. She detonated the missile anyway.

What followed was something that looked like a new star being born, a sphere of radiance that expanded in all directions. Two robots caught the edge of the blast, but... so did Anna.

Force-fields snapped into place to protect her shuttle, but the missile had gone off closer to her than she would have liked. It was like being tossed about by a tidal wave. They were knocked off course, stars streaking past in the canopy window. It took her a moment to get reoriented.

"Two of the drones are heavily damaged," Cassi said. "The third is coming around for a counter-attack."

Anna yawed to the right until her targeting reticle settled itself onto the final drone. The damn thing unleashed another stream of plasma, and she slid the shuttle downward to let it pass right over her.

Anna fired before she even had a targeting solution, releasing a series of orange flares into the blackness of space. She pitched the nose upward until every one of those sizzling projectiles was ripping its way through the small fighter.

Then she targeted the other two for good measure, pounding the until there was nothing left but scorched debris.

Gasping for breath, Anna slumped forward in her chair. She just wanted to lie down and sleep. "Status," she panted. "How quickly can we get back to the Destiny?"

"Anna..."

"What?"

Her screen lit up with an image of the Destiny as it tried to outrun the twenty little robots that kept hammering its shields. She was about to insist that they go back, but then she noticed the time-stamp on the video. This footage was almost three minutes old.

Eventually, several of the drones pulled the same trick of concentrating their fire on one spot. They managed to punch a hole through the shields and destroy the emitters that sustained them. And then it was all over.

With several of the shield emitters damaged, the drones had an easy time exploiting the weak spot. They overwhelmed the Destiny with a continuous onslaught until the ship exploded in a fireball.

Anna used her knuckle to wipe a single tear off her cheek. "Okay," she whispered. "Then we better find someone else who needs our help."

"No offense, An," Cassi said. "But we're in no position to help anyone. The hits we took destroyed our aft shield emitters and knocked out our warp engines. There's a small hull breach, and the cabin has been exposed to vacuum. If we go back into battle, we are *going* to die."

Massaging her eyelids with the tips of her fingers, Anna heaved out a breath. "Then I guess we should try to land this thing."

She swivelled around.

Cassi was sitting at the starboard console with a scowl that could curdle milk. "We try that," she said, "and we're just as dead. There's no way we make it back to the planet without attracting the attention of more drones."

"Then we take the Gate."

"And leave the shuttle here for them to salvage?"

Ticking off her fingers one by one, Anna pointed out the flaws in the other woman's objection. "First of all," she said, "they already *have* one of our shuttles. They got it when they took Jack prisoner, remember? Second, I think they have bigger concerns right now. And third, unless you think this little shuttle holds the key to their victory, it's not worth sacrificing two lives."

Cassi shrugged and then got out of her seat. "Works for me." She glanced toward the cabin door. "You ready to make the mad dash?"

"We better make sure we have a Gate that can receive us first."

Anna used her multi-tool to place a call to Justice Keeper HQ. The screen lit up with the image of Agent Thrin. "Ma'am?" he said. "Do you need assistance?"

"Our shuttle is damaged," Anna explained. "And we need to make an emergency evacuation via the SlipGate. Please be ready to receive us. I'm sending my authorization code." She tapped a sequence of numbers and letters into the screen and forwarded them to HQ via a secure text message.

"Code accepted," Agent Thrin replied.

"Open your Gate in exactly one minute."

"Confirmed."

She ended the call and brought up the app that controlled her own SlipGate. This would require a bit of finagling. If she requested a trip to Justice Keeper HQ before Thrin opened his Gate, all she would get for her trouble was an error message. And with the cabin's life-support compromised, she didn't have time to make multiple attempts. She set the destination and left the app open so that all she would have to do was push one button.

Rising from her chair, Anna paced to the back of the cabin. She paused near the set of double doors. "Okay," she said. "Get ready to activate your emergency life-support."

Cassi had one shoulder pressed against the wall. Her mouth quirked into the tiniest smile Anna had ever seen. "Ready when you are."

Stepping back to give the other woman some space, Anna tapped a button on her armoured vest. A sphere of flickering electromagnetic energy appeared around her body, so thin that she could easily see through it. It was a low-power force-field that would last for about a minute. Any bullet could easily punch through that barrier, but it was strong enough to trap a pocket of air around her.

Cassi was safe inside her own force-field, watching Anna with more than a hint of anxiety on her face. They weren't able to talk to one another. Trapping air also trapped sound.

Anna felt a mild tingle as her hand passed through the force-field to hit the switch that opened the door. Once the pressure seal was broken, air rushed out of the cockpit. She quickly pulled her hand back into the safety of her bubble.

And then she started down the steps, taking the force-field with her.

The artificial gravity was still working even though there was a fist-sized hole in the ceiling that let her look out on the stars. She made her way around the square table to the SlipGate at the back of the room.

Once she and Cassi were in position, Anna tapped that button on her multi-tool and ordered the Gate to send them both to HQ.

The trip through SlipSpace took only a few seconds, and when they arrived in a windowless room with no furnishings except a single console by the door, Anna dropped her force-field. She took a deep breath of stuffy air. Delicious, stuffy air!

Agent Thrin was a short man with dark, brown skin and thick hair that curled over his ears. "Travellers have arrived safely," he announced. "I'm locking the Gate."

"How bad is it?" Anna asked.

"Ma'am?"

She crossed her arms with a sigh and then strode across the room. "The battle," she clarified. "You don't get much of a chance to look at the big picture when you're dodging incoming fire, but what I saw didn't look good."

The young man was nervous. His eyes dropped to the console as if he couldn't bear to look at her. "You'll have to speak to Director Tal, ma'am," he said. "My job is to make sure no one gets through that Gate without proper authorization."

"Gotcha."

"She's waiting for you in the Prep Room."

Two seconds after she heard that, Anna was striding out the door. "Come on, Cass," she said. "Our work's not done yet."

Melissa had a moment of surprise when she stepped through the shuttle's airlock. It should have been bright outside; her eyes should have smarted. But they didn't. The tall trees that surrounded her – each one with green leaves so thick they almost formed a roof over her head – provided more than enough shade.

Jack was right in front of her on the mucky ground. He turned, offering his hand. "Come on," he said. "We have to get moving."

Melissa took it and stepped down.

The air was damp and much too warm, and she was distracted by the incessant buzzing, chirping and hissing of insects in the rainforest. At least, she thought that it was insects making all that noise.

Some of those trees were enormous: towering giants with trunks as wide as her living room. She saw colourful birds flitting from branch to branch. If they hadn't been in such a hurry, she would have wanted to take a picture.

Melissa looked up, blinking. Thin shafts of golden sunlight managed to pierce the ceiling of leaves. "How are we supposed to find our way in this?"

Glancing back over his shoulder, Jack answered that with a sly smile. "Well," he said. "the drop-ship we took down is about ten kilometres west of here. So, I suggest we go east."

The shuttle's nose had been crumpled slightly, and one of its wings was bent at an odd angle. The rock wall they had damaged stood about fifteen feet high with plenty of handholds for climbing.

Jack was the first one up, scaling the thing in a matter of seconds. He crouched on the top and looked back, waiting for her.

Grumbling under her breath, Melissa grabbed a small out-cropping of stone and began to climb. Her first instinct would have been to use Bent Gravity for a graceful ascent, but there were men who wanted to kill her in this forest. She had to conserve her power in case she needed it.

At the top of the tiny escarpment, Jack stood with his fists on his hips, inspecting the wreckage. "We won't be salvaging that any time soon," he muttered. "Well, we better blend in with the locals."

He was wearing the standard gear that Keepers always wore on tactical missions: black pants and a matching t-shirt, a light armoured vest and a backpack stuffed with meal bars. But with one touch of a button on his belt, his garments all changed to a deep, earthen green.

Melissa did the same, applying her own layer of camouflage. Doing so reminded her of all those lectures in her ninth-grade history class. She remembered one day when Mr. Camus had spent an entire class going over the tools and weapons that soldiers used in World War Two. The subject of camouflage had come up then too. Now, she was a soldier. And that didn't sit well with her.

Oh, she had been in combat situations before. The raid that she, Anna and Keli had conducted on that Antauran ship came to mind. But this was different. Their objective on that raid had been to confiscate or destroy contraband weapons. If there had been a way to complete that task without firing a single shot at an Antauran security officer, Anna would have embraced it. But today... Today, their mission was to stop the enemy by any means necessary.

The ground sloped gently downward as they made their way through the gaps between skinny trees that pricked Melissa with their branches. Her backpack got caught on one, and she had quite a time getting it free.

The only weapons she carried were a holstered pistol and a belt knife. And about half a dozen cartridges of ammo, if you counted that. "What if we get lost?" she asked. "Wouldn't it be smarter to stay with the shuttle?"

Jack was about ten feet ahead of her when he turned and gave her a sympathetic look. "The shuttle is an easy target," he said. "If there are more drones in the area, they'll probably destroy it."

Melissa pushed one branch out of her way, flinching when it snapped back and hit her right in the nose. "Why would they destroy a wrecked shuttle?" she asked. "Wouldn't that just be a waste of ammo?"

Jack dropped to a crouch with his back to her, retying the laces of his shoe. "They will destroy the shuttle," he began, "on the off chance that some clever, young Keeper might decide to use it as a hiding place while she waits for a rescue."

Melissa felt a touch of warmth in her face. Sighing, she wiped sweat off her brow with one hand. "Okay," she relented. "You've convinced me."

"Well, that's only one part of our predicament," Jack said. "We *could* use the GPS-service on our multi-tools to help the rescue parties find us, but any signal we send will be picked up by the Ragnosians as well."

"Couldn't we encrypt it?"

"We can encrypt the message, yes," he answered. "But the signal itself would be a beacon telling anyone who was looking right where to find us. Given the presence of our friends back there, I recommend radio silence."

Unscrewing the lid of her canteen, Melissa tossed her head back and took a swig. "Got it," she said a moment later. "We wander around until a poisonous snake bites us or we run out of food."

"Speaking of," Jack replied. "Go easy on that. We have to make it last."

"Right, how silly of me," she muttered. "We'll run out of water long before we run out of food."

Leaning one shoulder against a tree trunk, Jack folded his arms and greeted her with a smile. "It won't be so bad, kiddo," he promised. "Ta'leean is the nearest city. I say we go there and use a SlipGate to get back to Keeper HQ."

Melissa nodded.

Their first attempt at getting to safety had been the SlipGate aboard their shuttle, but the cabin's ceiling had a hole in it, and the Gate had scorch marks all over its surface. It wouldn't connect to the network. Jack had tinkered with it for over five minutes before giving up in frustration. He probably would have stayed longer if not for the fear of some opportunistic drone hurling death from above.

At first, his eagerness to leave the shuttle had seemed silly to Melissa, but now…It bothered her that she had to be *told* something that should have been obvious. She was a full Keeper now, not some cadet. But she'd had her badge for less than two months.

Her training this past year had focused primarily on how to deal with immediate threats. What to do when you were surrounded by men with guns. Long-term strategy wasn't exactly on the syllabus.

Melissa clicked her tongue in annoyance.

Her feelings were a mess of contradictions. On the one hand, she resented the fact that she was forced to take part in a military conflict, and on the other, she hated herself for not being better at it.

Jack led her through the rainforest on a course that took them steadily eastward, past Brazil nut trees with their thin green leaves. They wouldn't be called that here, but Melissa recognized the species. Alios, like all the worlds the Overseers had terraformed, was remarkably similar to Earth.

At one point, they had to maneuver around a patch of strangler figs that was next to impenetrable. That required a short trek through an ankle-deep stream – once again, she lamented her inability to use Bent Gravity to get across – and then a sprint up a steep hill where the branches of kapok trees hung low.

Up and down they went, over the uneven landscape. After an hour, Melissa's belly was rumbling. She opened her backpack to fish out a protein bar and wolfed the thing down in less than a minute.

The morning sun was slowly climbing to its zenith, and with every passing minute, the air grew hotter and more humid. Or maybe the increased humidity was only in her mind. Sweat drenched her body. She half wanted to take off the vest to relieve the heat, but that would leave her exposed if they ran into trouble.

She sighed.

It was going to be a very long day.

The double doors slid apart, and Anna strode into the Prep Room with a fury in her step. It was well past midnight now, but the Keepers who had run this operation were still frantic, still calling out status reports and relaying orders.

Larani stood by the round table with a hand over mouth, watching a holographic display of the battle going on above them. A semi-transparent image of Alios floated in the air with orange and green dots zigzagging all around it. And the green were starting to outnumber the orange.

Shutting her eyes tight, Anna drew in a breath. She shook her head. "It's not good, is it." As if she even had to ask. "I only saw my little corner of the battle, but I'm willing to bet that we're losing."

A sharp glance from Larani silenced her, but then the other woman visibly calmed herself. "You'd win that bet," Larani mumbled. "We're down to five cruisers, and we've lost eight of the orbital defense stations."

"Bleakness!"

"They're landing troops all over the planet."

Anna fell into a cushioned chair, sliding it backward across the floor tiles. "Okay," she said. "What about the reinforcements from Palissa? They should be here within the hour, shouldn't they?"

"They're not coming."

"What?"

It chilled her to the bone when Larani responded to that with grim laughter. The other woman brushed aside a lock of dark hair that had come loose from her bun. "Well, it seems the Ragnosians had reinforcements of their own," she rasped. "Another twelve ships that intercepted our allies in deep space and waylaid them. We're on our own."

"Reinforcements from Leyria?"

"Three days away at best."

Anna was numb inside. Her mind kept cycling through different possibilities. How did they protect over a billion people from this invasion? Evacuate? Surrender? It was clear that they couldn't win this fight. Alios would fall in the next twenty-four hours.

Larani was bent over with her hands on the table's surface. The poor woman looked haggard. "We have confirmed reports of drop-ships landing about fifty kilometres outside of the city," she mumbled. "I'm sending you and Agent Seyrus to join the Second Infantry Division. You will defend Arinas to the best of your ability."

It dawned on Anna that she probably looked as worn out as Larani did. Well, maybe that would give her a kind of ragged nobility. "I want my people with me for this one," she said. "Call back Rajel and Keli."

"I'll do what I can."

"Jack and Melissa?"

Shuddering, Larani looked up to study Anna with eyes full of despair. "I'm afraid their shuttle went down over the Haltorean Rainforest," she said. "We haven't been able to confirm whether or not they're still alive."

Anna winced, tears leaking from the corners of her eyes, streaming over her face. "Okay," she said, nodding. "Cassi and I are on our way. We'll hold the city for as long as we can."

Reclining in the captain's chair with one leg crossed over the other, Telixa frowned as she examined the hologram that floated in front of her. It was a wire-frame depiction of the planet below with little dots to indicate places where her ships engaged the enemy.

The Leyrians were breaking; she suspected that her forces would have control of this world in less than a day. But it was a costly campaign. Quite possibly the most costly she had seen in her entire career. She had lost almost half of her fleet, and the ships that she had sent to intercept the Leyrian reinforcements weren't doing much better.

It saddened her to admit it, but this little exercise had shaken her faith in Ragnosian military might. Occupying a world that barely managed to visit its own moon was one thing. Challenging a foreign power that was roughly equal in terms of science and technology was quite another. Not for the first time, she wondered if this campaign had been a mistake. Not that she had much choice in the matter.

She could practically feel Slade's eyes on her.

The man had not made his presence felt in over three days, but he could return at any moment. Unless her people found some way to remove the dormant virus that had settled into her nervous system, she was basically Slade's slave.

Idly, she contemplated sending a message and demanding the planet's surrender. But... no. Not yet. Best to wait until they were frightened and desperate. Then, when all hope seemed lost... Then she would offer the Aliosians a way out.

Melissa stopped with her hand on a tree, closing her eyes and catching her breath. Fat droplets of sweat rolled over her forehead. "Okay," she said. "Even Keepers need a rest now and then. Not to mention water."

A narrow, meandering path ran between two lines of trees to a babbling stream up ahead. Noon had come, and it was painfully hot. The shuttle had been just shy of eighty-five kilometres southwest of Ta'leean when it crashed. Melissa was eyeballing it, but she figured they must have traversed at least ten of those kilometres in the last three hours.

Normally, a Justice Keeper on foot would be able to cover twice as much ground in that time, but she and Jack had been forced to double back more than once when they encountered some impenetrable barrier. A thicket of trees that was just too dense to break through or a knee-deep bog teeming with poison dart frogs.

Jack stood on the path with one hand on the grip of his pistol, gazing off into the distance. He turned at the sound of her voice. "You need a rest, kiddo?"

Closing her eyes, Melissa nodded vigorously. "Yes, please," she panted. "And you should have a drink! You're no good to anyone if you get dehydrated."

Dropping to one knee, Jack unclipped the canteen from his belt and removed the cap. He took a good long gulp. "You're right," he said. "Rationing is one thing, but this heat will kill us if we're not careful."

"Damn straight."

"Hell," Jack added. "I'd offer to just stay here and let the sun go down a little if not for the Ragnosians who might ambush us at any moment."

Melissa sat down by a kapok tree with her legs stretched out, fanning herself with one hand. "Thank you for that image." As soon as the words left her mouth, she regretted them. She sounded petulant. "I'm sorry."

Jack smiled, then bowed his head and wiped the sweat off his brow. "Don't worry about it," he said. "We're both a little frazzled."

"Yeah, but you seem to be handling it better."

"Well, that's because I've been doing this a little longer. You might be a trained Keeper, Melissa, but you never planned on going to war. And you're way too young to have all this on your shoulders."

Tilting her head back with lips pursed, Melissa felt her eyebrows climbing. "Yeah, but I don't have to take my frustrations out on you," she grumbled. "I'm sorry that you got stuck with the rookie."

"As opposed to?"

Melissa took a moment to drink from her canteen before answering. "Come on," she said. "Wouldn't you rather be here with Anna?"

Jack was on his knees, scrubbing his fingers through his damp hair. "Oh, yeah," he said softly. "When I think about romantic getaways, this is *exactly* what I have in mind. Mud, mosquitoes...a total lack of basic hygiene."

"And people shooting at us."

"Well, that actually gets Anna a little randy."

"Ugh! TMI!"

"Hey, you asked. So-"

Jack stood up so quickly it made her want to jump. In a heartbeat, he was on his feet with one hand on his holstered pistol, scanning the forest through narrowed eyes. It was downright scary.

Melissa followed his lead, standing up and drawing her gun as well. She powered up the weapon and searched for some sign of trouble. Any sign of trouble at all. She didn't see any-thing; she didn't sense anything. Just trees, the odd bird and-

Something floated out into the open.

A small, blue sphere with a camera lens hovered about five feet above the path, recording both of them. With lightning-quick reflexes, Jack rounded on it and took aim with his pistol. "EMP!"

He didn't fire though; he just stood there with his gun held tightly in both hands, watching the thing. "That's a Leyrian search and rescue drone," he said. "I think help is on the way."

Only then did Melissa notice the slight whirring noise from the drone's anti-gravity stabilizers. It was so soft that all the other sounds in the rainforest drowned it out unless you knew exactly what to listen for. How could Jack have heard it over all that?

The drone projected a hologram, a six-foot-tall image of a man with white hair cut neat and short. Melissa recognized his green uniform. This man was part of the Aliosian infantry. "Fall in!" he bellowed.

"And you are?"

"I said fall in!" the hologram barked.

Lowering his weapon, Jack smiled and shook his head. "And I said who the hell are you?" he countered. "If you're here to rescue us, we're very much appreciative, but Mama always told me not to accept a ride from a stranger."

The holographic soldier crossed his arms and glowered at them. No doubt he was used to that being enough to coax any-one into obedience. "Well, permit me to introduce myself," he said. "Major Ari Tramon, at your service."

"Agent Jack Hunter," Jack replied. "Nice to meet you."

"The two of you have caused us a fair bit of trouble," Major Tramon explained. "Our sensors detected your shuttle crash-ing about twelve kilometres southwest of here. We've been looking for you ever since."

"Much obliged, Major," Jack said. "I assume you've come to give us a ride back to civilization."

For some reason, Major Tramon answered that query with a mocking grin. "Oh, we came out here to get you, all right," he said. "With those slimy bastards shooting us from orbit, I might add. But you ain't going anywhere until we're done with you."

"Sir?"

Chuckling softly, the Major nodded. "That's more like it, son," he said. "Now, your orders were to destroy that drop-ship. Orders you disobeyed. Thanks to you two, we've got about three dozen Raggies crawling through these woods. And you're gonna help us deal with them."

Melissa felt sick to her stomach. She should have known better than to think that she might get out of this without having to kill. The mantras that had been going through her head earlier came up again. She was a Justice Keeper. This was her job.

In all likelihood, she would have to take a life sooner or later. She had been aware of that from the moment that she first Bonded Jena's symbiont. So, if today was the day, then she would do what she had to do. And she would pray to God for forgiveness later.

"What did you have in mind?" Jack asked.

"The drone'll lead you back to a rendezvous point about five clicks southeast of here," Major Tramon said. "I'll be expecting you in about an hour. And, Agent Hunter, be punctual."

Chapter 12

Anna was about to leave the Prep Room when the comm system started beeping. For half a second, she entertained the notion that it might be Jack or Melissa calling to report in, but that was unlikely. Not necessarily because they were dead, but of all the people who might be calling, what were the odds it was one of them?

Still, curiosity – and maybe a touch of desperation – got the better of her; so, she settled into her chair and waited to see who it was. She was grateful for Seth's comforting presence. He eased her anxieties with soothing emotions.

Larani was at the round table, but she looked up when the noise started. The poor woman looked like she was ready to collapse from exhaustion. "Do we have an ID on the caller?" she asked.

"It's coming from a cargo ship that dropped out of warp about thirty seconds ago," Agent Sokai answered.

"What?"

Anna had to admit that she was just as puzzled. Granted, it was impossible for anyone traveling at FTL speeds to know what was happening until they dropped out of warp, but Alios had been sending out distress calls ever since this whole thing started. All civilian ships had been diverted to other safe ports. She found it hard to believe that the pilot of that cargo hauler had missed every one of those alerts. So, who would fly directly into a firefight?

"Answer the call," Larani said.

The screen on the wall lit up to display a grizzled man with a scraggly red beard and dishevelled hair to match. "Director Tal," he panted. "Please…I'm under fire. I need you to open your SlipGate."

"Who are you?"

Anna was on her feet in an instant, squinting at the screen. She shook her head in disgust. "I know who he is!" she growled. "That is Corovin Dagmath, the assassin who killed President Salmaro."

Larani's face was stone, her merciless gaze fixed upon the man who had thrown Antaur into chaos. It was clear to Anna that the other woman was contemplating whether she wanted to shove Corovin into a cell and leave him to rot until the Antaurans came to execute him. "If that's true," Larani said, "I can't imagine why I would let you into Justice Keeper HQ."

The screen went dark for half a second, and then Corovin flinched as he was jostled by the impact of incoming fire. He stretched up to tap a few controls above his head. "If you want to survive this battle," he said. "You *need* my help. I know Ragnosian tactics. I know Telixa Ethran, and I will tell you everything in exchange for asylum."

"Your offer is hardly tempting, Mr. Dagmath."

Corovin looked directly into the camera, his gray eyes wide with fright. "Please," he whispered. "With my knowledge, you have a fighting chance of getting through this. But I can't hold out much longer!"

"What do you think?" Larani asked.

"We can't trust him."

"Are you sure?"

"He offered to help us before," Anna said, "offered to trade his people's secrets in exchange for political asylum. And then he killed Adare Salmaro. You open that SlipGate, and he'll probably send a nuke through it. And besides, I'm not convinced that he's in any real danger."

"It wasn't my fault," Corovin protested. His teeth were clenched, his face red as he hammered on the cargo ship's controls. "Grecken Slade had a gun to my head. He made me kill the Antauran president."

The screen went black again, and when Corovin returned, his face was deathly pale. "Please," he groaned, "I'm begging you."

Shutting her eyes, Anna took a deep breath. "I'm gonna regret this," she muttered to herself. "We can't just let him die."

The other woman shot a glance toward her officers at the edge of the room. "Send a message to Agent Thrin," she barked. "Tell him to open the Gate."

Before she even finished saying that, Corovin leaped out of his chair and ran off-screen. The transmission ended ten seconds later. Anna could feel her heart pounding in her chest. She was more than a little worried that he might send a bomb through. Well, if he did, she would find out at any moment. All she could do was-

"Traveller has arrived!" Agent Sokai shouted. "And the Gate is locked again. I've sent a team of Keepers to meet him in the SlipGate chamber."

"I think I'll join them," Anna said as she walked out of the room.

The drone led them to a small valley where the trees had thinned just enough to let a little sunlight in. Soldiers in green uniforms were busy assembling rifles or checking on supply packs. One guy seemed to be logging everything on a tablet.

There were no vehicles that Jack could see. He couldn't help but wonder how they had come out here. Surely not on foot. His first instinct was to ask, but he decided against it. Right now, he and Melissa weren't in good standing with these people. No need to make it worse.

Jack strode through the camp, refusing to step aside for anyone who got in his way. In his mind, he saw Melissa following right behind him. The young woman kept glancing this way and that, and it was clear that she was more than a little uncomfortable.

It didn't take long to find the man in charge.

Major Ari Tramon stood underneath the branches of a fat wimba tree, checking something on his multi-tool. He turned at the sound of their approach and greeted them with a mocking smile. "Well now," he said. "Our two troublemakers."

"What's the plan, sir?"

The major blinked, startled by Jack's willingness to cooperate. "Just like that?" he spluttered. "No moralizing speeches about the sanctity of human life? The need to make peace with our enemies?"

Crossing his arms, Jack smiled and bowed his head to the other man. "You can say what you want about Keepers, sir," he began, "but we're not naive. If the Ragnosians are causing trouble, we'll deal with them."

"I'm glad to hear it," Major Tramon replied. "And the plan is simple. The Raggies went down about eleven kilometres west of where your shuttle crashed. We figure they'll employ the same strategy as you did: get away from the damaged craft to avoid being an easy target. Which means they're moving through this forest on foot. Now, the question is, 'Where are they going?'"

Stepping back with a hand on his sidearm, the major grimaced at the mud under his feet. "The only settlement in this area is Ta'leean," he said. "We suspect they'll be heading in that direction. Our people will intercept them before they get there."

Jack nodded slowly as he considered that. "Makes sense," he said. "Mind if I ask a question?"

"I suppose it was inevitable."

"Do we even know what the second dropship was carrying?" The incredulity on Major Tramon's face made him pause for a moment, but it was a good question, and he was going to get it out. "The first one housed two fighter drones. Can we be sure that the second one even had troops on board?"

Instead of answering, the major lifted his forearm and began tapping something into his multi-tool. Jack's tool buzzed a second later, and when he checked the screen, he saw an aerial photo of the crashed dropship.

"Zoom in," Tramon said.

Jack did so and noticed something in the mud around the troop carrier. Boot prints. So, the ship really had been carrying people. "We risked a flyby to be sure," Tramon went on. "And no small risk at that. The skies aren't exactly friendly at the moment. There are at least three dozen people in this forest who might get up to all sorts of trouble. Say one of them gets near Ta'Leean with a dirty bomb. I'm sure I don't have to explain the danger."

With a sigh, Tramon turned his back and faced the tree with fists on his hips. He shook his head. "Now, if those bastards had landed in an open field, we'd be able to track them easily with sensors." He kicked a rock with the toe of his boot. "But they happened to go down in one of the densest forests on this planet."

Jack stood with his arms hanging limp, his eyes fixed on the ground. "Yeah, well," he muttered. "Sorry about that."

The major turned slightly to look over his shoulder. "Ain't looking for an apology, Hunter," he said. "The point is that finding them isn't gonna be easy. And that's where you two come in."

"You want us to find them?"

Tramon extended his hand toward a group of people a short distance away. One of the men stepped forward, a tall guy with dark skin, curly hair and a thick mustache. "Let me introduce Captain Stefan Denathril," Tramon said. "He will be leading a team to locate the Ragnosians, and you'll be going along to provide backup just in case they get into trouble."

"Just to *find* the enemy?" Melissa inquired. "That's it?"

The major puffed up his chest and put himself right in front of her. "Let me make this perfectly clear," he said. "You will not engage the enemy unless you are fired upon. Now, given your...predilections...that shouldn't be a problem for you, Agent Carlson. But I do realize you Keepers have a complicated relationship with the chain of command."

Melissa held his gaze defiantly, refusing to budge an inch. Good for her. Jack could recall a time when she would have wilted under anyone's stare. He made a mental note to get her a cake or something. "If we're not supposed to attack them," she said, "then what exactly *are* you planning?"

"If you must know," Tramon replied. "Once you've confirmed their location, you will retreat to a safe distance. Captain Denathril will call in an air-strike and we'll blow those bastards away from above. Any of this causing problems for you, Agent Carlson?"

"All of it, actually," she said. "But I'll do it anyway."

"Now that's what I like to hear!" Tramon barked. "Grab your gear; have a snack, and if you feel the need to relieve yourself, now is most definitely the time. You leave in ten minutes."

When the armoured car came to a stop, Anna pushed the door open and got out. She was smack-dab in the middle of a wide thoroughfare between two lines of skyscrapers, a road that ran from the centre of town all the way to the edge. Bonavin Avenue should have been bustling with people, but there were no civilians on the street today.

Up ahead, a barricade of armoured vehicles, portable force-field generators and bullet-proof shielding stretched from one sidewalk to another. There were soldiers in tan uniforms scurrying about, working diligently in the early-morning light. A few of them barked orders to their subordinates.

Anna felt her mouth drop open, then shook her head in dismay. "They always told us this might happen," she mumbled. "Teachers...politicians. We always thought it would be the Antaurans invading our territory. But here we are."

On the other side of the car, Corovin climbed out of the back seat and stood up to glower at the barricade. The man was wearing the heavy black armour that he had stolen on Antaur. He had come through the SlipGate in that thing, prompting several Keepers to point guns at him. Only his head was uncovered. "That's why you're going to lose," he said. "You can't believe it would actually happen."

"Oh, we believed it," Anna countered. "Why do you think there were twenty-four heavily-armed space stations in orbit of this planet?"

"For all the good it did."

Glancing over her shoulder, Anna narrowed her eyes. "You're the one who decided to join a losing cause," she said. "Could have flown off anywhere in the galaxy and lived a quiet life."

Corovin strode forward, trailing his fingers over the hood of the car. He stopped a few feet ahead with his fists clenched behind his back. "Away from civilization?" he asked. "I'm not used to roughing it."

Anna sighed.

Cassi emerged from the car a moment later, shutting the door and giving the man a hard-eyed stare. "The last aerial scan showed dropships putting tanks down outside the city," she said. "We're supposed to stop them with *this?*"

"Have faith, Cass."

Corovin snorted.

Together, they went to join the soldiers at the barricade. A tall man looked up as they approached, took five seconds to assess them and then jerked his head toward the sidewalk. "Report to Captain Bosama."

The captain was an olive-skinned woman in her mid-thirties who wore her hair buzzed at the sides and thick on top. "So, you're the Justice Keepers they sent to help us," she said. "I'll let you know when I need you. For now, just stay out of the way."

"Yes, ma'am," Anna muttered.

"Are you sure this is where I'll be the most useful?" Corovin asked. He was looking out over the barricade as if he expected enemy troops to start advancing on them at any moment. Which they very well might. "As I said, I served in the Ragnosian military. I'm the only one who knows their tactics. And you want to risk that advantage by putting me out in the open like this?"

Anna stepped up in front of him, craning her neck to meet his gaze. There were days when she hated being short. "An assassin who's afraid to die," she said. "Well, at least I got my daily dose of irony."

"Just looking out for your best interests," Corovin said. "Which, in this case, just happen to be mine."

"If you two are quite finished..." Cassi said.

"Enemy approaching!" someone bellowed.

On the other side of the barricade, several blocks away, a Ragnosian hover tank advanced slowly down the street with its main gun pointed forward. Perhaps a hundred men and women in gray uniforms walked alongside it, each one carrying an assault rifle.

Crouching down behind the barricade, Anna let out a breath. Cassi's worries about whether they would be able to hold out against Ragnosian artillery popped into her mind. "Is this standard for them?" she asked.

Corovin knelt at her side, keeping his head down. "No," he answered. "Normally, they would begin with an air-strike. Demolish a few buildings, terrify the locals. I don't know why they've changed tactics."

"The infrastructure," Anna said.

"What about it?"

"Every Leyrian city is designed to be self-sufficient," she explained. "To provide an abundance of food, water and everything else that its citizens need. If your people want to hold onto this planet, they're gonna have to feed their troops. And the bulk of your fleet is half a galaxy away. Even with the SuperGates, those are some long supply lines."

Frowning as he considered her words, Corovin nodded. "So, they're trying to avoid damaging the infrastructure," he said. "That explains why they haven't resorted to orbital bombardment."

Down on one knee, behind the armoured cars, Captain Bosama lifted her forearm and spoke into her multi-tool. "Ragnosian army," she said in a crisp, clear voice. "You are hereby ordered to withdraw, or we will meet your aggression with deadly force."

In response to that, a hatch opened in the hover-tank's pointed front end, revealing a cylindrical tube underneath. A missile flew out, trailing smoke behind it as it barrelled down the street.

Anna felt a moment of panic.

Just before it hit the barricade, a huge wall of flickering static appeared, stretching from sidewalk to sidewalk and rising at least ten stories into the air. The missile struck the force-field and exploded in a brilliant flare of light. Anna had to avert her eyes.

Flames roiled, rising into the air, but none of them could breach the barrier. Once they died down, the force-field vanished. "We won't be able to withstand that forever!" Bosama shouted. "Rifles take aim!"

Soldiers who crouched behind the armoured cars lifted their weapons.

"EMP rounds, loose!"

A blizzard of glowing, white tracers pelted the tank, each one landing with a sharp, metallic *ping* that Anna could hear even at this distance. Sparks flashed over the vehicle's body, and Ragnosian troops threw themselves to the ground to avoid getting hit.

"No effect!" someone shouted. "The tank's armour is too strong!"

Bosama was actually grinning. Bleakness take her, Anna could swear that the woman was laughing. "As expected," the captain replied. "Heavy artillery, you're up!"

When she looked around, Anna saw people stationed on the rooftops of buildings on either side of the street. Each group had a portable cannon set up and pointed at the advancing tank. Unless Anna missed her guess, every last one of those things packed as much firepower as you might find on a shuttle.

Plasma bolts rained down on the tank like fireballs streaking out of the sky. After just a few shots, the vehicle exploded, sending shrapnel into the air. The Ragnosians tried to jump out of the way, but they too were vaporized.

Unable to help herself, Anna dropped to all fours and emptied her stomach onto the ground. She wiped her mouth with one hand. "Damn it…"

"Now who's afraid of death?" Corovin mocked.

The glare she gave him should have flayed his skin off, but he only laughed at her. "Take a good look, Justice Keeper," he said. "Do you think any of them are going to cry when they step over your broken body?"

"At least it's over."

This time, Corovin threw his head back and practically roared with laughter. "You think so, do you?" he shouted. "It was a clever move: using that fancy ammo of yours to disable the tank's shield generators, then hitting it with heavy artillery. But do you really think my people would just march their soldiers toward a firing squad without a plan?"

"That *wasn't* the main assault?"

"No," Corovin said. "*That* was about intimidation. Telixa was hoping you might be willing to just abandon the city if she made a show of force. Now that she knows you're willing to fight back, well..."

No sooner did he finish speaking than she heard the distinct hum of gravitational propulsion. Anna looked up to see a fleet of wedge-shaped drones flying over the road, coming right for them. Each one was small enough to fit in her lap, but she was certain that they-

The drones started spitting bullets.

Once again, the enormous force-field snapped into place, intercepting the incoming fire before it could hurt anyone. "Not bad," Corovin said. "It seems your people are *not* completely useless. But of course, those things can-"

The first few drones flew right over the force-field and began firing at the people on the other side. Leyrian soldiers went down from a hit to the leg or the arm or the chest. Some were protected by their body armour even if the impact knocked them off their feet. Others were bleeding profusely.

Staying low, Anna lifted her pistol in both hands and lined up a shot. She fired a bright, white tracer into the underbelly of a robot and sent the bloody thing careening into the side of a building.

Her allies were not idle.

Every soldier had their rifle pointed skyward, releasing a stream of EMP rounds that turned the space above the road into a no man's land for drones. In seconds, every one of those metal monstrosities was a smoking ruin on the ground. Cassi had to leap aside before one fell right on top of her.

Captain Bosama was huddled up against one of the armoured cars and snarling as if someone had just kicked her in the stomach. "Help the wounded!" she cried. "Get anyone who can be moved to cover, and-"

"Another wave coming!"

Sure enough, a second squadron of drones was on its way, releasing bullets that bounced uselessly off the force-field. "Rifles forward!" Bosama growled. "We're gonna hit 'em before they get close! Release our own drones, countermeasures protocol. Lower the barrier on my command...now!"

Half a second after the force-field vanished, a swarm of glowing bullets assaulted the incoming flyers, knocking many of them down before they could even get off a shot. Others bobbed and weaved to avoid being hit.

Egg-shaped security bots emerged from the gaps between buildings, flying out into the street to engage their Ragnosian counterparts. And since they weren't attacking living targets, they were able to use full-power ammunition.

The sky became a tempest of robots and bullets, and then, one by one, the drones began to fall to the ground. When it was over, maybe half a dozen wedge-shaped bots were left, and they immediately turned their attention to the Leyrian soldiers. One began a straight nose dive toward a small group who stood just behind the barricade. "Get out of there!" Anna screamed.

They ignored her.

Sprinting toward them at speeds that only another Keeper could match, Anna put herself in front of the group. She spun around just in time to see the drone coming right for her.

Her hands came up, and a Bending formed. The drone that should have impaled her with its pointed tip instead curved upward and sped off into the sky. It exploded maybe three seconds later. "What the…" someone stammered behind her.

Other drones were carrying out their kamikaze attack, crashing to the ground and exploding on contact, killing people who were too close to the blast. Each one detonated with about as much power as you would expect from a low-yield grade, but even that was enough to put down at least a dozen good people. A quick survey of the area told her that they had lost this battle.

She saw burned soldiers, bleeding soldiers and soldiers who were just plain dead. The moans and wails of the wounded froze her blood. She should be crying, but she felt numb inside.

Corovin was crouching by the front entrance of a hair salon, his face now hidden behind the blue visor of his helmet. He looked to her as if she might give an indication of what he ought to do next.

Bosama was still taking cover next to one of the armoured cars, clutching her rifle like it was some cherished, childhood toy. Her face was pale, her eyes frantic.

Anna ran to her.

Falling to her knees, she took the other woman by the shoulders. Bosama seemed to come back to reality. "We have to retreat," Anna said.

"We can't retreat," the captain insisted. "Our orders were-"

"Fuck our orders!" Anna growled. She was seething with teeth clenched, her cheeks stained with dust and grime. "They're gonna be sending another wave any minute now. If we stay, we're dead."

"The wounded…"

Anna shut her eyes and nodded slowly. They would *not* leave those helpless people behind. "Have your people collect the ones who can be moved," she panted. "Order your medics to do what they can for the rest. Agent Seyrus and I will stay behind to give them cover."

"But-"

"Just do it!"

Anna used her multi-tool to place a call to HQ. When Larani's face appeared, she breathed a sigh of relief. "We've been monitoring your situation, Operative Lenai," the chief director said. "How can we help?"

"Illegal weapons," Anna gasped.

"I'm sorry?"

"A few years back, there was a smuggling ring delivering weapons to colonists on the Fringe. Ben was part of it if you'll recall." The other woman nodded, but it was clear from her expression that Larani didn't like where this was going. "I'm guessing that many of those weapons are still here. Get them to me."

"Please tell me you're not planning to-"

Snarling like an angry dog, Anna trembled with frustration. "Damn it, Larani! Will you just trust me?" Bleakness take her, hadn't she earned that much? "I'm well aware of the danger."

"All right," Larani said. "Where do you want them?"

Anna turned to the soldiers who were carrying their wounded away on stretchers. She wasn't their commanding officer, but she *was* the only one here with any semblance of a plan. Which meant they were going to listen to her whether they liked it or not. "Fall back to Fifth Street!" she yelled. "We rebuild the barricade there!"

Chapter 13

The trek through the forest was long, hot and tiring. Step by step, they followed muddy paths that meandered in between the trees, paths with sections so narrow the whole platoon had to march single file. Melissa hated those bits the most. The tries always tried to scratch her with thin branches that felt like grasping fingers.

They skirted the edge of a small pond filled with brown water and then carefully made their way around a nest of snakes. She had to resist the urge to shudder when she heard them hissing. Bullets and battlecruisers were one thing, but snakes? Snakes were just creepy.

Worst of all, somewhere in the mid-afternoon, a sudden downpour drenched them all from head to toe. When she complained, one of the soldiers gave her a disapproving look and said, "It's called a rainforest for a reason."

Her boots were water-tight, thank God, but the rest of her was soaked. She decided to adopt a positive attitude. At least the rain offered some relief from the heat.

Three steps ahead of her, Jack stopped with his hand against a tree trunk. He leaned forward, peering into the shadowy area under the branches of two gigantic lupuna trees. "We're good," he said. "No hostiles."

A young man who stood behind Melissa with his rifle pointed down at the ground smirked at the back of her head. "Maybe the princess should take a look," he suggested. "Isn't it her turn now?"

Jack twisted around and directed a glare at the man who had spoken. "*I'm* telling you that the way is clear," he said. "If that's not good enough for you, maybe you should look for yourself."

Half an hour into their journey, Captain Denathril had decided that if he had two Keepers at his disposal, he may as well make use of their special abilities. Melissa was fairly certain that the man had no idea how spatial awareness worked – it didn't let you see *through* things – but she couldn't argue with the notion that a Nassai's panoramic vision might pick up a flicker of motion that eyesight could.

So, she and Jack were made to scout ahead. Or rather, Jack was. She had told him more than once that she was willing to take turns, but he insisted on being the first one to walk into any new environment. At first, Melissa thought that was just macho crap. But she was fairly certain that Jack would not be so protective of Anna.

Down the hill, they went, along a gloomy path where only thin shafts of sunlight managed to penetrate the leafy canopy above them. There were insects everywhere. Some of them buzzed around her head.

Wincing, Melissa shooed them away with one hand. "Why won't you let me take point?" she asked Jack. "My eyes are just as sharp as yours, and I know how to use my spatial awareness."

"I know that," he muttered.

"Then why?"

Jack couldn't stop, not without bringing the rest of them to a halt, but he sighed as he climbed up a rocky hillside. "Because you're my little sister," he said. "Or you may as well be. Other kids your age are starting college, not going to war."

Melissa began to climb as well.

The young soldier immediately behind her paused for a moment, and she was pretty damn sure that he was checking out her ass. "Maybe you should just take his kind offer," he said. "Think about it, princess. If someone's gonna get their head blown off, better him than you."

Melissa turned around.

She opened her mouth to speak, but Jack's hand on her shoulder quieted her. When she met his eyes, Jack simply shook his head and then continued on his way. Up the hill. To a small clearing.

Stepping out of the shade felt like stepping into an oven, but there was just enough space here for the platoon to spread out. Jack called a halt, and the platoon took a rest, gathering together in groups of two or three.

Captain Denathril came up the hill with a scowl that he seemed to reserve just for Melissa. One look at his troops, however, and he nodded with approval. "Well done," he said. "You got us this far."

They had a quick snack of protein bars and water. Melissa savoured every bite even if it did taste like peanut butter spread over cardboard. This was only the second meal that she'd had since jumping into a shuttle the night before. She was famished.

Some of the soldiers complained about sore feet which made her notice the lack of pain in her own. Well...the very *slight* pain. It was the sort that could be easily ignored if she focused her attention on anything else. She suspected that she had accelerated healing to thank for that. God bless Ilia.

Jack was sitting on a log with his elbows on his knees, his forehead pressed against laced fingers. The poor guy looked like he might pass out.

"You all right?"

He looked up, blinking at her. "Yeah, I'm fine." His words were hoarse. "Just a bit tired, that's all."

Melissa knelt down in front of him, sighing. "Make sure to eat, okay?" It sounded silly, telling him what to do, but she wasn't going to back down now. "And we have lots of water now. So, drink up."

"Looking out for me, are you?"

"I'm not letting my big brother go into battle on an empty stomach."

Unzipping his backpack, Jack retrieved one of the many protein bars that he had taken from the shuttle. "Good advice." He tore open the wrapper and started chomping away with gusto.

Once she was certain that he would finish the thing, Melissa began a quick circuit of the camp. Her stomach was fluttering at what she had to do next. There was a voice in her head that urged prudence, that told her no good would come from opening her mouth. She often listened to that voice.

But not today.

It didn't take long to find the young man who had been walking behind her earlier. He was tall and slim, pale with short, blonde hair in a crew cut. And he looked up when he saw her approaching. "Something I can do for you, princess?"

Melissa arched an eyebrow, holding his gaze for a long while. Eventually, the man lost his nerve and looked away. "You know, that's funny," she said. "'Cause I was gonna ask you the same thing."

"Look, I didn't mean-"

"I'm Agent Melissa Carlson," she said. "You're welcome to call me Melissa. But if it's a title you want, Agent Carlson will do. Not princess. Do we understand each other, Lieutenant..."

The man shut his eyes, a soft shudder escaping him. "Higsen," he said. "Lieutenant Doran Higsen. And I didn't intend any-"

Melissa crossed her arms and took a step back, refusing to break eye-contact. "Not really interested in what you intended to do," she cut in. "I've been putting up with micro-aggressions ever since I was a girl; I don't need them from you. Not when I might have to shield you from enemy fire."

"I understand."

Despite her better judgment, she put a hand on his shoulder, and the man seemed to relax a little. "Listen, Doran," she began in what she hoped was a soothing voice. "I get it. We're all scared. But we're all in this together."

She turned around and made her way back to Jack. Those butterflies in her stomach started flapping their wings when she saw that he was sitting up straight and watching her like a hawk. "Nicely done," he said. "I think I owe you an apology."

Melissa sat down next to him, folding her hands in her lap and shyly hunching up her shoulders. "Because you tried to dissuade me from talking to him?" she asked. "Don't worry about it."

Shutting his eyes tight, Jack shook his head. "No," he replied. "Stopping you from confronting Higsen was the right move. If you had done so while we were on the march, it would have slowed everyone down, and then Denathril would want to know what the hold up was."

"I see."

"You and I would get the blame for it, not his tactless lieutenant. No, I owe you an apology because I've been treating you like a cadet from the moment that we boarded the shuttle. But you're not a cadet anymore. You're ready for this, Melissa. I'm sorry it took me so long to see that. You can take point if you want to."

Melissa leaned over sideways, resting her head on his shoulder. "Will you still be my big brother?"

"I'll always be your big brother."

Their short break came to an end much sooner than Melissa would have hoped, and then they were moving again. Onward, down tree-lined paths that brought them near to the place where the shuttle had crashed. At least, it looked familiar to her.

Lieutenant Higsen was no longer right behind her, but every time they encountered one another, he gave her a nod of respect. Which set her mind at ease. She did manage a little light chitchat with the ones nearest to her in line. Getting to know them seemed like a good idea.

Lieutenant Amala Tharn was a short woman who had joined the mobile infantry to defend the outer colonies from Antauran raids. She had been thinking about resigning her commission in light of the new treaty. Melissa was torn between wishing that the woman had done so a few weeks ago so that she would be spared this, and being grateful that Amala was here with them.

Jonan Alderi had thought about joining the Space Corps. He said it was a great way to see things no one else had ever seen. The Fleet was always exploring new star systems. But even with simulated sunlight and plenty of exercise, Jonan couldn't stomach the long stretches of being cooped up on a ship. This way, he could still serve.

She wanted to get to know as many of them as she could – if nothing else, it would smooth over tensions between them – but Denathril kept insisting that they keep chatter to a minimum. And Melissa couldn't really argue with the man. They *were* searching for hostiles, after all. When it came time for someone to scout ahead, Melissa was the first to accept the task. She and Jack agreed to take turns.

The path they followed became a narrow ravine between two rock walls that stood at shoulder height. Inspecting that was easy; there wasn't much to see. But she made it a point to make sure there was nothing waiting for them on the other side.

Jogging out of the ravine, Melissa dropped to one knee with a hand on her pistol. She scanned the area with her eyes and with spatial awareness.

There were trees on either side of her, big ones with thick trunks that must have been at least a hundred feet tall. The ground was littered with dried up leaves, rocks and twigs. She sensed motion off to her left and almost drew her weapon, but it was low to the ground. A small animal, most likely.

"We're clear!"

Jack was the next one out of the ravine, and he clapped her on the shoulder as he passed. "Good job," he said softly. "I'll take the next one."

She nodded.

Another hour passed with little activity to speak of. She was sure that they were now further west than the shuttle's crash site by at least a kilometre or two. If they were going to run into the Ragnosians, it would happen any time now.

On several occasions, Captain Denathril had asked his people to take up positions on a high vantage point and scan the forest with binoculars. Each time they reported nothing out of the ordinary. Maybe the Ragnosians weren't headed toward Ta'Leean. They could have gone west, toward the distant shoreline.

The soldiers were starting to complain of fatigue. It began as angry mutters, but it didn't take long for that to escalate into full-on griping. Melissa was tired – she had gone more than twenty-four hours without sleep – but she knew she still felt strong enough to keep going. The benefits of carrying a Nassai. Really, it was boredom more than anything else that got to her. She thought about saying as much to Jack but decided to keep it to herself. If the others heard her, it might come off as gloating.

They were walking through a densely-wooded area, carefully maneuvering around trees, when Melissa felt something. A flicker of motion off to her right. She looked, but there was nothing there. Perhaps she had just imagined-

"I felt it too," Jack said.

He was standing on the path with one hand hovering over the grip of his holstered pistol, squinting into the trees. "Whatever it is," he muttered. "It's fast. And much too big to be an animal."

"One of Slade's minions?"

"If we're lucky."

She caught a glimpse of whatever it was racing from tree to tree. It had legs; she could say that much. Which meant it was human-shaped. And the only thing that would fit that description was… "A *ziarogat*," she whispered.

The line of soldiers had come to a stop, and some of them were watching Jack and Melissa with irritated expressions. "What's the holdup?" someone shouted. "Why aren't we moving?"

"Weapons up!" Jack shouted. "Hostile in the trees!"

With almost perfect synchronicity, they all turned on their heels and pointed their rifles into the forest. The one nearest Melissa was sweating, and she could tell that he was scared. "I don't see—"

Something leaped over them, flying across the path and dropping into the trees on the other side with only the slight rustle of bent branches. The soldiers tried to adjust their aim, but bullets ripped through one man's arm before he could even get his weapon up. He fell to his knees, placing a hand over the wound.

Some of the others opened fire, but they hit nothing.

Melissa had her gun clutched in both hands, her eyes flicking back and forth as she searched for a target. "I don't see it!" she yelled. "I don't sense it!"

"You won't," Jack said. "It's smart, and it knows the limits of your abilities. It will hide behind solid objects until it's ready to strike."

Bullets struck one woman's chest, knocking her to the ground. The two men next to her both stumbled out of the way, and then one of them went down from a single shot to the head.

Jonan was firing into the trees. His shots struck wood with a loud *thwack, thwack, thwack,* but so far as Melissa could tell, he didn't even touch the *ziarogat.*

In fact, the cyborg used the noise as cover to attack other officers further down the line. Screams of pain echoed through the forest. "Cease fire!" Jack bellowed. "Cease fire! Right the hell now!"

Jonan didn't listen, and neither did the others who were following his example. In all that chaos, many of them didn't even notice when the *ziarogat* jumped over them a second time. It shot several in the back before they could turn around.

Jack's teeth were clenched, his face flushed to a deep red, and there was fire in his eyes. "They're not trained for this sort of thing," he said. "I'm gonna lead the gat out of here."

"What?"

"Its primary function is killing Justice Keepers," he said. "If I reveal myself, it will focus its attention on me."

Panting as she tried to track the blur in the forest, Melissa felt a fat droplet of sweat rolling down her forehead. "I should go with you!" she protested. "We will have a better chance of killing that thing together."

"No!" Jack insisted. "One of us has to stay with the platoon!"

"You said you wouldn't treat me like a cadet!"

"I'm not," Jack assured her. From the corner of her eye, she could see that his face was grim. "Melissa, we don't know what the Ragnosians will throw at us. These are good men and women. I *need* you to protect them."

"Okay," she agreed. "I'll do what I can."

Stepping off the path with his gun in hand, Jack scanned his surroundings. There was motion off to his right. He could still hear the sounds of people crying out in pain. The damn *ziarogat* was taking advantage of that.

He saw it rushing from one tree to the next, getting ready for another attack. It was a male cyborg, shirtless with pale skin and a bald head. He could see a few scratches on its body, scrapes from the branches it had snapped.

"Hey!" Jack shouted.

The creature paused in mid-step and looked over its shoulder to study him with silver eyes.

Lifting one hand, Jack crafted a Bending that made the air ripple for half a second. When it fizzled away, he could see that he had the *ziarogat's* full attention. "That's right," he said. "You don't want them."

He turned and ran.

The sound of twigs snapping and leaves crunching was the first indication that the cyborg had followed him. Then, in his mind, he saw his pursuers as it leaped through the gap between two trees and thrust its fist out toward him.

Jack threw himself onto his belly just before a line of bullets sped over him. He rolled to his right and fell off of a rock wall. Landing with a grunt, Jack pushed himself up and took off again.

Spinning around, he lifted his weapon as he trotted backward. He fired, and the *ziarogat* leaped from the rock wall just in time to take a hit to the shoulder. It stumbled, thrown off balance.

Jack turned and ducked beneath the branches of a fat kapok. If he could keep some foliage between him and his enemy at all times, it would be much harder for either of them to get a clean shot.

He shoved his gun back into its holster and ran. The sound of footsteps behind him never lessened, not for an instant. Spatial awareness showed him momentary flashes of motion behind intersecting branches. Lead the thing away from the soldiers. Ordinary humans, no matter how well trained, were no match for one of these abominations.

He slid down a mucky hill, then leaped and flipped through the air.

Landing perched on a thick branch, he paused for half a second to catch his breath. Then he threw himself forward. Jack caught the next branch in his path and swung like a monkey.

The *ziarogat* seemed to have realized that he had taken to the treetops because it scrambled up the thick trunk of a shorea gratissma. Clinging to the wood like a squirrel, it thrust its right fist out toward him.

Jack dropped from the branch and let himself fall, flinching as bullets whizzed past above him. He landed in a crouch.

Staying low, he scrambled over flat rocks and made his way to a huge lupuna tree that was surrounded by muddy puddles. The damn thing was as big as a house at its base. It would provide him with adequate cover.

He would make his stand here.

It had been several minutes since Jack ran off with the *ziarogat* three steps behind him. Since then, the forest had been quiet. Well, quiet except for the moans of men and women who had been shot.

Melissa stood between two twisted trees, staring off into the distance. Drawing in a shuddering breath, she nodded once. "Okay," she said. "We need to plan our next move."

The infantry officers still stood in a line, and most of them were pointing their rifles into the forest as if they expected the *ziarogat* to return at any moment. Which it might do. Melissa didn't want to think about what that would mean.

Captain Denathril jostled several people out of the way as he approached her. "Tell me your assessment, Agent Carlson," he said. "Do we wait for Agent Hunter to return?"

"No," Melissa said reluctantly. "Agent Hunter can take care of himself. We carry on with the mission. That-"

She cut off when spatial awareness alerted to something behind her. Motion. A lot of it on the other side of the path. "Find cover!" Melissa screamed before ducking behind one of the trees. The others followed her lead, Captain Denathril included.

Seconds later, a volley of bullets zipped across the path. Some of them struck trees. Others flew right past. One or two managed to score a hit on some poor officer who could not find adequate cover.

Denathril was crouching behind the next tree over. "We found them!" he shouted, tapping away at his multi-tool. "Let's call in our reinforcements."

His face contorted a moment later, and Melissa knew that things were not going to go according to plan. "Comms are jammed!" he shouted. "Can anyone else get through?"

"Negative," one of his officers replied.

So, they were stuck out here. Alone. With no backup and an inferior position. The ground sloped downward in the direction that Jack had gone, but it sloped upward in the opposite direction, rising to a crest on the other side of the path. The Ragnosians were up there. This was not going to go well.

Jack ran around the lupuna tree.

On the other side, he found another dirt road that ran off into the west. Looking in that direction made his eyes hurt. The sun was well past its zenith now. Afternoon was fading to evening.

Pressing his back to the trunk's indomitable girth, Jack waited. Spatial awareness was useless to him with a humongous tree in the way. He was grateful for Rajel teaching him to listen. And listen, he did.

The creature's footsteps were soft, barely audible unless you knew what you were listening for. But he heard the soft squish of shoes on wet earth. The *ziarogat* was closing in on him.

As quietly as he could, Jack rushed across the path and took refuge behind a kapok. It didn't provide nearly as much protection, but if he could keep still, he might be able to avoid notice long enough to gain the element of surprise.

The *ziarogat* emerged from behind the lupuna.

It turned its back on him, gazing eastward as if it thought he might have gone that way. Jack expected it to start surveying the immediate area, but it didn't. It was transfixed by something in the distance. Was this a trap? An attempt to lure him out? If it was, Jack would have to spring it. Doing nothing would leave him at a disadvantage if his enemy found him. He crept out into the open.

The *ziarogat* rounded on him.

For a half a moment, there was something akin to shock in those glossy, silver eyes, but then the creature sprang into motion with inhuman speed. It strode forward and threw a punch.

Jack ducked, allowing the cyborg's fist to pass over him. He popped up and swung his elbow into the *ziarogat's* nose. That earned him a few seconds.

Jack spun and back-kicked, slamming his foot into the panel on his enemy's chest. Thrown backward by the force, the *ziarogat* went stumbling into the massive trunk of the lupuna tree. It wheezed on impact.

Jack ran for the kill.

He leaped and spread his arms wide, intending to finish this with a swift kick to the face, but the silver-eyed devil stepped casually out of his path. Jack landed with a grunt, his frantic mind trying to form a plan.

When he turned, the *ziarogat* was standing just a few feet away. It kicked a big rock with devastating force and sent the thing flying into Jack's belly. Pain flared up, making it hard to think. He was dimly aware of the cybernetic monstrosity raising its right hand to aim the wrist-mounted gun.

Jack fell backward half a second before three bullets whizzed through the space where his head had been. His backside hit the ground, sending another jolt of sharp pain through his body.

The *ziarogat* adjusted its aim.

With a thought, Jack put up a Time Bubble, a sphere just big enough to encompass his body and some of the ground beneath him. Beyond its pulsing surface, the cyborg was frozen in place with its arm extended, ready to loose a stream of bullets.

Gasping for breath, Jack drew his gun with his right hand. Then he rolled aside and let the bubble collapse. Bullets struck the ground where he had been, churning up clumps of dirt and pebbles.

Jack rolled onto his back.

He raised the pistol in one hand and squeezed the trigger. By instinct, the *ziarogat* shielded its face behind its left hand, and then a crackling wall of white static appeared to intercept Jack's bullets. Portable force-field generators only offered a few brief seconds of protection before they ran out of power, but they were a few seconds in which his enemy could not return fire.

"High impact!" Jack bellowed.

He pointed his gun at a thick branch that extended over the path, a branch that hung over the *ziarogat's* head like the out-stretched arm of a beggar. Without hesitation, Jack pulled the trigger.

The loud crack of wood splitting got the cyborg's attention. It looked up to see the falling branch and then jumped out of the way.

Curling his legs up against his chest, Jack sprang off the ground with core strength and landed on his feet. He thrust his hand out, swinging the gun this way and that as he searched for his adversary. The only thing he saw was a narrow path and a whole lot of forest.

Squinting as a bead of sweat rolled down his forehead, Jack hissed. "Come on, you bastard," he growled. "Show yourself!"

He started forward at a measured pace, clamping his other hand onto the grip of his pistol. "Standard ammunition." The red LEDs on his gun went dark. High-impact rounds were powerful, but their rate of fire was slower than that of plain old-fashioned bullets. Jack wanted to be able to unload a clip if he had to.

Noise to his right.

He turned and found the *ziarogat* coming out from between two trees. It leaped and kicked the gun out of Jack's hand, leaving him defenseless. The creature landed in front of him and tried to shove its fist in his face.

Crouching down, Jack flung one hand up to swat the *ziarogat's* arm aside. He used the other to punch the panel on its chest once, twice, three times and four, smashing its circuitry with his knuckles.

Jack followed that with a palm strike to the nose.

His opponent backed up, silver blood leaking from the cyborg's nostrils and spilling over its pursed lips. These things were tough, but even with all of those enhancements, it was still half human. Blunt-force trauma slowed them down. Jack moved in to press his advantage.

Without warning, the *ziarogat* raised its left hand and another force-field snapped into place mere inches away from him. It sped forward before Jack could react, mowing him down like an oncoming truck.

He was thrown backward, hurled into the thick trunk of the lupuna tree. Before he even started to fall, Jack raised his hands and crafted a Bending, carrying it with him as he descended. It taxed Summer, but he had no choice.

Jack landed on wobbly legs. The bullets that should have torn him to shreds curved upward in a graceful loop and flew back toward the creature that had loosed them.

He let the Bending vanish to find the cyborg standing there with holes in its chest, holes that leaked metallic blood onto its firm, six-pack abs. "No force-field?" he asked. "Guess you used up the last of your power supply."

It startled him when the *ziarogat* ejected a thin ammo cartridge from its gauntlet. It made no attempt to reload. The damn thing just stood there, watching Jack with a vacant expression. "Out of bullets, huh?" he teased. "Well, that's all right. I'd rather do this the old-fashioned way."

The *ziarogat* made no response. You might have thought it was a department-store manikin for all the life it showed. But the fight wasn't over. If Jack tried to run, it would hunt him down like a bloodhound. Not that he would leave this thing loose to go after others.

It was time to end this.

Jack strode forward with teeth bared, shaking his head in disgust. "You're not gonna stop until I put you down," he spat. "Well, come on, Fulgore! Let's see what you got!"

Spurred by his taunting, the *ziarogat* decided to meet him halfway. The holes in its chest were already sealing themselves. Jack wasn't sure *how* these creatures recovered from grievous injuries so quickly, but he had fought one of them before, and he knew the rules. A head-shot would do the trick, but he no longer had his gun. He felt a pang of fear when his enemy got within arm's reach.

The *ziarogat* offered a hard right-cross.

Leaning back, Jack batted its hand away with a casual flick of his wrist. The other fist came at him, nanobots emerging from the cyborg's gauntlet, linking together to form a blade.

Jack twisted his body, one hand flying up to grab the creature's wrist and point it skyward so that its blade hit nothing but air. He hooked one foot behind the *ziarogat's* knee and tripped it, throwing the ugly thing down onto its backside. His opponent rolled aside before he could press his advantage.

In less than half a second, the *ziarogat* was back on its feet and watching him with hatred in its gaze. It attacked once again, twigs crunching beneath its feet as it moved in for the kill.

It tried to slice at Jack's stomach.

He leaped, using Bent Gravity for extra height, and somersaulted over the cyborg's head. Flipping upright in midair, he dropped to the ground with a thud and then whirled around to face his enemy.

The *ziarogat* rounded on him.

Jack kicked its belly with all the strength he could muster, forcing it to bend double. He spun for a hook-kick, one foot wheeling around in a tight arc, striking the creature's ear and knocking it senseless.

Just have to hold on, he thought. *Give them time to get away. Anna...I love you.*

Chapter 14

Bullets rained down on them.

Some grazed trees; others punched right through trunks that were too thin to stop them. Some hit soldiers, and others whizzed past without doing any damage. Captain Denathril's people returned fire, but it was harder to get a good shot when your enemy had the high ground.

Melissa was crouching with one hand raised, a circular Bending deflecting bullets that should have pierced her flesh and sending them into the sky. "I need cover fire!" she screamed. Did anyone hear?

She let her Bending collapse.

Throwing herself sideways, she rolled across the mucky ground and landed face-down behind a tree. There was a vicious *THWACK* as something ripped through its trunk, and then splinters of wood fell onto her back.

Melissa looked up, blinking. "I can't do anything down here," she said. "Can your people distract them?"

Denathril had his shoulder pressed to the next tree over, his face red and contorted with pain. He seemed to have taken a hit to the arm. "They can," he croaked. "What are you going to do?"

Melissa narrowed her eyes. "Just trust me."

"Flashbangs!" Denathril shouted.

Two women with small launchers on the bottoms of their rifles pointed their guns up the hill and fired a pair of grenades. Both landed on the hilltop with a flash of blinding light and a deafening roar that pained Melissa's ears even at this distance. Ragnosian men fell backward. Others went down from Leyrian gunfire.

Melissa took advantage of the diversion.

She ran across the path and dove into the trees on the other side, staying low so that her enemies couldn't get a clean shot. Veering to her right, she moved around kapoks that grew out of the hillside at an odd angle, their trunks bent as they strained for the sky. She kept going until she was sure that she was out of the line of fire.

She charged up the hill as fast as she could, leaping over fallen trees, ducking under hanging vines, avoiding rocks that might trip her. Melissa drew her pistol, powered it up and hissed, "Stun rounds."

The LEDs on the barrel turned blue.

Somewhere in the back of her mind, she wondered if she ought to be using lethal ammunition, but she was in no mood to deal with moral quandaries. She didn't have to kill to keep her friends alive.

The land flattened out as she reached the hilltop, and the trees were spaced further apart. There were maripa palms up here and other varieties that she didn't recognize on sight. It would be harder to find cover, but she would make do somehow.

Melissa hid behind a Brazil nut tree with her pistol held in both hands, its muzzle pointed at the ground. Cautiously, she peered around the trunk.

At the top of the hill, a line of men and women in gray uniforms were firing down on Captain Denathril and his officers. None of them had seen her coming. She had been stealthy enough to avoid notice.

Melissa chose her first target.

Her bullet struck the shoulder of the man nearest to her, sending a jolt through his body that made him convulse and pass out. Her second shot hit the next man in line, and he went down just as quickly.

By now, the others had realized that something was wrong. The third man in line glanced in her direction and snarled when he saw her. He swung his rifle around with a feral growl.

Melissa ran into the open.

Bullets skinned the bark off the tree she had been hiding behind.

Without looking, she aimed and fired, releasing a single round that bounced off the man's chin. Electric current made him tremble. His rifle fell to the ground, and then he toppled over, falling down the hill.

The fourth Ragnosian was a woman who rounded on Melissa and took a step back in surprise. Her rifle came up with alarming speed, ready for a kill shot.

Power surged through Melissa's body as she put up a Time Bubble, a simple sphere that was just large enough to let her take two steps to the right. She could just make out the other woman as a blurry figure in gray who clung to her weapon the way a frightened child might hold a teddy bear. Melissa let the bubble collapse.

Multiple rounds sped past on her left.

The female soldier had only an instant to react with surprise before Melissa's next bullet stung her thigh. And then she too was falling, collapsing onto the man behind her and knocking him off his feet.

She knew she was in trouble when the other Ragnosians all turned their attention toward her. Many of them ignored the Leyrian soldiers and focused their weapon on her instead. She had to-

A figure in black flew over Melissa's head and landed right in front of her as if he intended to shield her from enemy fire. His hands came up, and Melissa gasped when she saw the air ripple. Another Keeper?

Bullets converged upon him, each one looping around and flying back toward the shooter. She heard the cries and shrieks of men and women who were pelted with their own ammunition. And that momentary distraction changed everything.

The man in black chose the nearest soldier and kicked the rifle out of his grip. He spun, one hand stretching out, a knife flying from his fingertips. It landed hilt-deep in the soldier's throat, and that poor fellow keeled over.

The next Ragnosian tried to get his rifle up.

Dropping to his knees, the man in black tossed another throwing knife that sank into his enemy's thigh. A shriek of pain from the wounded soldier was almost enough to drown out the sound of gunfire. In the blink of an eye, the newcomer was on his feet once again.

He jumped, sailing right over the wounded soldier's head and kicking the woman behind him. She fell to the ground with the man in black landing on her chest, pinning her beneath his weight.

Before anyone could react, he drew his sidearm and shot her right in the face. The other Ragnosians were forming a tight semi-circle around him, ready to unleash a storm of gunfire.

The man became a streak of darkness that resolidified just outside the semi-circle. He grabbed the nearest soldier, slit that fellow's throat and then threw the corpse into the next man in line. The rest fell over like dominoes.

Drawing his pistol again – he must have holstered in the Time Bubble – the man in black fired at one soldier. And the next and the next. Three perfect headshots that left three puddles of blood on the ground.

There were other Ragnosians, but none of them were trying to kill this stranger, and they weren't interested in Melissa either. In fact, the six who remained all turned tail and ran.

"Stop!" Melissa shouted.

The man in black froze in the act of pursuing them, turned and looked over his shoulder. His face was hidden behind a mask. "Mercy?" he asked. "Haven't you learned by now that leaving your enemies alive to trouble you never works in your favour?"

Gaping at him, Melissa felt the blood drain out of her face. "You're no Keeper," she whispered, shaking her head. "No Keeper would ever do what you just did. You're one of Slade's people."

"What I just did?" he scoffed. "I just saved your life."

"I could have handled it."

It bothered her when the stranger laughed. "Hiding behind trees?" he mocked. "Is that how you would have handled it? Your stun rounds are useless against body armour; so, you have to aim for an arm or a leg. And a hit to the extremities minimizes the round's effectiveness, meaning they'll wake up much sooner than they would have if you had just shot them in the chest. It almost seems as if you Keepers want to lose."

"You disgust-"

The man in black leaped, flying through the air on Bent Gravity and landing right in front of her. His hand lashed out to seize her throat. "We have unfinished business, you and I!"

Before she could wonder what that meant, she was being thrown sideways, away from the slope that led back to her allies. Her shoulder slammed into a tree, and then she fell to the ground.

Clutching her upper arm as she rose, Melissa winced from the pain. "Who the hell are you?" It came out as a rasping growl. "And what do you want with me?"

He was striding toward her, chuckling softly. "You'll find out," he said. "But first, a little privacy."

Melissa ran around the tree, feet splashing in muddy puddles. It wasn't so much an attempt to get away from him as it was an attempt to get *him* away from Denathril and the others.

She quickly discovered that she was in a small grove of maripa and babassu palm trees, each with flat, green leaves that caught the sunlight. There were puddles all over the place, some of them as deep as her ankle. Well, if she had to fight this guy, this would be a good place to do it.

She turned around and found the man in black passing between two trees as he entered the grove. He stopped, observing her for a moment, perhaps wondering what to do with her.

Lifting her chin, Melissa stared down her nose at him. "So," she said, her eyebrows rising. "What do you want with me?"

He reached up to remove the mask, peeling it away with an almost reluctant hand and then tossing it aside. Melissa gasped when she saw the face beneath.

It was Aiden.

Spreading his arms, he bowed to her like an actor on a stage. "Do you understand now?" He stood up straight and faced her with an oily smile that made her skin crawl. "I thought I would give you the chance to avoid the fate that awaits your friends."

"What fate is that?"

Grinning, he shook his head. "Melissa, please," he said, feet splashing in the water as he approached. "I think you know the answer to that. The Justice Keepers are corrupt. Ideologically broken."

Melissa had her fists up in a fighting stance, her mouth tight with anxiety as she backed away. "I'm not so sure about that," she hissed. "Aiden, you just killed six people for no reason."

"No reason? They were your enemies."

"You could have stunned them."

He stopped dead, pressing his lips together as he looked up at the palm leaves that hung over his head. "You know, I *am* a Leyrian too," he said. "I'm not exactly thrilled to have invaders on one of my colonies."

"What do you want?"

"Join our cause," Aiden beckoned. "Accept a real symbiont and the power that goes with it. Slade will welcome you…And we can be together."

Despite herself, Melissa couldn't help but smirk. "Well," she said. "Now, I know I'm a real Keeper. It's not official until one of you tries to make me go dark-side."

"Aiden, you don't have to do this."

"I *want* to do this."

Splashing through the puddles with every step, Melissa approached him slowly. "You want to murder people?" she countered. "Because that's what Slade will make you do. How could you possibly believe that I would *ever* be with someone like that?"

For the first time since this whole thing started, she saw something that might have been a crack in his confidence. Just an instant of hesitation, and then he was all bravado and bluster again. "Same old Melissa," he said. "Still looking down her nose at everyone around her."

"You really don't get it, do you?" she spat. "I never thought I was better than you, Aiden! You were the one who was obsessed with Bonding a symbiont, not me! I didn't leave you, Aiden; you *pushed* me away. And now you think I'm gonna swoon and fall into your arms because suddenly you can Bend space-time? As if that mattered to me at all? I never thought I was better than you, but you know what? I do now. Because only a miserable excuse for a human being would ever work for a monster like Slade. So, tell me, Aiden. Was it worth it?"

"Let's find out."

Aiden leaped, flying through the air on a wave of Bent Gravity, and landed right in front of her with a spray of water. The hatred in his eyes frightened her. "Don't hold back, my love," he said. "I won't."

He began with a high roundhouse kick.

Melissa ducked and felt a rush of air as his foot passed over her. Heart pounding, she backed away from him and rose with her fists up in a fighting stance. "I don't want to fight you."

Aiden came forward, punching.

Crouching slightly, Melissa reached up to seize his wrist with both hands. She lifted it above her head, spun around beneath it and then forced Aiden to bend double. A kick to the back of his knee knocked him off his feet.

Aiden toppled over, landing on his backside and grunting on contact. He rolled out of the way before she could press her attack. Not that she would have. She still had some hope that he might be saved. A moment later, he was rising and kicking a rock, sending it flying toward her with a touch of Bent Gravity.

Melissa batted the stone away.

That moment of distraction allowed Aiden to close half the distance between them. He jumped and kicked her square in the chest, driving the air from her lungs. She sensed a massive tree just a few paces behind her. If he could pin her against that, things would not go well for her.

Aiden was coming; she could sense him clearly, running toward her with his teeth clenched, snarling like a rabid dog. It was becoming more and more likely that words would not solve this.

Melissa jumped.

Curling up into a ball, she back-flipped and pressed her feet against the tree trunk. She pushed off and flew right over Aiden's head as he ran past beneath her. She landed in a crouch.

Touching the very rock that he had used against her, Melissa applied her own surge of Bent Gravity and sent it flying toward him. Aiden whirled around just in time to take a hit to the chest.

Melissa rose smoothly and turned to face him. Her stomach was in knots. Anxiety clawed at her insides, but she managed to keep it under control. "We can help you. You don't have to go back to Slade."

"That's funny. I was going to make you the same offer."

"I'll never serve him."

Without warning, Aiden drew his pistol and thrust the gun out toward her. She had only half a second to raise her hands and craft a Bending. The air began to ripple, and his bullets curved upward, flying off into the blue sky.

His laughter made her pause. She let the Bending vanish, and the blurry figure that was Aiden resumed its proper shape. He was just standing there by the tree, grinning and laughing at her. "You could have sent those bullets back toward me," he said. "But then Justice Keepers lose because they aren't willing to do what's necessary. I see that now."

"I *don't* want to hurt you."

"Your mistake."

"No," a new voice said.

Melissa looked around to find the shapes of men in green moving through the trees that surrounded this little grove. One by one, they stepped out into the open, each one carrying an assault rifle.

Their leader was a heavyset man with broad shoulders who wore the insignia of a Ragnosian lieutenant proudly on his chest. His visor was pulled up so that she could see his dark face. "What do we have here?" he drawled. "A pair of Justice Keepers?"

"I'm no Keeper," Aiden insisted.

The squad leader replied to that with a toothy grin. "Well, son," he said. "We got a good look at you doing all that fancy gravity bending. As far as we're concerned, it don't much matter why one Keeper is fighting another."

Melissa teetered on the edge of open panic; she had been in sticky situations before, but there was no way she could get out of this. Not against so many! Not when they were surrounding her on all sides. Her career before-

No!

She forced herself to ignore her fear and focused instead on her training. The squad leader was still talking, which meant she had a moment to assess the situation before all hell broke loose. She counted twelve men. Too many for one Keeper alone, but if Aiden could help her, that would mean six each. The odds were still very much against her, but she had a chance of getting out of this. A small chance was better than none at all. She could feel Ilia's pride.

She made eye-contact with Aiden and found that he was watching her like a hawk, waiting for some kind of signal. He winked. So, his allegiance was clear then. *The enemy of my enemy and all that.*

The Ragnosians had formed a ring at the edge of the grove with Melissa and Aiden stuck in the middle. One move – the slightest twitch from either one of them – would turn this place into a giant meat grinder. She needed time, which meant that she was going to have to rely on her Bending abilities. *Follow my lead, Aiden,* she thought at him.

Melissa erected a Time Bubble in the shape of a narrow tunnel that covered half the distance between her and Aiden. The distorted images of the soldiers were all perfectly still, frozen in place. None of them would have noticed that anything had changed. Her skin began to prickle.

An instant later, from her perspective, a second tunnel appeared, terminating less than a micrometre away from the edge of hers. Melissa broke into a sprint. She caught a brief glimpse of a very blurry Aiden coming to meet her. When they were within arm's reach of each other, they both let their bubbles collapse.

Melissa and Aiden joined hands.

They ran in a tight circle, linked to one another, each one extending their free hand to craft a Bending that would deflect incoming fire. It took a few seconds for the soldiers to track them – they would have seen two streaks of colour converging in the middle of the grove – but it wasn't very long before they were smack dab in the middle of a storm of gunfire.

Their combined Bendings formed a flawless cylinder around their bodies; bullets came at them from all sides, but every single one curved slightly and flew back toward the ring of men surrounding them.

Blurry soldiers fell, crying out in pain.

Melissa's skin was on fire. Her temples were starting to throb. She could not keep this up much longer, but fortunately, she didn't have to. She could see that only three of the twelve men were still standing.

Together, she and Aiden released their Bendings.

Melissa turned and ran for one fellow who was still on his feet near the edge of the grove. That man raised his rifle, shining a laser sight on her chest.

She fell to her knees, sliding along the mucky ground as bullets whizzed past above her. Scooping up a flat rock, she threw it at the man before he could adjust his aim. It hit him in the face, cracking his visor, and he stumbled.

In one graceful motion, Melissa was back on her feet and charging toward him. She jumped, raising her knee to strike the man's cracked helmet. Knocked senseless by the blow, he lost his balance and collapsed against a tree.

Melissa landed in a crane stance, one foot raised off the ground, and she scanned her surroundings.

All around her, men were rising. Some of them had only been grazed by the bullets she and Aiden had deflected. Her partner was busy dealing with a trio of soldiers on the other side of the grove, which meant she would have to handle the ones over here. There was one on her left and one on her right.

She chose the former.

Melissa ran for him, loping over mud and rock with inhuman grace. The hot wind burned her face. Noticing her at the very last second, that man swung his gun around frantically and tried to take aim.

Melissa fell backward.

Catching herself with both hands, she brought her feet up to strike the underside of the rifle before he could fire, tearing the weapon from his grip. It went flying off into the trees. Melissa rose into a handstand.

She pushed off the ground and flew backward, feet-first toward another man who was standing behind her. That guy had his back turned, focused on Aiden instead of her, but he must have heard something because he spun around just in time to receive a kick to the chest.

He fell hard on his ass, and Melissa landed on top of him, squatting on his chest. The poor dolt was wheezing. She almost felt sorry for him. Almost. There was no time for that sort of thing.

Drawing her pistol, Melissa shouted, "Stun rounds!"

That first soldier, the one who had lost his rifle, was reaching for his sidearm. He managed to get it free of its holster before Melissa's first shot stung his arm. A powerful surge of current made him flail about and then fall flat on his face.

She fired another shot into the leg of the man beneath her, knocking him out as well. With those two dealt with, she turned her attention to Aiden and found him breaking the bones of some poor man in a gray uniform.

There were dead bodies at his feet, and the puddles that surrounded him were red with blood. Melissa felt like she might be sick. The power of a symbiont should never be abused in that way.

A soft rustle in the trees made her look up to see Captain Denathril and his platoon coming into the grove with rifles at the ready. Stun rounds battered the few Ragnosians who were still standing, causing them to tremble and fall to the ground with a splash.

Aiden turned around to find himself surrounded by enemies. His face contorted into a snarl of rage.

"Who is this?" Denathril asked.

Melissa was bent over with her hands on her thighs, breathing hard. Her body was drenched in sweat. "One of Slade's lieutenants," she explained. "He has the powers of a Justice Keeper with none of the checks that would prevent him from abusing them."

Several soldiers choked up on their rifles.

Standing up straight, Melissa blinked and then looked around. "You didn't kill the Ragnosians," she said. "Not that I'm complaining, but why not? I'm sure Major Tramon would not approve of this."

Denathril had that stern expression you often saw on military types, but he nodded as if he had been expecting this question. "Between this place and the mess on the hilltop, you took out the bulk of their force," he said. "An air strike would be pointless now. We can take them back and interrogate them."

"Oh..."

Pointing his sidearm at Aiden, Denathril cocked his head as if he were deciding whether or not to shoot. "What about this one?" he asked. "If he is the danger you say he is, then perhaps it would be best to-"

"Try it!" Aiden snarled. "Your people will die screaming!"

Melissa faced him with her arms folded, smiling and shaking her head. "Oh, I don't think so," she replied. "My skin is burning; my head is swimming, and if I Bend just one more time, I'll probably pass out. You can't be much better off."

Aiden looked at her with murder in his eyes. Somehow, he seemed to see this as yet another betrayal. Was he really stupid enough to think she would run away with him just because she had grudgingly accepted his help when her very life was in danger?

"I got a message through to Fleet Command," Denathril said. "It seems that when the Raggies scattered, whatever they were doing to jam our transmissions was no longer in effect. Our forces have control of the local air-space for a moment. They've dispatched a shuttle to pick us up."

"What about Agent Hunter?" Melissa protested.

"I suggest we find him post-haste."

The shuttle arrived about five minutes later, retrieving most of the platoon and the unconscious Ragnosians. Captain Denathril and five of his best officers stayed behind to help Melissa locate Jack. And of course, they were stuck with Aiden too.

Denathril had suggested that they let the shuttle crew take Aiden, but Melissa was not willing to let him out of her sight. The guy might be exhausted, but he could push his symbiont further than any true Nassai would allow. Right up to the point where it killed them both. And he was just demented enough to try something like that if he thought that a holding cell was the alternative.

Aiden walked with an assault rifle pressed against the small of his back, and Doran Higsen was the man with his finger on the trigger. The good lieutenant would often flash a smile to let Melissa know that he had no intention of letting Aiden try anything.

It took about five minutes to make their way back to the place where they had been ambushed, another ten to follow the

234

trail of fresh footprints to the place where Jack had made his stand. By the time they got there, the sinking sun was casting golden rays over the forest.

When they found him, Jack was sitting on a boulder with his knees apart, gasping as he stared into his lap. He looked up to blink at them. "Ah," he said. "Bout time the lot of you showed up. You know, if I'm gonna kill a cyborg for you, the least you could do is *not* make me walk all the way up that hill."

The corpse of the *ziarogat* was stretched out at his feet with a knife sticking out of its forehead, silver blood flaking around the wound. It stared lifelessly at the heavens, but then even when that thing was alive – if you could call it that – it still had a dull, vacant stare. Melissa was just glad that it wasn't moving.

Jack stood up, a yawn stretching his mouth into a cavern, and then grunted when he noticed Aiden. "Didn't I meet you at her eighteenth birthday party?" he asked. "What the hell are you doing out here?"

"He's one of Slade's lieutenants now," Melissa explained.

"Oh," Jack muttered. "And here I thought it was just the machismo bullshit of an untrained doofus charging into a warzone to impress his girlfriend. Thanks for making it *so* much worse!"

Aiden stood tall and proud with his head held high. You would never have guessed that he had a gun barrel poking him in the back. "Joke while you can, Hunter," he said. "When the Inzari burn this galaxy to ash, I will be anointed as one of their servants, and you…You will be dust."

"Well, I'm glad to see that he's mastered the cliche bad-guy speech," Jack said. "The scenery could use a few more bite marks. Hey, Aiden; I have to ask. Did they make you pick one of those lame aliases?"

"I am called Razor now."

Covering his mouth with one hand, Jack shut his eyes and...tittered. It was almost enough to make Melissa forget that they were in a war-zone. "Seriously?" he exclaimed. "Razor? What? Was Double-Bladed-Lightsaber taken?"

Aiden took a step forward, snarling as if he meant to rip Jack's throat open, but a poke from Higsen's assault rifle calmed him down. "It seems I am your prisoner for the time being," he said. "Perhaps we should go before more Ragnosians arrive."

"He's right," Denathril agreed. "I can signal the shuttle to pick us up."

Chapter 15

The noonday sun was bright in the cloudless sky, casting silver rays that reflected off the windows of buildings on either side of the street. The air was quite warm, so warm you wouldn't be comfortable in much more than a bathing suit, but it was always hot in Arinas.

They had moved the barricade to an intersection much closer to the centre of town. Captain Bosama had managed to evacuate most of the wounded before another wave of drones came down on them. Anna and Cassi had done what they could provide cover, but a few people didn't make it.

Bleakness take her, even those few casualties had felt like a knife through the chest. She knew it was irrational; she knew it was impossible. She knew that if she gave voice to her feelings one of these soldiers would tell her that she was naive, but Anna wanted to save them all. Every last one.

She kept those feelings to herself. She was quite sure that she would punch anyone who started lecturing her on the realities of war, and now wasn't the time for squabbles. It had been over three hours since the last attack, but the Ragnosians weren't going to stay quiet forever.

Down on one knee behind the barricade, Anna held a set of binoculars to her eyes. "Damn it..." She lowered them and shook her head. "What are they waiting for?"

Cassi was on her right with a pistol held in both hands, its barrel pointed upward. "Maybe they're reassessing their strategy," she suggested. "They have to figure that we'll adapt if they keep hitting us with the same thing over and over."

Pursing her lips as she considered that, Anna nodded. "Maybe," she agreed. "But the latest reports say that they're gathering outside the city. They have to know they can't get any more drop-ships past our shuttles."

"Yeah…"

"So, why wait?"

On her left, Corovin studied the empty street through the blue visor of his helmet. "Never underestimate Telixa Ethran," he said. "That woman is never passive. You can be certain of that much."

"Well, that's a-"

"Operative Lenai!"

Anna twisted around to find Captain Bosama pushing her way through a group of soldiers. The woman wore thick sunglasses that seemed to cling to her face. "We just got some backup."

She stepped aside to reveal Rajel and Keli standing behind her, and Anna had to resist the urge to jump up and hug them both. *That* would be a very unsoldiery thing to do. Not the kind of gesture that would inspire confidence in the troops. Or so she thought, at least. She was pretty damn sure that her tactics were sound, but as far as presentation went…Well, she was making that up as she went along.

Rajel was smiling with his usual brand of 'in your face' confidence. One look at the guy, and you would never guess that he expected to be dodging gunfire any minute now. "Well," he said, "we're here."

Keli wore the same look of disapproval that she always adopted in situations like this. "Your people are frightened," she added. "Their anxieties shine like beacons in the night. I wonder if they will be capable of doing their jobs when the shooting starts."

"Great job, Kell," Anna replied. "I'm sure they feel *much* better now."

"Apologies."

Anna noticed the small, plastic tags on Rajel and Cassi's vests. Excellent. She was glad to see that they had each received one when they arrived. She herself was wearing one, and so was everyone else behind this barricade. "Well," she said. "All we can-"

"Drones approaching!" one of the lookouts shouted.

Sure enough, another squadron of wedge-shaped robots was flying down the street toward their position. In less than twenty seconds, they would be close enough to open fire. Anna wasn't worried about that just yet. The force-fields would protect them if they could keep those little bastards from getting too close.

Anna felt her eyebrows shoot up. "Now, the fun begins." She ducked low, tapping commands into her multi-tool. "Execute Program Fourteen."

Death Spheres rose from the rooftops on either side of the road, flying into the middle of the street. One by one, they reoriented themselves to point their lenses at the oncoming drones, unleashing orange particle beams that carved the drones into pieces. A few of them exploded in the air.

Red-hot shrapnel fell to the ground, burnt metal and scorched circuitry. Within ten seconds, every last Ragnosian drone was disabled, all without the Leyrian soldiers firing a single shot.

Sighing with relief, Anna tapped the little tag on her vest. Death spheres targeted anything that moved unless you happened to be wearing some kind of friend-or-foe ID that would tell them to ignore you.

Dangerous but effective.

"Drones destroyed," Lieutenant Tharee reported.

Rising from her chair in one fluid motion, Telixa frowned as she approached the display screen. "Every one of them?" she inquired. "You're telling me that not one drone got past their defenses."

"Yes, ma'am," the lieutenant replied. "The drones were destroyed at a distance of six hundred metres from their barricade. Too far for their explosives to be of any use."

Stroking her chin with the tips of her fingers, Telixa studied the readouts. "How very unexpected," she murmured. "We may have underestimated these Leyrians."

The screen displayed a simple map of the city. Arinas was essentially a disk with spoke streets extending from the centre. There were circular streets as well, intersecting the spokes at even intervals.

"Send another wave," she ordered.

"Ma'am?"

Telixa spun to look over her shoulder, raising an eyebrow at the audacity of anyone who might question her orders. "Another wave," she repeated. "Let's find out just how effective these defenses really are."

Lieutenant Tharee was a skinny man with copper skin who refused to look up from his console. "Drones sent," he said. "Approaching target. One point two kilometres. Zero point nine kilometres. Zero point eight... Drones destroyed."

"Show me a visual of their position."

The screen went dark and then lit up again with a still photograph taken by one of the drones in the first squadron. There were at least two dozen uniformed soldiers behind the line of cars, but Telixa paid special attention to the three people in front. Two Justice Keepers – you could tell because they never wore helmets – one with pink hair, and the other with strawberry-blonde hair in a ponytail. There was also a man in what appeared to be Antauran armour. She was quite certain that it was the suit she had procured for that useless assassin, Corovin Dagmath.

Telixa rounded on her chief of security, striding toward him with her hands on her hips. "And you're quite certain that this is the same Justice Keeper who raided our ship a few months ago?"

Lieutenant Commander Haron was a very pale man with a thick mustache and a receding hairline. "I am," he replied with a nod. "Several of my officers recognized her. She seems to have devised a countermeasure to our drone strikes."

"Clever girl," Telixa murmured.

Returning to her chair, she sat down and crossed one leg over the other. Her face was stern as she chose her next words. "Send in the troops," she said. "Tell them I want that barricade broken within the hour."

"Ma'am," Lieutenant Tharee replied. "If we do that, the Leyrians will strike them down with heavy artillery again."

"Yes, they will, Lieutenant," she replied. "I'm counting on it. Send down drop ships twenty-six, forty-five and eighty-three. Tell them to unload their cargo within a two-block radius of the Justice Keeper, preferably not in front of their guns."

"Ma'am," Ensign Cathali chimed in. "The Leyrians have over fifty assault shuttles and several wings of fighters patrolling the air-space above Arinas. It's very unlikely that our ships will get through even with an escort."

"I only need one of them to get by, Ensign. Just one."

Anna stood up, gazing into the heavens. Sweat-slick hair clung to her forehead. "Okay," she said, nodding. "We've shown them that they can't just sit back and bomb us from orbit."

Corovin was next to her with his hands on the hood of the car. The brief look he gave her might have been a disapproving glare. She couldn't tell with the visor covering his face. "Which means you should expect something worse."

Anna wanted to smack him. She could already hear some of the soldiers muttering about what that might be. The Bleakness take Corovin and his opinions. It only got worse when Bosama echoed his sentiments.

The least they could do was let the soldiers savour the victory for a few moments. People had to believe that a fight was winnable, or they would give up hope. Preparing them to fight the next battle was all well and good, but if you demoralized them, the next battle would be over before it began. Seth was proud of her for some reason. She would have to ask him about it later. "Operative Lenai?" someone said through her earpiece.

Closing her eyes, Anna tapped it so that she could reply. "I'm here, Stephen." She recognized the voice of an Earth-born Keeper who had been posted to Alios a year ago. He was her primary contact with the air support. "What's up?"

"Enemy fighters coming our way!"

Anna whirled around to face her people with a stern expression. "You heard that!" she yelled, striding toward them. "Looks like they're getting ready for an air-strike. Get out of the street!"

The soldiers all stood in little clusters of four or five, but they were all watching her the way a mouse might watch an approaching cat. A few of them sprang into motion with incredible haste, running for the skyscrapers on either side of the street. Every building in every Aliosian city was outfitted with force-field generators that were specifically made to defend against orbital bombardment. The Antaurans had been raiding this planet for decades.

Those who decided to seek shelter had barely made it three steps before Stephen's voice came through the speaker again. "Negative, ma'am," he said. "The fighters are all maintaining a high altitude. We don't think they're targeting you."

One of the lookouts was standing by the barricade and peering through a set of binoculars. He lowered them and shouted. "Ragnosians approaching!"

Sure enough, another platoon of enemy soldiers was escorting a hover tank down the street. The Leyrians took up positions behind the barricade, aiming their rifles with precision.

"Take out their shield generators!" Bosama shouted.

Something about this didn't feel right.

Dropping to a crouch, Anna tapped her earpiece again and frowned as possibilities tumbled through her mind. "What's happening, Stephen?" she asked. "Are they trying to tie you up?"

"Got a..." His voice was cut off by the buzz of static, and for a second, Anna feared that he might have been hit. "On my tail," he added when the distortion cleared up. "They have a..."

"Stephen?"

"Watch out for..."

"Stephen?" There was no answer. Suddenly, Anna was sick to her stomach with worry, and Seth's emotions echoed her own. Something was wrong here. One look at the approaching Ragnosians made it clear that they were outmatched.

Their shots rebounded off a force-field that popped up to protect the barricade, and Leyrian soldiers returned fire, pelting the tank with EMP rounds. Artillery cannons on the rooftop fired streams of plasma that eventually overpowered the tank's defenses. Just like the last time. But why would they use the same tactic twice?

"Keli!" Anna shouted. "Get over here!"

The telepath was crouching behind a streetlight a good twenty paces away from the barricade. She looked up with irritation plain on her face, then scurried over as quickly as she could. "What is it?"

"What do you sense?"

The other woman scrunched up her face with concentration. "Nothing much," she answered. "The soldiers approaching us truly believe that they are the main line of attack. Whatever the plan is, they're not in on it."

A sudden clap of thunder made Anna jump, and when the spike of adrenaline faded, she saw that the tank had been destroyed, smashed to bits by the heavy artillery just like its predecessor. The Ragnosian soldiers were in retreat.

"The pilots," Anna said. "What do you sense from them?"

"There are no pilots. Those fighter drones are automated, but I'm sensing a kind of urgency from..." Abruptly, she stood and pointed a finger into the sky. "There!"

A Ragnosian drop-ship descended from the open sky, flying low over the rooftops of skyscrapers. It slowed to stop above an intersecting street, hovering silently for a few seconds. "Oh, no..."

A hatch opened in the troop carrier's underbelly, and a large, metal triangle fell out. Thruster packs on the SlipGate slowed its descent until it dropped out of view behind one very tall building.

Turning away from the barricade, Anna loped up the empty street like a lioness on the hunt. "Let's move!" she bellowed. "Cass, Rajel, Keli, Corovin!"

The other two Keepers fell in beside her while Keli and Corovin struggled to keep up. Which would suit Anna just fine. A telepath was most useful when you didn't put her directly in the path of oncoming gunfire, and she wasn't entirely sure what to do with the assassin.

"Where are you going?" Bosama shouted.

"To save your ass!"

The street where the Gate had landed branched off from Bonavin Avenue on her right but not on her left. It took less than twenty seconds for her to reach the corner, and then she pressed her shoulder against the side of a building. The others caught up to her in short order.

Cautiously, Anna peered around the corner.

The Gate was standing in the middle of the road, sunlight gleaming off its polished surface, and its grooves were already glowing. A bubble appeared from out of nowhere with blurry figures inside.

When it popped, there were three tall robots standing side by side, each with long arms and legs. Their heads swivelled, scanners targeting Anna. She caught a glimpse of motion before ducking out of sight.

Bullets scraped the duroplastic off the side of the building before flying across the road to shatter the front door of a skyscraper.

Bracing one hand against the wall, Anna shut her eyes and formulated a plan. "All right," she panted. "I'm gonna give you cover fire. Cass, when they're distracted, you and Rajel hit them with everything you've got."

The other two nodded.

Drawing her pistol, Anna thumbed a switch to select EMP rounds, but before she could act, Corovin unclipped something from his belt. He threw it into the intersection, and then the drones were shooting at nothing, putting bullet holes in the buildings across the street. "Now!" the assassin yelled.

Aiming around the corner, Anna fired at the nearest drone. A single charged round struck the robot's chest, and then another. And then another, each one landing with a flash of sparks and a distinct crackling sound. The drone stumbled as its damaged circuits tried to compensate.

Throwing herself sideways, Cassi rolled along the crosswalk and came up on one knee. Her hand flew out in a blur, pointing a gun at her target. White tracers erupted from the barrel.

Corovin shoved Anna out of the way to let loose with his submachine gun. She heard the distinct ping of metal on metal and the sizzle of scorched circuitry. Then there was a crash as one of those mechanical beasts fell over.

One glance into the intersecting street, and it was clear that they were not out of trouble yet. The bots had been reduced to scrap, but the SlipGate was lighting up again. This time, when a bubble appeared, Anna could see humanoid figures inside.

It popped and left three shirtless men standing in the middle of the road, each with a metal panel fused into his chest, each with silver eyes that seemed to stare right through you. Behind them, two more robots scanned for targets. "Oh, Bleakness…"

Cassi had retreated to the safety of the street corner, but her eyes were feral. Haunted. "Not these things again," she whispered.

"Our primary objective is to disable the Gate," Anna said. "We leave it there, and they'll just keep sending bad guys through. Its security protocols won't respond to any of our multi-tools; so the only option is to hit it with something big and loud and messy."

"A few grenades should do the trick," Corovin muttered.

Brushing a lock of hair off her cheek, Anna heaved out a breath. "Keli," she said. "Work your mojo. Slow down the gats or stop them outright. Anybody gets a chance to take a shot, do not hesitate. You won't get another."

Anna rounded on their newest teammate and shoved a finger in his face, right up against the visor. Corovin jerked his head back in response. "You're more familiar with Ragnosian tech than any of us," she snapped. "Disable those drones. Hack their firmware, exploit a weakness. I don't care how. Just do it."

"Cass, you and I are gonna hit 'em from multiple angles, keep them shooting at us while the others work behind the scenes, And Rajel!"

"Hmm?"

Anna jerked her thumb toward the SlipGate. "Smash."

He replied with a menacing smile.

"Let's go to work."

Anna and Cassi went around the corner together. Not fifty paces away, the SlipGate was blocked by three *ziarogati* and two Ragnosian battle drones, big, brutish robots with round heads marked by a single round eye that lit up when it saw them.

The instant they stepped into the open, all five enemies raised their weapons. Anna was about to call on Seth when a Time Bubble that was not of her making surrounded her and Cassi. She could feel the other woman's hold on space-time.

"Now," she said.

Dropping to a crouch, Anna pointed her gun with one hand and fired. Precision was difficult since she couldn't see clearly through the edge of the bubble, but she didn't have to be precise. She selected each target on her side of the road and sent a glowing bullet toward it. Bullets that seemed to freeze in place the instant they passed out of her time-frame. Cassi did the same to the others.

The bubble popped.

Both drones and all three *ziarogati* stepped back as ammunition chewed through their bodies, the cyborgs trembling from the jolt of electric current. They had just bought themselves a few seconds.

Anna ran for the nearest drone.

She leaped and wrapped her legs around its waist, clinging to its body. The blasted thing's weapons were mounted on its wrists. It couldn't quite twist its arms enough to get a clean shot. But it did try to trap her in a bear hug.

Anna let herself fall to the ground.

With the gentlest tug of Bent Gravity, she slid between the robot's legs and popped up behind it. Aiming over her shoulder, she fired without looking and sent an EMP round through the back of its head.

The robot fell over.

Not ten feet away, Cassi spun to deliver a ferocious back-kick into the chest of a *ziarogat*. The cyborg was thrown backwards into the SlipGate, rebounding off the metal.

Cassi rounded on her enemy, lifted her gun and fired a shot that ripped through the *ziarogat's* shoulder with a spray of blood. Her next shot put a small hole in the creature's forehead.

The second robot began lumbering toward Anna, wrist-mounted guns extending for a kill shot. She grabbed the portable force-field generator Corovin had lent her, extended her hand toward the mechanical goon and erected a wall of flickering electrostatic energy to protect herself. Bullets bounced off of it.

Tapping a button on the generator, she sent the force-field barreling toward her opponent. It mowed down the drone like an oncoming train and knocked the thing onto its backside. That gave her the opening she needed.

Anna got up and ran for the curb, hopping onto the sidewalk and ducking into an alley between two buildings. If Ragnosian drones were anything like their Leyrian counterparts, this one would classify her as a priority threat and come after her first. She could kill it in here, where there was less chance of being caught in the crossfire between her people and whatever came through that Gate.

The alley was wide enough for three or four people to walk side by side. Plenty of room to fight. Now, all she could do was hope that the robot's programming worked as she had guessed it would.

Those hopes were answered when she heard the *clank* of metal feet drawing near. A moment later, the robot stepped into view, its eye glowing red.

Anna reached out to Seth.

A Time Bubble expanded until it was just large enough that she would be able to touch its surface if she stretched her arms out. Beyond it, the drone was a hazy figure with fists clenched, ready to fire those wrist-mounted guns.

Crouching, Anna brought her gun up in two hands and fired once. A glowing bullet appeared just outside the bubble, inching its way toward its target. The robot was fast, but even it wouldn't be able to react that quickly.

With a quick pivot, she fired again.

Another bullet appeared beside the first, following a slightly different trajectory. It would have to do. She couldn't remain in the bubble any longer. Releasing her hold on space-time, she let it dissolve.

The robot stumbled as one bullet hit its right wrist, and the other struck its left arm a little too high to damage the gun. Anna cursed. It was hard to aim when you couldn't see your target clearly.

Catching itself with a few shaky steps, the drone regained its balance, and then a small hatch opened on its chest, revealing yet another weapon hidden in there.

Anna leaped with the lightest touch of Bent Gravity, propelling herself right over the mechanized demon. Bullets rushed past beneath her. One almost grazed the sole of her shoe. She landed behind her enemy and quickly spun around.

The bot rounded on her.

Anna shot its knee before it could attack her. Blue sparks arced along the limb from ankle to thigh. The robot stumbled, almost losing its balance, almost falling right on top of her.

Throwing herself out of its path, Anna aimed without looking and fired another shot through the side of its head. There was a soft whirring sound as the drone fell flat on its face, and then it was still.

Anna sucked air into her lungs.

Her skin was tingling, but it wasn't painful. Not yet. She had been trying to avoid the use of her abilities, but these things were just too fast. Now, she had to help the others and pray that nothing pushed her to exhaustion.

The *ziarogat* stood before Corovin, watching him with dead eyes and blocking his path. With alarming speed, it thrust its fist out toward him and released several rounds. They bounced off his armour, each one landing like a punch to the chest, bringing with it an ache, and he was forced to back up.

The *ziarogat* adjusted its aim so that its fist was pointed at his face. He heard a soft buzz that suggested it had switched to one of those fancy ammunition settings the Leyrians used.

He tapped his belt.

A force-field appeared, flickering and crackling, and he hardly even noticed when a bullet flattened itself against the screen of static. With a gesture, he sent the force-field speeding toward his opponent.

He gasped when the cyborg jumped over it and kicked him in the face. The helmet protected him, but it was still disorienting. Corovin stumbled, the mechanized joints in his suit moving sluggishly.

The *ziarogat* was coming.

Corovin tapped a button on his wrist, activating a blade of nanobots that extended from the slot on his gauntlet. By instinct, he bent his knees and brought the sword up just in time to parry a high attack.

The cyborg jumped and brought its own nano-blade down in a fierce vertical slash that struck Corovin's weapon with enough force to make him retreat a few steps. Such strength! Who could have created these things?

The creature spun in a blur and kicked like a mule, pounding his chest with a black-soled shoe. Once again, he was staggering, struggling to keep his balance. Keepers might have incredible stamina, but even with the armour, his body was weakening.

With the merciless precision of a machine, his enemy came forward to slash at his belly. Corovin hopped backward but not quickly enough. The nano-blade tore a gash in his armour and left a shallow cut across his bellybutton. If not for the suit, his guts would be spilling onto the street.

Now, a voice whispered in his mind.

To his shock, the *ziarogat* froze in mid-step as if the very air had congealed around its body. *NOW!* the voice insisted. *I can't hold it forever!*

Detaching the submachine gun from his belt, Corovin pointed it and fired a single shot. A hole appeared in the cyborg's forehead, and silver blood spattered onto the street. Half a second later, the thing fell over dead.

But there were others.

Cassi was dealing with one, trying to stay one step ahead of its aim. So far, every one of its shots had scarred the edifice of a building. Cassi blurred into a streak and then resolidified behind her opponent.

She tried to shoot it in the back, but the *ziarogat* accepted the wound without even the tiniest flinch of pain. It twisted around to strike her cheek with the back of its hand. Cassi nearly lost her balance.

Closing the distance as fast as his suit would allow, Corovin thrust out his left hand and let loose a cloud of nerve gas from the tips of his fingers. The cybernetic abomination seemed to be surprised by this move, but it was not harmed in any way that he could see.

It jumped and struck Corovin's chin with the tip of its shoe.

He was thrown backward, arms flailing as he tripped over a fallen drone and fell on his ass. Through the visor, he had a glimpse of the gat standing over him. Apparently, it had decided to finish him before resuming its fight with Cassi.

It lifted its arm…and froze.

A bullet pierced the creature's skull and came out the other side with a trail of silver goo in its wake. And then the thing was dead.

More coming! Keli warned.

Turning his head with a high-pitched whir, Corovin watched as the SlipGate lit up again. Another bubble seemed to expand from an infinitely small point into something big enough to hold perhaps a dozen people. There was no telling what was inside. There was no way to win this-

Rajel soared right over him, landed on the pavement and sprinted toward the Gate. The blind man jumped effortlessly over any piece of debris in his path. He was a man on a mission, and he would not be deterred.

Springing off the ground, Rajel flipped over the bubble as it popped. He dropped a pair of grenades, landed with one foot perfectly balanced upon the very top of the metal triangle and then continued on without missing a beat.

The grenades landed at the feet of three more battle drones and two more *ziarogati.* Robots and cyborgs both looked down to assess their situation.

One of the gats made a dive for the sidewalk. One of the robots stomped toward the other side of the street. The others tried to spread out, but they didn't get far before a huge fireball engulfed them all.

Two of the drones were destroyed. One of the cyborgs was a mass of blackened flesh. And the Gate... The Gate had scorch marks all over its once smooth surface. But despite that, the grooves began to glow again.

"It's still functional," Corovin lamented.

"Admiral."

Telixa was sitting with her hands on the arms of her chair, staring mournfully into her lap. Taking this planet had taxed her forces more than it should have. Damn Slade for forcing her into this. She looked up at the sound of someone calling out to her. "What is it, Lieutenant?"

"Ma'am, someone is accessing the SlipGate."

"What?"

The young man with tilted eyes and short, black hair that curled over his ears was frantically pawing at his console. "They're using our access codes!" he wailed. "But it's not me! The next batch of drones isn't in position yet!"

Cheeks burning, heart pounding, Telixa hissed air through her teeth. "Who would do such a thing?" She had a feeling that she knew the answer.

Leaping from the top of the SlipGate, Rajel hit the ground and put himself into a Time Bubble, a long, narrow tube that extended from his body. He ran through it until he reached the very end, then let the bubble vanish and instantly put up another.

He ran to the end of *that* tunnel as well and only then did he let himself return to a normal time-frame. The very instant his bubble popped, he heard the roar of the grenades he had dropped exploding. Spatial awareness alerted him to flying shrapnel. One of the drones had been destroyed, and he was fairly certain he had eliminated one of those half-human things as well. He hated *ziarogati*.

Sadly, when the crackle of the fire died down, he heard something that unsettled him. SlipGates made a slight humming noise when an incoming traveler was about to arrive. The sound was unmistakable, and he was hearing it now.

The bubble arrived on the other side of the Gate.

It felt like a gap in the universe to him, a spherical region where the world ceased to exist. He had never really gotten used to that feeling. A hole in the world? Such a thing should not exist.

Whatever uneasiness he felt at the presence of the bubble was only amplified when it deposited its passenger onto the pavement. Rajel knew that silhouette all too well. "No," he whispered. "It can't be-"

Grecken Slade back-flipped over the Gate and landed right behind it. He turned and ran up the road toward Rajel.

Spinning to face the man with teeth bared, Rajel strode toward him. "You must be pretty damn stupid," he began. "Did you really think you could get past-"

Slade jumped right over him.

That in and of itself was galling. It was as if the other man thought he wasn't worth the bother. He was about to pursue, but Anna stepped out of the alley and screeched when she became aware of Slade's presence. "Destroy the Gate," she ordered. "I'll handle him."

Slade ignored her too.

"Let him go," Rajel said. "We have bigger problems."

Anna glanced in his direction, and the disappointment on her face was undeniable. "Think, Rajel," she said. "Why would he come here? Into all this chaos? He's going after the Prime Council."

She didn't bother to explain further; she just took off in hot pursuit of Slade. Rajel sensed that the others had dealt with the enemies that his grenades had failed to put down. The remaining battle drone was now a hunk of twisted metal with sparks shooting out of its chest-plate. The final *ziarogat* was frozen in place as Corovin rammed his nanoblade through its chest. Keli's doing, no doubt.

"Get some more grenades!" he said. "Quickly!"

Telixa clicked her tongue as she examined the latest sensor data. The display screen showed her a top-down view of Arinas, and the battle was not going as well as she would have liked. Her troops were attacking on multiple spoke streets, trying to break through Leyrian barricades, and so far, the Leyrians were holding. It was only a matter of time; she could already see the cracks in their defenses, but more than half of the ships in her fleet were disabled or destroyed, and her armies were scattered over the planet's surface. She might take this world, but she would pay a heavy cost for it. Perhaps it was time to try a new tactic.

Standing up with a sigh, Telixa approached the screen and then nodded once. "The time has come to make our presence felt in a more personal way," she said. "Lieutenant, broadcast a message on all frequencies. Holographic transmission where possible."

"Yes, ma'am."

Slade made a left turn onto a narrow street lined with small, vacant buildings, each one no more than two or three stories high. Not a spoke street. This one went on for about three blocks before ending in another intersection.

Anna was only five steps behind him and running at top speed. She threw herself into a dive, tackling him from behind. They both fell to the pavement, rolling apart.

Slade sat up, pressing a hand to his forehead. His momentary grimace of pain was quite satisfactory. "Foolish woman," he said. "You can't stop what's coming. This has all been ordained from the moment of creation."

Lying on her side in the middle of the road, Anna panted. "Yeah, yeah," she said. "Heard the speech already, Slade. Fate itself is on your side! We stopped you before, and we'll do it again."

"Did you?"

Anna hesitated.

The cruel smile on Slade's face made her shiver. "Did you really stop me before?" he pressed. "I found the Key, Anna. I opened the SuperGates. Has it occurred to you that everything you did was simply part of the plan?"

"If that's the case, then-"

She cut off when her multi-tool started squawking. The screen revealed that she was receiving a transmission on an open channel, one that was being broadcast across the entire planet. She had no intention of listening – not when she was face to face with a murderer who would use any distraction as a means to escape – but when she didn't play the message, Slade tapped a button on his multi-tool.

A hologram of a Ragnosian admiral appeared between them: a short woman with a bob of brown hair and red epaulettes on her uniform. Anna recognized her. She was the one who commanded the ship that had captured Jack. "People of Alios," she said. "Your planet has been liberated from an oppressive government. From this day onward, you are free. Those of us who purchased your freedom at a high price will not abandon you now. We will help you to rebuild and provide humanitarian aid."

"In exchange for our good efforts on your behalf, you will stand with us in opposing those forces that would drag you back under the yoke of tyranny. All agents of the former government will surrender themselves for arrest and investigation. All Justice Keepers will be summarily executed."

The woman's stoic expression was broken by a smile that she smothered again half a second later. "Your immediate and unconditional surrender will result in a cessation of hostilities," she said. "Further resistance will be punished. You have ten minutes."

The hologram vanished.

The End of Part 1

Interlude 3

"You're not spirits, are you?":

It was a question that he did not need an answer to. As he stood within the corridors of this ship of flesh, he realized that "spirits" was a term that came far short of what these creatures were. The walls seemed to pulse with an eerie, red light. The floor squished under his feet.

He was Petar now, a short man with a gaunt-cheeked face, hair so yellow it was almost white and a goatee to match. This body irritated him. It was not as strong as the others the creatures had offered.

Without warning, the Old Woman appeared in front of him and smiled like a proud mother watching her child play. "No," she said. "Not spirits. What your species calls a soul is nothing but a crude approximation of the truth."

He closed his eyes, taking that in, and then nodded. "What are you then?" he asked. "What are you really? If I am to serve your needs, it would help to know."

The Old Woman turned away and began walking up the hallway. He followed without hesitation. The woman was an image these creatures had projected into his mind – he had deduced that much – and if she was walking away, it was for a purpose.

She stopped at a seemingly inconsequential place; Petar saw nothing about this section of the tunnel that seemed any different from anywhere else inside this ship. But the Old Woman raised a hand.

A seam grew in the wall, rising from floor to ceiling, and when the flaps of skin split apart, he saw blackness on the other side. Blackness and stars? Were they in the heavens then? It only made sense. So many people believed the skies were the domain of the gods. Was that what these creatures were?

He approached the opening with arms folded, frowning as he peered through the gap. "I don't understand," he said. "Are you trying to tell me that you look down on my world from above?"

A sphere of blue and green floated in the endless darkness, oceans and land masses partly hidden behind swirling clouds. At this distance, he could hide it by raising just one hand. Perhaps these creatures *were* gods. They lived among the stars. They had mastery over life and death...

"That is not the world of your birth," the Old Woman said. "It is one of many that we have provided for your people."

"Why would you do this?"

"To observe the different ways in which your species might develop."

"To what end?"

She ignored the question, walking away from the window, and the opening resealed itself when she was gone. Petar followed her into an open chamber with a pool similar to the one he always woke up in when they restored him to life.

He dropped to one knee at the edge, inspecting the liquid. "This is where I always wake up." He dipped a hand into the goo, then pulled it free and watched as it dripped from his fingertips. "What is it?"

Standing beside him with her hands clasped in front of herself, the Old Woman chuckled. "The building blocks of a human body," she said. "Of every living creature on your planet, actually. From it, we can construct any vessel that you require."

"Any vessel?"

She nodded.

"Could you make me female?"

"If you wish it."

His lips writhed, revealing clenched teeth, and his face was suddenly warm. It had only been an idle curiosity – a question posed to test the limits of the Old Woman's power – but the thought of being a woman sickened him. "I do not," he said emphatically.

The Old Woman nodded again.

"What am I then?" he inquired. "If, as you say, you can place my consciousness in any vessel, then what is the essence of that consciousness?"

The Old Woman blinked as if she were surprised by the question. Perhaps she had not expected to hear such musings from a lowly human. He felt a ridiculous amount of pride in that. "Your language lacks the terminology to describe it," she explained. "But so long as you remain faithful, you need never fear death."

Gods indeed.

These creatures were powerful beyond his wildest imaginings. They had restored him more times than he could count, each time with a new face and a new name, but he was always himself. Desires from one life carried over into the next. Anger over a slight did not fade simply because he found himself in a new body.

After Dravis Trovan had died in bed, he had awoken to find himself wearing the face of a bald and corpulent man. They had left him on yet another strange world, this one populated by people who could read his very thoughts. That terrified him more than any of the painful deaths he had suffered.

"You said something to me once," he muttered. "Centuries ago, when they called me William. You told me that my people had to go to the stars."

"Yes."

"Why?"

The Old Woman was silent for a moment, standing at the edge of the pool with a blank expression. Finally, she deigned to give him an answer. "We need you to fight each other."

"To what end?"

She rested a hand on his shoulder, and he shuddered. It was the mind walkers that helped him to realize the Old Woman's true nature. She was nothing but a projection they forced into his thoughts; he knew that, and yet her touch felt as real as that of any flesh and blood woman. "All will be revealed to you in time, my son," she promised. "All will be revealed to you in time."

During the years that he had spent among the mind walkers, he had learned many things. There was an ancient language on their world, a dead tongue that few people still spoke, but he had learned it. Tha'kedian. Mastering it had been necessary to present an air of culture and sophistication.

That language had a phrase that came to mind whenever he thought about the Old Woman and her people. *Inza ri.* It meant, "the unknowable ones." He could think of no title more suited to these creatures.

Remaining on one knee, he bowed his head respectfully. "I will serve," he said. "I will be your voice and your hand."

"And in return, you will live,"

Part 2

Chapter 16

When the hologram vanished, Slade got up and showed her a menacing smile. He turned abruptly and took off in the direction of the Hub, where the Prime Council would be protected behind several layers of security.

Curling up into a ball, Anna sprang off the ground and landed upright with her fists clenched. She turned on her heel and ran after him. "Seriously?" she yelled. "You're not even gonna dignify me with a 'Bwahaha, my evil plan has come to fruition speech?'"

Slade paused just long enough to draw a pistol from his belt holster. Quickly, he rounded on her with his arm extended, the gun pointed right at her chest. Instinct kicked in, and Anna called upon her symbiont.

She fell to her knees, using Bent Gravity to pull herself along the road as bullets zipped past above her. Unclipping the grenade from her belt, she popped the cap with her thumb and threw it at Slade.

He became a streak of red and black, moving toward the sidewalk.

In the blink of an eye, Anna had a Time Bubble of her own – just a simple sphere – and through it, she saw a distorted Slade on the curb. The man was twisting around with his pistol clutched in both hands, ready to put a bullet through her.

Turning on her heel, Anna drew her gun and raised it in both hands. She fired and watched several bullets appear just beyond the edge of her bubble. She had no desire to kill, but she would make an exception for Slade.

Her bubble collapsed.

The instant that it did, she saw that Slade had a Bending in place. Anna had only a second to duck – a second granted to her by the momentary slowdown as bullets passed through the crumpled fabric of space-time – before her ammunition turned back upon her. The grenade went off with a deafening roar, spraying chunks of pavement into the air. One even grazed the back of Anna's head.

The Bending fizzled away to reveal a grinning Slade on the curbside. He seemed almost pleased. "You fight dirty!" he exclaimed.

Holstering her pistol, Anna squinted at him. "I learned from the best," she growled. "Let's get this over with."

Slade moved like a shadow sliding across the wall, chuckling as he came to meet her in the middle of the street. "As you like it," he cooed. "I must admit that I have been looking forward to this."

He spun for a hook-kick.

Anna ducked and felt it when his foot passed over her. The man whirled around to face her with a menacing grin. He threw a punch.

Catching his wrist with one hand, Anna clamped the other onto Slade's lapel. With a quick twist of her body, she flipped him over her shoulder so that he landed on his ass in the middle of the road.

Once again, Slade became a blur, and when he resolidified, he was standing right in front of her. His hand lashed out to seize her throat, lifting Anna off the ground. He threw her backward with a surge of Bent Gravity.

Air whistled in her ears as she was hurled toward the sidewalk. Her back hit the pole of a street lamp, sending a jolt of pain through her, and then she landed on the curb, groaning as she fought her way through the agony.

Anna winced, sweat oozing from her pores, running over her face in fat droplets. "Come on," she whispered to herself. "Focus, focus!"

Slade was closing in on her at an almost leisurely pace. His cruel laughter was like knives in her ears. "You do remember how this went last time, don't you?" She did, and the reminder did her no good. "This time will be the last time, Lihua."

That name...

Slade turned his body for a fierce side-kick.

Anna slipped out of the way, and his foot hit the pole instead, putting dents in the metal. The man brought his leg down with a yelp of pain. Which gave her the second that she needed.

Anna kicked his knee, making him stumble. Jumping, she flung her elbow into the side of his head. That made Slade retreat as he struggled to maintain his balance. He spun to face her, backing up along the curb.

Anna moved in to press her attack.

She jabbed his chest with one fist then the other and finished with an upper-cut to the chin. His head snapped backward from the impact. The pain made Slade scurry away with a hand up to shield his face.

Anna leaped and twirled in the air, kicking out behind herself with enough force to crush a human skull. But she hit nothing. Nothing at all. When she landed with a grunt, Slade was right next to her.

He grabbed the back of her collar, lifting her off the ground. His other hand settled onto her stomach, and then he spun her around and around in circles. The next thing Anna knew, she was flying face-first toward the lamppost.

She braced herself, slamming both hands against the pole to slow herself down, but the impact still winded her. In the haze of pain and dizziness, she was barely even aware of someone coming up behind her.

A foot struck her back, flattening her against the pole.

Anna cried out and then fell to the ground, rolling across the sidewalk toward the front window of a bakery. "Not this time," she wheezed. "You're not going to get me this easily!"

She was back on her feet again in an instant.

Giggling maniacally, Slade drew a long, curved knife from his belt and tossed it up with a flourish. He caught it so that the tip was pointed downward and then moved in for the kill.

He slashed at Anna's belly.

Anna hopped backward with a squeak, barely evading the cut. On his next attempt, Slade tried to plunge that blade into her eye.

Leaning back, Anna caught his forearm with both hands, holding the knife an inch away from her face. She made him bend double and then kicked his stomach hard enough to drive the air from his lungs. Then she sent him head-first into the front wall of the bakery.

Drunkenly, he turned to face her.

Anna spun, lashing out with a devastating hook-kick, her foot wheeling around to strike his cheek. Blood sprayed from Slade's mouth as he collapsed against the wall. He was panting, gasping as he staggered forward.

Backing away from him with her fists up in a fighting stance, Anna took a moment too steel her nerves.

She leaped, turning belly-up in the air and catching Slade's neck between her shins. Allowing herself to fall over sideways, she brought him down with her. The hand that held his knife was pinned underneath him.

Clenching her teeth, Anna snarled. Her face was on fire, her hair drenched with sweat. "The voice of the Inzari," she mocked, "Beaten by a lowly Justice Keeper. You're pathetic!"

Something yanked her away from Slade, an unseen force that dragged her into the middle of the road. Somehow, despite exhaustion and pain that would have brought most other Keepers to their knees, the man was still able to call upon Bent Gravity.

She sat up.

Grecken Slade was already on his feet and marching toward her with the knife in hand. There was no smile on his face now. No, now it was all business. He was going to finish it.

Anna got up, drawing her own belt knife and holding it with the blade pointed downward. "All right then," she whispered. "Let's get this over with."

So far as Rajel could tell, Admiral Telixa Ethran had every intention of making good on her promise to let the Alosians contemplate her offer of mercy. It had been over five minutes since the holographic transmission ended, and so far, nothing else had come through the SlipGate.

Two of Captain Bosama's men had come to join them, and they now stood in the middle of the road with one of those portable cannons pointed at the SlipGate. Rajel had called for backup the instant hostilities ceased, and the few minutes since had been a long stretch of stomach-churning tension. It was no easy thing to bring one of those big guns down from the nearby rooftops. He had been terrified that the artillery would not arrive until after Ethran's deadline had passed.

One of the military men glanced toward him.

"Do it," Rajel said.

The cannon released a spear of hot plasma that sped down the street and struck the SlipGate. The impact was just at the edge of his spatial awareness, but Rajel could hear the hiss of smoke rising from scorched metal.

Another blast followed the first and then another. Finally, he heard something that was part hum, part crackle and felt the build-up of static in the air.

Cassi was down on one knee by the curb with her head turned toward the Gate. She flinched at the noise. "The grooves," she said. "They're flickering."

"I assume that's good."

Corovin lumbered up the street with the whir of mechanical joints, his visor rising to reveal a handsome face with a neat goatee. "I'm pretty sure it means that the Gate is out of commission."

Rajel used one finger to slide his sunglasses up his nose, pressing them flat against his face. "All right then," he rasped. "The rest of you go back to Captain Bosama. She may need you."

"What about you?" Keli asked.

"I'm going after Anna."

The distant artillery was silent now. Anna noticed that for the first time. The fighting had stopped. This little street in the centre of town – a road that stretched on for four blocks at most – was mostly untouched by the violence. Store-front windows were still intact. There were no scorch marks on the buildings. Aside from the dent that Slade had put in one of the lampposts, you would never have known that violence had taken place here.

The former head of the Justice Keepers was striding toward her with purpose in his eyes. He meant to kill her. Anna could tell that much. There would be no offers to join his cause, not today. No, for Slade, this was pest control. Squash the bug before it became a real nuisance.

He slashed at her face.

Anna ducked and felt the stirring of air as his fist passed over her. She cut his belly with her knife, leaving a tear in his shirt and a cut in his skin. When she popped up, Grecken Slade was snarling.

Anna tried to slit his throat.

His free hand came up to seize her wrist while the one that held his knife plunged the blade down toward her heart. Only a quick twist of her body saved her. The steel went into her left shoulder instead. Hot fire piercing her body. She couldn't think.

Stepping back, Slade drove his open palm into her chest. A surge of Bent Gravity sent her flying backward down the street. She skidded to a stop when her feet touched the ground, barely managing to stay upright.

She pulled the knife from her flesh.

Squeezing her eyes shut, Anna shrieked at the lance of pain that went through her. "You know, I'm really getting sick of these things!" There was blood soaking her shirt. Now, she would have to fight without her left arm.

Slade was coming toward her, his black hair flowing in the wind. "I killed you on your father's farm!" he screamed. "I killed you at York! I killed you outside Thriadan! Do you remember that, Lihua? Raymond? Mari?"

"You're insane."

"Am I?"

He stopped in the middle of the road, his lips parting in a grin that belonged on the face of a demon. "Think back, Anna," he said. "You know I'm right."

Anna searched within herself for some indication that what he claimed might be true. It seemed ridiculous. Maybe there was life after death, maybe not – she didn't really have firm opinions on that issue – but there was nothing, not one shred of evidence to suggest that reincarnation was a thing.

Only…

Jena had killed Slade a year ago, but here he was, standing right in front of her, just as pompous as ever. Maybe he was a clone, but if he was, the Overseers had duplicated more than just his body. Somehow, they had reconstructed his memories and personality. So did they rebuild his brain, molecule for molecule, or did they locate his soul and stuff it into a new body? There was just no way to tell. But Slade's presence here meant that it was worth asking the question.

If the latter – if there really was such a thing a soul – then wasn't it at least possible that she had lived before? That she might have encountered Slade in one of those lives? She looked for something to confirm it. She asked herself whether the names he spoke felt like they belonged to her, and what she found was…nothing. She was Anna. Just Anna and no one else. And she was okay with that.

Anna held his gaze for a long while, sweat matting her damp hair to her forehead. She narrowed her eyes. "I don't know anyone named Lihua," she said. "Or Raymond…Or Mari! Now, you ask yourself something."

"What's that, my dear?"

"The Overseers brought you back. Isn't it possible that they put these memories in your head? That there never was a Lihua? Think about it, Slade. Why are there so many religions? Because people are afraid to die. And to stave off that fear, they will do just about anything."

"You don't know what you're talking about."

Anna hissed at a flash of pain in her shoulder. "Don't I?" she asked. "Why do you serve your Inzari if not the fear of death and the promise of something better? They are using you, Slade."

He growled like a caged beast.

Ten seconds later, he was sprinting toward her, oblivious to the wound in his belly that leaked blood onto his fine white shirt. Oblivious or apathetic. She wasn't sure which one it was.

He drew back his arm and threw a punch.

Anna ducked, allowing his fist to pass over her. Stepping to the left, she rose and brought her knee up into his stomach.

Anna jumped and slammed her elbow into the back of Slade's skull. Stunned by the hit, he stumbled along the empty road and finally managed to stand up straight. When he turned around, his eyes were wild with fury.

Then he was coming at her again.

Growling, Anna planted a foot in his chest. She pushed him away, forcing him to retreat until he was practically tripping over a manhole cover. Even with the accelerated healing of a symbiont Bond, all those wounds added up.

Anna leaped.

She flipped through the air, thrusting her leg out and bringing her heel down on the top of his head. That final blow made Slade fall over, landing on his ass in the middle of the street.

He was stretched out on his back, vacant eyes staring up at the sky. Some incoherent nonsense came out of his mouth, and then he groaned. Anna didn't want to get too close, but she was fairly certain that he was dazed.

Quickly, she drew her gun and pointed it at him. She held it tightly in one hand, her finger curled around the trigger. The LEDs were dark. No stun rounds for Grecken Slade. Today, she would end it.

Only...

She had no compunctions about killing this man. She had ended Wesley Pennfield's life, and his crimes paled in comparison to those of Grecken Slade. But it occurred to her that killing Slade might not be tactically sound.

Jena had ended his miserable existence, or so everyone had thought, and yet here he was, weaving his sick little schemes. She couldn't say whether this Slade was the original brought back to life or merely a clone of his predecessor, but one question did occur to her. If he *was* just a clone, then why not create more? Why not two Slades or three or ten?

On the other hand, if the Overseers had managed to "capture Slade's soul" and stuff it into a new body, then multiple Slades would seem to be impossible. Presumably, each soul was unique. So, if she killed Slade today, might that be the same as just letting him go? What good would it do if the Overseers just reincarnated him into a new body and set him loose again?

If there was something unique about Slade, something that could not be duplicated, then perhaps the smartest move was to throw him into a cell and let him rot. Anna sighed. Carrying him all the way to-

Her multi-tool started squawking.

"Receive message."

Once again, the hologram of Telixa Ethran appeared. The admiral was standing with her hands on her hips, glowering into the camera. "It seems that you have rejected our offer," she said. "We cannot be held responsible for the casualties if you persist in fighting us."

And just like that, the hologram was gone.

Somewhere in the distance, Anna heard screams and the distinctive *clanking* of metal feet. She was pretty damn sure that staying here would *not* be a good idea.

Groaning, Slade touched his fingers to the side of his head. He was still in pain, but it was clear that he was already recovering from the damage she had inflicted. There was no way she could take him with her.

Anna pointed her gun at him and fired.

His body spasmed from one shot through the chest and then another. Then, with one final gasp, his head turned, and his eyes glazed over. Sure, maybe the Overseers would just bring him back again, but she wasn't going to leave him to run free.

When she turned around, she was suddenly face-to-face with an old woman whose leathery skin was marked by liver

spots. A woman with thin, silver hair. "It is no use, my child," she said. "You cannot destroy the one who slayed the White Serpent."

And then she was gone.

Anna stumbled backward, nearly tripping over the corpse. Gasping, she raised a hand to shield herself from something that was no longer there. "Bleakness take me," she whispered.

Those footsteps were coming closer.

She could do no good in her current condition. Going back to the barricade would be unwise; she would only be a liability. She felt like a coward for thinking it, but it was the simple truth. She needed medical attention.

Worst of all, she didn't dare risk calling to let the others know she was alive. If any of those drones picked up the signal, they would be on her in no time. There was only one thing to do. Cautiously, she slipped out of sight and made her way back to Keeper HQ.

Chapter 17

It had been non-stop commotion in the Prep Room from the very moment that the attack began. How long had that been now? Larani couldn't tell. Except for the occasional bathroom break, she had not left this room in at least twenty-two hours. She was beyond tired.

Her officers all manned various stations throughout the room, all bringing the latest reports from the various battles taking place throughout this city. The Ragnosians were closing in. She could feel it. "Status report," she said raggedly.

Agent Telrin twisted his chair around to face her with one hand on his ear-piece. "The Ragnosians have resumed attacks on all vectors," he said. "We estimate that they'll break through at least one barricade within half an hour."

"As expected," Larani said, nodding. "Can we get any more of our people out there to reinforce those barricades?"

"No, ma'am," Telrin replied. "HQ is currently on a skeleton crew. We've sent every last body that we can spare."

Dropping into a chair, Larani bent forward and pressed a fist against her forehead. She felt like she was going to pass out. "Send a message to Fleet Command," she said. "Advise them that we should try to get as many civilians off-world as possible."

"We don't have enough ships to provide escort," Agent Sokai said. "Anyone who tries to flee will be gunned down before they achieve orbit."

"Better that than staying here as a slave!" Larani snapped.

Her people all turned away, resuming their duties. She wished she could have the words back, but she made no attempt to apologize. If she was honest with herself, she had to admit that her outburst wasn't just hyperbole. She knew what she would choose if her options were death or servitude as a second-class citizen.

"Ma'am," Sokai shouted.

"What is it?"

"Long-range sensors are picking up ships coming our way at high warp," the young agent replied. "It's hard to tell at this distance, but I'd say there are at least a dozen. And they'll be here in less than an hour."

"Ragnosian reinforcements?"

Sokai turned around and her eyes were bright with hope. "No, ma'am, I don't think so," she breathed. "These ships are coming from Antauran Space."

Larani was on her feet again in an instant and striding across the room. She laid a hand on Sokai's shoulder and leaned in to look at her screen. "The Ragnosians must have seen them as well," she said. "How are they reacting?"

Frowning, Sokai shook her head. "No change that I can see," she reported. "They're continuing to press their attack. Maybe their sensors aren't as good as ours."

"We're about to find out," Larani said. "Forward this data to Captain Taborn. We might be able to talk our way out of this."

The SlipGate bubble came to a stop in a bland room with gray walls. Jack couldn't see much except for what seemed to be the blurry figure of a man operating the controls. Melissa was next to him, and she looked nervous.

The bubble popped.

His mouth stretched into a yawn that he covered with one hand. "Status report," he mumbled, striding across the room. "The last we heard, the city was about two inches shy of falling to the enemy."

The young man behind the console looked up to study him with gray eyes, then nodded once in solemn confirmation of Jack's worst fears. "That's right, sir," he replied. "The Ragnosians are attacking on multiple vectors."

Melissa came up behind with teeth bared, hissing like a cat. "Well, we have to get out there!" she insisted. "They need our help."

"You're not going anywhere, and neither am I."

"Jack!"

His skin was still burning, though not as badly as it had been an hour ago. It felt like a thousand fiery pinpricks from head to toe. Every now and then, he experienced a sudden wave of dizziness. Summer was at her limit. "I'm about ready to collapse," Jack snapped. "And so are you. We won't do anyone any good by getting ourselves killed."

The Gate technician – Jack didn't know his name – grunted his agreement with that assessment. "Director Tal wants to see you in the Prep Room, sir. I suspect you'll be sent to Medical soon after."

Blinking several times to moisten bleary eyes, Jack yawned again. "Ooh, did you hear that, Melissa?" he said. "The Prep Room! That could be fun. If you like rooms…and prepping."

Outside, he found a gray hallway that was just as bland as the SlipGate chamber. They were in the basement, which meant no windows, and worse yet, the ceiling lights flickered. Damage to the power grid. Things were not going well around here.

Melissa walked beside him with arms folded. Her face had that pinched expression that Harry got whenever he disapproved of something. "I still say we should be out there with the others."

"Melissa, you're in no condition to fight."

"How many others have been pushed to exhaustion?" she protested. "Why should we get any special treatment?"

Jack put himself in front of her, resting his hands on her shoulders. The anger in her dark eyes was... Well, at the moment, she could give Anna a run for her money. "I get it," he said. "You've got that brand new badge, and right now, you're feeling the weight of all that responsibility. Melissa, a Keeper who collapses after two steps is not going to save anyone's life."

She sniffed.

The remainder of their journey was silent, and when they finally arrived at the Prep Room, the doors slid apart to reveal a very frazzled Larani behind the round table. The Chief Director had one lock of hair out of place, which, for her, represented a very serious lapse in decorum. "How are we holding up?" she asked.

"The eastern barricade has fallen, ma'am," Agent Telrin shouted over the din. "We have Ragnosians in the inner city."

"Are they headed for the Hub?"

"No, ma'am," Telrin replied. "They seem to be coming here."

Jack fell back against the wall, groaning at the thought of having to fight again. He covered his face with one hand, massaging his tired eyes. "Well, kid, looks like you just got your wish."

Despite her earlier protests about lending their failing strength to the cause, Melissa did not look happy. No, she looked haunted. She did not want to go back out there; that much was plain.

At the sound of his voice, Larani spun around and watched him through narrowed eyes. "Not just yet, Agent Hunter," she said. "There are still a dozen Keepers inside this building who are in much better condition than you. I won't send my people out to die in a futile struggle."

Melissa was blushing and staring down at the floor. Jack was pretty sure he knew why. Hearing Larani echo his earlier sentiments would have killed any notions she had of dying in some noble last stand.

"If it comes to it," the chief director went on, "I will send those of us who have not yet seen combat to guard your backs while you get the wounded through the SlipGate."

"Ma'am," Agent Sokai broke in.

"Yes?"

"The approaching fleet has entered the solar system. They'll be here in less than five minutes."

Biting his lower lip, Jack looked up. "An approaching fleet?" he asked, eyebrows rising. "Friends?"

"We certainly hope so," Larani muttered.

It was impossible to get any kind of detailed scan of something moving faster than light. The best you could say was that something was coming your way, and you could only discern that much by the ripple it made in SlipSpace. It was entirely possible that these newcomers were here to support the Ragnosians, and then...Well, if you were going to die for a cause, it may as well be a lost cause. More romantic that way. He felt a pang of grief from Summer. She hated it when he got somber.

"Captain Taborn has rallied the last of our Phoenix-Class cruisers," Sokai reported. "They're moving to engage the Ragnosian fleet."

"How many?"

"Four in total, ma'am."

"And the Ragnosians."

Agent Sokai looked crestfallen when she checked her screens. She steeled herself a moment later and spoke in a calm, level voice. "There are still nine Ragnosian ships in orbit," she said. "Three more joined their fleet about two hours ago."

Larani took a chair, crossing one leg over the other, and gripped the arms until her knuckles whitened. "No doubt those were part of the group that intercepted and waylaid our reinforcements."

Reinforcements? It took him a moment to remember a report from Fleet Command saying that Palissa would be sending all the ships it could spare. The fact that those ships had never arrived did not bode well.

"Incoming fleet is dropping out of warp!" Sokai exclaimed, "Reading thirteen- No, make that *fourteen* Antauran capital ships. Message incoming on all channels."

"Let's hear it!"

The air shimmered, and then a hologram coalesced above the round table. It was the image of a tall man with dark skin and a ring of white hair around his otherwise bald head. "This is Colonel Tharian Delvon of the Antauran warship *Striganath*. Alios is under our protection. We advise you to withdraw immediately."

Another hologram appeared, resolving into the image of Telixa Ethran. Jack felt an immediate sense of anger at the sight of her, emotions that were amplified by Summer. His Nassai was quite protective of him.

"Your alliance with the Leyrians is new," Telixa said. "Why die for people that you called bitter enemies only one year ago? Ragnos has no interest in your territory. Remove yourselves from this conflict, and we will overlook this incident."

Jack was afraid that the colonel might accept her offer, but any chance of that went up in smoke when the man laughed in her face. "Take a look around you, lady," he said. "You are severely outnumbered. Your troops are exhausted and battle-worn. You pick this fight, and you *will* lose."

"We shall see."

Both holograms vanished.

"What's going on up there?" Larani shouted.

A sphere of darkness popped into existence above the table, growing until it was large enough for Jack to stand in. It took a moment for him to notice that it was dotted with little white flecks. Stars.

Then ships were rushing back and forth through the blackness. The Antauran vessels weren't as sleek as their Ragnosian counterparts. They were fatter, blockier, but still armed with enough firepower to pulverize a city.

One of those fatter ships unleashed a pair of bright, blue particle beams from its rounded nose, particle beams that struck a Ragnosian battlecruiser but failed to penetrate its shields. The battlecruiser responded with its own particle beams, and soon the whole thing was just a mess of bright colours.

The image changed.

A squad of Antauran fighters, each one shaped very much like a boomerang, flew low over the dorsal hull of a Ragnosian vessel. They all released streams of blue plasma from the tips of their wings, and some of those shots eventually went through the shields, damaging the emitters underneath.

Swarms of automated fighters were attacking the Antaurans. One ship was taking so many hits that its shields were constantly active, making it look more like a star than a man-made vehicle.

All it took was one to break through.

A hundred drones flew through the gap, and the Antauran dreadnought crumpled like a soda can in the fist of an angry teenager. Where was Telixa? It sickened him to realize it, but a part of him was hoping that she would die here. Or at least that she would be taken as a prisoner of war. Summer felt terrible sadness at that. There were times when Jack honestly wondered how the Nassai could love him when she was privy to his thoughts.

He approached the table with a grim expression, breathing slowly to remain calm. "Can you show me which ship the admiral was broadcasting from?"

Agent Sokai turned just enough to make eye-contact and then nodded once. She began tapping commands into her console.

Once again, the image flickered.

Jack saw a huge Ragnosian battlecruiser against the darkness of space, a behemoth that fired green particle beams at its fleeing enemies. Suddenly, one of those fat Antauran ships came into view and let loose a storm of plasma bolts.

They hammered the battlecruiser's starboard hull, sending chunks of debris flying off into space. And then, for reasons that he could not understand, Jack felt pity for the woman who had held him captive. Yes, on some level, he hated her. Yes, some ugly part of him wanted payback, but he realized now that he would find no satisfaction in Telixa's death. The last thirty-six hours had been a colossal waste of life. Too many dead on both sides. And that disgusted him.

Summer was proud of him; he could feel it like warm sunlight shining down. Jack had the distinct impression that if his Nassai could speak directly to him, she would be saying, "This is why I love you."

"The Ragnosian ships are leaving," Sokai exclaimed.

Jack fell into an empty chair, throwing his head back and letting out a long breath. "It's done," he whispered. "Thank God…"

Melissa came over to stand beside him with a smile on her face. She gave his shoulder a squeeze. "Thank *you*," she said. "I don't think I would have gotten through this without you."

"I'm afraid your celebrations are premature," Larani said. "We still have Ragnosian armies in our cities."

"Armies without support," Jack interjected.

"They don't know that yet."

The sound of footsteps distracted him, and Jack turned around to find his girlfriend striding into the room with her left arm in a sling. Her face lit up as soon as she saw him. "Maybe," she said. "It's time we told them."

Turning away from the charred SlipGate, Cassi watched as some of Bosama's men went back around the corner to join their fellows. Anna gone, Rajel gone. Ragnosians all over the place. Needless to say, she was *not* in a pleasant mood.

It had been almost an hour since Anna had taken off in pursuit of Slade, and so far, they had heard nothing. Either she was dead, or she was maintaining radio silence for some reason. Cassi had thought about calling to check in, but every time the idea popped into her head, she dismissed it. The city was crawling with enemies. Ragnosians troops had broken through some of the other barricades. If Anna was maintaining radio silence, there was a damn good reason why.

In all that time, no one had come through the SlipGate. Cassi was fairly certain that it was inoperable. Still, she had been keeping an eye on it just in case.

Keli leaned against a building with her arms folded, frowning at the soldiers' backs. "So, with our fearless leader off fighting Slade," she began. "Who's in charge?"

Corovin had his visor up, and he replied to that with a sly little smile. "That," he said, "is a very good question."

"I'm in charge," Cassi said without hesitation.

They both looked at her.

Were they expecting some sort of explanation? Someone had to provide order in the midst of all this chaos, and the Bleakness would take her before she trusted that job to an unstable telepath or a treacherous assassin. "Keli," she barked. "What do you sense from the Ragnosians."

The other woman shut her eyes and concentrated. "They're afraid," she said. "The mood has changed somehow."

Cassi's multi-tool beeped. "I suspect we're about to learn the answer."

With a quick swipe of her finger, she answered the call and found herself looking at a very dishevelled Larani Tal. "Agent Seyrus," the other woman said. "I'm glad to see that you're all right. A fleet of Antauran ships has come to our aid. The Ragnosians are fleeing the system."

"I'm glad to hear it, ma'am."

"How is your team?"

Cassi took a moment to inspect her people. Corovin and Keli were both watching her. "A little banged up, but otherwise fine," she replied. "Those of us who are still here, anyway. Operative Lenai left to pursue Grecken Slade. I don't know her condition."

"She made it back to Keeper HQ," Larani assured her. "She's wounded, but she will make a full recovery. The threat posed by Grecken Slade has been neutralized."

Cassi nodded. "Operative Aydrius is also-"

A flicker of motion in her spatial awareness made her look up, and she found Rajel jogging toward them. He was breathing hard, but so far as she could tell, he was just fine. "Scratch that," she said. "Rajel is here."

"Good," Larani said. "We're broadcasting messages to the Ragnosian commanders. We'll be playing them over loudspeakers in a moment. We hope that being cut off from their support ships will be enough to make them surrender."

"Your instructions, ma'am?"

Exhausted, Larani looked away from the camera and let out a breath. "Remain with Captain Bosama until you are certain that the danger has passed," she said. "Then return here for your next assignment."

"Yes, ma'am."

The call ended just in time for her to see Rajel approaching her with concern on his face. "I wasn't able to find Anna," he lamented. "But I did find Slade's corpse lying in the middle of Releth street. It was clear that there had been a struggle. One of them had used a grenade."

"Rajel-"

"There were a couple Ragnosian drones inspecting the body." he went on. "I dealt with them."

"Rajel," she broke in. "Anna's fine-"

Corovin shouldered his way in between them, turning his back on her and clapping a hand onto Rajel's shoulder. "We won, Justice Keeper!" he shouted. "Your people came and scared mine away."

Cassi stepped up beside him with her arms crossed. She gave the assassin a glare and then returned her attention to Rajel. "As I was saying, Anna was wounded and went back to HQ. We're to help Captain Bosama deal with any remaining troublemakers."

"An easy task," Corovin scoffed.

"But one that we should take seriously."

"And then," he said with a wink for Rajel. "Perhaps you would like to join me in a celebration."

For a second, Rajel looked confused, but he quickly recovered, eyebrows rising above the rims of his sunglasses. "I suppose that will depend on exactly what you had in mind."

Cassi left them to flirt. She was in no mood to listen to it. She liked Rajel, but she was done chasing men who set their sights on someone else. On the adjoining street, she found Bosama and her officers gathered around the barricade. Many of them were staying low for fear that some enterprising Ragnosian might take a cheap shot. Cassi couldn't say that she blamed them.

She dropped to a crouch next to the Captain, frowning as she took stock of the situation. "They haven't pressed their attack?"

Bosama shot a glance in her direction and then blinked in confusion. It seemed the woman wasn't expecting to see Cassi. "They haven't fired a shot in over ten minutes," she said. "I think they know-"

She was cut off by the sound of a deep, authoritative voice coming through the loudspeakers on either side of the road. Those had been installed as part of an emergency alert system that could be used to direct an evacuation. When you lived on the Fringe, the possibility of an attack was a daily reality. That fear should have died a quick death now that the Antaurans were their allies, but it seemed Ragnos was eager to start a war.

The words were Vanasku. Cassi couldn't understand any of them, but she was fairly certain that she knew the gist of the message. "Your support ships are gone. Surrender or die." Well…essentially that but phrased more tactfully.

Several gray-clad Ragnosians stepped into the open from an adjoining street two blocks away. Each one was unarmed, and they all had their hands in the air. Behind them, the broken remains of a hover tank littered the ground.

"Well," Cassi whispered. "That went better than expected."

Chapter 18

Two hours later, Anna sat on a bed in the medical centre. She looked almost demure with her knees together and her eyes downcast. Not an adjective that Jack would ever have used to describe her, but there it was.

He sat in a chair with his elbow on the armrest, half his face covered by the palm of his hand. "Oh, God," he groaned. "I could sleep for a week."

"Me too."

"What happened?"

The question made Anna wince as if recalling the events brought a new surge of pain. "An encounter with Slade," she answered. Jack was immediately on edge. Hearing that name sent adrenaline flying through his system. "He decided to capitalize on all the chaos. He was going for the Prime Council."

"And he stabbed you?"

Gingerly, Anna touched her left shoulder. Even that fleeting contact made her hiss. "I'm getting sick of knives," she said. "Frankly, the only foreign object I want penetrating my body is you."

Several nurses smirked at her comment.

Jack was frozen in place with his mouth hanging open, his face burning with the heat of a thousand suns. "Really?" he stammered. "In front of everybody?"

"Eh... You knew I had a big mouth when you married me."

"I haven't married you yet."

"Aha!" Anna snapped her fingers. "'Yet!'"

Slouching to the point where he was almost falling out of his chair, Jack let his head loll. "I've never been a praying man," he muttered. "But I'm gonna have to start if I want to get through this with my sanity intact."

Anna hopped off the bed, standing over him with an impish grin. She bent forward, took his face in both hands and kissed him softly on the lips. "I'll let you in on a secret," she whispered. "I just like to watch you squirm."

"Well, I hope I gave a good performance."

"Always."

She sat in his lap as if no one was watching, slipped an arm around the back of his neck and snuggled up. "So, I hear you guys had quite an adventure," she murmured. "Is Melissa holding up okay?"

"I think so," he said. "You should have seen her out there, An. She was incredible."

"She had a good teacher."

Jack looked up to hold her gaze for a very long while and then allowed himself the barest hint of a smile. "Well, I had a good teacher too," he replied. "In fact, I had the best teacher a guy could ask for."

"Aww."

"And I hate to ruin this wonderful moment we're having," he said. "But Slade? Did you bring him in?"

With a heavy sigh, Anna stood up, turned her back on him and went back to the bed. She waited just long enough for Jack to worry. "I killed him," she said. "Put a bullet right through his chest. Two, actually."

Standing up was difficult, but Jack forced his limbs to move. He approached her from behind, wrapped his arms around her tummy and held her close. "I'm so sorry," he whispered, "That can't have been easy for you."

"You're not disappointed in me?"

"Never," he insisted. "Maybe, with any luck, this time, it'll stick."

"I don't think so...Right after I put him down, this old woman appeared to me and said I would never be able to destroy him. And something about a white snake?"

"Well, the ladies are always fawning over David Coverdale."

Anna spun around in his arms, sniffling as she nuzzled his chest. "Please tell me I didn't do all that for nothing." She trembled, and Jack held her for a little while, running fingers through her hair.

"I wish I could," he said at last. "But Isara told me the Overseers can bring people back as long as one of them is present at the moment of death, and it looks like one was there when you killed Slade."

"But how?" Anna protested. "I would have felt it with spatial awareness, wouldn't I? And if an Overseer was there, why didn't it intervene?"

"Maybe they have limitations we don't know about."

"Maybe...So, what do we do now?"

Smoothing a lock of hair off her cheek, Jack bent down to kiss her forehead. "Now, we recover," he said. "And then I suspect Larani has some work for us."

A meal, a shower and a nap were the only forms of relief Melissa had when all of the chaos died down. And even after four hours of deep, dreamless sleep, she still felt exhausted. Jack had been right. If she had gone out to fight again, she would have gotten herself killed. Running on adrenaline, she hadn't noticed at the time.

Now, she was sitting on a desk in an empty office, watching the two holograms that stood side by side in the middle of the room. Larani had been kind enough to give her a few minutes of comm time, and she had used it to call her family back home.

A transparent Claire stood before her with arms folded. "So, you fought in a war…" she said. "Like a real-life war."

Gripping the edge of the desk tightly, Melissa hunched over and let out a breath. "More like a battle," she said. "But yes… A real-life battle with guns and bombs. Let me guess; you think that's the coolest thing ever."

"I'm not an idiot, Melissa," Claire snapped.

The holographic Della glanced over her shoulder to frown at her youngest daughter. "We just heard the news last night," she said. "CBC won't shut up about it, and CNN is wondering if Earth might be invaded in the near future."

"Unlikely," Melissa muttered.

"Are you sure you don't want to come home, sweetie?"

She looked up to blink at her mother. "I can't come home, Mom," she said. "I'm not a cadet anymore. I have responsibilities."

Della's mouth twisted with obvious disapproval, but she said nothing. After years of dealing with Harry, Melissa half expected her to press the point, but her mother seemed to understand. "You should call your father," Della suggested. "If Earth has heard about what's happening out there, then Leyria *definitely* has."

"Yeah…"

That only made her more uneasy. Harry was a problem that she had filed away in the back of her mind. There had to be some way to get him out of his creepy deal with the Overseers. "How are you adjusting to life on Earth?" Melissa asked her sister.

Claire shrugged and let out a sigh of frustration. "School doesn't start for another month," she said. "I tried hanging out with some of my old friends, but they're afraid of me now."

"They're not afraid," Della insisted.

"Mom," Claire said. "I'm a telepath. Trust me when I tell you they're afraid."

"Just give them some time," Melissa said. "They-"

She was cut off by a burst of static and an unfamiliar voice coming through her multi-tool's speaker. "Agent Carlson," it said. "I just wanted to warn you that your time is up in two minutes."

Right now, her call was being sent through the Aliosian telecommunications network, to a SlipGate that forwarded it to Earth via a microscopic SlipSpace wormhole. Pretty much every Gate that they could spare was being used to let some-one make an off-world call. Some soldier who needed to tell his family that he was all right. Some clerk who had to requisition materials to rebuild damaged space stations and shuttles. She was lucky to get five minutes with her family.

Melissa stood up with a grunt, nodding to her mother. "You might have better luck getting through to Dad," she said. "Let him know I'm okay. And would you mind calling Jack's mother? I'm sure he'll do so when he gets the chance, but she must be worried sick about him."

"Of course," Della said. "Call again as soon as you can."

"I will."

Claire rushed forward to throw her ghostly arms around Melissa's waist. Melissa couldn't feel anything, but the gesture warmed her heart nonetheless. "I love you, Sis," Claire whispered. "Be safe."

"Love you too," Melissa said. "And right back at you."

And just like that, they were gone.

Wedge-shaped attack drones flew between the skyscrapers, casting shadows over the road as they closed in on their targets. One by one, they dove, striking the ground and exploding on impact, sending bodies into the air.

Anna woke up with a gasp.

She sat up with a hand over her chest, her mouth a gaping hole as she sucked air into her lungs. Her tank-top was drenched with sweat and her hair was a mess. Starlight came through the window behind the desk.

They had set up a small cot for her and Jack in a top-floor office. The hotel they had been staying at before the attack wasn't an option. The power was out in that part of the city. Despite the Ragnosians' best efforts to preserve the infrastructure, there was some damage to vital systems.

"Hey, hey," Jack whispered.

He sat up behind her, his arms encircling her. Sobbing, she let herself fall against him, and her tears left a wet spot on his t-shirt. "It's all right," he whispered. "I'm right here. I'm right here."

Anna forced her eyes shut, but the tears still flowed freely. She sniffled and nuzzled his chest. "I couldn't save them!" she whimpered. "I tried, but there were so many! They just fell all around me!"

Gently, he ran fingers through her hair. "I know," he murmured. "It's not your fault, Anna. *No one* could have saved them."

"I know, but…"

Together, they laid back down on the mattress, facing each other, each with an arm wrapped around the other. For a very long time, Anna just cried. All of those people…She had only known them for a few hours! She hadn't even learned their names! Why didn't she learn their names?

She couldn't say how long it took for sleep to find her. For a very long time, she just trembled while Jack held her close and whispered that he loved her and that it wasn't her fault. Seth was whispering the same thing in his own way.

When she finally did nod off, she was exhausted. And the worst part was knowing that all that grief would be waiting for her when she woke up.

At an hour past noon – which was 07:00 by the Leyrian clock; the date changed at dawn every morning – this little bar was almost empty. Blinds on rectangular windows were pulled up to admit the gray daylight of a winter afternoon, but that did very little to ease the sense of gloom.

Wooden tables were spaced out on the tiled floor, and there were flags on the dark-green walls celebrating Leyrian sports teams. It felt almost like the kind of sports bar you might find back home.

Harry sat at the counter with a mug of beer, watching the suds rise. It had been over thirty-six hours since the first reports came in from Alios, and his stomach was in knots. He had promised to let Melissa live her life, to stop trying to protect her. But that promise didn't make it any easier to let go. There was nothing he could do, of course. He couldn't break his promise even if he wanted to, but he could worry.

Behind the counter, a tall man with a dark beard and buzzed hair was transfixed by the images on the TV. Well, it was actually a screen of SmartGlass on the wall opposite the bar, but for all intents and purposes, it was a TV.

"Could you turn up the volume?" Harry muttered.

"Volume!" the man said gruffly.

"And the latest reports from Alios say that the Ragnosian fleet has been driven off by the sudden arrival of Antauran ships." The news anchor's voice possessed that quality they all seemed to get after a few years on the job. Bubbly and frank at the same time. He hated it. "However, casualty reports indicate that Leyrian forces suffered heavy losses. So far, over five thousand fleet and infantry officers have been confirmed dead. We've also lost nearly one hundred Justice Keepers."

Harry lifted his glass, shuddering as tears streamed down his cheeks, and downed half of it on one long gulp. "Damn it…" His mug made a *thud* when he set it back down on the counter.

The door jingled as someone came in, and he looked up to find Sora rushing toward him in a panic. "I came as soon as I could," she said, taking the seat next to him. "Harry, I don't even know where to begin."

"I'm glad you're here." He didn't sound glad; he sounded nonchalant, but he decided that it wasn't his job to perform the social niceties right now.

"I'm sure she's all right."

"That makes one of us."

He turned around to find footage of the battle above Alios on the screen. Leyrian ships spitting particle beams from their pointed noses, plasma bolts streaking back and forth. Had Melissa been on one of those ships? It seemed unlikely. Justice Keepers were more useful on the ground. The planet had nearly fallen.

Sora took his hand. His left hand.

He yanked it away with a hiss, and she wilted as if he had just called her the ugliest woman he had ever seen. Harry felt an instant sense of remourse. He was fairly sure that he could control the N'Jal, but he didn't want to risk it coming into direct contact with Sora. Not after...

Harry hated the thought of hurting her feelings. "It's not you," he promised. "I hurt my hand earlier."

"Oh."

They switched positions so that Sora could hold his right hand instead, and that seemed to placate her. "I've been worried about you," she murmured. "When we talked last night, you seemed so..."

Pursing his lips, Harry felt his eyebrows rising. "Distraught?" he offered. "Well, I'll get by, I suppose."

"I want you to do more than get by."

He looked at her and found her watching him with such concern in those big, dark eyes. "I want you to be happy, Harry," she said. "Ever since you got back from Antaur, there's been this cloud of doom around you."

"I just…It's been a stressful time for me."

"Are you going to tell me what happened to Claire?"

Lifting his mug to his lips, Harry took a slow sip of his drink. "Nothing happened," he assured her. "Claire's mother wants to spend more time with her and living here on Leyria has been hard on her."

He could see it in the way she looked at him; Sora wasn't convinced. But then why would she be? She had probably heard her fair share of dogs eating homework stories, or whatever the Leyrian equivalent was. She could spot a lie when she saw one.

He didn't relish the thought of telling her what a shitty father he was, but that wasn't what held him back. Sooner or later, she would find out about his little congregation. Maybe she already knew. But he didn't want the Overseers getting anywhere near her, and telling her about Claire would make that more likely.

"Is there anything I can do?" Sora asked.

Harry forced himself to smile even though he really didn't feel like it. "How about dinner tonight?" he offered. "My place? Around 13:00?"

She leaned in close to kiss his cheek and then pulled away with a smile that almost made him forget all his troubles. "It would be my pleasure."

When Anna woke up, Jack was still sound asleep with his arm wrapped around her. His handsome face looked so peaceful in the morning sunlight. She wanted nothing more than to kiss his forehead, but she resisted that urge. Jack needed his rest. She didn't want to wake him.

Five minutes later, she was standing by the window in gray track pants and a black tank-top, gazing out upon the city.

The glittering skyscrapers seemed to have survived the battle without much damage. She could still see gardens on some rooftops and windows that reflected the sunlight. She noticed the odd scorch mark here and there but nothing serious. Although things might look very different on street level.

A soft knock at the door got her attention.

In her mind, she saw it open just enough for Larani to poke her misty head through the gap. "Are you awake?" the other woman whispered.

Padding across the room on bare feet, Anna ran to her superior officer. She brushed a strand of hair out of her face. "I'm up," she whispered. "But Jack's still out cold. What can I do for you?"

Larani motioned her to step into the hallway.

When she did, she found it a little gloomier than she had expected. The lights were out, and the only source of illumination came from nearby windows. The building had at least two emergency generators; so, even if the city grid went down…

"To help people sleep," Larani murmured as if sensing her thoughts. She gestured to the glass doors in front of every office. "Not very good for keeping light out."

Anna nodded.

Larani might have spent the night on a cot or a couch in the lounge or curled up on the floor of the Prep Room, for that matter, but you would never know it to look at her. The chief director was groomed to perfection. Her black hair was done up with a clip. Her clothes, while somewhat plain, were neat and tidy. "Antauran troops are patrolling the city," she said. "They're using telepaths to track down those Ragnosians who have refused to surrender."

"You want us to join them?"

"Eventually," Larani said. "I've sent a few of our people who weren't on the front lines to back them up. But many of you need rest."

Crossing her arms, Anna leaned her shoulder against the wall. "I've recovered, for the most part," she said. "I can go."

In response, Larani poked her left shoulder, and she jumped back with a hiss. "So, you've recovered, have you?" Anna stifled the flash of anger she felt. The other woman had a point. "Don't push yourself too hard, Operative Lenai."

"Point taken," Anna grumbled. "So, what's next."

"I got a call from the Prime Council."

Blinking several times, Anna took a moment to process that. She shook her head slowly. "I'd almost forgotten the whole reason for this trip," she muttered. "I'm guessing she wants to go through with the debates?"

"Good guess."

Anna replied with a shrug of her shoulders. "Not much of a guess, actually," she said. "It's what I would do in her place."

Larani obviously disapproved, but she nodded just the same. "The Prime Council feels that the Fringe Worlds and Alios, in particular, need her support more than ever," she said. "So, despite the objections of her staff, several high-ranking military officials and myself, she has chosen to remain here to conclude her campaign."

"I take it you want Keepers guarding her at all times."

"For the moment, the Prime Council is safe inside a hidden bunker," Larani said. "We needed every Keeper we had to defend against this invasion. But if Sarona Vason insists on making public appearances, then I want the people who have the most experience in dealing with Grecken Slade to protect her. And that means your team."

Jack stepped into the doorway with one hand on the frame. "Sounds good to me," he said. "I'll take the first shift."

Chapter 19

Jack had no idea where the Prime Council's bunker was located. He had to take a SlipGate to coordinates he wasn't allowed to see, and when he arrived, he found himself in an underground complex without windows. Theoretically, this could be anywhere on the planet.

It looked kind of like Princess Leia's ship in the first five minutes of Star Wars; everything was white with doors that slid open. A man in a black military uniform led him through a series of twists and turns to a door that looked just like all the others.

When it opened, Sarona Vason was on the other side. She looked him up and down, frowned and then stepped back to let him enter. "Special Agent Hunter. I take it you are my guard for the day."

Shutting his eyes, Jack nodded to her. "Yes, ma'am," he answered. "For the next six hours, anyway."

Her quarters were fairly plain, all things considered. The sitting room had a round, glass table and something that resembled a kitchenette. There were also big, comfortable chairs.

Sarona went to the table and poured tea from a kettle into one of several cups with a floral pattern around the rim. "Larani says you have a head for politics," she began. "I must admit I found your tweaking Dusep quite amusing."

"Well, the best way to deal with an inflated ego is to point and laugh."

"Indeed."

Seating herself in one of the large chairs, Sarona crossed one leg over the other and watched him with a cup and saucer in hand. "Larani does not approve of my decision to remain on this planet and conduct the debates as planned. What do you think?"

Jack paced across the room with his arms folded, sighing softly. "Larani is one of the best Keepers I've ever worked with," he said. "But on this issue, she's wrong. After what this world just went through, you need to be here."

"Why is that?"

He gestured to a chair, waiting for permission to sit, and then Sarona smiled. "By all means, Agent Hunter," she said. "If you're going to be here all day, you may as well get comfortable."

"Do me a favour," he said. "Call me Jack."

The woman's eyebrows went up, but she hid a smile behind her cup. "Very well, Jack," she said. "My question?"

He sat down across from her with hands on his thighs, staring at the floor as he formulated an answer. "Well, the reason you need to stay is that the people need you," he began. "But I'm guessing that what you want to hear is that leaving would open you to all sorts of attacks from Dusep. He'd call you dishonest, irresponsible, cowardly…"

"My, you *do* have a cynical view of politicians."

"Ma'am?"

"Call me Sarona." She watched him like a hawk. "Everything about you suggests a dislike for authority figures, a trait that is well-documented in your service record, which I have read cover to cover. Cal Breslan. Cara Sinthel…Nice job, by the way. You *do* have a nose for sniffing out traitors."

"Thanks."

"But your answer to my question assumes that my decision to remain here was based on self-serving motives. Is it so hard to believe that I would stay because I care about the people of Alios?"

Blushing at the thought that he might have been rude, Jack closed his eyes and took a deep breath. "I meant no offense," he said. "Back home, politicians rarely do anything for altruistic reasons."

"And this extends to your police? Your military?"

"It's much the same," he answered. "When I was seventeen, two years before we made contact with your people, I went to Winnipeg's Pride parade with a friend from my high school. If you don't know, that's an event to celebrate homosexual relationships and a broad spectrum of gender identities."

"Ah."

"While we were there," Jack went on. "protesters from a militant religious group showed up with signs that said some truly repulsive things. I was maybe fifty feet away when one of those protesters approached a young gay man and began whacking him over the head with his sign. Not hard enough to wound. Just enough to irritate."

Reliving the story made him angry. He remembered trying to push his way through the crowd to help the young man. However, by the time he got close enough, it was too late. "So," Jack said. "The young man did what anybody else would do. He pushed the sign away. Didn't touch the protester at all. He just pushed the sign out of his face."

Sarona was frozen with her cup raised halfway to her lips. Jack could tell that she was hanging on his every word. "What happened?"

"The cops arrested the young man," Jack growled. "They said that touching the sign was an act of violence. Several people got angry and said that they should arrest the protester as well, but – wonder of wonders – the cops just *happened* to be looking the other way when he instigated the whole thing, or so they claim."

The Prime Council was silent for a moment. Finally, she looked up to meet his gaze. "Several dozen eye-witness accounts weren't enough for them?"

Jack answered that with a sad smile. "You don't get it, Sarona," he said, shaking his head. "The cops didn't see it because they didn't *want* to see it. Because the cops protect the powerful, not the innocent. And now…I'm one of them."

"Is that how you see the Justice Keepers?"

He stood up with a sigh, turning his back on her and shuffling over to the table. Even without spatial awareness, he would have felt her eyes on him. Carefully, he poured himself a cup of tea.

Slurping as he took a sip, Jack allowed himself a moment to savour it. The stuff was pretty good. Kind of a minty taste. "When I first Bonded Summer," he said, "when your people first came to Earth, I thought we were gonna clean house. Investigate all the dirty cops. Hold them accountable."

"But that didn't happen?"

"No," he muttered. "Instead, your government became obsessed with assuring the many disparate governments of my planet that you wouldn't impose Leyrian values on us. Every time I tried to make them revise that policy, it didn't go so well for me."

Returning to his chair, Jack frowned as something else occurred to him. "You want to know the worst part?" he asked. "The thing that makes me wonder if any of this makes any difference?"

"What's that?"

He scowled and shook his head. "Larani has been grooming me," he said. "Taking me to watch Dusep's press conferences. But that's all we did was watch. I'm starting to think that 'a head for politics' means a willingness to do nothing in the face of injustice."

The Prime Council looked as if she didn't quite know what to make of all this. "So, what would you do differently?"

Tossing his head back, Jack felt his eyebrows climbing. "Well, that is the question, isn't it?" he grumbled. "If you're thinking I'd resort to violence, of course not. But I'd do what I've already done. I'd speak out against him."

"And be censured for it?"

"It would be worth it."

Setting her cup and saucer down in her lap, Sarona regarded him in silence. It must have gone on for at least thirty seconds. Long enough to make him *very* uncomfortable. "You do realize," she said at last. "That repeated defiance of a court order could cost you your badge."

"What's the point of having the badge if the simple act of denouncing a bigot is off-limits? And now you see where I'm coming from; the rules protect powerful men like Dusep. They don't protect the immigrants and refugees he preys on."

He expected that to unsettle her or to offend her. He was prepared to hear that she would be sending a report to Larani detailing his unsatisfactory conduct. Jack Hunter was a screw-up. Pissing off his social betters was second nature to him. The one thing he did not expect from her was a fond smile and a chuckle. "It may displease you to hear this, Agent Hunter," she began, "but you *are* a Justice Keeper. To your very core."

This little side street lined with two and three-story buildings was quiet. Overhead, the morning sun shone down from a clear blue sky, and the tall elm and ash trees on each sidewalk seemed to drink in the light. It was peaceful, almost idyllic. You would never guess that twenty-four hours ago, this city had been a war zone.

Cassi moved cautiously, peering this way and that. "I doubt they're still here," she muttered. "If they were smart, they would have fled the city in the night. We should have shuttles scanning the nearby fields and forests."

Nearly a dozen men and women in uniforms camouflaged to match the buildings crept along with assault rifles at the ready. Their leader, Captain Saransin, paused to give her a flat stare.

The man was handsome enough: tall with chocolate-brown skin and hard eyes. "They're fighting a guerrilla war now, Agent Seyrus," he said. "If they're smart, they'll go to ground and try to damage the infrastructure."

She sighed.

Rajel was next to her, moving down the street with his pistol in both hands. As usual, he had that look of concentration, the one that said he was listening intently and that he wished everyone else would bloody-well shut up. Anna had wanted to come on this patrol, but everyone else – including the Carlson girl – had vetoed that idea. The fool woman was recovering from a stab wound!

Cassi had used her Bending abilities sparingly yesterday, and it was much the same for Rajel. They were the obvious choices for this assignment. Which annoyed her to no end. Rajel Aydrius was the last person she wanted to talk to right now.

He seemed to sense her displeasure, smirking as he came closer so that he could speak without raising his voice. "Is there some reason you keep glaring at me?"

"I'm not glaring at you."

"I beg to differ," he said. "I-"

She fixed him with a stare that would freeze his blood cold. The idiot took a step backward as if he feared that she might hit him. And if she was honest, she had to admit that the thought had crossed her mind. "Trust me," she growled. "When I glare at you, you'll know it."

A flush painted his face red, but he said nothing. Instead, he returned his focus to the task at hand. Good. Now was not the time to hash out their issues.

Every time they passed an alley, Cassi scanned it with her eyes and with spatial awareness. And every single time, she found it empty. There was no one out here. She was quite sure that the Ragnosians had left.

"I'm just saying," Rajel began. "It seems like-"

"Are you incapable of doing your job?" Now, it was her face that burned. "How is it that you outrank me when you can't even pay attention during a routine patrol? You do realize that we're looking for people who might start shooting at us!"

Creeping up the street with her gun in hand, its muzzle pointed downward, Cassi shook her head. "Idiot man," she muttered to herself, not caring if he heard. "Get your damn head in the game."

Up ahead, one of the soldiers came to an abrupt halt and signaled the rest of them to stay back. "One of the reconn drones is sending a warning," he said. "There's motion nearby."

Cassi focused on her spatial awareness, but she sensed nothing but the buildings on either side of the street. Whatever it was might be too far off for her Nassai to pick it up, but she could-

A flicker of movement on her left.

She spun to face the curb, thrusting a hand out to craft a Bending that made the air shimmer. A bullet appeared inside the patch of warped space-time, curving upward and speeding off into the sky.

Cassi threw herself into a dive, the Bending vanishing.

She somersaulted over the pavement and came up on one knee, pointing her gun at her attacker. One quick, clean shot. Her first round hit the leg of a man in a gray uniform, sending a jolt of electricity through him.

He went down to expose the next man behind him, but that fellow took a shot to the arm before he could aim his rifle. Flailing, he fell to the ground on top of his companion.

There were at least twenty hostiles coming out of alleys and around the corner from neighbouring streets. In seconds, they had the Leyrian platoon surrounded, and then, it was pure pandemonium.

Two of the gray-clad men pulled smoke grenades from their belts and tossed them into the crowd. The next thing Cassi knew, she was surrounded by a thick, gray fog that made her eyes water.

Motion ahead.

She stepped aside just before a bullet grazed her left arm and brought a shout of pain to her lips. The Ragnosians were hazy figures that fired into the crowd, but she could sense everyone as easily as she could on a clear, spring afternoon.

Cassi ran for one, fell upon her knees and slid underneath the bullets that he fired, pulled by Bent Gravity. Aiming her weapon, she squeezed the trigger, and down he went.

She was on her feet again in an instant and running toward the ring of men that had surrounded them. One guy must have heard her approaching footsteps because he swung his rifle around to aim for her chest.

Cassi spun for a hook-kick, her shoe striking the rifle and knocking it askew just before it went off. The soldier stumbled, trying to regain his balance. Whirling around to face him, she fired a shot into his leg.

He fell.

The one next to him reacted.

With a quick pivot, Cassi fired again and watched the bullet bounce off his chin. The jolt it delivered made the poor fellow drop his weapon and collapse, landing next to his comrade.

Motion behind her.

Cassi dropped to a crouch just before several rounds went through the space where her head had been. Thrusting her gun out behind herself, she pulled the trigger several times. The shadow in her mind staggered as she pelted it with ammo.

She ejected the empty clip from her weapon, grabbed another and slammed it into place within seconds. Then she was standing up, turning on the spot and searching for her next target. The smoke made it hard to distinguish friend from foe. Without any visible markings, one man in tactical armour looked very much like another. But the Ragnosians seemed to be wearing bulkier vests.

She caught a glimpse of Rajel leaping over a crowd of men to land behind them and hit them with stun rounds. One by one, they all passed out.

One of those silhouettes ran for an alley.

Snarling with teeth bared, Cassi took off after him, Her feet pounded the pavement, and she jumped onto the sidewalk. She slipped into the gap between two buildings but froze there. The alley was empty.

Cassi narrowed her eyes. "No," she whispered, striding forward. "It's not that easy. It's *never* that easy."

She had seen someone duck into this alley. She hadn't imagined it. But where could they have gone? The alley ended in a high chain-link fence that separated the buildings on this street from those on the next street over. But if one of the Ragnosian soldiers had gone that way, she would have seen it. She-

A sudden noise made her jump. It sounded like the scuff of footsteps. Someone was moving about in the narrow gap between the fence and the building on her left. Carefully, she moved through the alley.

Setting her jaw with determination, Cassi shook her head. "It's not gonna work," she whispered. "You're not gonna get away that-"

She gasped as she went around the corner.

Chapter 20

"The Ladarian Centre will be fine," Dusep intoned.

He was sitting in a conference room with hands clasped in his lap, a smug smile on his face as he looked out the window. "In fact," he added. "I think it will make a splendid venue for the debate."

Standing by the window with her back turned, Sarona Vason nodded. "Fine," she muttered. "Then we are in agreement."

Larani had been watching both of them as they hammered out the details of their final appearance before the election. Politicians back on Leyria were insisting that the Prime Council return home and complete her reelection campaign there. The Fringe was no longer a safe place, or so they insisted.

Larani herself had voiced similar objections, but the Prime Council had waved them away. She wouldn't say that she and Sarona Vason were close, but she knew the other woman well enough to know that she would disregard prudence in the service of her people. It was frustrating. Her Nassai echoed those sentiments.

The view through the window was a gloomy afternoon, where windows in nearby buildings were ominously dark. There were still sections of the city without power. The engineers were working as hard as they could.

Larani was hunched over the table and tapping their finalized instructions into a SmartGlass tablet. "The Ladarian Centre," she said with a nod. "I will have a security detail of three Keeper teams in addition to your own people."

"Now *that*," Dusep interjected, "is something I *would* like to discuss."

Larani exhaled.

He swiveled around to face her with a wolfish grin. "I don't trust Justice Keepers," he said. "I don't want your people guarding me."

Pressing her lips together, Larani did her best to stuff her irritation down into the pit of her stomach. "Be that as it may," she said coolly, "we have good reason to believe that Grecken Slade will make an attempt on the Prime Council's life."

Dusep threw his head back and rolled his eyes. "So, I'm supposed to rely on Justice Keepers to protect me from another Justice Keeper." He chuckled. "Can you see why I'm having a hard time trusting you?"

"The point is moot," Sarona said without turning away from the window. "My security detail has approved the presence of Larani and her team. And as I am the actual Prime Council, my people outrank your people."

"For now."

Larani cast a glance toward the one person in this meeting who, surprisingly, had not said very much. Anna sat at the head of the table with her arms crossed, eyeing Dusep like a cat who was just waiting for a rival to set foot on his territory. It was clear that the young woman had no love for politics. You could see it in the way that she glared at both candidates. To Anna, this was all pointless squabbling. She wanted to know what would be expected of her people, and then she wanted the meeting to promptly end.

"While we're on the subject," Dusep went on. "I was under the impression that you have Grecken Slade's corpse in your morgue."

Closing her eyes, Larani drew in a deep breath. "We have discovered," she began, "that the Overseers have the capacity to...resurrect Slade."

Dusep laughed, but his amusement died when he realized that no one else shared it. "I remember Agent Hunter making noises to that effect," he said. "I assumed that it was the backward superstition of a man from a primitive society."

Anna reclined in her chair, frowning at the man. "That's not surprising," she said. "Bigots always assume that foreigners are stupid, and it usually comes back to bite them in the ass."

Rising from his seat, Dusep gestured toward Sarona. "You see?" he said. "No sense of decorum! No respect! I'm supposed to trust my safety to her?"

Anna showed him a cheeky grin.

Once again, Larani had to stifle her irritation. Whatever satisfaction she might have felt at Anna zinging this man withered when Dusep did what he always did, turning the situation to his own political advantage.

"Save your speeches, Jeral," Sarona muttered. "There are no cameras here."

Dusep opened his mouth to say more but quickly shut it again. "We're in agreement then," he grumbled. "Two days from now, at the Ladarian Centre. And then, our people can decide what future they want."

When the meeting finally ended, and Dusep stormed out of the room, Anna took a moment to let the anger drain out of her. She truly loathed that man. And it was a unique kind of loathing. As much as she despised Slade, she had to admit some small amount of grudging respect for him. If nothing else, he was a worthy adversary. But Dusep...Dusep was nothing more than a petulant child who rose to prominence by appealing to xenophobia and tribalism. It sickened her to realize that her planet was a place where such tactics worked.

With a sigh, she went out into the hallway.

Jack was waiting there with his arms folded, and he smiled when he saw her. "Got the details sorted out?" he asked. "Have they settled on a venue and all that?"

Anna stepped forward, closing her eyes and breathing slowly. "Yup," she said with a curt nod. "Our team will be one of three Keeper units assigned to work security."

"Sounds fun."

"You've been guarding her for almost six hours now," Anna said. "Maybe it's time we switched."

Jack squinted as he peered through the conference room door. "Nah, it's fine," he said, shaking his head. "I can stay with her the rest of the day."

"I'm sure you can," Anna countered. "But I might have a better use for your talents. We've got Corovin in a holding cell, and I'd really like to find out why he came here. Feel up to doing a little detective work-"

"Sure, if you-"

Jack cut off when Anna's multi-tool started buzzing and beeping. A quick swipe of her finger answered the call, and then a light-blue sound-wave appeared on the screen, pulsing whenever the caller spoke. "Anna," Rajel said. "We've got a problem. A squad of Ragnosians ambushed us."

"Is everyone all right?"

"Yeah, we're fine," Rajel said. "But Cassi's missing."

Anna looked up, and her eyes widened. "That can't be good," she whispered. "Jack, call Melissa. I want her guarding the Prime Council."

"On it."

"Sit tight, Rajel," she said. "We're on our way."

Side by side, Jack and Anna ran down an empty street, both dressed in black with light-armoured vests and holstered pistols. The buildings on either side of them weren't exactly tall, but Jack could see towering skyscrapers looming in the distance.

Up ahead, a cluster of men and women in heavy body armour stood in the middle of the road, and Rajel was with him. The guy looked frantic, his face flushed, his chest heaving with every breath. "No!" he said. "Get the drones here now!"

"As I was saying," one of the soldiers replied in tones that made it clear they had had this conversation before. "Many of the drones were damaged during the battle. Those we have left are patrolling the city, looking for enemy forces. We can't just divert them away from that task to find one Justice Keeper."

"And I said-"

"Whoa," Jack cut in.

The soldier – a captain by the insignia on his chest – did a quick about-face at the sound of his voice. "I'll tell you the same thing I told him. We can't just send a drone to find your friend!"

Grinning sheepishly, Jack lowered his eyes. "And I'm not going to press that point." He approached the group with his hands up in a mollifying gesture. "But let's just take a moment to remember that we're all on the same side here."

Rajel shut his eyes, and a fat tear slid over his cheek. He sniffled, shaking his head. "She was angry with me," he mumbled. "Said I wasn't doing my job."

"It's okay," Anna replied. "No one blames you. Just tell us what happened."

Wiping that tear away, Rajel shuddered. "They ambushed us," he began. "Came out of the alleys and the side streets. I wasn't really watching Cassi; I figured she could take care of herself, but when the dust settled..."

"She was gone," Anna said.

"Yeah."

Wrinkling her nose in distaste, Anna shook her head. "I don't like this," she said. "Cassi wouldn't just run off in the middle of a battle, and if one of those bastards hit her, we'd have found her body by now."

Jack strode forward with his lips pursed. Uniformed men and women shuffled out of his way. "Maybe something drew her away."

In his mind, he saw Anna behind him with fists on her hips. The scowl on her face made her feelings on that matter clear. "Which means it was a trap," she said. "Probably with the intent of getting their hands on a Keeper."

Jack spun to face her, his eyebrows shooting up. "Yeah, but why?" he asked. "They have no support ships. It can't be Telixa wanting more test subjects; she's gone. And they have to know that Keepers make terrible hostages."

Anna nodded.

Baring his teeth with a growl, Rajel stepped between them. "It doesn't matter why they took her!" he insisted. "Our only priority is getting her back!"

"All right," Anna said. "We won't accomplish anything by standing around here and arguing about it. Let's split up into teams and search the area. Back alleys, neighbouring streets. Look inside buildings as well."

Anna chose Jack as her partner, and together, they inspected the nearby alleys and side streets. It was slow going. There wasn't much of anything that could be used to hide a body. No garbage or refuse. Even now, Jack still marveled at that. He had gotten used to the cleanliness of Leyrian streets, but even the back alleys were almost pristine.

Some buildings had outdoor waste disposal units that were periodically emptied by maintenance bots, but none were large enough to contain a body. Leyrians didn't generate a lot of trash. Food containers were all recycled, collected once a week and sent back to the processing plant to be sterilized and reused. The same was true for shampoo bottles or cleaning products or just about anything else.

He was in one narrow alley when something got his attention.

Jack sank to a crouch with his hands on his knees, frowning at the ground. "I don't like this," he said, shaking his head. "Is that what I think it is?"

Anna was in front of him, but she turned around in response to his question. Her face hardened when she saw what he had noticed. "It sure looks like it."

There, on the ground, was a small spot of something that looked a hell of a lot like dried-up, silver blood. A spot no larger than the tip of his index finger. Not that he would be stupid enough to touch it without gloves.

Clamping a hand over his mouth, Jack shut his eyes as he ran through scenarios in his head. *"Ziarogati,"* he whispered. "Maybe the Ragnosians had one. But why wouldn't it attack with their main force?"

Anna turned her face up to the sky, blinking slowly. "Maybe that's what happened to Cassi," she said. "Maybe its job was to lure any Keepers away from the fight so that the ordinary soldiers wouldn't have to deal with them."

"Maybe."

"Whatever the reason, I think we're on the right track."

They moved deeper into the alley until they were blocked by a chain-link fence. On the other side, Jack saw buildings from the next street over, but there was no indication that Cassi had gone that way.

There was, however, a narrow gap between the fence and the two buildings on his side. When Jack explored it, he found something that froze his blood.

A dead *ziarogat* with a bullet hole in its forehead.

This one had once been a small woman with dark skin and a round, girlish face. Like all female *ziarogati*, she wore only a pair of gray pants and a thin tank-top. And she was bald.

About ten feet away, an unconscious Cassi was lying stretched out on the ground. There was dried blood on her forehead and in her pink hair. When he saw her, Jack had to resist the urge to panic. She wasn't moving! Was she even breathing?

"Anna!" he said. "Help me!"

Melissa sat with arms folded in the small chair they had given her in the corner. The Prime Council's security bunker was abuzz with activity. There were men and women in black fleet uniforms and green infantry uniforms all clustered around Sarona Vason.

The Prime Council herself wore a green jacket over a white blouse and kept her long, silver hair up in a braid. "We owe you all a great debt of gratitude," she said to her assembled guests. "One that we will not forget."

About two dozen Antauran officers in crisp blue uniforms stood before the Prime Council. Their leader, Colonel Tharian Delvon, answered her kind words with a smile and a nod of respect. "We honour the alliance that we made with your people," he said. "And now, it's time to plan our next move."

Melissa wasn't sure she liked the sound of that. As far as she was concerned, the next move should be rebuilding Alios's defenses and repairing the minor damage to its infrastructure. This sounded more like sabre-rattling.

The hologram of a man with sun-darkened skin, graying hair and a thick, salt-and-pepper mustache stood next to the Prime Council. Melissa recognized him as Sal Thrios, the Leyrian Defense councilor. She didn't know much about him, but being stuck in the corner gave her plenty of time to look stuff up on her multi-tool.

Sal Thrios had served in the Space Corps for over twenty years before going into politics. He had been named to the position of Defense Councilor just under five years ago, shortly after Leyria had made official first contact with Earth. As Melissa understood it, he was safe and sound back on Leyria, but this was a high-level strategy meeting, which meant that his presence was required. "Colonel," he said. "Are you suggesting that we initiate a counter-attack against the Ragnosians?"

"More than suggesting," Colonel Delvon replied. "My government's position is that Ragnos declared war on *us* when they murdered our president. We've exercised restraint with the understanding that your people would not want to enter an armed conflict, but now that they have attacked you as well..."

Breathing deeply through her nose, Sarona nodded as if she had been expecting that response. "I'm still hoping that we can avoid outright war," she said. "They've seen what they're up against now."

"With respect, Madame Prime Council," the colonel replied. "I consider your stance on this issue to be dangerously naive. The Ragnosians knew of our alliance, and they were willing to test your defenses anyway. Failure to respond will only invite further aggression."

Sal Thrios grunted, and the look he gave Sarona made it clear that he didn't think she would like what he had to say. "I'm afraid I must concur, ma'am," he said. "We must acknowledge the reality that we are very likely in a state of war, whether we want to be or not. The Ragnosians have displayed a pattern of aggression. They've trespassed in our space; they've kidnapped our citizens. They've assassinated the Antauran president, and now they've attempted a full-scale invasion of our colony."

The colonel puffed up his chest and thrust out his chin. "Quite frankly," he began, "our patience is not without limits. If you are unwilling to participate, my government may initiate the counterattack without you."

Melissa felt cold inside.

"Before we do anything rash," Sarona began. "What if I were to offer you the man who killed your president?"

The Antauran's exchanged glances.

Uh oh...

"We have him here," the Prime Council explained. "In a holding cell. We're not sure what to do with him; so, we offer him to you as a gesture of good faith."

Colonel Delvon looked skeptical, but he forced a smile and said, "You understand that I will have to consult my government," he said. "But the gesture is appreciated."

Jack ran to Cassi.

His heart was pounding. Going up against a *ziarogat* alone was dangerous for any Keeper. He had barely survived his few encounters with those half-human devils. And if Cassi was dead... He wasn't sure how, but he knew he'd find some way to blame himself.

The instant he got within three feet of her, she sat up and touched her fingertips to the scab on her forehead. "Bleakness take me..." Her eyes fluttered. "Jack... Anna. Are the others all right?"

Anna stood with her hands in her pockets, smiling with obvious relief. "Yeah," she said, nodding. "Everyone's fine. We were worried about you."

Dropping to one knee beside Cassi, Jack frowned as he inspected her wound. "You did good, Cass," he said. "I gotta say, taking on a gat with no help from anyone? You're really kicking it up a notch."

He expected a grin or a smart-ass quip, but instead, Cassi shuddered. She glanced toward the chain-link fence and then scuttled away from it as if she expected a rabid dog to leap from out of nowhere. Jack didn't sense anything with spatial awareness, but he looked anyway and found nothing there. "Cass, what's wrong?"

She grimaced, pressing a hand to the side of her head. "Nothing," she grunted. "I guess the *ziarogat* psyched me out. I managed to get a shot off as it threw me into the wall. The next thing I knew, you guys were standing over me."

"Scary, scary," Jack said.

"We should get you to the med-centre," Anna added. "Just in case."

Cassi kept looking toward the fence with obvious trepidation. Her face was white as snow. "What?" she stammered. "Oh, yes... The med-centre. Probably a good idea."

Something about this didn't sit well with Jack. In all the time he had known her, Cassi had never been the sort of person who jumped at shadows or struggled with her words. Granted, a bonk on the head could leave you dazed, but aside from that scab, she didn't even seem to have much of a wound. Maybe her symbiont had already healed the damage, but if that was the case, she would be fully coherent. Unless there was internal hemorrhaging. Now, that was a scary thought.

He performed a quick scan of his surroundings and found Cassi's pistol lying on the ground. Retrieving it with one hand, Jack offered the other to help Cassi get back on her feet. "Come on," he said. "Let's get you checked out."

Interlude 4

A square window with metal grating allowed just enough sunlight to make the conference room uncomfortably warm. The Leyrians, Antaurans and Ragnosians had all learned to control the temperature of their dwellings and workplaces, but it seemed that Earth was lagging behind on that score.

He was George S. White now: a tall and broad-shouldered man with a square jaw and short, brown hair. A man of some means who had turned a modest inheritance into a sizable fortune through skillful investment in the New York Stock Market.

It was such a plebeian name, George. That he shared it with the man who currently sat on the throne – his throne! - did little to reduce his dislike of it. He had been Dravis, Vindronic and Gaozu of Han! Names that had commanded respect from his enemies. And now, he was George. A name as modest as the three-piece suit he wore to blend in with these people.

Two men sat side by side on the other side of the wooden table, both dressed in the brown uniforms of the British army. One was just into his middle years with little flecks of gray in his dark hair; the other had a leathery face and deep creases in his brow. "Well, gentlemen," the younger man began. "I trust you won't mind if we conclude our business as swiftly as possible."

"Of course not, Major," George replied. "I don't wish to take up too much of your time; you must be exceedingly busy."

"That would be a monumental understatement," the older man replied. "Half the streets are still blocked up. Getting around this city is a bloody nightmare, and now – when we should be planning a counter-attack – I'm here listening to you lot."

Such arrogance... What would either of these men think if they knew they were in the presence of William the Conqueror? George exchanged a glance with his partner.

Roger Pennfield was a tall and slender man who appeared to be in his late thirties, a spindly fellow with spectacles that sat just a little too far down his nose. In reality, he was much older than he appeared.

After centuries of working alone, George had petitioned the Inzari for their blessing to recruit others. Roger had been the first. Though, at the time, his name had been Lord Henry Pennfield. His decision to pose as his own descendant was foolhardy. Anyone who saw a painting of the late Henry would note the uncanny resemblance. However, claiming to be the last scion of a reclusive family did make it easier to access his vast fortune. So, George was willing to give the other man some latitude... for now.

"We appreciate your patience, Colonel," Roger said in a voice as dry as the Sahara. His face remained perfectly expressionless. "We would not have asked for this meeting without good reason."

"Oh, he's got a reason, does he?" Colonel Fenton spat. "Well, go on then. State your case, and be quick about it."

Roger answered that with a smile that didn't quite touch his eyes. "We wish to help you kill Nazis," he said simply.

"You want to kill Nazis?" the colonel barked. "Well, don't let us stop you! By all means! Put on a uniform."

With considerable effort, Roger stood up, making it a point to lean his weight on a wooden cane. He watched the colonel over the rims of his glasses. "I'm afraid that certain infirmities make that impossible," he said. "But I've dedicated each of my factories to the war effort. We've been providing you with munitions for almost two years now."

"At considerable cost," the major grumbled.

"We wish to change that," Roger said. "Henceforth, we will be providing you with munitions free of charge."

The two men sat there with their mouths agape. George was so amused that he had to suppress the urge to laugh.

Major Harrison stood up with his thumbs hooked around his belt. The man looked like he had swallowed a bee. "Well," he began. "We are, of course, very appreciative. But if you don't mind my asking, how can you afford this kind gesture."

"My finances can easily absorb the cost."

"And I will lend my support as well," George added.

The major offered a curt nod and then gestured to his companion. Colonel Fenton was still dumbstruck, but he regained his wits when he realized that everyone else was waiting on him. "Yes," he said. "A wonderful gesture. We'll pass your message along. Thank you, sirs."

The streets of London were a mess; nine months of bombing had left many of them utterly impassable with rubble littering the roads. Some buildings were scarred with black scorch marks. Others had been reduced to piles of brick and wood.

George walked down a narrow lane of townhouses with his hands inside his jacket pockets, frowning as he inspected the damage. A part of him couldn't help but feel some connection to these people. They *were* his, after all. He had founded the dynasty that was now ruled by his incompetent namesake.

Idiot man! Endorsing that buffoon Chamberlain. Peace in our time indeed. So far as he knew, George was the oldest living human being in the galaxy. He had been a king and a beggar, a soldier and a serf. He had seen men kill each other with swords, with guns, with ships that traversed the stars! And in all that time, one truth remained constant: you destroyed your enemies completely or they destroyed you. There was no middle ground. Men like Hitler saw weakness as an invitation to attack.

Roger was at his side, limping with the cane. "I must be mad," he muttered. "to let you talk me into this fool's plan. Do you know how much money I'm giving up?"

George felt his lips quirk into a smile. He shook his head slowly. "I thought that you were a wiser man, my friend," he said. "You have seen the power of the Inzari. You have passed through death and returned, and yet you still fret over such petty concerns."

A blush put some colour in Roger's cheeks. George's words must have stung. The man usually kept a tight rein on his emotions. "I still have to live on this world," he said. "My means are finite."

"And easily replaced."

"So, you say…"

Shutting his eyes, George drew in a deep breath. He turned his face up to the sky and let the sun beat down upon him. "Don't be so dour, Roger," he replied. "If earthly possessions matter so much to you, you may have mine."

The other man stopped short and looked over his shoulder, squinting through the lenses of his glasses. "You would give away your fortune so easily?" His surprise was not a good sign. It seemed that Roger had grown fond of the trappings of this world.

Such things were to be expected, George supposed; the other man had spent most of his four hundred and thirty years here

319

on Earth. He had been allowed to visit the other worlds – one could not do the Inzari's bidding without a broader perspective – but Roger always returned here. And when his services were not needed, he hid himself away and tended to his family's fortune.

"I have named you my sole beneficiary," George promised. "I think that George S. White is not long for this world."

"What do you mean?"

"Come," George said. "I will show you."

It took nearly two hours to find their way back to his town-house in Belgravia. Twice, they had to turn back when rubble made a street impassable. Everywhere they went, people hurried about their business, often exchanging furtive glances. It had been over a month since the last bombs fell – and with the sun up, it was highly unlikely that the Germans would attack – but that fact did little to ease the tension.

When they finally arrived at George's flat, his doorman reacted with a sneer at the sight of Roger. Jeffery was a tall man with a leathery face and a ring of gray hair that puffed out over his ears. "Mr. Pennfield will be joining us again, sir?"

Straightening his tie with one hand, George shut his eyes and shook his head. "Yes, he will, Jeffery," he replied. "And I would advise you to put aside your animosity."

He stepped inside and found himself in a well-lit hallway with white walls and freshly-polished floor tiles. At the end of that hallway, Stella – his maid – looked up and sneered at him. Her face was too pretty for such a mean expression. She was a pale woman with auburn hair that she wore in a braid and sharp, brown eyes that seemed to drill through you. "Well," she said, trying – and failing – to disguise her Leyrian accent with a thick, Irish Brogue. "Look who it is! Has Mr. Pennfield finally decided to commit himself to the cause?"

"'Mr. Pennfield' knows his place," George cautioned. "You should learn yours."

She showed her teeth in a way that made him think of a hissing cat. "Well, far be it for me to question the Inzari." She spread her black skirts in a curtsy, bowing her head in a mockery of respect. "If they believe that Roger is a dutiful servant, who am I to argue?"

There were days when George wondered how long it would be before Stella pushed him to the point where he killed her. The Inzari would not restore her if he told them not to. They cared little for which servants he chose to employ. As long as he carried out their orders. Truthfully, he would have killed Stella long ago if not for the fact that she was the most proficient killer he had ever met.

Decades ago, when she was still calling herself Ariana Tamolo, she actually managed to kill a Justice Keeper on her own. That was how George had found her. That was why he brought her into the service of the Inzari.

He shivered at the thought.

Who would have imagined that the Leyrians would choose to Bond with the life-forms that the Inzari had abandoned on their primary moon? Even the Inzari had been surprised by *that* development. Learning that his masters did not know everything was as frightening to him as the abilities a human gained by joining with these Nassai. One day, he would have to devise a method for dealing with the Justice Keepers.

"Come," he said, ignoring Stella's anger. "You should see this as well. Jeffery, see to it that we are undisturbed."

"Yes, sir."

He led them down a set of stairs to a basement with a black-and-white checkerboard floor. It was a rather inelegant portion of the house – just one large room beneath all of those above – with little in the way of furnishings except for a backup refrigerator. But there was one thing that drew the eye.

Right in the middle of the room, a solitary metal triangle stood with its topmost point almost brushing the ceiling.

Light shimmered along its gleaming surface, and the sinuous grooves that covered almost every inch of it had a hypnotic effect.

"Come."

George stood with his back to the SlipGate, flanked by Roger and Stella, and waited for the bubble to surround them all. Within seconds, they were rushing through a tunnel that seemed to go on forever.

The bubble arrived in a place that was almost as dark as the tunnel had been, and when it popped, George found himself in a dome-shaped chamber with walls of flesh that gave off a faint red glow. Part of the floor had come up to form a triangle behind them, but it quickly shrank to nothing.

George paused for a moment to watch Stella through narrowed eyes. "Come," he said, stalking off through a round opening in the wall.

A narrow tunnel ran through the bowels of the ship, its floor rising and falling in gentle, rolling hills. There was a wet, gurgling sound all around them, and the walls had a slimy texture.

It didn't take long to find an open chamber very much like what he thought of as the "Gate Room." The only real difference here was the presence of a deep pool of goo. Both Stella and Roger had seen this place before, when they pledged themselves to the Inzari. Dying was part of the process, though the Inzari had brought them both back in their original bodies. George sometimes wondered why they had not done the same for him, but in truth, he couldn't even remember the face of Liu Bang. His mental image of the man he had been came from drawings and other such renditions.

The others had been here more than once. Stella was over a hundred years old, and Roger more than four times that. Every few years, they entered the pool so that the Inzari could preserve their youth. George never bothered with such measures.

Whenever a body became too infirm, he simply let it die and found himself in a new one.

Roger and Stella gasped when they noticed the man strapped to the wall.

Karl was a tall man with a toned physique. Much too pale, and his blonde hair was so fair you could almost call it white. But otherwise, he was a truly handsome man. The very definition of Aryan perfection. That would make things easier.

The man's shirt was unbuttoned, and his pants were torn in several places. Snarling, he struggled against the restraints that held him in place. Thick bands of skin grew out of the wall and encircled his wrists.

"There's no need for that," George said in German.

Karl screeched with impotent rage.

Standing by the entrance with a stiff posture, Roger frowned at the captive man. "What is he doing here?" There was far too much disdain in his tone. "Surely you don't mean for this man to join our ranks."

"Don't be a fool," George replied. "I've had telepaths probing his mind, uncovering every last detail of his life."

"For what purpose?" Stella demanded.

George didn't answer her with words. Instead, he reached into his jacket and drew a small revolver from an underarm holster. Pressing the barrel to the side of his head, he cocked the hammer and pulled the trigger.

A fog of confusion filled his mind. It was always like this. Somehow, he knew that it was always like this, though what he meant by *it* was somewhat elusive. All he could say was that he had done this before. Many times.

At first, he gave no thought to the warmth that surrounded him, but then he realized that he was submerged in some strange liquid. A liquid so thick he had to struggle to swim through it.

His head broke through the surface, and slime dripped from his face. Blinking, he took stock of his surroundings. It all came rushing back. He was George, but... No. No, George was dead. He was Karl now.

Splashing and coughing, he emerged from the pool without a stitch of clothing on his body. He could not say how much time had passed, but he was willing to guess that it couldn't have been much more than a few minutes. Roger and Stella were still standing over his former body, carefully avoiding the puddle of blood that surrounded his head.

The other Karl was still struggling against his restraints, but he gasped and went still when he noticed his naked twin climbing out of the pool.

Wiping the goo off his face, Karl chuckled. "Much better," he said in Leyrian. He didn't want to risk using an Earth language on the off chance that his doppelganger might know it. "Wouldn't you agree?"

"You're planning to impersonate him?" Roger inquired. "Why? Who is this pitiful wretch?"

Grinning, Karl offered a shallow bow. More of a tip of the head. "He's your German counterpart, Roger." Revealing that little nugget had an effect on Roger. He was a loyal Englishman through and through. Oh, he served the Inzari, but he still loved his country, and he despised the Nazis. Not that George... Karl could blame him on that point. "We need to make sure that the Reich is properly supplied with weapons."

"And why is that?"

"We have to keep the war going. The Inzari have taken an interest."

Pacing a circle around him with one hand over her mouth, Stella paused to admire his new body. "Tell me," she said. "Why should the Inzari care about a war on a planet so primitive my people could conquer it with just one ship?"

Roger stiffened at that and glared daggers at her. The man knew that the Leyrians were technologically superior, but loyalty to England meant loyalty to Earth. Hearing such things would not sit well with him.

"You might say that the war is a microcosm of the Grand Experiment." Karl let out a peal of laughter that made his doppelganger whimper and look away. "Preliminary data that will give them some indication of what to expect."

The other Karl began to writhe, pulling at the straps of skin that bound his wrists. His feet kicked, and his head thrashed. But the only thing that came out of his mouth was a series of unintelligible shrieks.

"Ah yes," Karl said, stooping to retrieve the pistol that George had dropped when he died. "I suppose, dear brother, that it is time for our association to end."

The other Karl's eyes widened.

The last thing the poor man saw was the barrel of a gun, and the ship groaned as a bullet drove itself into the wall.

Chapter 21

Jack wasn't the sort of guy who got very fussed about architecture, but even he had to admit that the Ladarian Centre was kind of cool. The building was essentially two concentric cylinders about three stories high. The inner cylinder was a large auditorium where speakers stood on a stage in the centre of the room.

The outer one was a concourse that formed a ring around the auditorium. Bridges on the second level extended from the inner cylinder to a walkway along the outer wall, each one leading to a platform where one could watch the stage from above. There were twenty-four of them like spokes on a wheel. One for each hour of the day, or so he had been told. He was on one of them now.

Jack stood on the bridge in blue jeans and a brown coat, gripping the railing as he watched the crowd below. "Everything looks fine from up here," he said over the comm channel. "But you can tell these folks are getting restless."

Several hundred people milled about on the white floor tiles, speaking in hushed voices as they waited for the chance to take their seats. The stagehands were making their final preparations, but the debate was on schedule to begin in half an hour. Nothing stood out to him at first glance – there were no obvious red-flags that would indicate a threat – but he still felt uneasy. Slade would try something; that much was certain.

Anna's voice came through his earpiece. "All right," she said. "Stay put. I'll join you in a few minutes."

He couldn't blame the people for feeling anxious. After what they had been through in the last week, it was a natural reaction. And Larani was asking a lot of them. These people weren't Justice Keepers; they were civilians. Summer offered comforting emotions.

He looked up to find Anna standing on the bridge in a pair of black pants and a matching t-shirt, a pistol conspicuously visible on her hip. Her face lit up when she saw him. "Hey, you," she said. "Ready for the big show?"

"As ready as I'll ever be."

"Don't stress," Anna said. "Once people see that Sarona has actual evidence and data on her side, they'll recognize Dusep for the clown he is."

Jack sighed.

He admired her optimism – he really did – but he couldn't share it. Maybe it was her Leyrian upbringing, but Anna genuinely believed that if people were given enough information, they would make the right decision. Perhaps that was because her people had a long history of making good choices. No poverty, no prejudice: Leyria sure was a great place to live. At least that was what the brochure said.

In reality, some of those old prejudices were starting to rear their ugly heads once again. Anna wasn't blind to them – she knew that her people had been flirting with some dangerous ideologies – but a part of her still believed that it was just a few bad apples, an aberration that could be corrected. Jack wasn't so sure. He had witnessed first-hand what happened when such ideologies took root on Earth.

Everybody told him that you had to work within the system if you wanted to see real change. So he put on the nice clothes, attended the press conferences. He tried to do as Jena did; he still remembered the way she had cut Slade's legs out from under him in that very first meeting. But Jack Hunter was no Jena Morane. She could slice through the bullshit with facts and *make* people listen. Jack tried to follow her lead. He had taken that approach on Antaur, and it almost sabotaged the treaty. Maybe there were people who could get results by playing by the rules. Jack wasn't one of them. But he couldn't bring himself to say anything that might deflate his girlfriend's optimism. So, he just changed the subject. "We need to talk about Cassi."

Anna shut her eyes, drawing in a deep breath. "Whatever you say," she muttered. "So, take me through it one more time."

"Something's wrong with her."

Anna stood with one hand on the railing, frowning as she turned her head to look out on the crowd. "That's what you said this morning," she replied. "But you said it was just a feeling."

"Well, something else occurred to me," he said. "On a hunch, I went and checked the armoury records this afternoon. Her gun came back with an almost full magazine. There was only one bullet missing."

"Which she used to shoot the *ziarogat* in the head."

"Exactly."

Anna blinked.

Jack turned away from her, pacing along the bridge and gesticulating as he spoke. "Think about it," he said. "How many times have you fought a *ziarogat?* Three? Four?"

She was there in his mind's eye, watching him with a skeptical expression. "That sounds about right," Anna grumbled. "But what does it matter? Are you saying that Cassi couldn't win?"

Turning on his heel, Jack faced her with all the confidence he could muster. He didn't like casting doubt on his friend, but something was off here. "How many bullets did you spend trying to kill the thing?" His voice grated, but he couldn't help it. "Don't know about you, but I've emptied entire magazines just to bring down *one* of those bastards."

"Yeah, but we don't know what happened," Anna countered. "Maybe Cassi didn't use her gun until she was sure she could get a kill shot. For all we know, there could have been ten minutes of fisticuffs before she even drew her weapon."

"But that's my point, An!" he protested. "So, she kills that thing with her very first bullet just before she makes a headfirst collision with the wall? She lines up the perfect shot while she's flying through the air, and the gat doesn't use a force-field to protect itself? Even for a Justice Keeper, that is some *damn* good luck."

Anna touched fingertips to her temple, wincing as if this topic gave her a headache. "Sweetie, I really want to believe you," she began. "But nothing you said is technically impossible, and Cassi has told her story several times. There are no holes."

Jack approached her, resting his hands on her shoulders and sighing softly. "It's not too late," he murmured. "We can switch places. Send me in there to watch Sarona. Cassi comes out here to help with the ambush."

Anna looked up at him with those deep blue eyes, and he knew that he was not going to like the answer. "Honestly," she said, "I would take your suggestion. But I need you out here with me when Slade comes. Cassi's good, but you're better. And you've gone up against him before."

Closing his eyes, Jack drew in a shuddering breath. "All right," he said, nodding. "If you think that's best."

Two seconds after he finished speaking, a voice came over the PA system. "Hello, everyone. We'd like to thank you for attending this evening's debate. We ask you now to kindly take your seats. Opening statements will begin in fifteen minutes."

People began filing into the auditorium with considerable haste, eager to take their seats and be away from this place. Or maybe they were just eager to see the debate. Right then, Jack didn't really care which it was. The only thing that mattered is that they would not be out here when Slade arrived.

The tension backstage was palpable. Larani watched as Sarona Vason reviewed her talking points on a tablet. The Prime Council had not spoken to anyone else or even looked up for at least fifteen minutes.

They were all gathered in a small, windowless room with a set of stairs that led up to the stage. Both candidates, their aides and seven Justice Keepers: all packed into a tight space and struggling not to bump into one another.

Dusep was nodding as one of his aides discussed his strategy. There was too much noise for Larani to hear what was being said, but she kept an eye on him nonetheless. If her instincts were correct, he would try to use the recent attack to stoke fear in the people.

Cassiara stood with her back to the wall, glowering disdainfully at everything in sight. After working with Jack for the better part of a year, she seemed to have picked up some of his dislike for politicians. Odd, that. Cassiara had been very politically active even before she joined the Justice Keepers. Her psych profile indicated an aptitude for reading other people. That was one reason why Larani had paired her with Jack. So, what had the young woman so on edge?

"Agent Hix," Larani said.

The man who stood beside her, nervously clutching the fabric of his shirt, shot a glance in her direction. "Ma'am?"

"Calm yourself," Larani said. "Everything's going according to plan."

"Yes, ma'am."

A stagehand poked her head into the room and said, "Candidates, we're ready for you." So, it was time to begin. Larani signaled her people to move, and they filed out of the room before Dusep and Sarona could so much as take one step toward the door. She followed them.

The auditorium had a simple design: several hundred seats on an inclined plane, all facing a stage with two lecterns. Every one of those seats was filled. The people spoke in hushed voices, some casting furtive glances toward the stage.

There were three Keepers beside each lectern, and they all stood perfectly still with a stiff, formal posture. Some of them scanned the audience as if they expected a man with a gun to pop up at any moment. Larani couldn't blame them. If everything went according to plan, Slade would never get anywhere near this room, but that man had a way of foiling even the best plans. Cassiara nodded as she took position behind Dusep's podium. And then it was time for the candidates to come out.

Sarona was the first one to emerge from the little room, waving as she stepped onto the stage. She was greeted with considerable applause and even a few whistles. Well, at least the Prime Council still had some ardent supporters. That was a good sign.

Dusep arrived thirty seconds later, and it dismayed Larani to see that the applause he received was no less enthusiastic than Sarona's. He took his position, gripping the sides of his lectern and staring down the crowd like a man who expected to go into battle.

The moderator, a plump woman with curly gray hair who wore a beaded necklace over her blue dress, placed herself between the two of them and nodded to the audience. "Welcome to the final debate of this year's campaign season," she said. "We thank those of you who have joined in person, and those of you watching at home. The issues facing our people have never been so complex. We will need decisive leadership in the years to come. This is your chance to decide who should lead the Systems' Council as we take on these new challenges."

She stepped forward, glancing first to Sarona and then to Dusep. "Each candidate will have two minutes to respond to each question, at which point, their opponent will be allowed a one-minute rebuttal. So without further ado, let's begin."

With a wave of her hand, the moderator summoned a hologram that displayed the first question. Nothing but black text on a white background, but it was large enough for everyone to see it clearly.

"Councilor Dusep," she began. "Your stance on immigration is well-known by this point. For over two centuries, it has been our policy to welcome anyone who is willing to live by our laws. Why should we change that policy now?"

Dusep set his jaw and nodded as if he had been expecting this question. "Thank you," he began. "That policy was initiated during a time when we had the luxury of open borders. The Antaurans were at least fifty years behind us in terms of military technology. The Salusians had only just discovered steam technology, and we welcomed them into our society with open arms."

"The situation is no longer what it once was. The galaxy is more connected than it has ever been before. Where once we were separated by unimaginable distances, now – thanks to the recently discovered SuperGates – we can reach almost any star system in a matter of weeks, if not days. The Ragnosians can be on our doorstep tomorrow, and those of you here on Alios know this first-hand. We can no longer tolerate the risk posed by unmitigated immigration."

To her credit, the moderator managed to keep a smooth face as she held Dusep's gaze. "Thank you," she said. "Prime Council, your rebuttal?"

Standing tall and proud, Sarona faced her audience with the dignity of a queen. And then she smiled. "It is through diversity that we grow stronger," she said. "Consider our new alliance with Antaur, an alliance that so many of you doubted not two weeks ago. If not for that alliance, many of you would be dead or prisoners right now. I believe-"

"And would the alliance have been necessary," Dusep cut in, "if we had focused on securing our own borders rather than expending so much energy on primitive worlds like Earth? I ask you-"

"Councilor Dusep," the moderator snapped. "Please do not interrupt."

Anyone who believed in democratic norms would have been suitably chastened by that, but Dusep replied with a mocking smile. It made Larani's blood boil.

"Prime Council," the moderator went on. "I will allow you to start again with a full minute for rebuttal."

"Thank you," Sarona said. "As I was saying…"

The more Jack watched the debate, the more certain he felt that things were not going to go well. He had seen this before. He had been quite young when many of Earth's nations started embracing fascist talking points, but he recognized the pattern.

There were screens on the walls in the concourse, and each one displayed Sarona Vason and Jeral Dusep verbally sparring with one another. Now and then, he caught a glimpse of Larani, and he could tell that she saw it too. The audience was starting to buy what Dusep was selling. People were still freaked out in the wake of the attack, and really, could you blame them?

There were still Ragnosian troops hiding out on this planet, waging a haphazard guerrilla war. Cut off from their support ships, they weren't much of a threat, but that did nothing to ease people's anxiety.

He noticed Cassi behind Dusep, glaring daggers at his back. She hated that douchebag; that much was obvious. Jack was relieved to see that she was guarding him instead of the Prime

Council. Which only made him feel guilty. He wanted to trust Cassi, but her story just didn't sit right.

He was on the upper floor of the concourse, standing on the outer ring that went all the way around the building. One of the large screens that hung from the ceiling showed a closeup of the moderator as she asked her next question.

Melissa came up to stand beside him, frowning as she listened. "It's not going well for the Prime Council, is it?"

Chewing on his lip, Jack shut his eyes and drew in a breath. "Sure looks that way," he muttered. "And then you know what happens next."

"Do you really think he'll show?"

She meant Slade, but that particular change of subject was so abrupt that it got Jack's attention. He took a moment to actually look at his friend, to see the tension in her face, the stiffness of her posture. "He'll show," Jack said. "He always does. Are you nervous?"

"No," Melissa replied. He had to give her some credit; for half a second, he almost believed her, but then her shoulders slumped and she leaned against the railing. "A little."

Jack felt his lips curl into an almost imperceptible smile. "Don't let him psych you out, Melissa," he said. "I saw you in action, remember? Believe me when I tell you that you're ready for this."

She stood up a little straighter, looked out upon the concourse with more resolve. "Thank you," she said with a curt nod. "I guess I should get into position."

No sooner did she finish speaking than Jack heard a buzz in his earpiece. Anna's voice came through loud and clear. "Greeting committee, get ready. We just registered an EMP that disabled one of the building's force-field generators. Southwest side."

"Confirmed," Jack said. "I'm on my way."

Before he even knew it, Jack was running along the outer ring on the upper level, passing bridge after bridge, each one leading to a door where one could observe the auditorium from above. There were skylights above him, each one showing a blue sky with thin, swirling clouds.

Glass shattered as a figure in black broke through, descending like a phantom to land on a nearby bridge. The newcomer had his back turned, but Jack could already see that he had long, dark hair.

"It's him," Jack said. "Begin Phase One."

Grecken Slade whirled around at the sound of his voice.

"Hey, Greck!" Jack called out. "Welcome to the party."

Chapter 22

Jack stood on the edge of the bridge with his feet apart, his gaze never wavering. "Glad you could make it," he said. "Should be a wicked good time."

In the middle of that bridge, Slade raised both hands into a fighting stance. The man chuckled under his breath. "I was wondering which one of you I would have to kill," he remarked. "I'm glad it's you."

"So, that's it?" Jack exclaimed. "Just straight to business? We're not even gonna bother with the pleasantries? How's your mother?"

"Dust beneath the soil of China."

Pressing his lips together, Jack nodded slowly. "Poetic," he said. "Have you ever considered putting that on a card?"

Slade came at him in a rage, glass crunching under his feet. Most of it had fallen to the lower level, but there were a few shards on the bridge. A hazard that Jack made note of. "You think I don't know what this is?" Slade bellowed. "You're stalling!"

"Aw, damn! You figured me out. Oh well...Let's fight."

Slade punched him in the face, filling his vision with dancing silver flecks. The man spun for a back-hand strike.

On instinct, Jack ducked and felt a fist pass over his head. He waited for Slade to come around, then drove his open palm into his chest. A sharp wheeze filled the air as his opponent staggered.

Jack jumped and snap-kicked, the tip of his shoe striking Slade's nose with a spray of blood. The other man stumbled backward across the bridge. Now to end this while the son of a bitch was still dazed.

Jack raced forward.

He threw a punch.

Slade's hand came up to swat his forearm and deflect the blow. The next thing Jack saw was four knuckles coming at him.

He bent backwards, one hand flying up to grab Slade's wrist. With his free hand, he reached for his holstered pistol.

Slade must have caught the motion because he rolled his wrist to pull free of Jack's grip. Retreating half a step, he spun and back-kicked, driving a foot into Jack's chest. The pain was unbelievable.

Jack looked up in time to see a black shoe striking him across the face. His vision went dark again, and nausea made him want to empty his stomach. He struggled to think, to remain focused.

In his mind, Grecken Slade was only a silhouette painted by spatial awareness. Just a shadow, a shadow that came forward and began another high roundhouse kick.

Jack raised his forearm up beside his head, intercepting the other man's ankle. That threw Slade off balance for half a second. Stepping forward, Jack delivered a mean right-hook to the cheek.

Slade collapsed against the railing.

Growling, Jack leaped and flew as straight as an arrow over the other man's head, his arms outstretched like Superman. He landed on the bridge and somersaulted across the floor tiles, one piece of glass cutting his shoulder. There were flags on the far side, positioned on either side of the door that led into the auditorium.

He sensed that Slade was chasing him, intending to tackle him from behind and force him to the ground. Rage flared up inside Jack. He grabbed the flagpole, then spun around and swung the circular base at his opponent's head.

Slade crouched down, casually raising one hand to catch the flagpole before the base could make contact. The man's face was twisted into a haggard snarl that betrayed his murderous intentions.

Slade shoved the pole forward like a spear.

The momentum forced Jack to back up, and then the tip of the pole went right into the wall beside him, shattering tiles on impact. "Come on, Greck," he said. "Didn't your mom ever tell you it's not nice to break stuff?"

"I will kill you."

"Uh huh…"

Falling onto his backside, Jack brought one foot up into the other man's stomach, producing a squeal of pain. He trapped one of Slade's legs between both of his, and then – with a twist of his body – he flung Slade down to the floor.

Jack was not prepared for the surge of Bent Gravity that sent him up toward the skylight. He almost passed right through it, but then he was falling, passing the bridge and descending to the lower level.

He called upon Summer to reverse gravity's pull for a few seconds, and that slowed him enough for a gentle landing. Down here, the concourse was a wide open ring around the auditorium with multiple bridges overhead. There were windows on the first floor that looked out on a garden.

Standing up straight, Jack shut his eyes tight. He tapped his earpiece to activate the microphone. "Anna," he said. "I think it might be time for Phase Two."

It startled him when Slade leaped from the bridge and sailed right over his head. The other man descended to land crouched on white floor tiles. Odd…Why wouldn't he go into the auditorium now that nothing stood in his way? Why not go after the Prime Council?

Slade rose in one smooth motion and then turned to face Jack with a mocking grin. "You didn't think you could get away that easy, did you? I'm going to kill you, Jack. Once and for all!"

"Because all those other times you killed me didn't take?"

"Actually, yes."

Jack blinked in surprise, then took a step back. "Just so that we're clear, you know that you're bonkers, right?"

Any witty rejoinder that Slade might have offered was cut off by the sound of feet pounding the tiles. Anna came running around the bend at top speed, sliding to a stop a few paces behind Slade.

Cocking his head, Slade giggled. It was a positively terrifying sound. "Well, now," he purred. "I was wondering when your bitch would show up. You know, it occurs to me that I always kill her first and make you watch, Jack. Maybe the key to ending this is to do it the other way around."

Something was wrong here.

The last time they had confronted Slade together, he had been terrified of facing both of them at the same time. But now, he was all bravado? What could have changed? The answer came to him like a blade of ice through the heart.

Slade had an ace up his sleeve.

It didn't matter. They had planned this little ambush, and now they were committed. There was nothing to do but see it through.

"Now!" Jack screamed.

Anna was about ten steps behind Slade, watching the whole scene play out. She could see it on Jack's face; she knew that her partner had reached the same conclusion that she had. Slade should have been hesitant to fight both of them together, but instead, he was gloating. That could only mean that he had something nasty planned.

The instant Jack screamed, Slade rounded on her with a murderous snarl. He came at her like a wolf loping across the planes, eager to sink his teeth into her throat. Maybe that should have scared her, but it didn't.

Anna turned her body for a roundhouse kick that struck his chin. She spun, lashing out with a back-hand strike. All she felt was one hand seizing her wrist and another settling onto the back of her collar.

Then she was soaring face-first toward the wall.

Tumbling through the air, Anna slammed her feet into the tiles. She pushed off and back-flipped, landing with a grunt.

When he saw his girlfriend careening toward the wall, Jack rushed in for the kill. Slade turned around to face him, cackling with an almost child-like glee. He threw a hard punch.

Jack's hands came up, catching the man's fist. He pulled his enemy close and then kneed him in the groin. That brought a wheeze of pain to Slade's lips. Jack punched him in the face.

Falling over backward, Slade caught himself with both hands and brought his feet up. Jack hopped back in time to avoid a nasty blow. But then his opponent flipped upright and hissed.

Slade jumped with a powerful kick.

Once again, Jack raised his hands up in front of his face, intercepting the other man's shoe. The impact stung his palms, and he was forced to retreat a few steps.

Slade used Bent Gravity to slide across the floor like a ghost on the wind, taking Jack by surprise with a palm-strike that hit him right between the eyes. Everything went dark, and dizziness made it hard to stand.

Jack crumpled to the floor.

The sight of it filled Anna with rage, and Slade's cruel laughter made it worse. The man stood over her boyfriend, ready to offer a final blow. Unable to restrain her fury, she screamed as she charged in.

Slade looked up to see her coming.

Anna tried to flatten his face with her fist.

Twisting out of her path, the man put one hand on her forearm and the other on her shoulder. Then he sent her on a collision course with the window. There was nothing she could do to slow her momentum.

Anna crashed right through the glass, shards falling all around her as she stumbled through a garden of yellow tulips. She felt the sting of shallow cuts on her body. Nothing that Seth couldn't handle. But she had to get back in the fight before...

Groaning, Jack stood up to find Slade standing with his back turned and peering out a shattered window. The man sighed, shaking his head. "You know," he said. "I am going to miss your antics."

Jack narrowed his eyes, anger boiling within him. "It's not over yet," he growled. "So, why don't you quit gabbing and fight?"

Slade whirled around to face him with that slimy smile. "If you insist," he said. "I suppose all things must come to an end. Do you remember the first time that I killed you, Guo-Dong? Do you remember watching her die?"

"Huh?"

Slade offered a high kick.

Jack ducked, allowing the other man's foot to pass over him. He rose just in time to see Slade coming at him with a vicious back-hand strike.

Turning his body, Jack caught the man's arm with both hands. He slammed the back of one fist into Slade's belly, then brought that same fist up to strike the man's nose with a sickening *crunch.*

A kick to the back of Slade's knee knocked him off balance. The son of a bitch fell to the floor and then rolled away before Jack could press his attack. "I am growing weary of this," he muttered as he got back up.

Anna came through the window with a beastly flying kick.

Startled by the motion, Slade turned around only to receive a black boot to the face, a blow that sent him sprawling backward with arms flailing. Blood stained his black, silk shirt. In that moment of confusion, Anna was on him like a wolf on a rabbit.

She landed ten feet away from Slade, then charged in and jabbed his chest with one fist then the other. Jumping with a feline screech, she slugged him right in the face. The guy looked like he might pass out.

Anna threw another punch.

Leaning back, Slade caught her wrist with one hand. His other hand grabbed a fistful of her shirt, and then he was twirling her around and around in circles. Jack was about to help when suddenly Anna came hurtling toward him. Slade was trying to knock them both down like a pair of dominoes. He really should have known better.

Jack reached for her.

Anna took his hand, and then he swung her around in a wide arc, Seth and Summer working together to keep her aloft, to undo Slade's Bending and create one of their own. It was accomplished without a single word spoken. Four minds acting as one. When they completed their circuit, Jack released her.

Anna flew across the concourse at blinding speed, kicking Slade in the chest. That brief moment of contact was all that she needed to apply a Bending.

Slade was thrown backward with incredible force, hurled right into the wall that separated the concourse from the auditorium. He hit so hard the tiles cracked, tiny bits of ceramic falling to the floor.

Slade followed them a second later, landing on all fours. He was groaning, breath rasping from his lungs. When he looked up at them, there was a thin trail of blood leaking from the corner of his mouth. "I...I'm going to..."

"To kill us?" Anna said. "Yeah. We heard you."

Shuddering, Slade managed to stand, but within five seconds, he nearly fell right back down again. He was able to stay on his feet but only barely. Jack readied himself for another round, but the other man surprised him.

Slade bolted for the auditorium and ducked inside.

With a casual shrug, Jack stepped forward. "Shall we?" he asked, gesturing to the door.

"We shall," Anna replied.

Together, they followed Slade and found themselves in a circular room where five rows of seats formed concentric rings around a central stage. Every last one of those seats was empty, and the only thing on that stage was an inactive SlipGate.

Slade was halfway down the aisle, seemingly frozen in midstep, as if the shock of what he saw had unnerved him. "Very clever," he murmured. "I don't give you two enough credit."

"Well, it was mostly Anna's plan," Jack said.

"Don't be so modest," she countered. "You came up with the idea. You were always the devious one."

Jack blushed at the compliment, then shut his eyes and nodded. "Fair enough," he said. "But you planned out the details. No one does logistics like you do."

"Aw!" Anna linked arms with him, resting her head on his shoulder. "We really do make a good team."

Seething with rage, Slade rounded on them. His teeth were clenched, his lips drawn back, and he looked like he might explode. "If you are quite finished with this saccharine nonsense!" he spat. "Perhaps we can resume killing each other?"

"Are you sure you wanna keep fighting, Greck? Wouldn't a nice, comfy holding cell be preferable to *Face-Punch 5: Revenge of the Fist?*"

Slade's answer to that was a shriek of impotent rage, and then he shot up toward the circular viewing platform on the upper level. He ran through one of the twenty-four doors that connected with the bridges outside.

Tapping his earpiece, Jack felt a smile blossom. "Hey, guys," he said. "It's time for Phase Three."

Not wasting a second, he and Anna ran back out to the concourse. They heard the thunder of Slade's footsteps on one of the bridges, but those footsteps came to an abrupt halt, leaving the room in silence.

A moment later, Slade leaped from that bridge and descended to the ground floor, landing near the window that Anna had shattered earlier. He couldn't even take one step before Melissa dropped down from above.

She landed in a crouch right in front of him, then stood up to block his exit. Her face was split by an ear-to-ear grin. "Going somewhere?" she asked.

Rajel jumped off a nearby bridge with his arm around Keli's waist, and together, they floated gracefully to the floor. "We went to all this trouble to plan your party," he said. "It would be rude to leave now."

Slade glanced this way and that, backing away from them. It didn't take long for him to realize that he was surrounded. "Foolish children!" he barked. "You really think you can stop me?"

"Five of us," Melissa said. "One of you."

"Go go, Power Rangers," Jack sang.

This time, Slade's laughter wasn't gleeful; it was cruel, menacing. He turned around with his head down, and then looked up to fix dark eyes on Jack. "Rest assured that I will kill you one day."

"Well, it's nice to have something to look forward to."

"But," Slade continued. "I have no quarrel with Carlson's daughter, the telepath or your blind friend. Order them to step aside and I may forget this impudence."

Anna strode forward with a smile on her face, shaking her head in dismay. "You're not getting it, are you?" she muttered. "There's no scenario where you walk out of here a free man. We're taking you in, and there's nothing you can do to stop it."

"Oh no?"

Grabbing a handful of his shirt, Slade ripped it open and sent buttons flying. The fabric fell away to reveal a simple black tank-top underneath, and that was when Jack noticed a strange mass of veiny flesh encircling Slade's bicep.

As if sensing his attention, it seemed to ooze down his arm and settle onto Slade's right hand, where it bonded with the skin. Jack felt a sudden rush of panic. It couldn't be. Could it? His mind searched for a reason – *any* reason – to doubt what he was seeing, but he just couldn't escape the grim truth.

Slade had a N'jal.

Chapter 23

Melissa had known this was coming; for over a year now, she had been expecting exactly this. She had tried to tell her father that there was a design in all this, that God had a plan, but of course, he didn't listen. People seldom listened to her, it seemed. That was one reason why she usually stayed quiet. But she had known.

Sooner or later, they were going to go up against Overseer technology, and they needed someone on their side who could balance the scales. Harry should have been here, but he wasn't. And now they were on their own.

Bending her knees, Melissa leaped and somersaulted through the air, bearing down on Slade. The man stepped aside so that he wouldn't be where she landed. Her feet hit the floor with a loud smack.

Melissa began a high kick.

Slade ducked, and her foot went right over him. Melissa spun for a back-hand strike that would take his head off. Her fist hit nothing but air.

When she came around, Slade was right in front of her.

He kicked her stomach, forcing her to hunch over. The next thing she saw was a fist colliding with her face, and then the pain overwhelmed her. She was barely aware of two hands grabbing her shirt.

Before she could react, Melissa was soaring up to one of the bridges, propelled by Bent Gravity. Her vision cleared in time for her to see Rajel at the apex of a jump that would bring him down on Slade from behind.

Slade thrust one hand out behind himself and released a rippling force-field that met Rajel in midair. He was thrown down to the tiles, groaning on impact.

Jack drew his gun.

With a dismissive flick of his wrist, Slade unleashed some kind of electric pulse that made sparks flash over Jack's body before he could aim the weapon. And all of that happened in two seconds.

Melissa's back hit the side of a bridge. Then she fell, reacting quickly to slow her descent. Power surged through her body as she and Ilia crafted a Bending of their own.

Shaking his head to clear the fog out of his mind, Rajel snarled and pushed himself up on extended arms. "May the gods scorch your soul!" He was on his feet and running toward Slade in an instant.

The man spun around to face him.

Rajel opened with a fierce right-cross.

Leaning back, Slade brought one hand up to deflect the blow. His other hand took a thick clump of Rajel's hair and pulled his head down. A knee came up to smash Rajel's nose, and then he was being thrown sideways.

Rajel slid across the tiles until his back hit the base of a window. Then he spasmed and coughed.

Fury coaxed Anna into motion before she even had a plan formed. She ran at Slade, ready to put her fist through his skull. Her blood was on fire. Her mind was frantic, but she knew one thing for sure, this was going to end now.

Anna threw a punch.

Slade caught her fist with one hand, and then she felt the tiny fibres of his N'Jal digging into her skin. Pain erupted in her body: a fiery sting that went from the top of her head all the way to the tips of her toes. It felt like being boiled alive in hot oil. She could barely even think.

Tears blurred her vision, but she could see that Slade was smiling. "Oh, how I have longed to teach you your place." His expression changed. It almost seemed as if he were listening to something no one else could hear. "And now the telepath attacks my mind."

He lifted Anna off the floor and threw her.

The pain faded as soon as he broke contact, but she couldn't focus, couldn't recall what she was supposed to do. She collided with Keli, and the two of them went down in a heap. The other woman moaned beneath her.

Anna rolled off of her.

The haze receded from her mind, and she saw Melissa in the middle of a leap that would bring her face to face with Slade. The former head of the Justice Keepers giggled as he raised his hand and released a force-field.

Melissa, however, actually climbed higher into the air as if pulled by some invisible tether. The force-field went past beneath her. She drew her gun, firing a storm of bullets before she even began to fall.

Slade raised both hands to shield himself, a force-field snapping into place to intercept Melissa's ammo. Round after round bounced off the pulsing barrier.

"EMP!" Melissa shouted.

Anna felt a twisting sensation of warped space-time just before Slade blurred into a streak of colour. He became solid once again near the window and the white tracer's that Melissa unleashed hit the floor instead.

The girl landed half a second later.

A force-field came barreling toward Anna, and she braced herself for the impact. But then Jack put himself in front of her and raised both of his hands to erect a Bending. The air shimmered like heat rising off the pavement, electrostatic energy coursing along the patch of warped space-time. It curved back upon itself, sped across the concourse and hit Slade with enough momentum to send him flying.

He crashed into a window, shattering the glass.

"This ends now," Jack said.

Jack's skin was tingling. A slight prickle that wasn't exactly what he would call painful, but it was difficult to ignore. Using his powers earlier hadn't taken much out of him; he and Anna had worked together to play with gravity, and so they had shared the load. But reflecting the force-field? That was a different story.

It dawned on him that Slade had been using his Keeper powers quite liberally. The man should be exhausted, but he just kept going. Was that another gift from his masters? Either way, it didn't bode well.

Step by step, Jack approached the broken window.

Rajel was lying on his stomach about five feet away from it. He looked up when he sensed Jack's approach and blinked. "I'm coming with you," he wheezed, getting back on his feet with some difficulty.

"No," Jack said.

"But-"

"This ends now."

Jack stepped through the opening, into a garden of tulips. Slade was out there, lying in the dirt with a hand over his heart, whimpering from the pain. "Well," he said. "This has been fun."

Sucking air into his lungs, Jack closed his eyes and did his best to fight his way through the fatigue. "Here's how it's going to end," he rasped. "We're not gonna kill you. We know better."

"Do you now?"

"They'll just bring you back," Jack muttered. "You know that cell you kept Keli in for the better part of twenty years? That's where you're going to spend the rest of your miserable life."

Slade laughed.

Bending over, placing his hands on his knees, Jack smiled and shook his head. "We won't let you die," he went on. "We'll keep you nice and sedated, twenty-four hours a day, each and every day...forever."

"You always were a tad short-sighted," Slade looked like a man who was ready to fall into a deep, peaceful sleep. Even with all of his enhancements, there were still limits, and his body had endured a great deal of punishment. "You put in all this effort to capture me, but, Jack...It was never about me."

"What are you talking about?"

Slade lifted his left hand to display the multi-tool on his gauntlet. With a deft swipe of his finger, he summoned a hologram. The debate was still going on half a world away. Sarona and Dusep were still behind their lecterns, and the Prime Council was articulating one of her many talking points. "You thought that by luring me here," Slade began, "you were neutralizing the threat to your precious politicians. But let me tell you something, Jack; I came here just to keep you busy."

He thrust his N'Jal into the air.

Larani was worried.

Not about the debate – that was actually going well; Dusep's constant defiance of democratic norms did not endear him to the audience – but if Anna's scheme was going according to plan, several of her people would be fighting Slade now. She should be out there with them. Until recently, she had been the only one who could best him in single combat. But the others insisted that protecting the Prime Council had to take priority, and Larani could not argue.

From the back of the stage, she watched as Sarona stepped out from behind her lectern and approached the audience. "History has shown us," the Prime Council began, "that whenever our actions are guided by fear, invariably we make mistakes."

"There is a difference between fear and caution," Dusep cut in.

The moderator gave him a glare that should have peeled the skin off his back. "If you are incapable of restraining yourself, councilor," she said in a voice as cold as ice. "I *will* mute your mic."

Several people clapped.

Dusep went beet-red – so the man *was* capable of feeling shame – but he made no further comment. He did snarl when he caught Larani watching.

Sitting back with one leg crossed over the other, Larani smiled at the man. *Yes*, she thought. *I see you for what you are, and now, they do too.*

"Make no mistake," the Prime Council went on. "We will defend ourselves if that is necessary. Consider that even when we were severely outnumbered, we were able to hold out against the Ragnosian fleet long enough for help to arrive. Our technology is second to none. But I believe that we can pursue other options."

She sighed, her shoulders slumping as she stared out at the crowd. "The Ragnosians have made a costly mistake," Sarona said. "One that I do not believe they will be eager to repeat. Now is the time to build bridges."

"Councilor Dusep," the moderator said. "Your rebuttal?"

"Just one question," he replied. "How do we build bridges with people who hate us?"

The Prime Council raised her hand and turned toward the moderator with a smile on her face. "May I answer the councilor's question?"

"Certainly."

Returning to her lectern, Sarona folded her hands on top of it and frowned at her opponent. "Sir," she began. "Many people over the centuries have asked that question. I would argue that the entirety of human history might be described as disparate groups learning to make peace with one another. Precedent is not on your side."

And with that, the auditorium erupted with applause.

Tapping quickly on her multi-tool, Larani called up the latest live-polls and saw that Sarona was pulling ahead of Dusep. When the debate began, the vote was split with fifty-five percent of people favouring Dusep and only forty-five supporting Sarona. In the last hour, Sarona had almost reversed those numbers. Data was still coming in from the homeworld and from the other colonies, but if sentiments there were at all similar to what they were here, there was every chance that Sarona might win a second term. Larani was almost ready to breathe a sigh of relief.

Almost.

She more than half expected one of Slade's agents to show up. Anna's last message said that their plan to lure Slade to the Ladarian Centre had been successful. It would be a difficult fight if any of his lieutenants joined him. She wanted nothing more than to check in, but that would only serve to distract Anna. She trusted her people.

"Councilor Dusep," the moderator began. "If elected, how will you guide the Council when the time comes for peace negotiations with Ragnos."

Dusep had regained some of his composure, but it was clear that he did not like that question. "I don't believe that peace with Ragnos is possible," he said. "People who think otherwise are deluding themselves. The fundamental philosophies at the cores of our two societies are diametrically opposed. We cannot-"

A flicker of motion distracted Larani.

Cassiara winced, touching her fingertips to her forehead. She looked almost as if a sudden migraine had taken her by surprise. Perhaps it would be wise to relieve the young woman in the next intermission. There were other-

Cassiara drew her pistol.

"No!" Larani shouted.

The other Keepers leaped into action. Agent Solin rounded on Cassiara and tackled her to the floor. As she went down, she managed to get off one shot. Just one...But it was one too many.

The bullet pierced Dusep's right shoulder with a spray of blood, causing him to collapse upon his lectern. It went into the crowd and killed a young woman with raven-black hair before anyone could figure out what was happening.

Then the screaming started.

Sarona whirled around with her mouth agape, trembling with fright. Several of her aides surrounded her and ushered her off the stage. People were shrieking as they exited the auditorium.

Agents Solin and Taresi were holding Cassiara down, but she squirmed as she tried to free herself. No Bent Gravity? Curious. Surely Cassiara could have flung them both off of her with very little effort. Unless...Unless her Nassai did not consent to this plan. So, she wasn't one of Slade's people then. But if that was the case, what would possess her to do such a thing? "Why?" Larani demanded.

Cassiara looked up with tears on her inflamed cheeks. "He was a threat to all of us!" she cried out. "He couldn't be allowed to win the election! I served my people today! I served my people!"

To her dismay, Larani noticed that not everyone had fled. There were reporters gathered at the base of the stage, and they all had cameras pointed at Cassiara. Many of them were white-faced and slack-jawed, but they did their jobs.

Why, girl? Larani thought. *You cost us everything.*

"I served my people!" Cassiara screamed.

Jack was numb.

He saw it all on Slade's hologram. He watched as Rael Solin tackled Cassi, watched as her gun went off. It all seemed to play out in slow motion. The bullet ripped through Dusep's shoulder. The man collapsed. And that was when Jack finally understood.

The data they had recovered from Leo's castle, the plan to kill Sarona Vason: it had all been a ruse. Just a little sleight of hand to keep them looking in the wrong direction. It was basic stage magic! He should have seen it coming.

After all, what good would killing the Prime Council do? Sarona Vason was hardly the only dovish politician in the Hall of Council. If she died, somebody else would step into her shoes, and the outpouring of public sympathy would make it that much easier to implement their agenda. But Dusep dying at the hands of a Justice Keeper... *That* would pretty much confirm every one of his crackpot theories. The Keepers were out of control! They had to be reigned in. The political establishment would not tolerate an iconoclast like Dusep. They would do anything to silence him.

All the pieces fell into place.

Slade had won.

Standing among the tulips with fists clenched at his sides, Jack felt his mouth drop open. "How?" he whispered, shaking his head. "How did you make her do it?"

A wicked grin spread across Slade's face. "Funny you should ask." With alarming speed, he literally *flew* off the ground and closed his hand around Jack's throat. His free hand took some kind of injector from his belt, and then he plunged the needle into the side of Jack's neck.

It felt like venom spreading through his body.

Jack squeezed his eyes shut, trembling from the hot sting. "Get off me!" He put a hand against Slade's chest, shoving him away.

The other man stumbled, almost losing his balance, but when he looked up, he was smiling. "Now, now... Let's not be rude." He thrust a hand out, fingers splayed, and the N'Jal seemed to pulse against his palm.

A wave of nausea hit Jack so hard he dropped to his knees and emptied his stomach right there "What..." He blinked the tears out of his eyes. "What have-aaah!"

The queasiness became a pulsing headache that felt like burly men pounding his skull with sledgehammers. Jack fell onto his back, fingers grabbing fistfuls of hair as he shivered. "Stop it!"

Somewhere in that never-ending storm of agony, he became aware of Summer. She was terrified. No, that word didn't do it justice. He had never felt such icy dread from his Nassai. Not even when he was seconds away from dying.

Anna ran through the shattered window, snarling at Slade. "Stop it!" she screamed. "Bleakness take me, stop it right now or-"

"Ah, ah, ah," Slade admonished.

With a flick of his wrist, he made Jack cry out in pain. Ants were crawling all over his body. Thousands of ants with a fiery bite. Except he knew they weren't actually there. Somehow, Slade was firing specific neurons in his brain, tricking him into experiencing sensations that weren't real.

The evil bastard stood there giggling while Anna looked on in horror. "You're going to let me go, my dear," he said. "Because the only way to stop me would be to fight your lover."

Slade crouched next to Jack, smoothing damp hair off his forehead. "You are mine now," he said. "Serve me, and the pain will go away. Resist…"

"Fuck you."

Slade made a fist with the N'Jal.

Jack flinched as shards of glass dug into his skin. Hundreds of them. He could see them sticking out of the back of his hands, protruding from his shirt. He could feel the hot blood leaking from the wounds.

"Serve me!"

"Fuck you."

The glass was gone – even the rips in his shirt were suddenly mended – but in its place, the nausea returned. Jack felt the bile rising to his throat. Rolling onto his belly, he puked in the dirt.

Baring his teeth, Slade hissed. His face grew redder and redder with every breath. "Serve me!"

Pushing himself up on extended arms, Jack narrowed his eyes. "You may as well call me Peter," he growled. "Because I deny you three times! I'd rather endure an eternity of torture than give you an inch!"

Slade stumbled as if somebody had straight-up slapped him. The shock on his face was unmistakable. He had not expected that response. In that moment, Jack felt a little thrill of victory. He could still defy this bastard.

"Very well," Slade murmured. "Live as you have chosen then!" He gestured with the N'Jal and the pain returned. Jack couldn't think. He was barely aware of Anna rushing to his side.

The others followed her out into the garden.

Slade was retreating, and even through all the anguish, Jack could tell that he was frightened. "All of you, stay back," he said. "Let me go, and I will give him a reprieve. Pursue me, and I will leave him like this, suffering endless pain until one of you finally puts him out of his misery."

"Don't listen to him," Jack croaked.

"You better hope they listen."

Clenching his teeth, Jack felt tears spilling down his cheeks. Every breath was agony, but he forced the words out. "Never mind me," he panted. "I'm expendable. The mission is more important. Take him down!"

With spatial awareness, he saw Anna come forward. She was close enough that he could see the fury in her eyes. "You heard him," she said. "Keepers, stand ready."

Melissa and Rajel took positions beside her.

"Loose!"

Together, the three of them launched themselves at Slade, forcing him to retreat through the tulips. "Insolent fools!" Slade raised a hand to put a force-field in their path, a crackling barrier that turned him into a blurry figure.

It took a moment for Jack to process the new sensations that he felt... or rather, the sudden *lack* of sensation. The pain was gone. He felt perfectly normal. Now, *that* was an interesting development. If he was right, it meant that Slade couldn't just turn it on and leave it on. He had to actively concentrate to make Jack suffer. *And he probably can't kill me either,* Jack realized. *If he could, he would have done it the instant that I refused to serve him. If we can get the N'Jal away from him...*

He noticed Keli crouching by the window. The telepath had her eyes closed as she massaged her temples.

A force-field sent Rajel sailing over Jack's head. The poor guy collided with the wall, then dropped to the ground in a heap.

Melissa and Anna were attacking Slade from both sides, forcing him to divide his attention between them. If they could just keep him busy for a few seconds.

Drawing his pistol, Jack forced himself to stand. He tried to aim his weapon, but a sudden blinding headache washed over

357

him. He was barely even aware of falling to the ground again. It felt like someone had jammed an ice-pick into his skull.

The pain faded enough for him to feel it when Slade jumped over him. The other man ran to the shattered window, ducking into the building with Anna and Melissa in hot pursuit. "He's going for the SlipGate!" Jack shouted.

The others probably knew that, but he had to do *something*. He couldn't just sit here and let Slade escape. Captain Hold-A-Grudge punished him for his defiance. Another wave of pain knocked him senseless.

Take him down, Anna! You can do it!

He knew that Slade had escaped when Anna returned two minutes later. That damn headache was still there, and it was getting worse. All that effort for nothing.

Jack wanted to cry.

Chapter 24

Jack was in a daze as they wheeled him through a hospital on a stretcher. He saw light after light scrolling past on the ceiling. Doctors in blue scrubs surrounded him, and he knew that they were talking about his condition, but he couldn't bring himself to focus. Any attempt to do so only made the headache worse.

Maybe he was wrong. Maybe Slade *could* just turn the pain on and leave it on? How long had it been? An hour? Surely, the man wouldn't keep concentrating on Jack for that long.

Anna was right behind the doctors at the foot of his stretcher. He could hear her trying to break through so that she could see him. "Operative Lenai," one man said with a glance over his shoulder. "Please give us some space."

And then Slade was there.

Somehow, he had replaced the female doctor on Jack's left, and of course, he was wearing that stupid purple coat with the gold embroidery. His face was split by the ugliest grin Jack had ever seen. "Oh, we're going to have such fun now."

"Slade…"

One of the doctors looked up at the sound of Jack's voice, and the look that he gave his colleague did not bode well. "He must be delirious."

"No," Jack protested. "He's here."

Slade threw his head back, roaring with self-satisfied laughter. "They can't see me, Jack!" he exclaimed. "Oh, but you can! Rest assured that I'm quite real and that you and I will be spending quite a bit of time together."

"No."

Slade leaned over the stretcher, and that vile grin of his became a rictus. "I'm going to be right here," he whispered. "Day in, day out...Driving you mad."

Jack winced, trying to sit up, but several hands pressed down on his chest, holding him in place. "Cassi!" he spluttered. "He did this to Cassi! You have to help her! It wasn't her fault!"

The doctors looked skeptical.

Anna finally managed to shoulder her way between two of them, and she looked like she was ready to peel strips off someone's hide. "Slade injected him with something. We don't know what it was."

"Hmm," Slade murmured.

Just like that, Anna vanished. One moment, she was there, and the next, she was gone. "No!" Jack called out, but all that did was make the doctors restrain him again. He heard something about a sedative. Great! Now they thought he was crazy.

All the while, Slade kept giggling. "I wonder if that might be the worst torture of them all," he mused. "If I made it so that you could never see her, never hear her voice or feel her touch-"

"I'll kill you!" Jack snarled.

One of the doctors hopped back.

"Not you," he assured the poor man. "I was talking to Slade. He's making me hallucinate somehow. I'll try to ignore him. Where's Anna?"

"She's right here," the doctor said softly.

Shutting his eyes, Jack made no effort to stop the tears that flowed freely. "I can't see her," he explained. "Slade is doing something, preventing my brain from recognizing her somehow."

"Agent Hunter, listen to me." The voice belonged to the female doctor that Slade had replaced. She was back, for some reason. Jack breathed a sigh of relief when he saw that Anna was there too, watching him with horror on her face.

That was when he noticed Keli leaning against the wall, wincing as she pressed a hand to the side of her head. "Whatever he's experiencing," she grunted. "I can promise you that it's real."

"You're stopping it?" Anna asked.

"I'm picking up some kind of telepathic signal," Keli whimpered. "It's alien, unlike anything I've ever felt before. But I can block it…for now."

"Jack," the doctor said. "We have to sedate you. Do you understand?"

He nodded.

"It's the best thing we can do until we find a more permanent solution. It will keep the pain away."

Shuddering, Jack turned his head so that his cheek was mashed against the pillow. "Do whatever you gotta do, doc," he whispered. "I could use the nap."

As the last traces of twilight faded from the sky, Larani looked out upon the city of Arinas. Most buildings were inhabited once again, tiny lights shining in distant windows, but she did notice a few that stood like silent shadows. Engineering teams were still in the process of restoring the city's infrastructure.

The door banged open.

Larani's shoulders slumped, her head hanging as she let out a breath. "You know, I was wondering how long it would take you to pay me a visit." She did not need spatial awareness to tell her who had just stormed into her office.

Sarona Vason stood in the open doorway, flanked by two of her personal security staff. The Prime Council still wore the black pants and green jacket that she had donned for the debate. "Larani."

"Sarona."

"How did this happen?"

Bracing one hand against the window, Larani sniffled as a single tear ran down her cheek. "I don't know," she whispered, shaking her head. "Agent Hunter is in the hospital. Slade infected him with something that lets him inflict pain at a distance. We suspect he did the same to Agent Seyrus."

Larani turned around.

The Prime Council watched her like a disapproving school teacher. "That's your excuse?" she asked, raising an eyebrow. "Slade used some kind of mind control?"

"We believe so."

"Larani, your agent may have just cost me the election. There are members of the Systems Council who think she should be sentenced to life imprisonment." Larani should have been shocked by that – no one had received such a harsh sentence in two centuries – but she wasn't. "If I'm honest, I have to tell you that I'm inclined to join them."

"Surely you don't think that's justified?"

Sarona just stood there with her mouth agape, and Larani instantly regretted her question. "She *shot* a man because she disagrees with his politics!" The other woman was on the verge of shouting. "The Justice Keepers are supposed to be apolitical. Always. And yet one of you just attempted an assassination to prevent a man she doesn't like from taking office!"

Closing her eyes, Larani kept her breathing steady as she took all of that in. "I take it Dusep has survived the ordeal?" Her voice was ice. The Prime Council might take that as disappointment, but right then, Larani didn't care.

"He's in critical condition."

"Then I wish him a full recovery."

Sarona began to pace across the office, growling and shaking her head. "I do *not* understand this!" she barked. "We had this locked up. You saw the polling data. If Agent Seyrus wanted to prevent Dusep from taking office, all she had to do was keep quiet and wait. Now, she's all but assured his victory. *Why* would she do that?"

"Exactly!" Larani replied. "This is Slade's doing."

"'Slade's doing...'" Sarona grumbled. "That seems to be your answer to everything. And even if you're correct, the fact that Slade keeps getting away with his little schemes is proof that *you* are not up to the task of bringing him in. How many times has Grecken Slade caused a political fiasco in the last year? That incident in Denabria with the woman who looks just like the late Director Morane? Disrupting our negotiations with Antaur? Now this? He's one of yours! Larani. If you can't even control your own people, then Dusep's distrust of the Justice Keepers may be justified."

Facing Larani with fists on her hips, Sarona frowned. "Council will be in session tomorrow morning," she began. "I will be attending remotely. They're going to vote on whether or not to invoke Article Thirty-Two of the Justice Keeper charter."

Larani swallowed.

"So," Sarona went on, "you better give me something solid that I can take to them, because if you don't, you may not have a badge in a week."

Jack was sound asleep in a hospital bed, and at first glance, he looked peaceful. His eyes closed, his chest rising and falling with a slow and steady rhythm. You would never have guessed that he had been in agony a few hours ago.

Given his condition, they had put him in a private room. Just four white walls and a bed. Nothing to look at except possibly the view through his window. He had a nice view of the garden behind the hospital.

Anna sat in a chair with her elbow on the armrest, her face buried in the palm of her hand. *My fault,* she thought. *I never should have let him get close to Slade.*

It would never have occurred to her to think that Slade might have such a weapon. And she trusted her partner. Jack could handle himself – she knew that – but she never should have let him confront someone as crafty as Slade on his own. Her own body had been overwhelmed with pain and exhaustion. Jack had said that he wanted to face Slade alone. She listened, and he paid for it.

The door opened just a crack, and Melissa poked her head into the room. When she saw that Jack was asleep, she came in. "They've got Cassi in lockup," she whispered. "They wouldn't let me talk to her."

Anna nodded.

"Is he?"

"He's sedated."

Anna stood up, and Melissa came over to give her a hug. She found herself sobbing into the girl's chest, her tears leaving a wet spot on Melissa's blue shirt. "I'm sorry," Anna whispered. "I'm so sorry."

"None of this is your fault," Melissa replied.

Backing away from her, Anna sniffled and wiped a tear off her cheek. "Yes, it is," she insisted. "I knew what Slade was capable of. I should have seen it coming! I should have..."

The young woman watched her with a flat expression. Anna recognized that look; it was the one Harry gave you when he was about to tell you that you were being an idiot. "None of us saw this coming," Melissa said softly. "Not me, not Rajel, not Keli."

"And that's the problem," Anna hissed. "He's always one step ahead."

Melissa scowled as she took in the sight of Jack lying there. "Do they know what Slade did to him?"

"Not yet," Anna muttered. "They put him through all kinds of imaging scanners, but so far, they haven't been able to determine what it is."

"We'll find out," Melissa promised. "And we'll fix it."

Anna wished that she could be so certain. It was pretty clear that Slade was able to inflict pain on Jack with the N'Jal. That probably meant that the injection had contained some kind of Overseer technology. She wasn't sure if even the most cutting edge medical science could contend with that. She was halfway through the process of explaining her fears when Melissa's eyes lit up.

The girl smiled, shaking her head. "Overseer tech!" she shouted and then clamped her mouth shut when she realized that she was being too loud. "Don't you see? We have the solution! If it's Overseer tech, my dad can get it out of him!"

Anna leaned against the wall with arms folded, frowning down at herself. "I know you mean well," she began cautiously. "But I'm not sure I want to take that risk. It didn't go so well for your sister."

"That was an accident."

"I know," Anna said. "But Harry's not a brain surgeon. And that's assuming that the problem is in Jack's brain. We don't know. He could make things worse."

Sighing, Melissa put one hand on her hip and held Anna's gaze for a very long while. "Why can't you just trust my dad?"

"Because I don't like the choices he's been making lately," Anna snapped. "And it's not just the N'Jal. It's everything he's done in the last year. Yesterday, I got a report from Denabria saying that your father is now running some kind of cult."

She fell into the chair again, tilting her head back and blinking at the ceiling. "And I know we've been here before," Anna went on. "We should have trusted Ben; we didn't, and he paid for it. The similarity is not lost on me."

"But…"

"But we don't know how a N'Jal works," Anna said. "What's that story you guys like so much? The one with the hobbits? I seem to remember that a key plot point is that the Ring has a corrupting influence on anyone who uses it."

Melissa stood by Jack's bed with a hand over her mouth, watching him sleep. "You think that the N'Jal is corrupting my father?" The girl spoke in a cool, serene voice. Despite that, it was pretty clear that she was not happy with the direction that this conversation was going in. Anna had no desire to pick a fight, but she was too damn tired to be diplomatic.

"The point is that we don't know," Anna said. "It's Overseer tech. For all we know, they can use it to subtly influence his mind."

A knock at the door interrupted them, and then Dr. Venaray stepped into the room. He was a short and slim man in his early forties, a handsome guy with tanned skin and wings of gray in his dark hair. "Come take a look at this."

When she followed him out into the hallway, he handed her a tablet displaying a representation of Jack's nervous system. There were little red dots all over the place. Anna had no idea what she was looking at. "Does this mean you found the problem?"

"It's a virus," the doctor murmured. "Or at least it behaves like one, using Jack's cells to replicate. When it's dormant, it binds itself to the sensory and autonomic ganglia of the nervous system. We suspect that it's activated by the telepathic signal your friend detected earlier."

"So, how do we stop it?"

"I'm not sure," Dr. Venaray answered. "There are various anti-viral agents that we could try. We might be able to devise a treatment that separates the viral DNA from Jack's cells – similar methods have worked against *truisia* and the HIV infection on Earth – but I've never seen genetic engineering like this. If this is Overseer technology, it may adapt to any treatment we try."

Anna exhaled, falling against the door-frame. "Okay," she whispered. "So what are the risk factors?"

The doctor's frown did not exactly fill her with confidence. "We won't know until we gather more data," he said. "But there may be another option."

"I'm listening."

"Well, to be blunt, We do nothing." Anna opened her mouth to say something, but the doctor raised his hands defensively before she could get a word out. "Jack's immune system is producing antibodies at an accelerated rate. We suspect that his Nassai is trying to fight the infection."

"Can she do that?"

"We don't know," Dr. Venaray said. "But the safest course of action might be to let her try."

"Well..." Anna mumbled. "That's something."

The only window in this little cargo hauler looked out on Alios: a beautiful gem of a world with continents covered in lush, green vegetation, perfect, sapphire-blue oceans and swirling clouds dancing over it all. Isara saw her faint reflection in the reinforced glass. A shadow staring back at her.

"He's asleep," Slade growled.

Isara felt her mouth tighten, then shut her eyes and nodded slowly. A shame. Hunter might have been a valuable ally, but now that was impossible. "Don't you have anything better to do?"

There was a time to be vicious, but endlessly tormenting an enemy who had been so thoroughly defeated was just crass. It spoke to an inner cowardice, a fragility that she found repugnant. Victory alone wasn't enough for Slade; no, he had to constantly remind his enemies of their defeat. Anyone who truly believed themself superior would not feel the need to indulge in such vanity.

With proper motivation, Jack Hunter might have been brought into the fold. The virus could have been used toward that end. But with Slade, it was just a sledgehammer to bolster his ego.

She turned around.

Slade was sprawled out in the cushioned seat that served for a captain's chair, his booted foot propped up on the arm, and his lazy smile made her want to stab him. "That boy has given me no end of grief," he spat. "I will make him suffer for every slight."

"Pathetic."

With a heavy sigh, Slade got up and strode toward her, his eyes fixed upon her with violent intent. "*You* should rethink your tone, Isara." He lifted his right hand to display the N'Jal on his palm. "Or I may have to teach you a lesson."

Pressing her lips together, she looked up into his eyes and blinked. "Please do," she said.

He chuckled.

"So, what now?"

He pinched her chin with one hand, tilting her face up. If he tried to kiss her, she would kill him. And it wouldn't end there. She would travel to the Inzari's regeneration chamber and destroy it. She-

"Now," Slade said. "We watch as history unfolds."

Chapter 25

Jack walked through a world of endless mist, mist without texture or temperature, mist that seemed to go on forever. It clung to his body, swirled around his legs and streamed from his fingertips.

He stopped dead.

Chewing his lip as he took in the sight, Jack nodded. "Well," he mumbled. "That's new." His head was still ringing, but the pain was a distant thing, easily ignored. Why did this place seem so familiar?

The answer came to him in a moment of vivid clarity. This was how he had met Summer all those years ago. Was she here too? He hadn't seen her, and he felt as though he had been walking around for hours.

As if in answer to his question, the mist parted to reveal Summer standing there in a simple pair of blue jeans and a flannel shirt like the ones his mother used to wear. A long braid of golden hair fell to the small of her back. "Yes, I am here," she said. "Your mind is still reeling."

"What happened?"

"Slade infected you with a virus," she explained. "It can activate certain neurons, trick your brain into thinking that you're experiencing a wide range of sensations, most of them unpleasant. I'm fighting it now."

Touching his forehead, Jack grimaced as the memories came flooding back. "That sounds like something Slade would do," he muttered. "So, give it to me straight, Doc. Do you think you can kill this thing?"

The look on Summer's face made him think that he didn't want the answer to that question. "We shall see," she replied. "But fighting this virus is tiring. I have little energy to spare for conversation."

"Hence the decor?"

"You will have to accept my apology."

Jack put his arms around her, pulling her close. It surprised him when she squeezed him just as hard as Anna would. "Don't stay on this sinking ship," he whispered. "If you can't kill the virus, I want you to leave me and take a new host."

She pulled out of his embrace almost violently and looked up at him with eyes that blazed. "Do you honestly think so little of yourself?" Jack wasn't sure if he was supposed to answer that. "Would you give up your life so easily?"

"Summer, I don't want you to suffer," he said. "And I don't want to live a long life as Slade's chew toy. I had a good run. Better than I deserve, really."

His Nassai turned her back and stalked off through the mist, stopping when she was just out of arm's reach. "I hear things even while your mind slumbers," she said. "Even if I cannot defeat this virus, the doctors are working on other options."

She spun around to face him, and he almost took a step back. Jeez…And he thought *Anna* had mastered the death glare. "I will *not* abandon you, Jack Hunter," she insisted. "Because of you, I understand what it means to have a best friend. So, we are going to get through this. We're going to live a long, happy life with Anna and Seth. And one day, you and I will bring Grecken Slade to justice."

"Well, when you put it like that-"

He cut off when the setting suddenly changed. The mist was gone, as was the void that contained it. He was looking at the inside of a green door with a window of frosted glass. There were sneakers on the floor: pink ones that belonged to Lauren and gray ones that he had worn as a teenager.

Jack stumbled backward from the door, raising his hands up in front of his face. "Whoa, whoa, whoa..." He let his arms drop a moment later. There was no danger here. "What's with the trip to Flashback Town? I thought you said you were too tired for virtual reality shenanigans?"

No one answered him.

"Summer?"

Still no answer.

He turned around to find that this was indeed the house he had grown up in. A set of stairs went up to the second floor, complete with one of Lauren's sweaters draped over the railing. Mom was always getting on her case about that.

On his right, the dining room was in pristine condition, white curtains fluttering in the breeze that came through an open window. There were placemats on the wooden table but no utensils.

Jack crept through the hallway, trailing his fingertips along the wall. He could feel the rough texture. Whatever Summer was doing, she had gone out of her way to make it vivid. But why?

Poking his head into the family room, Jack saw that everything was as it should be. The room was empty, but his father had left a Jays game playing on the TV. There were throw pillows strewn about on the gray couches, and the recliner had a half-finished bottle of beer in its drink holder.

Bracing a hand on the wall, Jack closed his eyes and took a deep breath. "All right, Summer," he said. "I appreciate the nostalgia, but I'd rather you focus on killing the virus. So, why don't we get to the point of this little vision?"

"In here."

That was not Summer's voice. That was a voice that Jack thought he would never hear again. And it was coming from the kitchen.

That, too was just as he remembered it: linoleum floor tiles and white cupboards encircling the room. One dish in the sink – most likely his father's – and a whole lot of magnets on the fridge. It even smelled like home.

An oval-shaped table sat in the light of a massive bay window that looked out on the backyard. One of the chairs was tucked neatly into place, but the other one...The other one had been claimed by an unexpected guest.

Ben Loranai looked good for a dead man: still slim and fit and handsome in black pants and a matching t-shirt. His hair was left loose to fall to the nape of his neck, and he saluted Jack with a beer bottle. "Hey, buddy."

Anna smoothed a strand of hair off Jack's forehead. He was still sound asleep, or so it seemed. After the first day, the doctors had decided that constant sedation wasn't good for anyone, not even a Justice Keeper. So, they had switched to a drug called *Thaladine,* which induced a sense of peace and euphoria. Jack slept a lot, and when he woke, he was only half lucid. So far as she could tell, Slade had given up on torturing him, but that might just be the drugs.

The screen of SmartGlass across from the foot of his bed displayed a newscast on the election. Anna kept the volume low, but she could still hear the anchorwoman who stared directly into the camera. "As there are only two candidates," she said. "This will be a straight popular vote. Right now, reports are coming in from districts across Leyria, Palissa, Salus Prime and the Petross space station."

Globes appeared as a graphic over her right shoulder. The anchorwoman drew in a long breath, then closed her eyes and prepared herself to say something she obviously did not want to say. "Preliminary results show Jeral Dusep with a sizable ten-point lead."

The image changed to a shot of Dusep in a hospital bed not unlike Jack's. The man was unconscious. He looked so helpless, not at all like the despot who had built his career on attacking immigrants and foreigners. "The councilor remains in stable condition, but he is expected to make a full recovery."

Anna paced across the room with her arms crossed, heaving out a breath. "Damn it, Cass," she whispered. "Couldn't you have resisted him? All you had to do was say no."

She spun around.

Jack was still asleep, but his head lolled as he murmured something unintelligible. Every time he made a noise, Anna perked up. She knew that there was nothing she could do, but she wanted Jack to know that he wasn't alone.

Leaving the room was hard. The doctors had agreed to let her stay the night, and she had slept fitfully in the bedside chair. But there were still moments where she had to go down to the cafeteria for a meal or sneak out to the restroom. And every second that she was gone was filled with anxiety that Jack might wake up and find her missing.

She had taken a few hours, yesterday, to visit Cassi at Justice Keeper HQ. Or rather, she had tried to visit Cassi. Melissa had been turned away when she made the attempt, but Anna figured they wouldn't do the same to an operative who had carried a badge for seven years. Not when that operative was Cassi's supervising officer. But to her surprise, the guards refused to budge. The prisoner was not to receive visitors.

That pissed Anna off something fierce. She had marched right into Larani's office and demanded that the chief director order those guards to let her in. It did no good. Even Larani was not allowed into that cell. That didn't bode well for Cassi.

Anna fell into a chair with a heavy sigh. "You need to wake up now," she muttered. "It's not going well, and I don't know if I can fix it without you."

Jack didn't answer her.

Closing her eyes, Anna sighed as she forced herself to acknowledge an ugly truth she had been avoiding. "It's my fault," she said. "You tried to warn me, but I didn't listen. You'd think, one day, that I'd learn to trust your instincts."

The door opened to admit Larani, who sighed when she saw Jack. "I should have visited sooner," she said. "I'm sorry."

"It's been a crazy few days."

"Indeed," Larani said. "The Hall of Council finished its deliberations earlier this afternoon." Now that was surprising. From what Anna had heard, those deliberations had started yesterday morning. Had they really taken more than twenty-four hours to decide whether Larani would retain her position? "They've chosen to delay the vote until after the election. For the moment, I will retain my position."

Anna forced a smile. Right then, she didn't feel like smiling, but it *was* good news. "I'm glad to hear it," she said. "And Cassi?"

Larani gripped the metal bar of Jack's bed, hunching over as she peered out the window. "Cassiara has been stripped of her badge," she said. "In one month's time, she will stand trial for attempted murder."

"Is there anything we can do?"

"No," Larani said. "It took some doing, but I was able to persuade the medical staff to run some tests. I think they were afraid that Cassiara might hurt them. They found no evidence of the virus that Slade used on Jack."

"What?"

"Cassiara is perfectly healthy."

Anna was on her feet and pacing in an instant, gesticulating as she worked it all out in her head. "Cassi's not a traitor," she said. "Slade must have infected her when she was missing. That was five days ago now. Maybe her body had more time to fight the virus."

Turning around to face her with arms folded, Larani answered that with a skeptical frown. "Perhaps," she said. "But that argument won't convince a jury."

"We have the evidence of what Slade did to Jack."

"And no evidence that he did the same to Cassi."

Grinding her teeth, Anna felt a wave of heat in her face. She touched her fingertips to her forehead. "It never bloody ends," she spat. "Look, I'm pissed at her too, Larani, but we can't leave her to rot in prison!"

"We may not get a choice in the matter," Larani replied. "As far as the public knows, Cassiara acted of her own accord. Even if we can somehow prove that she was under duress, the prosecution will bring up Jack's refusal to accede to Slade's wishes."

They were cut off by another update from the newscast. The anchorwoman was staring into the camera with a positively dire expression. "We have now received the final results from Leyria and Palissa, showing Jeral Dusep with a fifty-three percent and sixty-one percent majority, respectively. In light of the numbers that we have already received from the other colony worlds, we can now safely say that Jeral Dusep is the next Prime Council."

"And," Larani said. "We have bigger concerns."

This was just a dream.

Five minutes ago, Jack had been talking to Summer about the virus that Slade had planted in his body. A virus that could make him hallucinate, experience sensations that were not real. If Slade could do that, then why couldn't he control Jack's dreams as well. This was his doing.

Either that, or it was a reaction to his body trying to fight the infection. Jack had experienced more than his fair share of fever dreams, and some of them turned the trippy factor up to eleven. A dream, a hallucination: it didn't matter which. But whatever it was, there was no way that Ben Loranai was sitting at his kitchen table and drinking a bottle of Labatt Blue.

Jack leaned against the doorframe, tossing his head back and rolling his eyes. "Oh, great," he muttered. "Just what I need. One of Slade's hallucinations."

"Well…"

"What? You're gonna tell me you're the real Ben?"

Chuckling softly, Ben stood up and set his beer down on the table. His smile… Well, it was good to see him smiling again, even if it *was* just one of Slade's tricks. "Well, that's the thing," Ben said. "The only reason we can *have* this little chat is because, when you wake up, you won't be sure that any of it was real. So, confirming my identity might get me in trouble."

"With who?"

"Na uh," Ben said. "Spoilers."

Pursing his lips as he studied the man, Jack felt his eyebrows rising. "So, let me get this straight," he began. "You came all the way back here just to tell me that you can't tell me anything?"

"I came back here to tell you to stop blaming yourself for my death. It wasn't your fault. One of my biggest regrets is blaming you for all the crappy decisions that Larani and the others made."

Jack walked across the kitchen with his hands in his pockets, smiling sheepishly. He shook his head. "Well, as mind screws go," he said. "This one seems fairly benign."

"That's because it's not a mind screw."

Opening a cupboard, Jack took out a glass and inspected it. He ran the tap, filled the glass and took a drink. Cold and delicious, just like always. He was starting to wonder if this *was* just a dream.

"Let's review the facts," he said. "The last time we spoke, you were pissed because I didn't tell you about Leo's reunion tour.

And you know what? You were right to be mad. Because not two days later, Leo killed you. So, if it's okay with you, maybe we don't do the whole Jack of Contrition thing."

Ben hopped up on the counter, gripping the edge with both hands. His soft laughter eased some of Jack's anxiety. "You know, I miss this side of you," he said. "You don't do the snarky quips as much these days."

"Well, I'm trying to be more professional."

"But you see, Jack; that's the problem."

Jack opened his mouth to speak, but the setting changed again before he could get a word out. Now, he was standing on a catwalk overlooking some kind of warehouse. The lower level was filled with big metal crates stacked on top of each other. Ten bucks said that every one of them was filled with drugs or guns or some other form of contraband. It was the standard operating procedure for bad guys.

Ben stepped up to the railing, holding it tight as he looked out upon a veritable treasure trove of illicit goods. "You recognize this place?"

Biting his lip, Jack nodded as he took in the sight. "Nicolae Petrov's warehouse," he muttered. "You and I raided it two years ago."

"And *you* ended up with a month-long suspension," Ben said. "Ah, those were the days! I miss the Jack who was willing to piss off his colleagues when he knew he was right, and I think, deep down inside, you do too."

Ben turned away, walking along the catwalk with one hand on the railing. "Wanna know the best part about being dead?" He stopped when he was just a few paces away. "It gives you a lot of time to consider your regrets."

Jack stood there with his arms crossed, staring at his best friend's back. "Yeah," he said. "I would imagine. But it's good to know I'll have plenty to keep me busy when my time comes."

Abruptly, Ben spun around, cocked his head to one side and raised an eyebrow. "Do you want to know what I regret?"

"Smuggling weapons on the Fringe?"

"Nope."

"Breaking up with Darrel?"

With a heavy sigh, Ben leaned one shoulder against the wall. "Well, that one I'll give you," he said. "But it's not why I came here. You see, Jack, I regret what I said to you before I died."

"You wanted to review the facts? Let's review them. I wasn't angry because you didn't tell me about Leo. No, that wasn't it. I was angry because you didn't tell me soon enough. But honestly now, would an extra twenty-four hours of looking over my shoulder have made any difference?"

"I guess we'll never know," Jack whispered.

Ben strode toward him, metal clanging beneath his feet. He spread his arms wide. "But there's a bigger problem," he said. "And there's just no way to put this delicately; so... You're off your path, buddy."

Forcing a smile, Jack looked down at his shoes. "I'm off my path," he mumbled. "Well, there's one I haven't heard before."

"You were never meant to be the guy who toes the line, Jack. That's not you, and you know it. You're the guy who tells the emperor that he's not wearing any clothes. And I know what you're thinking: 'What's Ben doing referencing an Earth fable that he almost certainly never heard?' Well, maybe I broadened my horizons after dying. Or maybe this is all just your mind trying to work out an emotional issue you've been ignoring. Does it matter? If this is just a dream, what does it mean that you're having it?"

"I don't know, Sigmund," Jack replied. "Why don't you tell me?"

Ben's response to that was a smug smile. "Tell me something," he said. "Did you agree with the arbiter's decision to confiscate my multi-tool? Or with Larani's decision to deny me access to the advanced armour?"

"No. Why should Keepers have a monopoly on power?"

"Right," Ben agreed. "And then you weren't exactly thrilled with being censured for voicing a political opinion. Sure, the Justice Keepers are supposed to be neutral, but neutrality has a way of benefiting those who already have power."

Just like that, they were in the rainforest, standing in ankle-deep puddles that formed in the small dips and craters in this uneven landscape. Massive trees rose up all around them, blocking out the sun.

Splashing as he paced over to the body of a dead Ragnosian soldier, Ben put his fists on his hips and shook his head. "Then there was that troop carrier," he said. "The one you refused to shoot down even though you had been ordered to do so."

Jack fell back against a tree trunk, shutting his eyes and trying to stifle his irritation. Despite his best efforts, a low growl rumbled in his throat. "I get it," he snapped. "Jack is a screw-up. Story of my life."

Turning slowly, Ben gave him a look that called him an idiot. "If that's what you're taking away from this," he said. "Then you haven't been paying attention."

The other man came splashing over to him and held out a closed fist. "The point is that you keep finding yourself at odds with the philosophies of the institution you work for. And that being the case, maybe you need to ask yourself whether this…" He let his fingers uncurl to reveal a Justice Keeper badge in the palm of his hand "…is something you actually want."

"And if it isn't?"

"Then I think you need to make some changes."

Before Jack could reply, the other man clapped him on the shoulder. There was sadness in Ben's eyes. "I wish that I could stay longer," he said. "But you know the whole cosmic order thing. They're not keen on us interfering with mortal affairs. Just do me a favour, okay? Tell Anna it wasn't her fault either."

Interlude 5

(47 years ago)

Her name was Alida: a beautiful young woman, with a bob of short, brown hair, who slept peacefully next to him. Her eyes fluttered open, and she smiled up at him. "You're doing that thing again."

For the last five years, his name had been Sorin. Five years spent arming colonists on the Leyrian Fringe Worlds while his associates did the same on the Antauran side of the border. This sector of space was dry kindling, ready to ignite at the tiniest spark. Just as the Inzari wanted it.

He was a man of average height now, slim, with a dark complexion and almost no hair to speak of. Except for a short goatee. Lying next to Alida with the blankets pulled up to his chest, he allowed himself a contented smile. "And what thing is that?"

"That thing where you start worrying."

Sitting up with a sigh, he scrubbed a hand over his face and his smooth, bald head. "I'm not worried," he said. "Or I won't be once Tysan picks up this shipment."

Alida sat up and nuzzled his shoulder, giggling softly. It was the innocent giggle of a girl who found herself besotted with a foolish old man. He had heard it many times. And he *was* old, though he didn't look it. "He'll be here," she assured him. "He always comes through."

Sorin nodded.

"Are you sure we're doing the right thing?"

Glancing over his shoulder, Sorin frowned at her. "We're doing the only thing we can." It was an answer he had given more than once. The only possible answer, though he had never explained why. Alida knew nothing of the Inzari. One way or another, those weapons would find their way into the hands of men who wanted to fight. If the Inzari wanted war, there would be war. There was just no getting around it.

"But the news reports keep saying we'll be responsible for an interstellar war."

He sneered, unable to hide his contempt. "Reports written by people who don't live out here," he snapped. "The Antaurans are gonna keep coming, and if we don't stand up to them, they'll take world after world until they've surrounded Leyria itself."

It was true.

Bleakness take him, it would probably still be true even without the Inzari guiding events. The Antaurans were eager to expand their empire. He had seen it thousands of times now. On Earth, on Leyria, on Ragnos. Humans lived to make war. They didn't need the Inzari to help them with that.

It dawned on him that he had thought a Leyrian curse. That happened sometimes. He had to adopt the speech patterns of the local culture, and that usually entailed thinking in those patterns. But he had thought it with such passion. He felt genuine hatred for the Antaurans. And that scared him. These weren't his people; this wasn't his cause. When exactly had this become personal for him?

He already knew the answer.

The answer was sitting right next to him.

Gently, he laid a hand on Alida's cheek and then kissed her forehead. "Sleep," he murmured. "This will all be over tomorrow."

When she dozed off again, Sorin got out of bed, draped a robe around himself and put on a pair of slippers. He stepped out into the cabin on the little cargo hauler he had appropriated for this assignment. After five years, the ship was starting to feel like home.

There wasn't much to see: just a round table and four seats, all bolted to the floor. The bulkheads were an ugly colour. Not quite gray, not quite brown, but somehow able to capture the dreariness of both.

He paced across the room to a small cupboard on the wall, opening it to reveal a bottle of Leyrian brandy inside. Pouring himself a glass, he sighed as he inhaled the aroma.

He tossed it back in one quick gulp, the alcohol burning his throat, then poured himself another. It did little to soothe his anxiety. Their ship was parked on a moon orbiting one of the gas giants of a star system about ten lightyears away from Palissa. A place so remote that there should have been no chance of attracting any unwanted attention. But the Justice Keepers had been merciless in their pursuit of smugglers. He despised the Justice Keepers.

Those idiots on Leyria honestly believed that if they could prevent weapons from making their way to the Fringe Worlds, it would squelch any possibility of a conflict with Antaur. Leyrians were idiots. There would be war. Sooner or later.

"You have become distracted, my son."

He shivered at the sound of a familiar voice.

Turning around, he found himself face to face with the Old Woman. She smiled at him like a proud mother. "You have done well," she said. "But you have grown attached to the girl."

"The girl is harmless."

"We disagree," the Old Woman replied. "It is time that you severed the connection. Your task here is finished."

Lifting a half-filled glass up in front of his face, Sorin shut his eyes and drew in a rasping breath. "I have served you faithfully for over two thousand years," he whispered. "I have damned my soul more times than I can count. For you. Please…Let me have this brief reprieve."

He realized that he was begging. He had never been the sort of man who begged for anything, but he did so now, and that frightened him even more than the revelation that he had taken Alida's cause as his own. He loved her.

When was the last time that he could truly say that he loved someone? Paleen? No. His marriage to Paleen had been nothing more than a political alliance, a necessary step in Dravis Trovan's rise to prominence among the Tareli aristocracy. Matilda? Was it even fair to call her his wife?

The original William of Normandy had been smitten with Matilda. So enamoured that he actually drubbed her when she refused to be his bride. Though most tales of that event were exaggerated. Sorin had never loved her. After stepping into William's shoes, he had been forced to pretend, but it was never real.

Qi? Yes, he had loved Qi, and Lu had killed her for it. Qi had died in misery while Sui Bian tended crops on Old Feng's farm. The worst part was that he couldn't even remember her face.

But he loved Alida.

And that terrified him.

The Old Woman studied him with those inscrutable eyes and then shook her head slowly. "You have a greater purpose," she said. "Your work must continue."

"Surely one of the others could-"

"They are but tools," she said. "*You* have been chosen to be our voice. Return to us now, my son, and claim your destiny."

Clenching his teeth, Sorin trembled as the rage flared hot within him. Would these creatures never be done with him? "I have served long enough," he growled. "You once told me that my people must go to the stars. Well, they have gone to the stars. My task is complete. I will serve you no longer. If that means giving up immortality, then so be it. I should have died a long time ago."

Just like that, the Old Woman was gone.

No arguments. No further attempts to persuade him. She was just gone. And that left him feeling cold inside.

Sorin woke in the middle of the night to an alarm blaring. His first thought was that The Justice Keepers had found him. But that made no sense. He had dropped the weapons yesterday; there was nothing to find. Perhaps they had arrested Tysan, and through him, they had found their way to Sorin. It didn't matter.

Leaping out of bed and tossing the blankets aside, he landed with bare feet on the ship's cold floor. He scrubbed at his face with the back of one hand. "What is it now?" he growled.

Alida sat up with the blankets clutched to her chest. "What happened?" she asked, squirming across the mattress to lay a hand on his back.

"I don't know."

He pushed his way into the ship's cabin, then ran up the small set of steps to the cockpit. Through the window, he saw tall palm trees under the starry night sky. They had landed on Palissa.

The ship's systems lit up when he spread his hands along the control console, lights coming on overhead. But he didn't need sensors to see the streak of blue flashing out of the sky, striking trees and setting them ablaze.

Bracing his hands on the console, Sorin leaned forward and squinted through the window. "Antaurans," he whispered. "They're attacking."

Alida came into the cockpit behind him, wrapped in the blankets and holding them close. "Here?" she whispered. "Why would they?"

He stood up straight with teeth bared and growled like a feral dog. "They probably know we've been delivering weapons to the militia." Tysan's camp was a few kilometres away, hidden in the forest and shielded from orbital sensors by stealth technology.

A crescent-shaped ship swooped low over the trees, firing streams of blue plasma from the tips of its curved wings. Not at them. But Sorin heard the explosion a short ways off. "That was a dread-wing," he snapped. "We need to leave this place."

Alida was already pulling a black t-shirt over her head. "Bleakness take me if we will!" She buckled her pants, then opened a small compartment to retrieve a pistol. One of the few security measures this ship offered. It would not even have been there if not for Sorin's insistence on taking precautions.

Looking up at him with a strand of dark hair falling over one eye, Alida blinked. "Come on," she said. "Tysan needs us."

"We can't go out there."

"Why not."

Crossing his arms, Sorin backed up until he was practically sitting on the control console. He shook his head in dismay. "If we do," he said. "We'll be killed."

"I'm willing to take that risk."

Alida was out the door and headed to the air-lock before he could protest. There was nothing to do but follow her and pray. Sorin was not a praying man, but he would put aside his pride for her. The only problem with that, however, was the stark reality that the Inzari had no interest in keeping Alida alive.

Outside, the palm trees were thick and domineering. Alida was always ten steps ahead of him, hopping over exposed roots, ducking low under branches, moving with a purpose. "This is foolhardy!" he called after her.

She turned back, looking over her shoulder, the pistol held tightly in one hand. "Go back to the ship if you're so inclined."

And then she was off again.

Sorin followed.

Less than two minutes passed before the dreadwing rushed past again, spitting bolts of hot plasma that set the forest on fire. Sorin could hear the crackling and smell the acrid smoke. If they tried to walk into that inferno, it would consume them.

Flames licked the trees and filled the night with a fierce orange glow. The heat they gave off was intense, but Alida showed no sign of slowing down.

Stepping forward with a hand up to shield his face, Sorin groaned. "We have to get back to the ship!" he shouted. "We're not safe out here!"

His lover started looking for a way to circumnavigate the blaze. At one point, she hopped onto a large rock, but that exposed her to the heat. She fell backward, very nearly cracking her skull open. Thankfully, she landed on her bottom.

Sorin went to her.

Dropping to one knee beside her, he snarled with barely-restrained anger. "Don't be a fool!" The words were out of his mouth before he had a chance to reconsider them. "In all likelihood, Tysan is already dead!"

"You don't know that!"

"Look around you, woman!"

Alida sat up and slapped him across the face, leaving a hot sting on his skin. His vision blurred for a moment, and when it cleared again, he saw her face in the firelight. There was contempt in her eyes. "I am not stupid," she hissed. "I will not abandon our friends when we have the power to-"

She cut off when something stung the side of her neck. A small dart that sank into her skin. Pulling it free, Alida blinked a few times as she tried to get a sense of what had happened. Then she passed out from the tranquilizer in her system.

"No!" Sorin called out.

Another dart hit him.

He had just enough time to look around and find a hooded figure standing between two trees. A wraith-like being who let out a peel of rich laughter as she strode toward him on nimble feet. Sorin wanted to curse her, but he couldn't get the words out. Everything went black.

He awoke to find himself lying on the sofa in the cabin of his ship. Slowly, the fog receded from his vision, and he recognized the dull gray ceiling above him. Dizziness put any thought of moving out of his head.

He looked around to find Sari – that was what she called herself now – standing by the door to his bed-chamber. Her hood was drawn back, exposing her pale face and the long braid of dark hair that fell to her shoulder-blades. "You've carved out a nice little life for yourself, haven't you?"

"What..." His mouth didn't want to form words. "What...What did you...do to me?"

"Just a mild tranquilizer."

"Where is...Alida?"

Sari pointed to a corner where Alida was slumped against the wall with her legs stretched out before her. But she wasn't asleep. Even with his head spinning, Sorin could see that Alida's skin was gray and pallid, her eyes glassy and unfocused. She was dead.

The thunder of weapons' fire outside matched the thunder in his own heart. His rage should have had him on his feet and strangling Sari, but he couldn't move. He just could not move. "Why?" he mumbled.

Sari turned her head to smile at him. "The Inzari warned you that your work was not yet complete," she said. "They told you to sever ties with her, and you refused. Since you would not do it yourself, they sent me to do it for you."

"I...I hate you..."

"Yes," Sari purred. "I'm sure you do."

He forced himself to sit up. The dizziness almost made him fall over, and he raised a hand to his temple. "You didn't have to kill her," he whimpered. "You...You didn't have to go that far."

"You had your chance to leave her willingly," Sari said. "You refused. Now live with the choices you have made."

Fury had him on his feet in a second. He ran toward her – stumbled toward her – only to receive a swift kick to the belly. He was barely even aware of his shoulder hitting the deck.

When he rolled onto his back, Sari stood over him. Her cruel smile belonged on the face of death itself. "Oh, by the way," she said. "This *isn't* a tranquilizer."

And then she shot him in the head.

Bit by bit, he became aware of his own existence. Bit by bit, he felt sensation creep into his mind. He was in the sludge again, the thick ooze that the Inzari used to build him a new body every time he died. Normally, instinct made him struggle until his head broke through the surface. This time, however, he chose to stay put.

Sadly, he didn't need to breathe while he was submerged in this stuff. It sustained him somehow. He couldn't kill himself, but he could refuse to cooperate. Maybe then the Inzari would do the deed for him. He wanted to die.

He waited, but the Inzari seemed to sense his plan.

The goo writhed all around him, spitting him out like a bad meal. He landed on the shore of the strange pool, covered in slime. It dripped from his chin, from his nose, from the tips of his fingers.

Slowly, he looked up.

The Old Woman stood over him with a proud smile on her face. "Welcome back, my son," she said.

Pawing at himself, he discovered his new visage. A long nose, thick eyebrows and a bald head. Not the sleek, smooth skin that Sorin had displayed. No, this time, he had a ring of hair from ear to ear. A man in his middle years then. His hands were pale, and so was the rest of him. "What do you want of me?"

"We have work for you on Ragnos."

There was no fighting it. Not here, in this place. So, he followed the steps that had become routine after two thousand years. He found clothes in a neighbouring chamber, and then, once he was dressed, a SlipGate rose out of the floor to propel him into his new life. The bubble rushed through its endless, dark tunnel, and when it finally popped, he was standing in a city of tall buildings in the shadow of an island that seemed to float on nothing at all. The latest display of Ragnosian vanity. He paid it no mind.

The very first thing he did was make his way to the slums. They weren't hard to find. And then it only took him ten minutes to locate a gun, put the barrel against his head and pull the trigger.

He awoke in the ooze and struggled his way to the shore. There was no point in resisting. Coughing and sputtering, he climbed out of the pool and remained on all fours as the slime dripped from his body. He was tanned now, his face slim with gaunt cheeks, his muscles taut and hard.

Once again, the Old Woman greeted him. "Welcome back, my son."

He ignored her.

The very instant he had strength enough to stand, he walked into the next chamber and put on what appeared to be Leyrian fashions. Soft, cotton pants and a tight t-shirt. The Gate arrived as soon as he was presentable, and sure enough, it deposited him in the middle of Denabria. He walked to the nearest subway station and threw himself in front of a speeding train.

He awoke in the ooze and scrambled his way out of the pool. He was fat now, his skin bearing a distinct copper complexion. Scrubbing the slime out of his jowls, he looked up to find the Old Woman waiting. "Welcome back, my son."

He found his clothes and waited for the SlipGate. He wasn't even sure what planet it brought him too, but it took him all of ten minutes to find a knife and open his veins.

He drowned himself, ingested poison and picked a hopeless fight with violent criminals. He took mind-numbing drugs until the overdose killed him, and when that did not work, he set his own house on fire. Each time, he woke up in the ooze. Each time, the Old Woman greeted him with the same infuriating words. "Welcome back, my son."

Did the Inzari think he would relent?

He refused to give them the satisfaction. Perhaps he had to kill himself in a way that made it impossible for the Inzari to revive him. He dreamed up the most destructive death he could imagine, and then – at the earliest opportunity – he flew a shuttle straight into the corona of a star.

It did no good.

He woke up in the ooze again and wept as it spat him out. The Old Woman never acknowledged his pitiful display. She just said what she always said. "Welcome back, my son." Why wouldn't they just let him die?

He endured death after death to no avail, and then at some point, long after he had lost count of how many times he had taken his own life, he began to think that perhaps he was trapped in his own personal Hell.

He spoke the truth of the Inzari to anyone who would listen. Maybe if he exposed their plans, they would finally decide that he wasn't worth the trouble of keeping alive. It didn't help. People laughed at him or called him a madman. After a few months of that, Sari showed up to put a knife in his back. He laughed as the cold darkness swallowed him. If the Inzari had sent one of their agents to kill him, it meant they were finally done with him.

He died with a smile on his face and awoke in the goo, unable to scream or wail. Despair claimed him then. He knew that he could not find it within himself to take his own life again. Why endure the pain if it only led him back here?

Slowly, he climbed out of the pool and struggled onto the shore, soft flesh pulsing beneath his hands. The air was warm and wet. Muggy like a hot, summer day. The Old Woman…Where was the Old Woman?

For the first time, he was alone.

With cautious hands, he traced the outline of his face. His face…No. Surely, they would not have done that to him. Not after everything else.

Down on all fours he sobbed as the truth became clear to him. He didn't need a mirror to recognize this face. He knew it all too well. He was Sui Bian once again: the one body that he hated above all others, the symbol of everything the Inzari had taken from him. "Why?" he croaked.

Suddenly, the Old Woman was there, standing over him with her fists on her hips. Her scowl was horrifying. "You needed a lesson in humility," she said. "Henceforth, you will wear this face until we decide that you have earned the right to another."

"Please, no…"

"Rise, my son. Groveling does not become you."

He got up and stood before her, shaking his head slowly. "I hate you," he rasped. "You must know that."

"We do not need your love," she said. "Only your obedience."

"What do you wish of me?"

Sari emerged from an opening in the wall, stepping into a chamber with a grin that made him want to skin her alive. One day, he would make her pay for what she had done to Alida. "You should be grateful," she said. "You might actually enjoy this assignment."

"What assignment?"

"It seems our friend Mr. Pennfield has managed to get his hands on the body of a dead Justice Keeper," she explained. "And more importantly, on the symbiont the Keeper carried. His preliminary experiments look quite promising."

He hesitated.

Of all the things she might have said, he had not expected *that*. It didn't relieve his pain, but it was enough to hold his interest. "What do you want me to do?"

Chapter 26

Jack's eyes fluttered open.

He was lying in a hospital bed with his hands folded over his chest, staring up at the ceiling. And he was *bone* tired. Every muscle felt like it had turned to jelly. "Whoa," he said. "That was a head trip…"

Anna and Melissa were at the foot of his bed, both standing with their backs turned as they watched the TV. They both spun around to greet him with bright smiles. "Hey!" Anna exclaimed. "You're awake!"

Sitting up, Jack winced as the fatigue hit him like an oncoming truck. "Barely," he panted. "But my vision is pleasantly Slade-free; so, I'm gonna assume that Summer killed the virus."

Anna blinked. "You know about the virus?"

"Summer told me," he explained. "Some time between my chat with the talking fox and that brief trip to Oz. Which reminds me, shouldn't you all be in sepia?"

Anna walked around the side of his bed and leaned over to give him a kiss on the forehead. "I'm glad you're feeling better," she said. "The doctors put you in the scanner this morning. They say the virus is gone."

Melissa stood there with her hands clasped demurely in front of herself, her eyes fixed on the floor. "But there is bad news," she added. "Dusep won the election."

"I figured."

"He's awake now," Melissa went on. "And making statements about how this is a brave new day for Leyria and its colonies."

Jack felt his mouth stretch in a yawn. He gave his head a shake to clear the fog out of his brain. "Well, we can deal with the fallout tomorrow," he mumbled. "Today, I just want to celebrate being alive and pain-free."

After hugging him, Melissa left so that he could rest, but she was gone less than five minutes before a doctor came in. Some guy named Vanaray who looked like he belonged on an episode of that *ER* reboot that lasted half a season. "It's good to see you awake, Agent Hunter," he said. "I take it Anna filled you in."

"She did," Jack replied. "I'm told you gave me a clean bill of health."

"Do you have any questions?"

Jack narrowed his eyes as he studied the other man, nodding slowly. "Actually, I do," he said. "Were you able to get any samples of this virus from my blood or tissue or anything like that?"

"We were."

"Can you make a vaccine?"

Closing his eyes, the doctor took a deep breath and then let it out again. "We have been looking into that," he said. "But this is Overseer technology. And there are similar infections that can remain dormant in the body for years without triggering an immune response."

Gripping the bars on either side of his bed, Jack steeled himself against another wave of fatigue. "Slade *will* use this bug against people who don't have the benefit of a symbiont," he muttered. "I want to take that bullet out of his gun."

"A laudable goal," the doctor replied. "We'll do what we can."

"Thanks."

Telixa Ethran marched through the corridors of her ship like a woman on her way to an execution. She didn't inspect the battle damage that her crew was still hurrying to repair; she didn't make eye-contact with anyone she passed. She just kept her head down.

Eventually, she came to a set of double doors that parted like the Sinner's Gate and then stepped inside to find herself in a plain room with cream-coloured bulkheads. There was nothing here except a small worktable and a single chair.

Ten seconds after she arrived, holograms appeared: men and women in dark-gray uniforms, each with admiral's epaulettes on their shoulders. Jhai Thoro, a big man with a thick, bushy mustache, harrumphed when he saw her. "Do you have anything to say for yourself? Any explanation for why you just handed us the worst military defeat we have suffered in *thirty* years!"

She had nothing to say.

She had no excuse because there was no excuse. The attack on Alios had been an abysmal failure, as she had known it would be from the very start. Oh, for a little while there, she had hoped that they might pull off a miracle. The Leyrian defenses had broken faster than her experts had anticipated. She'd had a fleeting hope that they might just be able to hold the planet long enough to fortify their position. But then the Antaurans came, just as she had expected. Under normal circumstances, she never would have authorized such a foolhardy plan. But Slade had her in his pocket now.

He appeared to her often, inflicting pain whenever she questioned one of his edicts. She couldn't tell anyone about the virus. If she did, he would leave her to suffer endless misery.

Jessi Vataro frowned, then stepped forward, his hologram intersecting with Jhai's so that their arms passed through one another. "You have dragged us into a conflict that we have little chance of winning!"

"The Leyrians are pacifists," Telixa muttered. "They'll deliberate for months before they decide to retaliate."

"Who said anything about the Leyrians?"

Jessi waved her hand and the entire room became a hologram. It seemed to Telixa that she was standing in the middle of empty space, surrounded by a thick, inky blackness speckled with stars. Only the presence of the worktable spoiled the illusion.

Several large Antauran frigates converged on a ring-shaped space station, firing blue particle beams that pounded its shields. Telixa recognized the installation. Drenovat Station. The Antaurans had made an incursion to her side of the galaxy.

Telixa shook her head. "How many?" she stammered. "How many?"

Jessi paced a line in front of her, snarling like a cornered cat. "They've struck four targets in our territory in the last twenty-four hours," she spat. "And I'm sure you realize that the alliance you failed to prevent will drag the Leyrians into the war whether they welcome it or not. Especially in light of the political situation there."

"Then we strike back," Telixa replied. "And we strike back hard."

The other woman froze in mid-step and then rounded on her. "Are you insane?" she bellowed. "There is no way that we can survive a protracted conflict with both Leyria and Antaur. My analysts predict that if we go to war, Ragnos will fall within eighteen months. I say we sue for peace."

"I believe," Toran Jaal put in, "that Admiral Ethran made that impossible when she attacked Alios. Even if we were to formally disavow her actions, the Antaurans still want revenge for the death of their president, and the Leyrians will be more than happy to go along with it."

Just as Slade wanted.

Ragnosian fighters were swarming the Antauran ships, spitting green energy bolts, but the Antaurans launched fighters of their own. It was chaos out there.

"She should be stripped of rank!" Jessi shouted. "After this fiasco…"

Toran, however, was more patient. He tapped his lips thoughtfully and then said, "Even the best commanders suffer defeats. Admiral Ethran's long career of service counts for something. For the moment, our concern should be devising a counteroffensive."

Telixa sighed. "Have your analysts assess the most viable targets in both Leyrian and Antauran territory," she said. "We meet to compare notes in three days."

The admirals all looked at her with grim resignation.

And then their holograms winked out.

The quarters that they had given Anna aboard the *Moonlight Dancer* – quarters that she shared with Jack – were a little cramped. The small sitting room offered just enough space to maneuver around the couch and the small square table with four chairs. Its walls were a dull gray and ridged in places.

Anna would say that it suited her mood – she was definitely feeling some glumness – but the truth was that her emotions were all over the place. Not so much gray but a rainbow of colours swirling together into an ugly brown sludge. There was sadness over Cassi, and a little anger too; there was guilt over her failure to anticipate Slade's plan, fear of the direction that her society seemed to be going in and a profound sense of relief at the knowledge that Jack would be all right. All of that combined into a general tightness in her chest. She chose to focus on the good feelings.

In pajama shorts and an old blue t-shirt, Anna stepped into the bedroom with one hand on the doorframe. "Hey, you!" she said. "What'cha thinkin' about?"

Jack was sitting on the foot of their bed. He looked up at the sound of her voice and blinked. "Well, I *was* gonna take a crack at the Hodge Conjecture, but now I'm distracted by the overwhelming cuteness."

"Aw…"

"You make it very hard to get any work done."

Stepping forward, Anna wrapped her arms around his neck and held him close so that he could rest his head on her chest. She ran her fingers through his hair. "That is a good thing," she whispered. "Larani gave us both some time off, and I've decided that I want to spend every second of it taking care of you."

"Oh yeah?"

"Mmhmm. So, how 'bout I give you a nice relaxing back rub so you can fall asleep?"

Five minutes later, Jack was lying on his stomach with his cheek pressed against the pillow, sighing as she gently kneaded his shoulders. "You know, I think we got this backwards," he murmured. "I'm supposed to be doing this for you."

Anna trailed kisses over his spine until she reached his shoulder. Then she nuzzled the side of his neck and whispered in his ear. "Silly boy. You know how much you like taking care of me when I'm stressed or tired? Well, that vice is pretty damn versa."

"Huh…when you put it that way…"

"I'm sorry."

Jack twisted around just enough to give her some side-eye. "For what?" he asked. "If you're questioning your back-rub skills, let me assure you that you've got nothing to worry about."

She sat up straight, shivering when she realized that it was too late to back out of this conversation. "I should have listened to you," she whispered. "You tried to warn me about Cassi, but I…"

Jack rolled onto his back and sat up, pulling her into a warm hug. Damn it! She was *supposed* to be taking care of him, but she couldn't stop herself from crying as she buried her nose in his chest. His hand settled onto the back of her head, gently stroking her hair. "It's okay, Anna," he said. "It's okay. You've got nothing to apologize for."

She looked up at him with tears on her cheeks. "You're very wrong about that," she whimpered. "I'm the reason for all of it, Jack. I'm the reason Dusep is Prime Council; I'm the reason Cassi is rotting in a cell. If I had just listened to you..."

She pulled away, wiping the tears off her face, and then shook her head. "I swore I wasn't going to do this," she growled. "I wasn't going to make it about me when you were the one who endured three days of torture."

Gently, he cupped her face with both hands and then kissed her on the lips. It was a warm kiss, tender but passionate, and for a few seconds, she almost forgot the tempest of emotions in the back of her head. When he finally broke the kiss, she was breathless.

"You think I'm mad because you trusted a friend?" Jack said. "You think I'm upset because you didn't immediately buy into the house of cards that I constructed from gut feelings and some *very* circumstantial evidence?"

"But you were right."

"So what?"

She froze. That was not the response she had been expecting.

Closing his eyes, Jack took a deep breath. "Anna, I had a hunch," he said. "It's my job to tell you when a situation doesn't feel right, but you're the team lead. It's your job to decide if we're gonna move forward anyway."

She nodded.

"And yeah," Jack went on. "I got the right answer. But that doesn't mean my math was good. I'm glad you trust my instincts, but I don't want you to just accept what I say without challenge."

Anna fell into his arms.

Jack held her tight, trailing his fingertips over her back, sending shivers through her. He kissed her forehead. "You've got nothing to apologize for," he whispered. "And we are gonna get Cassi out of that cell."

"Yes, we are."

"So, will you do something for me?"

"What's that?"

He smiled, chuckling softly as he touched his nose to her forehead. "Will you just cuddle with me for a little while?" he asked. "I think I'd feel safer falling asleep in your arms."

"I'd love to."

Like every other passenger ship, *Moonlight Dancer* had windows. Normally, they were used for looking down on a planet from orbit, but there was nothing to see when you were traveling at FTL speeds. Just endless black in all directions. The light from the stars they passed slid along the edge of their warp field to the point where space was most crumpled, a point that was always directly in front of the ship. The pilots looking out from the cockpit would see what appeared to be an infinite tunnel with a light that never came any closer, but everyone else got the void.

Even with the dismal view, Melissa decided that this was a good place to put her thoughts in order. She was worried. Worried about her father and the rumours of what he had been up to lately. Worried about Claire and her new-found telepathy. Worried about what might happen if the Leyrians decided to turn on immigrants.

The sound of footsteps announced Larani before she came around the corner from a nearby corridor. Melissa sensed her as a faint silhouette just on the edge of perception. The other woman paused, then turned to go.

"You don't have to," Melissa said.

Larani froze.

Melissa closed her eyes and let out a breath. "I just came here to do a little thinking," she said. "But I would not mind the company."

Larani stepped into the small viewing area, frowning at the blackness on the other side of the reinforced glass. "You couldn't sleep either, could you?" she muttered. "There are days when I wonder if we'll ever be able to sleep well again."

"In my experience, you can get used to anything."

"Yes," Larani agreed. "But I have yet to decide if that's a good thing."

With a few cautious steps, she came up beside Melissa and stood with her hands folded behind her back. "I wanted to tell you that you acquitted yourself well during the conflict," she said. "I am very proud."

Melissa allowed herself a small smile. "Thank you," she said. "But I spent most of my time with Jack worrying about whether I might have to kill someone."

"That's what makes you a Justice Keeper."

Tiny streaks of light shot past on the other side of the window, each one resolving into a distant star. The ship had dropped to sub-light speeds, most likely so that it could make contact with the nearest outpost and adjust course if necessary. There was no sound and nothing to feel. At one moment, they were hurtling through space at several billion kilometres per second, and the next, they weren't.

"So, what happens now?" Melissa asked.

Larani was as still as a statue, her face a mask of iron-willed determination. "We do our job," she said. "The same as always."

Chapter 27

"War."

Harry paced across the stage, waggling his finger at the people who filled almost every seat in this auditorium. Word of what he had been doing was spreading. Everyone wanted a look at the preacher who used force-fields and claimed divine knowledge from the god damn Overseers. "I bet many of you are spoiling for that."

Spinning to face his audience with fists on his hips, Harry frowned. "But that is *exactly* what the Overseers want."

A young woman in the third row shot out of her seat. She was pretty and short, with long blonde hair and a round face. "What?" she asked. "We're just supposed to take your word for that?"

Harry smiled, bowing his head to her. "I get it," he said. "By now, you all know about my little gift. The man who can wield Overseer technology. But what does that matter? It doesn't make me anything but a man with a gadget."

The young woman blushed, closing her eyes and nodding slowly. Clearly, he had articulated her thoughts. Well, maybe that could add to his mystique. Harry didn't want this job, but so long as he was stuck with it, he would do it right.

"If the Overseers want us to go to war," Harry insisted. "Then we *have* to be a people of peace. Our very survival as a species may depend on it."

"How do you know?" someone shouted.

Shutting his eyes tight, Harry drew in a breath and then shook his head. "Because the Overseers are liars," he answered. "The scriptures say that I've come to deliver you from them, and I tell you now that they are deceivers."

A few people got up, awkwardly shoving past their neighbours as they made their way to the aisles. Harry ignored them as they walked out the door. Not everyone who came here was a fan. Some of them wanted to see the charlatan who claimed to be a divine messenger.

He hated this job; he hated it with every fibre of his being, but there was nothing he wouldn't do for his daughters. And if he was going to be a preacher... Well, Harry was the sort of man who did a job right regardless of how he felt about it. His friends might not trust him anymore, but he could use this to do some good.

Harry stepped up to the edge of the stage, tilting his head back to look through the skylight. "Dusep wants war," he went on. "All those people who protest outside the spaceports? The ones who keep harassing helpless refugees? They want war. But war will kill us."

There were members in the crowd, people exchanging glances. He was getting to them; he could tell. Not everyone agreed, but they didn't have to. Being something of a spectacle gave him some clout; he could use that to get his point across.

He saw a young woman in the front row, a tiny wisp of a girl who kept frantically flipping through the pages of a book. The Covenant of Layat. Harry recognized it now. He had seen the cover enough times. Was the girl frightened? Was she searching for something that might refute his words? Or confirm them?

Dropping to one knee at the edge of the stage, Harry looked down on her. "Don't be afraid," he said. "You know who I am." That sounded sufficiently religious for his purposes.

The young woman looked up at him with wide eyes, and then, as if realizing who she was speaking to for the first time, she averted her gaze and began turning pages with wild abandon. He wasn't going to get a response out of that one.

He had the distinct impression that nothing he did here would make a dent in the Overseers' plans, but maybe Jack, Anna and the rest had rubbed off on him. If trying to persuade these people was futile, he would do it anyway.

He tried not to look at Sora, who stood at the side of the room with her arms folded, deliberately refusing to even glance in his direction. His girlfriend didn't like this "new job" of his, and she had made no secret of that fact.

Standing up straight, Harry took a moment to consider his audience. He nodded once and then said, "We're finished for the day. Come back tomorrow, and we will speak again."

With that, several hundred people got up and began making their way towards the exits. Less than five minutes later, the only one who remained was Sora.

She studied him for a long moment and then sighed as she strode toward the stage. "I almost think you're starting to believe your own press," she said. "Harry...You can't honestly think that this is right."

"I think it is necessary."

He meant that but not for the reasons that she was probably assuming. She didn't know about Claire. Not the full story, anyway. All she knew was that Claire had decided to go back to Earth and live with her mother. "We both know the way things are going," Harry added. "If I can do even the smallest thing to get us off this collision course, you're damn right I will."

"By lying to people?"

"Who says I'm lying?"

Sora threw her hands up and then shook her head in dismay. "So, you *are* starting to believe your own press!" Grumbling to herself, she took a seat in the front row and then gave him a stare that probably made her students buckle down and get to work.

Harry sat down on the edge of the stage with his hands on his knees, gazing down into his lap. "I can use this thing, can't I?" He wiggled his fingers to emphasize the N'Jal. "How do you know I'm not the one the Covenant specifies?"

It was probably the stupidest thing he had ever said. At this point, he wouldn't blame her for breaking up with him. But here they were...

"I'm an atheist," Sora replied.

Well, that put it all in perspective, didn't it? He felt sick to his stomach. Because deep down inside, he *agreed* with Sora. She was right; he *was* lying to people. But he was doing it to save his kid, and for Claire – or Melissa – he'd deliver everyone in the galaxy into the fires of Hell.

"Look," Harry said. "Why do we talk about this tom-"

He looked up to find Melissa standing in the doorway. The look on his daughter's face broke his heart. "So, it's true," she said, marching down the length of the aisle. "I heard rumours, but..."

Closing his eyes, Harry nodded. "It's true," he admitted. "And I've heard a thing or two about your exploits as well."

"This was the price, wasn't it?" Melissa said as she neared the stage. "This is what they made you do in exchange for saving Claire."

Sora was hunched over with her arms folded, but she turned a penetrating stare upon Melissa. "Claire..." she gasped. So much for secrecy! It was only a matter of time before she put it all together.

"We'll talk about it at home," Harry assured her.

"No, I think we'll talk about it now."

Harry blinked.

He wasn't used to such assertiveness from his daughter. Well, he knew that saving Claire meant damning his soul. There was no point keeping it secret any longer. "They wanted me to preach," Harry mumbled. "They didn't care what."

Sora was on her feet and striding toward him in an instant, and he could tell that if his next words didn't satisfy her, their relationship was done. "Who wanted you to do what?" she asked. "Specifics, Harry."

Melissa spared him the effort. "Dad made Claire into a telepath with that thing," she said. "But he botched it, and Claire was dying. So, he cut a deal with the Overseers to save her."

"Bleakness take me," Sora whispered.

"I'm guessing," Melissa went on, "that they'll go after Claire if you don't hold up your end of the bargain."

Harry set his elbow on his knee, touching his fingertips to his forehead. "They've never said anything to indicate that they have any interest in Claire," he replied. "But I can't imagine they'll take it well if I renege on my promise."

"You actually spoke to the Overseers..." Sora trailed off.

"It was-"

Before he could finish his sentence, Sora turned on her heel and walked right out the door. Harry should have felt something. Well, he did feel something: a dull ache in his chest. But it wasn't much. The truth was that he had been resigned to this for a while now. He had made his choice; now, he had to live with it.

An overcast sky loomed over the Hall of Council, splitting a cold drizzle down on the old building with its narrow, arch-shaped windows. The people who gathered on the steps were all wearing thick winter coats. It was a typical winter day in

Denabria. The temperature hovered just a few degrees above freezing.

Anna stood at the back of the crowd with her hands in her coat pockets, ignoring the chill rain as it pelted her face. *Perfect weather for an inauguration*, she thought to herself. *It suits him.*

A bunch of reporters stood clustered together on the bottom step, exchanging glances and speaking in hushed voices. Their many cameras – small, disk-shaped devices – hovered over them, waiting for a good shot.

They didn't have to wait long.

The doors opened, and several dozen councilors came out, forming into two lines on either side of the entrance. Dusep emerged a few minutes later with the Prime Council's staff on hand. His other arm was wrapped up in a sling.

He approached the podium at the top of the stairs, frowned and then nodded to his audience. "We begin a new chapter today." He said it so simply. Anna had expected a booming voice and gesticulation. All the trademarks of a man who fancied himself a dictator. But for some reason, Dusep was remarkably calm. "Today, we start putting our own people first."

A few people clapped.

"We have suffered much in these last few months," Dusep went on. "We have endured much, given away too much, suffered insults to our dignity too many times. We are a great people – a people who have left prejudice buried in our distant past, a people who have gone to the stars – and we will suffer these indignities no longer."

This time the applause was louder.

So, it begins.

Standing as tall as he could, Dusep faced the crowd with a stony expression. "A week ago," he said, "one of our colonies suffered a brutal attack at the hands of the Ragnosian Confederacy. This atrocity will not go unanswered. I have just received word that our Antauran allies have struck several bases on the borders of Ragnosian space. We must stand with them!"

Bringing his fist down on the lectern with a loud *thud*, Dusep snarled. "Half a galaxy stands between us and them, and still they attack us." He shook his head slowly. "Rest assured that this is not about resources. If they wanted minerals or hydrogen, they would find any number of empty star systems closer to home. No, this is about hate. They come here because they hate us!"

People started to cheer, thrusting fists into the air.

"We will not yield to their hatred!" Dusep shouted. "As of this moment, we are at war!"

All the cheering stopped as people realize the implications. Anna felt sick to her stomach. The battle on Alios was only a small taste of what they would endure. The Ragnosians weren't going to back down in the face of aggression. They would step up their attacks. This war might eventually come to Leyria itself.

And the alternative was just as bad. If the combined forces of Leyria and Antaur managed to overpower Ragnos, would her people show mercy when their blood was hot? Somehow, she didn't think so.

Dusep wasn't finished with his tirade. He stepped forward with teeth bared, snarling like a wounded animal. "For years now, I have said that the Justice Keepers were dangerous," he spat. "And the recent attempt on my life only proves my point. We have held a special session of Council, and we are proposing new regulations to make sure that no Justice Keeper is ever in a position to abuse their power again."

Anna swallowed, then shut her eyes and nodded to herself. *You had to know that was coming*, she lamented. *Oh, Cassi...*

"It's a new day on Leyria, my friends," Dusep intoned. "For the first time in a very long time, your government is going to take care of *you*."

Harry was lying in bed with his hands folded over his chest, staring wistfully at the ceiling. His room was dark except for a small lamp on his nightstand, and the drizzle kept rattling on his window.

He was unhappy – there was no denying that – but it was smothered with a dreadful sense of despair. He was stuck in this position now, and he had no one to blame for it but himself. His friends had tried to warn him about the N'Jal, but he had refused to listen. Because in a world of Justice Keepers and telepaths and men with gadgets, the ability to use Overseer technology had made Harry Carlson special. He realized now how vain that was. But it was too late.

His friends distrusted him; Claire feared him, and Melissa…Melissa saw him as a problem to be managed. His girlfriend was gone, and he was stuck playing the role of fake messiah to a bunch of idiots who were desperate for some kind of leadership. And all because he had been stupid enough to think he could fix anything. That he could protect his girls from a strange and hostile galaxy.

Making Claire into a telepath had been unintentional, a mistake brought on by the foolish belief that Harry Carlson – a man with no medical training – was qualified to go poking around in another person's brain. Once that mistake was made, the deal with the Overseers became inevitable; there was no way he was letting his daughter die.

A knock at the door made him look up, and he found Melissa standing just outside the bedroom. "I'm sorry about confronting you in front of Sora." She took a few steps into the room and stood there with her eyes downcast. "I didn't mean to cost you your relationship."

Harry sat up, grimacing. A heavy sigh escaped him before he could stop it. "It's not your fault," he muttered. "If our roles were reversed, I'd be pretty mad at me too."

"Still…"

Ignoring his aching knees – getting old was a dreadful experience – Harry went to the dresser and studied himself in the mirror. He looked haggard, his eyes marked by dark circles, his hair dishevelled. "Honestly, Missy, it was only a matter of time. You don't become a false messiah and expect your girlfriend to stick around."

"Missy…" she murmured. "You haven't called me that in forever."

Bent over with his hands on the dresser's surface, Harry smiled and shook his head. "Old habits die hard," he said. "Harder for me, I suspect."

"I thought we should talk."

Harry turned around to lean against the dresser. "Yeah, I had a feeling you'd want a follow-up." It was hard to keep the irritation out of his voice. He wasn't annoyed with his daughter; he was annoyed with himself. "Look, Melissa, I know you don't approve, but I don't have to tell you how dangerous it might be for Claire if I didn't keep up my end of the bargain."

Melissa sat on the edge of his bed, seemingly fascinated by something in her lap. He recognized that look of anguish on her face; it was the one she always got when she was about to say something that other people wouldn't want to hear. "I don't disapprove. I understand why you're doing this."

"Your bosses won't feel the same way."

"Yeah, but I can think for myself."

"So, if you're not here to tell me you disapprove," he began, "why do you look the way you did whenever you brought home a D on your report card?"

Melissa hugged herself, rubbing her upper arms as she drew in a breath. "Because I'm gonna tell you something you'll like even less," she said slowly. "I wanna be there with you when you hold these little services."

"Absolutely not!"

"Dad, people are talking about you," she said. "And they don't all have nice things to say. Larani and the others...They won't understand why you have to do this. Maybe Jack – and he might be able to persuade Anna – but the others? Not gonna happen. Somebody has to watch your back."

Covering his face with one hand, Harry massaged his eyelids. He looked up and blinked at her. "And if that someone is you," he countered, "it will be the end of your career."

Melissa regarded him with nothing less than pure serenity; it was almost scary. "Funny thing about Keepers," she replied. "The Nassai choose us because we're willing to sacrifice our careers to do what's right."

"Yeah, but *I'm* not willing to let you make that sacrifice."

"And I'm not giving you a choice."

Harry plodded over to the bed and sat down beside her. He put a hand on his daughter's back. "Carlson and Carlson," he said softly. "We should take the show on the road! Between my tricks and your Bendings, we'd make a killing."

Melissa leaned her head against his shoulder, and he gave her a hug.

Chapter 28

The detention centre was on the sixth floor of Justice Keeper HQ. Melissa hated coming here. Double doors slid apart to reveal a reception area with a horseshoe desk. As always, there were three Keepers on duty, but she only recognized one.

Special Agent Taro Paleen looked up to frown at her, but then he nodded. "Agent Carlson," he said in a brusque voice. "You know I can't let you in to see the prisoner, right?"

Standing before him with hands clasped in front of herself, Melissa bowed her head respectfully. "I was hoping," she began, stepping forward, "that you'd make an exception for me."

He shook his head.

Melissa let out a sigh of frustration. "You can't just keep her isolated forever!" she protested. "It's inhumane."

"The orders come from the Prime Council himself," Taro explained. "Frankly, Larani had to fight just to hold onto Cassi. Dusep's people wanted to dump her into a maximum-security facility. They don't trust us anymore."

"Well, be that as it may-"

The door slid open again, and this time it was Anna who strode into the room, glowering at everyone. She was followed by a man in a red coat and high-collared shirt, a handsome fellow with high cheekbones, tanned skin and buzzed hair. "You're going to let me in there," Anna declared.

Taro rose from his seat and towered over her with arms folded. "Like I just told Agent Carlson," he said. "We've been over this a dozen times. The prisoner is not to receive any visitors."

Anna stepped up to the desk with a smile, nodding as if she had prepared for exactly this eventuality. "Yeah, I'm not interested in Dusep's wannabe dictator routine," she replied. "Cassi has rights, one of which is the right to an attorney. So, unless you want her to walk right now, you'll let Mr. Devarin into that cell."

Lifting his chin to stare down his nose at her, Taro grunted. "I suppose I can't argue with that," he said. "But I don't see why I should allow *you* into the cell."

"Article Nine of the Justice Keeper code says that a supervising officer may visit the accused Keeper for the purpose of conducting an investigation."

"We aren't investigating this."

"Bleakness take me if we're not." Anna tapped at her multitool, producing a hologram that shimmered into existence between them. It was too far off for Melissa to read it, but she recognized black text on a white background. "An order," Anna said. "Signed by Larani Tal herself. The way she sees it, her career is over in a month anyway; so, why not do some good in the meantime?"

Taro closed his eyes, breathing deeply, and then nodded his acquiescence. "Very well," he muttered. "I'll let you in."

"Agent Carlson will be coming with me."

Melissa gave a start at the sound of her name.

The three keepers stepped aside, allowing Anna to approach the doors behind the desk. They slid apart to reveal a long cellblock with doors on either side of the corridor. Anna went through without a second's hesitation.

Melissa followed with the lawyer on her heels. Most of Justice Keeper HQ was exactly what you would expect from an office building: long hallways painted in soft colours, offices of glass and chrome. But the detention centre looked like something out of *Star Wars*.

Anna strode up to the third door on the left, pressing her palm to the scanner on the wall. There was a brief warbling sound as the biometrics read her handprint, and then the door slid open.

Cassi's cell was the same as the others she had seen. A round table stood in the middle of the room, directly underneath an overhead light. There was a small window of reinforced glass in the back wall, a window that looked out on an overcast sky.

Cassi herself was dressed in gray sweatpants and a blue t-shirt, all without pockets that she might use to hide a weapon. And there was a collar around her neck. It was there to prevent her from Bending space-time, but it sickened Melissa to see it.

Cassi sat on the edge of her bed with her hands clasped in her lap and looked up when she heard them enter. She blinked as if she didn't believe her eyes. "They let you in? I thought..."

Anna rushed across the room.

Cassi was on her feet in an instant, and the two women embraced each other. "I thought I would never see anyone again." Cassi sobbed. She trembled in Anna's arms, breathing hard.

"It's all right," Anna murmured. "We're here now."

Cassi shook her head forcefully, tears streaming over her face. "It's my fault, Anna," she whimpered. "He got me. He got me, and I broke!"

Anna was running a hand over the other woman's back, whispering soothing noises. "It's not your fault," she insisted. "Anyone would have broken after what he did to you."

"You must hate me!"

"No."

Melissa approached them reluctantly.

With a glance over her shoulder, Anna gave her a curt nod of approval, and then she joined the others in a group hug. Cassi clung to her, weeping against Melissa's chest and shivering. Anger and grief welled up inside Melissa. She had never been a vengeful person, but she would make Slade pay for this.

Finally, Cassi pulled free of their embrace and wiped her tears away with the back of one hand. "Who's this?" she asked, noticing the lawyer for the first time.

He waited by the door with a stiff posture, trying his best not to look awkward. "Charl Devarin," he answered. "I'm your attorney."

"I didn't think they'd let me have one," Cassi mumbled.

Anna backed away from her with arms folded, snarling and shaking her head. "Jeral Dusep is the kind of man who holds a grudge," she said. "But, this time, we can use that against him. He's not gonna risk letting you walk on a technicality."

Mr. Devarin strode forward with a grunt of disapproval. He stopped about five feet away from Cassi and forced a smile. "I think we've got a pretty strong case," he said. "I can't get your badge back, but given the facts of the case, we can argue that you were acting under duress."

"Will that work?" Cassi inquired.

"Special Agent Hunter is willing to testify on your behalf," Devarin explained. "He was infected with the same virus that Slade used on you. And the account he gave of his experience would sway any jury."

Cassi sat down on the bed, covering her mouth with one hand. She closed her eyes and nodded. "I didn't dare imagine…"

"You'll have to sit tight," Devarin cautioned. "Be meek and polite to the guards. You're going to be a model prisoner, the very image of contrition."

Cassi nodded.

Anna sat down at the table, setting her elbow on its surface and resting her chin on the knuckles of her fist. "We have to play this smart," she said. "If we follow the law to the letter, everything will work out."

Cassi was staring into her lap, shuddering with every breath. "Even if it does," she muttered. "What'll happen to me? My life is over. From now on, I'm the woman who shot the Prime Council."

"We'll deal with that after the trial," Anna said.

"No matter what happens," Melissa added. "We will always be your friends. We know the truth."

"How's Jack?" Cassi asked.

Anna's eyebrows shot up. "He's coping about as well as can be expected," she answered. "You know him. Cover the pain with a smile and a quip."

Cassi put her elbows on her knees and covered her face with both hands. And then she started sobbing again. "But he didn't break, did he?" she moaned. "If he had, he'd be in here."

Anna went over and threw her arms around the other woman. "It's all right," she whispered. "It's not your fault."

Once again, Melissa found herself standing in the background, exchanging glances with the lawyer as she waited for the appropriate moment to say something. A moment that might not come. It was all right. She didn't necessarily have to *say* anything; she could just be here for Cassi.

It startled her when Mr. Devarin turned to her with a thoughtful frown. "Keep her morale up," he advised. "She's going to have to convince three arbiters and nine jurors that she is truly remorseful."

"I'll do what I can," Melissa promised.

She and Anna stayed with Cassi for another half hour. They gave hugs and assurances; they made sure that Cassi knew she wasn't alone in this, that she had allies fighting for her on the outside. And they reminded her that they would be coming back as often as they could.

Eventually, the cell door opened to reveal Taro standing just outside. He informed them that their time was up and unceremoniously showed them out. The look on Cassi's face as they departed was pure anguish. It was clear that she hadn't had any visitors before today. Almost two weeks in total isolation. And everyone said that the Leyrians did not engage in cruel and unusual punishment.

Melissa stood in the cellblock with one hand on the wall, frowning into the distance. "I can't go yet," she said. "There's one more thing I have to do."

Anna gave her a disapproving look. "You sure that's wise?" she asked. "Melissa, he's dangerous."

"I know."

"You want me to come with you?"

Squeezing her eyes shut, Melissa shook her head. "No," she whispered. "This is one of those things I have to do alone."

With some reluctance, Melissa started forward. Despite her veneer of bravery, she had no desire to do what she was about to do, but there was no avoiding it. Oh, sure, she could pass this off as someone else's problem. No one would blame her – she had been a cadet less than two months ago – but avoiding this confrontation felt cowardly to her.

Melissa went to a door at the end of the cellblock and pressed her palm against the scanner. A green line went up and down, reading her handprint, and then the whole thing flashed red. "Access denied," a feminine voice said through the speaker.

"By who?"

"Larani Tal."

In her mind, she sensed the silhouette of Anna coming up behind her. The other woman nudged Melissa aside and pressed her hand to the scanner. Half a second later, the door slid open.

Anna smiled and then nodded once to her. "You can do this," she said. "I'll be right out here."

Working up her courage, Melissa went through and found herself in a cell that was almost identical to Cassi's. The man who sat at the table, however, was *not* a friend. Her skin crawled at the sight of him. The door shut behind her, locking her in.

They had put Aiden in sweatpants and a black tank-top. He sat there with hands folded on the table's surface and looked up slowly when she came in. "I was wondering when you would pay me a visit."

Melissa stood before him for a long moment, doing her best to remain serene. "Why?" It was the only word that she could force through her lips. Being in a room with this man brought all the hurt she had buried back to the surface.

"Why what?"

Sitting across from him with one leg crossed over the other, Melissa arched an eyebrow. "You have to ask me that?" she shot back. "You know what I want to know."

He leaned back with hands folded behind his head, grinning triumphantly at the ceiling. "Why did I accept Slade's offer?" he said. "Why did I Bond one of the fallen symbionts?"

"Well?"

His mocking laughter made her feel like a child. All those insecurities – the fears that motivated her to keep her opinions to herself – came rushing into her mind. "You're a smart girl," Aiden said. "You tell me."

"My guess is vanity."

Clasping his chin with one hand, Aiden tapped his lips with his index finger. "Yes," he said as if musing to himself. "They *have* taught you well. You've learned that sense of smug superiority."

"Are you going to tell me or-"

"I have come to realize," Aiden said, "that the philosophy that governs our people is flawed. The Justice Keepers serve flawed ideals. Our world requires correction."

Melissa sat back in her chair with arms folded, shaking her head slowly. "You killed half a dozen people," she rasped. "Slaughtered them like helpless animals right in front of me."

"Enemy soldiers."

"Does that matter?"

Once again, Aiden laughed, only this time it was cruel and bitter. "It should," he insisted. "They invaded one of our worlds, Melissa. Killed our people. I say they got what was coming to them."

"And that's why the symbiont never accepted you," Melissa hissed. "If that's how you think, it's no wonder that a Nassai wouldn't want you. A Justice Keeper has to care about a Ragnosian as much as they would a Leyrian."

"And why should they?" he countered. "The Justice Keepers *are* Leyrian. Why shouldn't they prioritize their people above anyone else?"

Melissa leaned forward with her hands on the table, staring intently into his eyes. "So, I should be loyal to Earth above all else?" she asked. "Is that how it works?"

Aiden held her gaze for a very long while. "You're a Leyrian now," he said. "This planet has given you and your family a lot, Melissa; you owe it your allegiance."

Melissa stood to go, frowning at him, but when she turned, he laughed again. "Think on it, Melissa," he called after her. "Think long and hard."

And she did think about it, despite a strong desire to do anything but. Aiden's sentiments weighed heavily on her mind. Not because she thought they had any merit, but hearing him articulate such ideas left her questioning her own powers of perception. How could he have believed such things for so long without her noticing? Maybe she was just a moon-struck girl.

Three hours later, as she entered a fabrication centre to repair some damage to one of her shirts, it was still on her mind.

It would probably still be on her mind several hours after she should have fallen asleep.

Pushing her way through the door, Melissa closed her umbrella and hunched up her shoulders against the chill. The drizzle outside was light but persistent, and every drop was ice-cold. Novol had called while she was on her way here, asking to meet with her. She decided this was as good a place as any.

The fabrication centre was huge, taking up most of the city block. A wide corridor, just inside the front entrance, ran in front of several "stores," each one specializing in a different kind of product. Some built or repaired furniture; others mended clothing or produced new garments. And others still maintained electronic devices. It was kind of like a big shopping mall but without all the advertising everywhere.

Heeled boots clicking on the tiled floor, Melissa strode through the corridor with a bag in one hand and her umbrella in the other. She closed her eyes, shaking her head in dismay. *He was right there under my nose. I didn't see him.*

The automated tailor's shop was on her right.

She went in to find it empty, but the lights brightened, and a serving bot not unlike the one she had at home came to life. He studied her with glowing blue eyes, cocking his head as if fascinated by her presence. "Something we can help you with, ma'am?"

"Just some light fraying on the hem of my shirt," she said. "A little touch-up, that's all."

There was nothing inside the shop except a couple of chairs and a small alcove in the back wall. A series of touchscreen stations allowed people to choose from a variety of new garments. All the work would be done out of sight. She could wait here – it wouldn't take long – or get something to eat from one of the many restaurants in the food court.

With a curt nod, the robot stepped aside and ushered her deeper into the shop. "Please place your garment in the receptacle." She did as she was told, fishing her black shirt out of the bag and placing it on a shelf in the alcove. A compartment opened in the wall, and the shelf retracted. "Scanning now," the robot said. "Estimated repair time approximately ten minutes. Would you like some music while you wait?"

"No, thank you."

She was there less than three minutes before Novol arrived, stepping into the shop with his eyes downcast. His thick winter coat was wet, and his black hair glistened, fat droplets rolling over his forehead.

Melissa rushed to him with a grunt of disapproval. "Didn't you bring an umbrella?" Before he could answer, she was heaving out a sigh of exasperation. "Boys... You never do grow up."

He looked up to blink at her, and then – to her shock – his face lit up with a grin. "At least you're in good spirits," he said. "I heard about what happened on Alios."

"What did you want to talk about?"

He stepped back with a shrug of his shoulders and then sheepishly averted his gaze. "There's just no easy way to say this..." Melissa was pretty sure that she knew what was coming. Her rational mind insisted that it was too soon, that she was still dealing with all the baggage from Aiden, but her heart was racing. Maybe... "I want to help with the war effort."

That hit her like a splash of cold water in the face. "What?" she stammered. "I mean... You really want to go up against your own people?"

"I'm Rathalan," Novol said. "I joined the military because it was either that or a long life working three jobs just to make ends meet. And that's assuming that work is available. Ragnos means nothing to me. They're not my people; they're the people who conquered my people."

Melissa nodded slowly, taking that in. "Okay," she said. "But why are you coming to me? Isn't there, like, a recruitment centre? Or something?"

Novol let out a breath and then lowered his eyes. A touch of crimson in his cheeks made her regret her question. "I'm not a Leyrian citizen," he muttered. "And they're not gonna trust me."

"How can I help?"

"Talk to Director Tal," he suggested. "If nothing else, I might be able to give you some valuable intelligence."

Leaning one shoulder against the wall, Melissa shut her eyes and exhaled through her nose. "Okay," she mumbled. "I'll do what I can. But if things keep going the way I think they're going, Larani won't be in charge much longer."

"I heard about what happened on Alios."

"God damn Slade." Melissa nearly bit her tongue. She wasn't prone to profanity, but after everything that had happened, she was on the ragged edge. How could they beat someone who was always ten steps ahead? That question had been in her mind ever since the disastrous attempt to capture Slade.

"I was talking about the attack," Novol said softly. "I heard you had to go into battle."

"Yes." The implications dawned on her, and her heart sank. No, he wouldn't be interested in pursuing... whatever this was. Novol might say that he had no loyalty to Ragnos, but it couldn't be easy looking at someone who had done violence to the people he had called comrades just a few months ago. "Novol, I'm sorry. I want you to know that I didn't want to fight-"

He surged forward, gently taking her face with both hands and kissing her on the lips. It was a soft kiss: tender and loving, filled with affection.

Breaking contact, Novol closed his eyes and shuddered. His nose touched hers. "I'm sorry," he whispered. "I should have asked first."

"The answer would have been yes."

Novol wrapped his arms around her, holding her close, and she leaned her head against his shoulder. "Thinking of you and combat," he muttered under his breath. "It's not something that anyone should endure, Melissa."

"I didn't have to kill anyone," she whispered.

"Thank the Spirits for that."

For a very long while – several minutes, at least – Novol just held her. She suspected he would have stayed like that for most of the night if the serving bot didn't waddle over and say, "Your garment is ready, ma'am."

"So," Novol said. "Dinner?"

Corovin's cell was dark and cramped: a box just big enough for him to stretch his arms out. There were no comforts here, just a bench that he could sit on or sleep on and a toilet he could use to relieve himself. He wasn't sure exactly where he was; all he knew was that the Leyrians had taken him somewhere on a starship. Presumably to their homeworld. The rumours had all said that they were a benign people. Perhaps those rumours were wrong.

Corovin sat on the bench with his legs stretched out so that his feet almost touched the door, his head thrown back so that he could look at the ceiling. He wasn't sure how long he had been there. Someone had come several hours ago to feed him. Or had it been several minutes? Time had no meaning in this place.

The door slid open, and a black-uniformed guard stood over him, wearing a look of disgust. "Get up!" the man said. "Now!"

Slowly, Corovin rose to his feet. He lost his balance and had to brace his hands against the wall to prevent himself from falling over. "Are you going to execute me?"

He didn't get an answer.

Instead, they slapped a pair of manacles on his wrists and forced him to walk with his hands together and his head down.

That might have been uncomfortable, but his body ached so much already that he didn't notice.

Three guards in heavy body armour guided him through a gray corridor with the barrel of an assault rifle pressed against his back. There was nothing to see. Just plain walls and doors that clearly led into other cells.

They made a left turn into a hallway that was identical to the last one except for the lack of doors. Two minutes of dragging his feet with every step brought him to another junction, and then they turned right.

This hallway was much shorter than the other two, with a large metal door at its end. One of the guards marched up to it and removed his glove so that he could press his hand against the palm scanner.

The door opened with a hiss, admitting them into a plain room with nothing but a SlipGate in the middle. The lead guard activated it with one of those pocket computers that the Leyrians wore on their forearms. Corovin had never seen a portable device that could control a SlipGate. He was beginning to realize that underestimating Leyria would be a grave mistake.

The grooves along the Gate's surface began to glow with vibrant light. Corovin approached the device, spun around and put his back to it. The guards surrounded him a moment later, right before a bubble enveloped their entire group.

Then they were rushing through an endless tunnel.

Without warning, the bubble emerged into a room that Corovin didn't recognize. He couldn't see much through its surface. Just an unbroken haze of brown and red, but there were several people present. More guards, he suspected.

When the bubble popped, his suspicions were confirmed. These guards wore blue uniforms and neat caps on their heads. There were half a dozen of them, two of which – he realized – were women. They carried nothing but small sidearms, and not one of them had drawn their weapon. "This way," one said.

Corovin didn't argue.

He could see daylight through arch-shaped windows in the wall; it was gray and overcast, but after weeks in a cell, it was the blessed light of paradise itself. Where was he? Somewhere on Leyria?

Once again, they herded him through corridors, only these had lush red carpets and cream-coloured walls. He saw no one except the members of his entourage, but it was clear to him that this was a government building of some kind. Perhaps the halls had been cleared in anticipation of his arrival. *We wouldn't want the assassin getting his hands on a hostage.*

He didn't bother keeping track of the twists and turns that led him to his final destination, but he knew that he had arrived when the guards clustered outside the door and ushered him through at gunpoint. He did not attempt to resist. This wasn't the venue for conducting an execution, which meant they had brought him here for another purpose. He might still be able to bargain his way out of this mess.

Inside, he found a long table with rounded corners sitting in the light of three massive, arch-shaped windows with brown muntin. Sheets of rain on the glass made it hard to see what was outside, but he recognized the outlines of skyscrapers. Many of them had lights in their windows.

A man with copper skin and short, dark hair sat at the head of that table. He had one arm in a sling, and it was clear from his momentary grimace that the wound pained him. Corovin knew this one. He had been briefed on the key figures in Leyria's government while he was still in Telixa's employ. This was Jeral Dusep, and the golden shepherd's crook propped up against his chair meant that he was now the Prime Council.

"Ah," Dusep said. "Here he is."

There were others gathered around the table; some were obviously politicians, but others wore the dark-blue uniforms of Antauran fleet officers. Not good. One of those, an older fellow with pink cheeks and silver hair, stood up to study Corovin. "Yes, that's the one," he said. "I've seen the video many times."

Corovin shut his eyes, his head sinking as the last flicker of hope went out. They were talking about the video of him killing the former Antauran president. So, he was being offered to the Antaurans as a gesture of goodwill. And they would kill him.

Rubbing his jaw with one hand, Dusep narrowed his eyes. "I will honour the agreement that you made with my predecessor," he said. "The assassin is yours. All we ask is that you commit half a dozen ships to the defense of Alios until we get the defense grid up and running again."

"Done," the old Antauran said.

Corovin stumbled forward, but the manacles delivered a shock. He fell to his knees, crying out. When it was over, he was panting. "I can offer you intelligence," he gasped. "I know the locations of several key Ragnosian installations."

"I think not," a female Antauran said. "The morale boost that our troops will gain by witnessing your execution is worth more than any unreliable intelligence you might offer."

"Shall I have him delivered to your ship?" Dusep asked.

Before anyone could answer, the door slammed open with enough force to make it bang against the wall. Guards leaped out of the way to make room for a small woman in gray pants and a red, short-sleeved blouse, a woman who wore her short red hair up in a ponytail. "Didn't invite me to the party, Jeral," Lenai said. "I'm offended."

The Prime Council was out of his seat in an instant, his face flushed with anger. "This has nothing to do with you!" he barked. "How did you even know about this meeting?"

Crossing her arms, Lenai strode across the room with a smile on her face. "Melissa told me about Sarona's plan to turn him over to the Antaurans," she answered. "I've been keeping an eye on the situation. I'm afraid this man is under my protection."

Dusep's lips parted in a sinister snarl. "You have no authority over this," he spat. "Guards! Remove this woman from the room!"

Lenai paused, glancing over her shoulder to arch an eyebrow at the men and women who approached her. "Oh please," she said. "Try."

Dusep was beside himself, shaking his head as if he didn't know what to make of her bravado. "You're insane," he spluttered. "There are nine armed people in this room. Even a Justice Keeper couldn't deal with that many."

"No, an ordinary Justice Keeper couldn't," Lenai replied. "But I'm no ordinary Justice Keeper. I'm Anna goddamn Lenai." Earth slang? Where might she have heard a phrase like that? "This man put his life on the line to protect my team, and the Bleakness will take me before I let you execute him."

Dusep opened his mouth to speak, but she cut him off by tapping commands into her pocket computer. A hologram appeared, depicting what Corovin could only assume was some sort of legal document. "And the Supreme Court agrees with me!" Lenai went on. "Article Twenty-Four of the Charter of Rights and Freedoms: any person in the custody of Leyria or any agency acting on Leyria's behalf must be granted the same basic human rights as a Leyrian citizen. You can't execute Corovin without a trial. And you can't turn him over to anyone who would."

"I can do-" Dusep began.

Lenai stepped up to him with fists clenched, craning her neck to gaze into his eyes. "Go ahead," she urged. "Give the court exactly what it needs to remove you from office. It'll be the shortest term in history."

"This is outrageous!" one of the Antaurans bellowed.

"You're jeopardizing the treaty." That from one of the Leyrian politicians. And soon, they were all speaking over one another. For a second there, Corovin thought that the room might descend into a shouting match, but then Dusep raised his hand for silence.

Anyone who saw the look on the Prime Council's face couldn't be blamed for thinking that Lenai had pummeled him with fists instead of words. The man recovered his composure in a heartbeat and then nodded to her. "Very well," he said in a voice as sweet as honey. "But we both know that no Leyrian court will try a man for crimes he committed against the Antauran people. We'll begin extradition proceedings tomorrow."

"While you're doing that," Lenai countered, using her pocket computer to produce yet another document. "You might want to have the Fleet admirals speak to their officers about following protocol with regard to the treatment of prisoners. This is a writ, signed by Larani Tal and sanctioned by three Supreme Court arbiters. The Justice Keepers will be taking point in the investigation into Corovin's crimes. He is to be transferred to one of our detention facilities immediately."

"Now, you go too far!"

"And furthermore," Lenai said over the Prime Council's objections. "We will be speaking with Corovin extensively about the treatment he received while in the custody of the Space Corps. And if we find that any of our officers violated his human rights, there will be criminal charges."

Corovin was gasping.

He looked up to see Anna standing over him and offering her hand. Taking it, he let her pull him to his feet. "He'll be coming with me now," she declared. "Thank you ever so much for your time."

He almost forgot to breathe. Was this really happening? He was beginning to understand why Telixa found these Justice Keepers so frightening. Such idealism was dangerous. It made one unpredictable and willing to die for all the wrong reasons. Still, if it saved his hide, he wouldn't complain. In fact, he had to admit a grudging respect for Anna. Perhaps putting his fate in her hands was a smart move after all.

Chapter 29

k woke up with a gasp.

He sat up, groaning, and rubbed his eyes with the tips of his fingers. "God damn it." His voice was raw and rough. Adrenaline kept whipping through his system, making his every muscle taut.

One look around the room and he could see that it was still utterly dark. The windows, now fully opaque, kept out the city lights. They would not become transparent until morning.

Anna sat up behind him, wrapping her arms around his tummy. Inhaling slowly, she nuzzled the back of his shoulder. "That's the third time this week," she said in a voice filled with sympathy. The feeling of her warm skin against his was almost enough to help him relax. Almost but not quite.

Squeezing his eyes shut, Jack nodded. "Yup. It's official," he muttered. "Definitely gonna need some therapy."

"I think we could all use some."

Sighing, Jack twisted around to slip his arm around her shoulders and pull her close. Anna rested her head on his chest. "I'm sorry," he whispered. "I didn't mean to wake you."

"Sweetie, I'm more worried about *you*."

"I'll be okay."

Anna looked up at him, and even in the darkness, he could sense the contours of her face. Her eyes were wide with concern. "Do you want to tell me what happened? Was it a nightmare?"

Together, they lay back down, facing one another and holding each other tight. "Not a nightmare," Jack explained. "Just as I'm about to fall asleep, when my mind is ready to drift away, something jolts me awake. It's like one moment I'm relaxed, and the next, I'm as tense as a spooked cat. Like I'm afraid to let my guard down."

"Because of Slade?"

Just thinking about it brought out a mix of emotions that he didn't want to deal with right now. Anger and fear and a profound sense of helplessness. "I'm used to people shooting at me," Jack said. "Or trying to stab me. But this... He could make me hurt just by thinking it! He didn't even have to *be* there!"

He didn't realize that he was on the verge of shouting until he finished speaking. It made him cringe inside. The last thing he wanted to do was take his frustrations out on Anna, but she didn't seem to be offended. She just held him closer, pressing her body against his as if she were trying to protect him. "I'm sorry," he whispered.

And then the dam broke.

He was weeping, trembling in her arms and clinging to her for dear life. "I thought I knew what that bastard could do!" he sobbed. "I thought I knew how bad it could get!"

"Come here," Anna murmured.

Rolling onto her back, she let him rest his head on her chest. Well, that was new. Jack wasn't used to the role reversal, but she was running her fingers through his hair, and that soothed away some of his tension. "I'm right here," Anna whispered. "No one's gonna hurt you. We're together now."

It pleased him to realize that he was smiling. Smiling because he believed her. There was a reason why Anna insisted on sleeping naked together as often as possible. He could still remember what she had told him when she first suggested the idea. "Clothes protect you from the outside world," she had said. "But when I'm with you, I don't need any protection. You're the one who keeps me safe."

At the time, he had been so flattered that he scooped her up in his arms, carried her to the couch – the extra thirty seconds it would have taken to walk to the bedroom were an unbearably long wait – and spent the next hour making love with her. But it wasn't just flattery; he realized now that he felt the same way. Nothing could hurt him so long as he was safe in Anna's arms. She was the one who kept him safe.

He listened to the soft beating of her heart. *Thump-thump...Thump-thump.* Within minutes, he was on the edge of sleep again, and this time, he let go.

Jack woke up a few hours later, feeling somewhat rested. It was still dark, and he had the distinct impression that dawn was at least an hour away. There was something he had to do, something that he should really stop putting off, but the sound of Anna's steady breathing made him pause. She needed him as much as he needed her; he wasn't going anywhere right now.

Fourteen hours later, Jack was sitting at his desk and listening to the rain pattering against the window behind him. Dusk had come early, as it always did in the winter months, and the last traces of daylight were fading from the sky.

Anna appeared in his doorway, pausing after taking two steps into his office. She smiled at the *Star Wars* and comic book posters on the walls. "You know, I keep meaning to tell you this, but I'm glad you finally decorated your workspace."

"It suits me."

Approaching his desk with her hands clasped behind herself, Anna frowned at him. "And now it's stern lecture time," she said softly. "What are you doing here when Larani specifically gave you a few weeks off to recover?"

433

He looked up at her, blinking several times, caught off-guard by the question. "It's nothing serious," he said. "I just wanted to go over some of the old case files I worked on with Cassi."

That was a bald-faced lie, but he wasn't quite ready to tell his girlfriend the truth. And he didn't want to be in the apartment when she came home from work because that would require him to come up with an excuse for why he was going out alone at night.

"You looking for something in particular?" Anna asked.

"It was just a hunch." Jack reclined in his chair, scrubbing his hands over his face and then threading his fingers through his hair. "And it turned out to be nothing."

He could tell that Anna wasn't satisfied with his answer, but thankfully, she didn't push. "Okay," she said. "Don't stay too late. I'll have some soup waiting for you when you get home."

And then she was gone.

Jack sighed regretfully. There was nothing he wanted more than to go home and eat that bowl of soup, but the anger was bubbling within him, simmering just beneath the surface. Sometimes, when he closed his eyes, he could see the mocking grin on Slade's face, and it made him want to put his fist through a wall. No one made him feel helpless! No one! It was about time he did something about that.

He ended up staying in his office until long after everyone else had gone home. He would have to come up with something to tell Anna later. The guilt he felt over lying to her almost overshadowed the slow-burning rage that tightened his chest. Maybe he should just come clean. Anna wouldn't like it; there would almost certainly be a fight, but at least he wouldn't be deceiving her.

Still, Jack was fairly certain that if she knew what he was planning, she would try to talk him out of it. And he had to do this.

With midnight only two hours away, he finally worked up the nerve to go downstairs, and then he ended up wandering the streets in the cold rain. Jack had no particular destination in mind; he just had to kill time.

The rainfall left small puddles on the road for cars and buses to splash through. The buildings in this sector of the city were mostly used by worker co-ops that specialized in software or construction or God only knew what. As such, they were mostly empty at this hour. He saw the odd person on the sidewalk, but he never made eye-contact, and anyone that he passed was happy to ignore him. Eventually, he tapped a few quick commands into his multi-tool, ordering it to transmit a signal into SlipSpace. He didn't know if anyone was listening, but he was pretty sure that he would not have to wait long to find out.

He followed the street westward until he reached the grassy hillside that led down to the marina. Wet earth squished under his shoes as he descended the gentle slope and approached the waist-high stone wall that looked out upon the ocean. Black waves lapped at the boats that were waiting at the end of several wooden docks. Pleasure boats that people could rent for a day out on the water. That was the only reason that anyone went sailing on this world; the Leyrians only shipped cargo on shuttles or through SlipGates.

Summer was apprehensive. Every time he thought about this plan, his Nassai expressed misgivings in the form of fear and anxiety. He hadn't spoken to her about it, but he knew that Summer wanted him to tell Anna everything.

Spatial awareness alerted him to the fact that he was not alone long before he heard the squelch of grass under boots. A wraith-like figure came down the hill behind him and stopped just a few feet away, never letting herself get within arm's reach of him. "Jack Hunter," she cooed. "This *is* a surprise."

Shutting his eyes tight, Jack tilted his head back and let the rain fall upon his face. He drew in a ragged breath. "I didn't know if you would come," he grated. "Guess that means I owe you."

He turned around.

Isara stood before him in a thick winter coat with the hood pulled up to hide her face. "I almost didn't come," she informed him. "Do you have any idea how hard it is to navigate the Leyrian capital when you are one of the most wanted people in the galaxy?"

Jack smiled down at himself and then shook his head ruefully. "Don't pretend you haven't been here ever since we got back from Alios," he said. "Slade was bound to have *someone* keeping an eye on things. I figured it was you."

"Incisive as always," she murmured. "So, what can I do for you?"

"A month ago, you made me an offer."

"Yes?"

Jack stepped up to her, narrowing his eyes. A sudden shiver went through him. "I'm in," he growled. "We kill Slade together."

Isara looked up, allowing a tiny bit of light to penetrate that hood. "He's more powerful now than ever before," she said. "You challenged him with four of your strongest allies, and he still eluded your grasp. What makes you think that you and I will fare any better?"

"You and Jena are like night and day," he replied. "But you do have one thing in common: you're two of the most cunning individuals I've ever met."

"And you are prepared to do what is necessary?"

Turning away from her, Jack braced his hands on the stone wall and hunched over. He shuddered. "You know what he did to me?" he spat. "What he did to Cassi?"

Isara was there in his mind, watching him warily. She stretched out a hand as if to lay it on his shoulder but then let it drop. "I know." The way she said it reminded him so much of Jena. It never occurred to him that she might be capable of sympathy.

"Then you have your answer."

"Very well, Jack Hunter."

He straightened and stared off into the distance, nodding slowly as thoughts coalesced in his head. "It's not just about me," Jack said. "Because of him, the whole galaxy's at war. Someone has to stop him."

"Stopping him will not stop the Inzari."

"It'll be a start."

"Yes," Isara said. "Perhaps it will."

When Jack finally got home, he was wet and cold and tired. His heart was heavy because now he had to lie to the person he loved more than anyone else. That could wait until tomorrow. Midnight had come and gone nearly an hour ago. By now, Anna should have been sound asleep, which was why it was a shock when he opened the door and found her sitting on the couch in pajama pants and a tank-top.

Anna looked up to study him, and he could tell that she was worried. "Did you sort out whatever you had to sort out?"

He shut the door as quietly as he could.

Standing before her with his arms hanging limp, Jack couldn't find the strength to lift his eyes from the floor. There was no getting around it; he couldn't lie to her, and any insistence he made to the contrary was just self-deception. "I need to tell you something."

"What's up?"

Breathing deeply through his nose, Jack took a moment to gather his courage. "You remember that deal Isara offered?" he began. "She and I team up to take down Slade? I took it."

"I know."

He blinked.

Anna was smiling as she stood up and sauntered over to him. Her arms went around his neck, and despite his wet clothes, she stood up on tiptoe to kiss him. "You're Mr. Detective Guy when it comes to suspects in the interrogation room. I'll give you that. You see things I miss sometimes."

Stepping back, Anna stared up at him with a stern expression. "But if you think I don't know *you* backwards and forwards," she said, her eyebrows rising. "Well, then you really haven't been paying attention. And here's a plot twist for you: I'm in."

"In?"

"Your plan to kill Slade. I'm with you."

Jack fell back against the door, blowing air through his lips. "Didn't see that one coming," he muttered under his breath.

"Well, at least I can still surprise you."

"Yeah, but I don't get it," he protested. "Aren't you the one who's always saying that Justice Keepers have to revere a life?"

Anna turned her back on him, pacing across the living room to the window that looked out on the balcony. She stood there for a little while with arms crossed. "How many people will this war kill in a year?" she asked. "A hundred thousand? A million? *Ten* million? Slade did that."

Turning slightly, she looked over her shoulder with fury in her eyes. "You want to save lives?" she said. "Maybe the best way to do it is to protect people from history's greatest mass murderer."

Jack strode forward with his mouth agape, then shook his head slowly. "So, you knew that I would go to Isara?"

"I didn't know when," Anna admitted, "but I've been expecting it ever since we got back from Alios. The first night you go 'out for a walk' without explanation? Well, it was pretty obvious what was going on."

"And you're not mad at me for keeping it from you?"

Anna spun around to face him, lifting her chin as she appraised him. "I am," she said, nodding. "But in light of everything that's happened, I guess I forgive you."

"Well, thank God for that."

"And you kind of scored some points by coming clean before I dragged it out of you. So, good on you for that."

He sat down on the couch arm with his hands on his knees, head hanging with the weight of his fatigue. "Did anyone ever tell you that you're the best girlfriend ever?" he asked. "There really should be a trophy."

"Someone may have mentioned it."

"Well," he said. "I really wanna go to bed, but seeing as how we just made a murder pact, I'm not up for cuddles."

"I'll make some hot chocolate," Anna said. "I have a feeling we could both use a long night of talking about our anxieties."

Chapter 30

Emptying a bag of popcorn into a big bowl, Della looked up to peek through the French blinds over her kitchen window. With summer drawing to a close, the days were getting shorter. The trees behind her property were dark shadows under a deep-blue sky.

Standing over the kitchen sink in track pants and a tank-top, Della peered into the darkness. She gave her head a shake. "Melissa will be fine," she told herself for the thousandth time. "Stop worrying about things you can't control."

The news reports about what was happening on the edge of Leyrian territory were sketchy. It was hard to get reliable information when your people didn't have spaceships of their own, and the Leyrians weren't exactly forthcoming. She knew that her daughter had survived the battle on Alios; she knew that Melissa had returned to Leyria, and that would have to be enough for now.

"Mom?" Claire called out from the living room.

"Coming!"

Della took the bowl of popcorn, turned away from the window and marched out of the kitchen. "Don't start without me!" Claire would be starting school next week, which made it the perfect time for her to catch up on all the Disney movies she had missed while living on Leyria.

A large rectangular doorway separated the living room from the kitchen, and on the other side, Della had white couches spaced out on a hardwood floor. Pale curtains over the windows provided some privacy.

Claire was sitting on one couch in red pajama bottoms and an old t-shirt, hunched over and rubbing her temples with the tips of her fingers. The look of pain on her face almost made Della drop the bowl.

"Sweetie, what's wrong?"

Claire looked up at her with large dark eyes that glistened. Tears spilled over her face. "I can feel them," the girl whispered. "Something has changed."

"Feel who?"

"The Overseers," Claire croaked. "Their presence comes through stronger than it ever did before. They are watching us, Mom."

Della sat down in the easy chair with the bowl in her lap, shaking her head as she fought through her own terror. There were only two possibilities that she could see: either Claire's new telepathic abilities were having some kind of negative effect on her. Or...Or...Or the Overseers really were watching. "Where are they, honey?" It was a stupid question, but it was all that she could think to ask.

When Claire looked up, her face was deathly pale. She took a moment to collect herself before answering. "Everywhere..."

"You have been honoured."

Slade moved with purpose through the tunnels of an Inzari ship. The soft floor seemed to give way a little under his feet. The air was moist and warm enough to make his thigh-length red coat most uncomfortable.

Valeth was at his side, glancing at everything like a wide-eyed schoolgirl, mystified by the experience of being in the presence of her gods. "Yes, Lord Slade," she mumbled. "I thank you for this honour."

"I shall need your assistance," he informed her. "In truth, you are the only one I can trust."

She nodded.

The tunnel opened into a large, dome-shaped chamber with a pool of brown goo in the middle. One look at the ooze and Valeth froze in place with a hand over her mouth. "Grace of the Inzari," she whispered. "Is that what I think it is?"

She had only joined his cause a year ago; as such, she still wore her original body. She had never set foot inside an Inzari ship before. Slade had told her of the blessings they offered – eternal youth, health and vitality – but now, she would see proof of their power with her own eyes.

Before he could answer, the Old Woman appeared from out of nowhere, and Valeth stepped back, gasping in shock. Which meant that she saw the apparition too. The Inzari could be selective about who they spoke to.

The Old Woman favoured them both with a gap-toothed smile. "Long have we watched this one," she said, gesturing to Valeth. "You bring us a most dutiful servant, my son."

Removing his coat, Slade let it drop to the floor. He began undoing the buttons of his white linen shirt, and when it was open, he tossed that aside too. "Did you get what you need from him?"

"We did."

Closing his eyes, Slade drew in a long, slow breath. "Then we are ready to proceed." He turned around to find Valeth watching him with her mouth agape. "Do not be afraid. Now, you will see proof of all that we have promised you. The gun?"

With some reluctance, Valeth opened her handbag and reached inside to retrieve a small pistol. She handed it to him and then whispered, "Are you sure about this?"

Tilting her chin up with two fingers, Slade bent forward to kiss her forehead. "Be at peace," he said. "All will be well, I assure you. Did you procure the appropriate attire for my re-emergence?"

"Yes, Lord Slade."

"Then I will see you again very soon."

He backed away from her, retreating until he was almost at the very edge of the pool. Then he lifted the gun, pressed its barrel to the side of his head and pulled the trigger.

The tip of Harry's pen slid across the paper with a scratching sound. Paper: a rare commodity, here on Leyria. But for Harry, it made the writing process more real. He put his thoughts in order. After everything that had happened – his mistake with Claire, his deal with the Overseers, Sora leaving – he needed the catharsis. He was-

A knock at the door startled him.

Harry looked up through the living-room window, but the curtains made it hard to see anything. Now, who might that be? One of Melissa's friends, no doubt. He was pretty sure that she was done with Aiden, but it didn't take an eighteen-year-old girl long to find a new boyfriend.

He went to the door and pulled it open to find Sora standing on his porch. Her face lit up at the sight of him. "Can we talk?"

Standing there with one hand on the door-frame, Harry shut his eyes and hung his head. "I thought you had nothing left to say to me," he muttered. "In light of my new job as a preacher and all…"

A frown tightened Sora's mouth, and then she looked away, seemingly fascinated by something in his garden. "I needed some time to process," she mumbled. "But I get it now. I know why you have to do this."

"Well, that's something."

Without invitation, Sora slipped past him and strode into the house. She stopped at the foot of the stairs, looking back over her shoulder to watch him from the corner of her eye. "Harry," she said. "If you think I'm gonna judge you for protecting your daughter…"

Harry shut the door. He wasn't quite sure what to make of all this; in truth, he wouldn't have blamed Sora for choosing to leave him, but unless he was mistaken, she had decided to stick it out. "So, does this mean…"

She closed the distance between them in two quick strides, threw her arms around his neck and then kissed him. It went on for what felt like several minutes, and when she finally pulled away, she was smiling. "Does that answer your question?"

Breathlessly, Harry nodded.

She fell into his arms with her cheek pressed against his chest. "So, if you're going to be up there preaching," she said. "I guess I'll be in the first row, cheering you on."

"I can live with that."

"But there's something that confuses me."

Harry gestured to his couch.

Seating herself with hands folded in her lap, Sora looked up at him with deep, brown eyes. "The Overseers were figures of myth," she began. "If not for the message beacons that they left behind, many people wouldn't even believe that they exist. So, what do they want you to preach for?"

Harry sat down beside her, grunting at the slight ache in his lower back. "That's the funny thing," he said. "I wasn't lying the other day. They don't care what I preach so long as I preach *something*."

"That would make sense," Sora muttered. "When we made contact with other worlds, we discovered that the Overseers had left message beacons for them as well. But the messages they gave to Antaur were completely different from the ones they gave us."

"How so?"

"They told us that all human beings were created equal. Men and women, dark skin or light: it didn't matter. They said that they brought us to Leyria so that we could learn to live in peace and harmony with one another."

Harry nodded. That went a long way toward explaining Leyria's progressive outlook on such matters. At least it was cultural meddling with benign intent. Then again, he wasn't sure the Overseers ever did *anything* with benign intent. "What about Antaur? What did they tell them?"

"They told the Antaurans that they were the pinnacle of evolution," Sora explained. "The best that humanity had to offer."

And so, Antaur had developed a stratified society based on genetic purity. He was starting to see a pattern in all this. A different message for each world, and no message for Earth. Jack's theory that Earth was some kind of control group in an experiment was looking more and more credible.

Harry stood up, slipping his hands into his pants' pockets and pacing over to the window. "Different messages for everyone," he said. "Almost like they're trying to make us believe different things."

"But why?" Sora protested. "How do you form a coherent religion out of such radically different ideologies?"

"Maybe they don't want one religion," Harry mumbled. The answer hit him like a flash of lightning that illuminated the night sky. "Maybe they want dozens of religions! Hundreds of religions!"

"But why?"

"I don't know." Harry leaned forward with one hand braced against the window. "But I suspect that finding out will be the key to understanding this game they have us playing. I think…I think I would like to see these message beacons."

They stayed together for several hours, talking and reconnecting. Finally, with midnight approaching, Sora decided to go home. When he was alone with his thoughts again, Harry found himself musing on the question of the Overseers' intentions.

He went for a walk to clear his head. The near-constant drizzle – the hallmark of a Denabrian winter – had abated somewhat. Following a spoke street toward the centre of town, Harry saw the outlines of tall buildings against the night sky.

Streetlights came on whenever he got within a hundred feet of them and turned off when he left them behind. Pure darkness provided better sleep. And even though Leyrian windows could turn opaque, this was one more way in which they tailored their environment to maximize health. With his Earth sensibilities, it made him think a prowler was nearby every time the light outside his house turned on. He didn't want to go for walks at night for fear that he was disturbing people, but right now, he needed the air.

Eventually, houses gave way to small buildings that stood two or three stories high. How long had he been walking? Half an hour, at least.

He turned off into a park with a fountain in the middle. A circular walkway formed a ring around it with paths branching off in all four cardinal directions. This seemed to be as good a place as any. The fountain was still; there were no crickets or cicadas in the nearby bushes, not in winter. The silence was downright eerie.

Raising his left hand with fingers splayed, Harry focused on the N'Jal. He sent a signal into SlipSpace, a transmission so faint and erratic that it would read as background noise to any human who might be listening.

It wasn't long before his call was answered.

Just like that, his ex-wife was standing before the fountain with her hands clasped together, her head bowed in a demure posture that the real Della would never adopt. "A good evening to you, my son." She looked up at him with eyes that held him transfixed, eyes that kept him pinned in place by the force of her stare. "How can we be of assistance?"

"What do you want?"

Della blinked. "We have told you," she said. "We wish you to guide your people toward renewed faith and belief."

Holding his coat closed with one hand, Harry approached her with a smile on his face. "No," he said, shaking his head. "Not that. I'm talking big picture. What do you want from humanity?"

The ghostly Della regarded him for a moment, her brows drawn together as if she were considering whether or not to answer his question. Finally, she nodded as if the matter were settled. "Some things cannot be unlearned, my son," she replied. "Are you sure you want to know?"

"I am."

"Well, then I should think the answer would be obvious," Della said. "We want you to kill each other."

Epilogue

Amino acids became proteins; proteins became cells; cells linked together, and within minutes, a fully-formed skeleton was floating in the pool of organic goo. Muscle tissue came next, along with organs, veins and arteries, neurons, synapses and nerves. Skin covered the body from head to toe, and hair sprouted from its scalp.

Bit by bit, consciousness seeped into his mind. He was angry; it was the first coherent thought he had. Angry, yet satisfied. He became aware of the blissful warmth all around him and felt no immediate desire to leave it. He knew where he was. The pool. Yes, he was submerged, but he didn't need to breathe in here. The pool nourished him.

Eventually, like a sleepy man on a lazy Sunday morning, he realized that he could not remain still any longer. So, he swam for the surface.

His head broke through, and the goo trailed over his face, dripping from his chin and his nose. Dark hair clung to his head. It was shorter than what he was used to, but he welcomed the change.

His eyes fluttered open.

Grunting, he emerged from the pool with ooze sloshing over his body in waves. His bare feet touched the fleshy floor of the Inzari ship. He very nearly stumbled. The lack of a symbiont would take some getting used to, but it was a problem that would soon be rectified.

Valeth was waiting for him with a folded towel in her hands. Her eyes were as big as teacups. So, the transformation had been successful then.

His former body was stretched out on the floor, stripped naked and lying on its side. A pool of blood had formed around the head, but it was shrinking, draining away as the Inzari ship consumed it. There was no need to waste organic tissue.

Crouching next to the corpse, he took its hand in his. That brief moment of contact alerted the symbiont to the presence of a viable host. The corpse's skin began to glow, and within seconds, it was as bright as the noonday sun.

The radiance latched onto him, flowing over his hand and up his arm, along his shoulder, his chest, and down to the tips of his toes. It washed over his face, and he threw his head back, closing his eyes as he delighted in the tingling sensation. It passed quickly. The Bonding was complete.

The corpse of Grecken Slade began to sink into the floor, consumed by the ship. He was eager to watch it go. Never again would he be forced to wear the face of Sui Bian. At long last, his penance was over.

Valeth approached him with the towel, then dropped to her knees and bowed her head. "Lord Slade..." she gasped. "You look different."

He took the towel and began wiping the goo off his face. "Slade no longer," he said. "That man is dead, and good riddance."

"Yes, my lord," Valeth replied. "But if you will forgive my impertinence..."

He made no effort to stop the lazy smile that grew on his face. Tossing his head back, he breathed in the warm, muggy air. "Be at ease, Valeth," he said. "You may ask your question without fear of my taking offense."

"What will you call yourself?"

Instead of answering, he pinched her chin with thumb and forefinger and turned her face up so that she was made to look into his eyes. And then he felt something that he had not experienced in a very long time.

With surprising gentleness, he brought her to her feet. His lips came down on hers roughly, and she let out a squeak. Her eyes widened, but shock lasted only a moment, and then she was returning the kiss with a fervour that matched his own. Lust pushed every thought out of his brain.

Her dress fell away with little difficulty.

He took her right there on the floor while the pool bubbled and the Old Woman looked on with mild curiosity. Valeth seemed to be oblivious to her presence. Or maybe she was just distracted. He could not say how long it lasted, but Valeth was in no hurry to be done. A part of him wanted to laugh. How long had it been since he had enjoyed the touch of a woman? Years? Decades.

Finally, he rolled off her, sated and content. He had to resist the urge to chuckle when Valeth grabbed her discarded dress and clutched it to her body. It was a bit late to be modest, but he made no comment.

"My question?" she said in a breathless voice. "What will you call yourself?"

Lying on his back with hands folded behind his head, he smiled up at the ceiling. "Where are you from, Valeth?" he asked. "Where did Isara find you?"

Valeth sat up with the dress held to her chest and looked over her shoulder. Dishevelled hair fell over one of her eyes. "From Antaur, my lord," she answered. "I never left that world until the day Isara brought me into your service."

Biting his lower lip, he nodded slowly. "Very well then," he said. "There is a figure from your mythology that I have always liked. Craxis."

Valeth took one look at his body and then grunted her approval. "Fitting," she said. "You have chosen well, my lord."

"Let us see how well," he murmured. "The mirror."

She fished it out of her handbag and gave it to him. Craxis lifted it to inspect his new face. There was still a bit of goo on his forehead, but otherwise, he was quite pleased with how he looked.

He took a moment to admire his new features: a strong jawline and soft, pale skin. Sharp blue eyes and dark hair with messy bangs that crisscrossed over his brow. Yes, he would enjoy wearing this face.

Tossing his head back, Craxis laughed, and his cackles echoed through the ship.

The End of the Tenth Book of the Justice Keepers Saga

Dear reader,

We hope you enjoyed reading *Cry Havoc*. Please take a moment to leave a review, even if it's a short one. Your opinion is important to us.

Discover more books by R.S. Penney at
https://www.nextchapter.pub/authors/ontario-author-rs-penney

Want to know when one of our books is free or discounted? Join the newsletter at http://eepurl.com/bqqB3H

Best regards,

R.S. Penney and the Next Chapter Team

About the Author

Richard S. Penney is a science-fiction author and futurist from Southern Ontario. He graduated from McMaster University with a degree in mathematics and statistics. Rich knew that he wanted to be a writer ever since he was a child, when he would act out complex stories with his action figures.

He has worked in a number of different fields, including banking, teaching and software QA.

In 2014, Rich published his first novel, *Symbiosis,* the first volume of the Justice Keepers Saga. The story was one that he had been planning to write ever since he was a teenager. The Desa Kincaid novels grew out of a tandem story that Rich started on Theoryland.com, a Wheel of Time discussion site.

Rich has been an environmental activist since his early twenties, and he has given talks on sustainability in Greece and Australia.

Contact the Author

Follow me on Twitter @Rich_Penney

E-mail me at keeperssaga@gmail.com

You can check out my blog at rspenney.com

You can also visit the Justice Keepers Facebook page
https://www.facebook.com/keeperssaga
Questions, comments and theories are welcome.

Lightning Source UK Ltd.
Milton Keynes UK
UKHW022223050221
378341UK00011B/549/J